Di Morrissey is one of Australia's most successful writers. She began writing as a young woman, training and working as a journalist for Australian Consolidated Press in Sydney and Northcliffe Newspapers in London. She has worked in television in Australia and in the USA as a presenter, reporter, producer and actress. After her marriage to a US diplomat, Peter Morrissey, she lived in Singapore, Japan, Thailand, South America and Washington. Returning to Australia, Di continued to work in television before publishing her first novel in 1991.

Di has a daughter, Dr Gabrielle Morrissey Hansen, a human sexuality and relationship expert and academic. Di's son, Dr Nicolas Morrissey, is a lecturer in South East Asian Art History and Buddhist Studies at the University of Georgia, USA. Di has three grandchildren: Sonoma Grace and Everton Peter Hansen and William James Bodhi Morrissey.

Di and her partner, Boris Janjic, live in the Manning Valley in New South Wales when not travelling to research her novels, which are all inspired by a particular landscape.

www.dimorrissey.com

Di Morrissey
The Silent Country

PAN
Pan Macmillan Australia

First published 2009 by Pan Macmillan Australia Pty Limited
1 Market Street, Sydney

978-1-250-05336-7

Internal illustrations by Ted Hutchinson © Ted Hutchinson
www.tedhutchinson.com

To Sonoma Grace . . . my first grandchild.

*With the hope that you will experience the natural
beauty of Australia and know a country which has been
cared for, respected and left for generations to enjoy and
appreciate. And that you too, will fight to keep it so.*

Acknowledgments

To Lloyd Wood, (and lovely Margaret) who shared the story of his outback expedition which inspired the idea for this novel.

To my family who share my days and to those we remember with love.

Special love to my children Nick and Gabrielle (and all their extended families who love them too).

Darling Boris, thanks for being there for me every minute of every day. I love you.

Elizabeth Adams. Thanks for all your advice (even that unasked for!) and being a shoulder and a friend through life's daily tribulations. And for being such a fantastic editor. Your input is invaluable and I even enjoy our arguments!

There are so many kind and helpful people who took time and trouble to answer questions, show me places, share knowledge:

My friend Susan Bradley for sharing her passion and knowledge of the North. Graeme Sawyer, Lord Mayor of Darwin and fighter for the environment. Ian Morris, Ecologist and Conservationist who shared his deep understanding of the landscape of Kakadu, Arnhem Land and its people. Françoise Barr, Archivist, Northern Territory Archives Service for her help in the Darwin Archives. Keith Adams (see www.crocodilesafariman.com) and my good friend, the Honourable Malarndirri (Barbara) McCarthy, M.L.A., Member for Arnhem.

To everyone at my publisher, Pan Macmillan – James Fraser, father of the lovely Casey, for being supportive, understanding and always ready with a laugh; Ross Gibb, our fearless leader; my great buddy Jane Novak who is a tower of strength when we hit the road and whose awareness and sensitivity to indigenous issues has been helpful; Roxarne Burns, Jeannine Fowler, Elizabeth Foster, Katie Crawford, Jane Hayes and Maria Fassoulas and all the phenomenal sales team; everyone at the warehouse and the fabulous reps; and Rowena Lennox for her meticulous copy editing.

And of course, the wise and wonderful Ian Robertson, gourmand, raconteur, family man and friend who also happens to be my lawyer.

There has come a time when we can no longer remain silent, but speak up for our country which is being sold, abused, mined, depleted, drained, over-worked, over-loved, its plants and animals becoming endangered and exterminated faster than we can know them.

Our country is silent. So we must speak and act to save it.

This novel is set prior to the Federal Government's intervention in 2007 into the Northern Territory.

DM
July 2009

I

IT WAS A SHORT, dead-end street lined with small white cottages. Years before, children had ridden bikes and scooters along the quiet road in safety. Now cars lined it, or were parked on the grass and double parked at the rear of the houses in a small laneway. Children's laughter was absent. Men and women came and went in a hurried, sometimes harried, manner. Lights frequently burned late into the night.

Behind the tiny street rose a large tower spiked with aerials, antennae and metal dishes. Around it were large grey cement studios surrounded by a bitumen parking lot filled with trucks, vans and a helicopter landing pad. The shadow of the Network Eleven tower fell across the red rooftops, a sentinel that dominated the surrounding residential suburbs.

A car pulled up and double parked outside the cottage with number 8 on its letterbox. A girl jumped out and hurried up the path, opening the front door where a small stencilled sign said 'Our Country'. The noise inside contrasted with the silent street. Chatter, people calling to each other, ringing phones and, from what was once a bedroom, voices on a tape that was being rewound forwards and backwards to edit.

She tossed her car keys in a bowl on the table inside the front door. Like all the other key rings there, it had a tag attached to it for identification. She strode into the kitchen and poured herself a cup of coffee from the large coffeemaker. A man was making himself a piece of toast.

'Morning, Stu, I've parked behind you. You must have got here early.'

'I've been editing all night. What've you got on this week, Veronica?'

'Chasing stories. We're a bit thin on the ground. Everything seems a bit too peaceful and dull.'

'That might change. Andy was looking for you.'

'I'm travelling. See you, Stu.'

As he took a bite of his toast he watched the pretty senior producer stride down the hallway. The word 'petite' certainly described Veronica Anderson. She was average height but with a narrow frame and tiny bones, yet her slim shape belied her energy and vibrant personality. She was strong, too. He'd seen her lift camera cases, help a crew carry equipment and she never seemed to tire. She was firm and determined but could also be a lot of fun. Veronica had a gutsy laugh and could tell a good story. At twenty-nine she was younger than some of the production team she oversaw, but everyone liked and respected her.

She went into what had been the lounge room of the house, which now served as the central production office.

In the centre was a large table covered in newspapers and magazines with a dozen chairs pulled up around it. The rest of the room contained a sofa, a small desk with a computer, phone and fax machine, filing cabinets, a large whiteboard and two TV sets both going at once. A tall, distinguished-looking man with glasses pushed back on his dark, grey-streaked hair was rifling through a pile of files and newspaper clippings.

Veronica put down her coffee. 'Morning, Andy. How was your weekend?'

Andrew Fitzgerald, the executive producer of *Our Country* and Veronica's boss, answered in a soft, well-modulated voice. 'Quiet. Did you go out raging? Dancing? Indulge in riotous behaviour?'

'Nothing of the sort.'

'Pity.'

'If you recall, you gave me a fat file on Aesop Gardiner to read. And I planted some herbs.'

'How nice. So what'd you think of slippery Aesop and his dubious art collection?'

'He's got one of the world's best collections of fake Buddhist art. I don't know that it's a story for our audience though.'

'I like the fact that those big sculptures were found in a machinery shed in a Victorian country town. What on earth did the locals think about that? And have you had any other ideas?'

'Why don't we wait till the rest of the team arrives for the morning powwow?' she answered as she flipped through the newspaper cuttings one of the researchers had collected as possible story ideas.

'I'd like to bounce some thoughts around with you first,' said Andy warmly. He liked to tease and chat with Veronica on a one-to-one basis before the rest of the program staff came in. While he regarded Veronica as a great

3

producer, organiser, a details person, he knew that if there were a potential story where he needed someone to get people to open up and talk freely, Veronica was the one to do it. As she worked behind the camera and was not a familiar TV face but a sensitive young woman prepared to listen, people seemed to want to share their stories with her. And while she was adept at uncovering information, she never abused people's trust but was candid and sincere, getting them to agree to talk on camera, allowing them to tell their story.

Veronica, thought Andy, could easily have faced the cameras. She was very attractive in a classical way, long dark hair, wide brown eyes, a heart-shaped face and a slender, shapely figure. He often thought she looked feather-weight, as if she'd blow away in a decent wind. But Andy knew of her terrier-like determination, her tireless energy and drive and how forceful she could be. Anyway, Veronica preferred to work behind the cameras because, as she had told him, 'I get to determine what makes a good story. It's my call and my responsibility and I like that.'

When it came to fighting in the trenches, Veronica would be his first choice to have beside him and, with this in mind, he said, 'Maybe we have to start rethinking our audience. The new regime is sure to start shaking things up.'

The network had recently been bought by a very rich entrepreneur, William Rowe, who'd made his money in mining among other enterprises. He had a reputation as an astute businessman, but was also a generous philanthropist who had donated millions to various Australian charities and was the patron of several cultural organisations. Indeed, he had been rewarded with an AO as much for his services to charity as for his successful business dealings.

Veronica and Andy had recently attended the full station staff meeting when everyone who worked at Network Eleven had been summoned to the main studio. This meant the people in administration, the creative departments, wardrobe, make-up, props, electrics, the technicians, the editors, as well as the staff of the big weekly and monthly shows. Veronica listened to William Rowe who, dressed in a suit and flanked by several younger men, also in suits, addressed the staff and suddenly she felt as though she was working in a bank. These were not media men. Mr Rowe, AO, made big promises to improve ratings, break new ground and promote and use cutting edge technology. He assured the staff that he had no intention of sacking anyone, as long as they produced quality shows and he asked for their co-operation to regain the number one ranking in TV land – 'despite the severe financial constraints of the current climate'.

'That means no extra funding. How're we supposed to make better programs with less money?' hissed Veronica.

'T'was ever thus in television,' Andy had whispered back. Veronica now reminded Andy of the impending budget cuts as she thought about some of the stories she wished they could afford to cover.

'What do you think is going to happen under Big Bill's regime? The rumour mill is working overtime.'

'Probably pub gossip. But I have been called to a meeting on Wednesday after next. Heads of departments and programs. In the main board room.'

'That sounds ominous. Do you think our program will suffer?' she asked. 'Become more tabloid? Having money restrictions on travel means no more far-flung locations. Do we stick to suburban backyards?' Veronica was aware that while their ratings were good and *Our Country* had a loyal audience who enjoyed the quirky, intelligent and offbeat stories about Australian places and people, new management always wanted to tinker with a tried-and-true formula.

'New blood likes to reinvent the wheel on occasion and we shall see,' said Andy, confirming her thoughts. 'But that is my concern. You and the team just concentrate on finding stories that are different from those that everyone else does. No state of the roads, disaffected youth or shonky builders for us.'

Competition, beat the others to an interesting story, that's what it all came down to, thought Veronica as she collected her papers from her tiny office.

The rest of the production team wandered into the central office and took their seats around the old pine table. Three researchers – two young women and a young man, two road producers, one of the editors, Tom, the new cameraman and Howard, the head of the camera department, spread coffee cups, notepads, files and mobile phones around the table. The two reporters who appeared on camera and who generally sat in on these meetings were both away on stories. Veronica didn't miss their presence since they weren't really involved in the creative side of the program and they didn't make decisions on what stories to cover. Shelley was brittle, ambitious and bitchy. Kenneth – never Ken – walked around with an air of importance and a constant Bluetooth earpiece, a BlackBerry as well as a smart phone, which were never turned off. Veronica was amused by his self-importance as he really had little to do except read an autocue and convey earnest pieces to camera, many of which were edited out. *Our Country* was a show that didn't rely heavily on the talent of the presenter, but allowed the story to tell itself.

Veronica sat on Andy's right and ran the meeting. The researchers each made several suggestions for story ideas that were discussed, dismissed, put in a possible pile or given a green light to be followed up later. Suggestions and jokes were made, all the staff enjoying the swift repartee that existed between the closeknit members of the professional team.

Andy leaned back in his chair, fingertips pressed together with an air of having seen and heard it all before. It was a tactic that made the researchers want to dig a bit harder and try to come up with clever and original ideas. Veronica listened, made notes, fired questions to the researchers about how they thought each story could work, who would be interviewed for it, what visuals they had in mind and what they thought the impact of the story would be on the audience. Howard was consulted about the availability of camera crews and the best way to cover the story from his point of view.

'I think we should be very careful with our budget at the moment, so helicopters are out,' said Veronica. 'Accommodation is the local motel, not starred resorts. While our show is national and we want to include as much of the country as possible, when it's way beyond woop woop – like the Buccaneer Archipelago,' she raised an eyebrow at Irene, one of the researchers, 'then we must use stringers. We know plenty of good ones all around the country, although there have been mistakes.'

Howard nodded, acknowledging the fact that he'd once hired an unknown young man in an outback town to shoot some footage which had proved to be unusable.

'And we want to get away from picture-postcard kind of stories. And eccentric characters. I know there are a lot out there but let's cull them. Injured animals, unusual pets, animals with party tricks are also off the list. And while we want to cover environmental stories, we can't ignore the big end of town either. We need meaty stories. Gutsy stories. Heart-wrenching stories that mean something, that make grown men weep and rate through the roof. But stick to the facts. Start digging. Don't take any story at face value. There's often more than meets the eye. Right, Andy?' Veronica turned to Andy who was staring out the window looking thoughtful.

'That's for sure,' he agreed. 'Maybe you might want to think about story segments with a theme – towns, groups, people doing something together. People with things in common, people who are diametrically opposite but are flung together. Find people who've made their lives succeed despite what misfortune has been thrown at them. People who've found their dream and are living it. Think about stories that can run the length of the show instead of different short segments. Think about digging deeper, we're not a shock investigative show but that doesn't mean we shouldn't scratch below the surface. Basically, viewers are interested in other people.' He grinned and sat upright. 'Shouldn't be too hard.' He got up from the table. 'Bring the list in when you're ready,' he said to Veronica, then he nodded to the others and went back to his office.

'Are we running out of stories or has everything been done?' asked Tom, the new cameraman.

Veronica glanced around the table. 'There's a bit of pressure 'cause of the new boss. Just because we've been a popular show and have rated well for six years doesn't mean that we aren't stale in his eyes. We just have to be more creative. He's brought in number crunchers but no new talent or fresh ideas, so we don't really know at this stage what he's after. Okay, let's go through your ideas and come up with a shortlist.'

Veronica listened to the debate among the team over the merits and flaws of each idea. While she was senior producer, she did occasionally file stories but she went out on the road less now, since her promotion. Previously, it was her and Eddie. The two of them were a great team. He was the cameraman and she was producer and journalist as well as running the sound equipment as Eddie had taught her.

They'd been mates, part of the gang initially, but after a few road trips covering stories, just the two of them slogging it out during the day chasing interviews and lining up shots, sitting around at night sharing a few drinks and their life stories, dreams and opinions on everything, inevitably, they'd become lovers.

But after fourteen months it had fallen apart. They briefly tried living together but that hadn't worked. They were happier in their own space and they began working less and less together, each being sent out on different stories and then, with her promotion, she'd left the studio infrequently. She knew Eddie had been unfaithful to her during their time together and he'd had no trouble finding new relationships once they split up. She'd been hurt and become reclusive and she found that she was relieved when he was transferred to another station interstate. Everyone at work was tactful enough not to mention Eddie in her presence.

Now that her anger towards Eddie had dissipated she remembered the fun and good times, so when she glanced over to where Tom was sitting, it irked her that he was using the sunflower mug that Eddie had always used. Veronica rose and went into Andy's office to give him the shortlist of ideas. He was looking at his computer.

'Just had a reminder email about the TV and Film Pioneers' Reunion on Saturday night. I think I'll go this year.'

'You're a pioneer, Andy?'

'Listen, I might appear doddery and decrepit but there are people who come to this annual get-together who were there when TV started in this country in 1956. I was just a kid at school when television started in Australia but I remember standing outside the local electrical shop that had a TV in the window. We used to go down at night and watch those early shows till Mum and Dad got a set.' Andy smiled at the memory. 'I loved some of those old programs, mostly American of course. It was a big deal when we started making our own Australian shows. Many of the people who come to the Pioneers' Reunion were responsible for that. You should come along,' he said suddenly.

'To the reunion? What for? I wouldn't know anyone,' said Veronica.

'It might sound like a gathering of boring old people but some of them are legends with a stack of anecdotes,' said Andy. 'I'm just thinking . . . we might find a story there that we can use in *Our Country*.'

'Then you don't need me. You suss it out and let me know if you want me to follow it up. Get that ol' story antennae working.' She smiled and wiggled her fingers on top of her head. It was a continuing joke between them that Andy could smell a story a mile before anyone else had twigged to its potential.

'I think the show needs a fresh perspective, a new generation to look at it. Do you have big plans for this Saturday evening?'

'Not big, but plans.' Veronica had planned to get a pizza and a DVD.

'Come along, Veronica. Keep me company for a bit. Just join us for the cocktails, milling around and watching the old clips from some of those early programs. You don't have to stay for the dinner and speeches.'

She knew Andy's invitation wasn't that of a lonely older man seeking her company. She was very fond of him as well as respecting him enormously as an experienced journalist and producer. He was wise in handling the sometimes temperamental creative talents working at the network. Andy had been widowed for five years and his children were scattered around the globe. His marriage had apparently been a very happy one and he'd planned to retire and travel, but after his wife's illness and death he chose to stay on at work. Veronica socialised with Andy within the context of their work and mutual interests connected with the show, the staff and the station and occasionally she accompanied him to an opening night at the theatre or a movie premiere. But this reunion was a bit out of their normal routine.

'So what are the clips they show? Like blooper reels, funniest film mistakes?'

Andy chuckled. 'No, but I wish I knew what happened to some of those. These are just surviving clips from the National Archives of classic early TV dramas . . . *Whiplash, Riptide, Homicide.* And some of the old hands who worked on them are still around.'

'And movies?'

'Yeah, they sometimes have film clips. Not the real early stuff – you know Australia made the world's first full-length feature film more than a hundred years ago – but these clips will be from films of the 1960s and seventies.'

'All very nostalgic, I suppose,' said Veronica politely.

'For those who worked on them. That's just a short portion of the evening, twenty minutes or so while we're having drinks, catching up, before a few presentations and then a long dinner. I'd be interested in your reaction to the clips. There's always a good story in the Aussie film industry, what we're making, not making, what we should be making. Sometimes a modern name turns up to present an award, say a few words.'

'Umm. Let me think about it.'

'Just come for the drinks, meet a few people. I wouldn't expect you to sit through dinner with the old farts.'

Andy knew that Veronica had been interested in film making a short while ago when she was with Eddie. They'd talked about making a documentary one day. Andy didn't pay much attention to the social life and romances of his staff but as he had a closer working relationship with Veronica and liked her, he was more aware of her personal life. Andy hadn't been sorry to see Veronica and Eddie split up, though he hated to see her feel so wounded. But Eddie was wrong for Veronica who was loyal and trustworthy to the back teeth, while Eddie wasn't, so it had been Andy who had pulled strings to get Eddie transferred interstate after the break-up. Not that Veronica knew it. Had Andy's wife been alive she might have accused him of interfering in Veronica's life. But he was pleased to see Veronica blossom in her new role with the extra responsibility and the way she managed the staff with grace and firmness. But she didn't party with the team the way she had before her promotion and now kept her private life to herself, which led to some speculation on occasion. Only Andy knew she spent most evenings alone reading material for work or writing scripts and ideas.

'Can I let you know in a day or so, Andy?'

'See what better offers come in? Please yourself. But I want you to think about a story linked to our film industry. Got to be an angle somewhere,' said Andy.

Finally, Veronica agreed to meet Andy at the City Bowling Club on Saturday evening to spend an hour or so at the Pioneers' Reunion. She'd had a surprise dinner invitation from her sister, Sue. Sue had asked to make it late-ish, around nine pm, after her children were in bed. As Veronica and her sister both had busy lives they didn't socialise as much as Veronica would have liked, but she hoped this was not another attempt to line her up with some friends of hers. Veronica had suffered a few painful dinners in restaurants with her well-meaning sister.

Both Sue and Philip, her husband, were high fly-ers. Sue was a lawyer, working in a firm specialising in environmental law and Philip was a senior executive in an engineering firm and while both were highly successful, it came at a cost. Veronica found her sister's lifestyle was one of stress and being constantly exhausted by work and the need to care for her husband and two girls aged four and two. But Veronica enjoyed her sister's company and since it fitted in neatly with Andy's invitation, she decided to join him first for an early drink at his nostalgia evening before dinner with Sue and Philip.

At the club she was ushered to the main dining room where a banner was strung across the small stage announcing 'The Annual TV & Film Pioneers' Reunion'. The bar was packed with women dressed in cocktail dresses and men in suits. All wore name tags. To one side was a large TV screen where black and white images of old-fashioned television ads were playing. Andy spotted her hovering near the doorway and came towards her.

'Great you came. You look lovely. So, a big dinner date?'

'Just dinner at my sister's house. I don't see her all that often, we both lead busy, busy lives, so I'm looking forward to it.'

'Let me get you a glass of wine.' They headed to the bar, where several people greeted Andy and gave Veronica, in her short black dress, approving looks.

'This is Alec Blair, a film director friend and Jim Winchester, who is a news editor,' said Andy. The men shook Veronica's hand.

'You must be Andy's right hand, eh?'

'We've seen some of your stories, Veronica. Good work.'

'Oh, thank you,' answered Veronica, quite touched. 'Andy's great to work for.'

'With,' corrected Andy. 'I thought she should come along to get a sense of the industry she's part of and see where it all began.'

'Times have changed, but a good story, told well, is the core of any show, whether it's news or drama,' said Jim. 'Technology is really the only difference between the old days and now.'

'I don't think that film techniques have changed as much as television has,' commented Alec.

'Alec directed some of our first TV dramas,' said Andy. 'Let's go and have a look. They're still running some of the old Artransa ads, then we'll see a couple of the shows that were made at these studios.'

'What's Artransa?' asked Veronica as they all took their drinks and sat at a table near the TV screen.

'It was the first big purpose-built studio complex constructed to make TV productions. It was out on the Wakehurst Parkway at the old blinking light at Frenchs Forest.'

'They made mostly TV ads to begin with, but they were like small movies,' said Alec. 'Then we got overseas co-productions and money for drama. Some overseas actors came to Australia to star in those early TV series.'

'Had to have an OS star, even a third rater. Producers wouldn't use our top-notch talent. Didn't think that they would have the drawing power. But they learned, eventually,' said Andy to Veronica. 'Have you heard of Peter Graves? He came out to do an Australian "western" and went back to star in the original *Mission Impossible* TV series. Here, take a look at this gem.'

Stippled gum trees were still and silent. Sunlight glittered on the sheen of leaves as if a huge lamp was shining through the lonely bushland setting. Like the crack of a rifle a spindly branch snapped, falling heavily to the ground. No breath, no movement, no man had caused this sudden severing.

Then, racing through the trees, came six horses pulling

a flimsy mail coach. Perched atop the driver's seat sat a tall, broad-shouldered man wearing a shirt laced up with leather strips, surprisingly immaculate tight moleskin trousers and a bush hat jammed low over his eyes. He lifted a long bull whip and cracked it above the galloping horses.

Thick bullock-hide straps, which suspended the coach above the large wooden and iron wheels, were designed to cushion the ride over the rough dirt track. But inside the swinging, squeaking, swaying coach, a woman passenger fanned herself looking hot, faint and seasick.

Then, dramatically, the horses reared and snorted as they were suddenly reined to a shuddering halt. In the middle of the track appeared a dishevelled rider on a strong black horse, a kerchief tied about his face. He aimed a menacing rifle at the coach.

'Stand, driver. Throw down your gun. I am Captain Starlight.'

'I'm Chris Cobb and I carry mail, not gold,' answered the coach driver in a strong American accent.

'Your weapon.' The bushranger cocked his rifle, pointing steadily at the coach driver.

The driver took his pistol from his belt and threw it to the ground.

As the frightened woman in the coach huddled into a corner of the padded seat, her gentleman companion stuck his head from the window.

'Mr Cobb, what is this? Surely not a hold-up?'

'Afraid so, Mr Harris. This cowardly man prefers not to show his face yet claims to be the famous Captain Starlight.'

'Oh, dear, oh my,' moaned the woman.

'Tell your passengers to throw out their valuables or I'll take them myself. And the mail bags, Mr Cobb,' came the muffled response.

The masked rider edged his horse closer to the coach's passenger door so he could see the occupants, his rifle still aimed at the coach driver. 'Hand over your valuables. Watch, wallet and your jewellery please, madam. Throw them onto the ground, there.'

Anxious to appease the bushranger, the portly man threw down his wallet and fumbled with his watch as the woman undid the clasp of the locket around her neck and tearfully handed it over.

'And now the mail bags, Mr Cobb.'

The handsome man frowned. 'I have built my reputation by delivering mail and passengers safely and on time,' he began as he turned to reach for the large sacks tied to the roof of the coach.

The bushranger was impatient. 'Just throw them down and you can be safely on your way.'

But the driver moved swiftly, lifting his long bull whip, snapping it with a flying crack.

The stinging sharp tail whipped across the bushranger's face cutting through the cloth of his kerchief and causing a deep cut which began to bleed profusely. Another crack and the whip was wrapped around the bushranger's shoulders, sending him tumbling from his horse as Christopher Cobb, the dashing American owner of Cobb and Co coaches, leapt down and, snatching his rifle, stood over the now helpless bushranger . . .

'The coach driver was Peter Graves?' asked Veronica. 'Was that about the gold rush days?'

'*Whiplash* was the story of Cobb and Co, the coaches that trundled around the bush then. Started by Chris Cobb, an American,' said Andy.

'They took a real story and loosely based the series on it. Wasn't too bad,' said Jim.

'I'm told that Peter Graves, who played Chris Cobb, was a nice man but those *Whiplash* scripts he had to work with were abysmal,' said Andy.

'That's because they were written by Yanks who'd never been here. Someone told me that one of the scripts called for a herd of ferocious killer sheep!' laughed Alec.

'Ah, now look at this. Who could ever forget Ty Hardin,' said Jim as the next black and white clip appeared on the screen.

'Who?' asked Veronica.

'Yankee actor called Ty Hardin. We called him Try Harder. He was so keen to come out to Australia and star in a show he put his own money in it. But he never did become a big star,' said Jim.

'Rule number one of show business, Veronica. Never use your own money,' said Alec.

The ocean was calm. Small foam-crested waves brushed against the hull of a sleek white yacht cutting through the waters off the Great Barrier Reef. On the deck stood the tanned, bare-chested skipper, a captain's white hat with gold trim crammed on his blond hair. His white pants were rolled casually above stylish canvas deck shoes. Lifting his binoculars the sun-baked Californian peered towards the horizon as a shapely brunette in a bikini emerged from below deck.

'Hey, Moss, where's the island?'

'We're still some distance away. Just checking for reefs, but I'm wondering about that boat out there. Looks like it could be in trouble.'

'My goodness, it just looks like some sort of canoe.' She shaded her eyes and squinted.

He handed her the binoculars. 'I've heard that there are pirates in these waters masquerading as native fishermen in trouble. Keep out of sight. But pass me my gun.'

'Your gun? You mean there could be trouble? What do they want from us? We're just sailing to a deserted island to explore, right?'

'Sorry, Trisha, I must have forgotten to mention I've been chartered to look for a cache of weapons left by the navy during the war. There's also supposed to be gold stashed on one of these islands. You'd better cover up. I have a feeling we're going to have company on this trip.'

Veronica giggled. 'I can see why this show, *Riptide,* never took off. Those lines are excruciating. But he was a good-looking guy and the location looks nice.'

'Yeah, they shot some stock footage on the Barrier Reef, the rest of the series was shot around Pittwater and in the studio,' said Alec.

'So when did they start all those successful Aussie TV shows you hear about, the cop shows?' asked Veronica.

'Once Hector Crawford, you must have heard of him Veronica, started his production company in Melbourne in the 1960s he began using local stories with local stars. Well, the shows made them stars. Serious actors from theatre and film wouldn't work in TV,' said Jim.

'Interesting. Seems the reverse these days. TV is where movie actors cut their teeth now,' said Veronica.

'Look, here's where many started.' Alec pointed at the TV screen.

In a dark street, late at night, the illuminated sign of Russell Street Police Station glowed faintly. A 1964 Holden, its engine throaty, swung to a stop and its doors opened simultaneously before three tall men in suits and hats stepped from the car.

In the cluttered and busy police headquarters Inspector Jack Connolly finished briefing his team, Detective Sergeant Frank Bronson and Detective Rex Fraser.

'And so, gentlemen, it seems we have a rather nasty piece of work on our hands. While this man remains at

18

large the streets of Melbourne cannot be safe for men women or children.'

'And it's not just them who are threatened,' commented Detective Fraser.

'Yes, homosexuals have also been targeted and they deserve the same protection as every other citizen,' commented the inspector. 'Now, we have a tip-off where this bloke could be dossing down. Here's the address. Take back-up with you.'

In the early hours of the morning, in a dark laneway off Gertrude Street in Fitzroy, three homicide detectives wearing overcoats and hats, with guns drawn, placed themselves on either side of a doorway. At a nod from Connolly the other two slammed their shoulders into the door, kicked it open and plunged into the darkness.

Shots rang out.

'Now that's one television program I've heard of,' said Veronica, 'Although I can't say that I know much about Hector Crawford. And that dialogue. It certainly wasn't terribly PC, was it?'

'Jeez, how long did *Homicide* run, Andy?'

'Eleven years or so. Ended in seventy-seven when the networks started bringing in cheap American shows.'

'*Homicide* was a good cop show, reckon half this room worked on a Crawford Production of some sort,' said Jim.

'Yep. Where many in the industry learned the ropes. Technicians today don't get the same training,' said Andy, glancing at Veronica.

'Digital cameras make it too easy, no control, no imagination. I thought it was pretty slick when video tape came in, but you talk to some of the old hands here, the feature film boys, the lighting cameramen, they say film still looks best on TV,' said Alec.

'My crews carry gear that could fit in a handbag. The

equipment's so light that we even have a couple of female camera people, don't we, Veronica?' said Andy.

'That's right,' she said, suddenly thinking of Eddie, who maintained video could look as good as film if you had good lighting.

'How's your station going?' Jim asked Andy. 'Is the network still rating?'

'Yes. But some shows might go now that Big Bill has taken over.'

'Oh, you mean William Rowe, the mining magnate. I thought he was supposed to be a huge philanthropist. But maybe not to employees, huh?' said Jim.

Veronica waited for Andy to respond to his friend's question but he merely shrugged. 'There're always rumours in the television industry.' He turned back to the TV screen. 'This next clip is from a good Aussie movie, though it was directed by a Brit and starred an English girl. I love this film.'

Silver water, floating above the wavering horizon, glimmered, shimmered, then slowly faded. Two small figures, ciphers in a barren land, gazed at the expanse of pale yellow dust between them and the distant oasis. There was no sound. Nothing but the arid expanse of desert surrounded them. From the sky they were mere specks among the dunes and saltpans, ants' trails of footprints behind them.

The girl stopped. Before them a straggly tree, a sparse clump of grey shrub and a dip in the earth loomed as dramatically as a city building in the pink-brown surroundings. Was this tiny gully hiding a stream? They slipped and skidded into it, finding only sand. The girl lifted a handful and let it dribble through her fingers. The small boy began to weep.

As they stood there, the girl suddenly jolted and grabbed her brother's shoulder, staring at the apparition that had appeared from behind the skeletal tree. As alien as they must have appeared to the man standing there, so was he to them. Scrawny, lean, his black body daubed in clay, he stared at them, the whites of his eyes wide.

The girl took in his dusty curls, his curious, fearless expression, his naked body clothed only in a woven band around his hips and loins. Dead lizards, tongues protruding, hung from it. He held a spear and a wooden implement and as they studied each other he spoke softly in a language she'd never heard before.

'Water. Please, we want water. Can you help us?' she asked.

The young man answered in a gurgle of words.

'Tell him we want water.' The boy tugged at her.

'Water. We need water. Can't you understand that?' she said, a desperate note of exasperation in her voice.

The stranger merely stared.

The little boy stepped forward, tilting back his head, jabbing his finger in his mouth, swallowing and cupping his hand.

A wide smile broke out on the Aborigine's face. In his rapid language he seemed to be explaining as he stepped into the sandy indentation by the scrubby bush and began digging with the wooden tool.

Dampness soon stained the sand and a small puddle formed. He showed them how to place their hands, straining the water through their fingers as they knelt to lap the precious moisture.

He watched the girl's pink tongue greedily suck at the water, her lips moist, her strange fair lashes closed on her golden skin. She sat back on her heels and stared at their saviour and saw in his eyes a softness, a hesitant pleasure in the curve of his lips revealing bright white teeth.

'It's going to be all right,' she told her little brother.

*

'Oh wow, that's so beautiful.' Veronica continued to stare at the screen. 'Was that David Gulpilil? He's amazing.'

'*Walkabout*. 1971. Yep. I think it was his first role. I reckon it's a movie that still holds up. You having another wine, Veronica? And you fellows, another beer?'

'No thanks, Andy, I have to drive.' Veronica was thoughtful. 'I'll have to try to get that movie on DVD. Must have been hard filming it, it looks a pretty desolate setting.'

'You been outback, Veronica?' asked Jim.

She smiled. 'I'm a city gal, but I have done the odd story in the more remote parts of Australia.'

'Sometimes it pays to get off the beaten track. You look at places with new eyes,' said Jim.

'You're right,' agreed Veronica. 'I had a friend who was a cameraman and he said the world looked different through the lens of a camera. Sometimes you don't really see things that are right there in front of you.'

Andy knew she was talking about Eddie and stepped in. 'I've been trying to suggest to Veronica that there must be a story, a new angle, about the Aussie film and TV industry. And I don't mean hearing your reminiscences,' he grinned at his friends.

'Aw, I dunno about that. I covered some pretty hot stories in my time and Alec, you could spill the beans on some well-known characters,' said Jim.

'Our show isn't about that kind of stuff and you know it. But any ideas are welcome,' said Andy.

Veronica glanced at her watch. She was surprised to find she'd been enjoying the humorous shop talk and the warm company of these older men who'd been part of the TV landscape almost since its beginning. 'I'll have to make tracks to my sister's for dinner. She doesn't entertain very often so I mustn't be late. Thanks for the drinks and the invitation, Andy. And it's been a real privilege to meet you, gentlemen. Perhaps I might come round and pick your brains some time.'

'Anytime, Veronica.' The men shook her hand and smiled and watched her thread her way through the room.

'She's a bright young woman. Very nice. Hope she doesn't fall in love and leave you, Andy.'

'We've been down that road,' answered Andy. 'I'm afraid she's one of this new generation, work is their life. No balance. Not that I'm complaining because she's a very talented producer. Hey, we should find our tables, dinner is happening by the looks of things.'

Andy shook hands with his fellow guests as the waiter began pouring wine. He knew the old TV and film hands at the table save for a man sitting on his right. He introduced himself.

'Andy Fitzgerald, Network Eleven.'

The man with white hair and a neat silver beard smiled as they shook hands. 'Colin Peterson. I'm a bit of an interloper, can't claim to be much of a TV or film industry person. Did a bit of scriptwriting once. You still in harness?'

Andy thought the man probably had a good twenty years on him, which made him around eighty. He nodded. 'Yep. Still working.'

'What show do you work on?'

'*Our Country.* Wednesday nights.'

Colin nodded. 'Of course. I love it. About Australian places and people. You've had some really interesting stories. Where do you get your ideas?'

There was general chat around the table as the dinner was served and by the time dessert appeared, everyone at the table was mellow and sharing stories.

Andy turned to Colin. 'So, you said you did some scriptwriting, which show?'

Colin leaned back in his chair, 'Ah, nothing you've

ever seen. But tell you what, it was the highlight of my life. A wild outback adventure.' For a moment the silver-haired man with the flushed face and slightly crooked bow tie looked like an enthusiastic young man.

Andy lifted his glass of red wine. 'Do tell. What was it? A feature, a doco?'

'It was in the fifties. I was hired to write the script for a documentary film which was supposed to showcase the Australian outback to the world prior to the 1956 Melbourne Olympics. There was a mixed group of us. Off we went on this crazy expedition making it up as we went along.'

'And how did it come out?'

The older man looked wistful then he straightened up. 'Well, it was all a bit of a saga. Good and bad memories. But I've never seen anything as wild, beautiful or as mystical as the wilderness of the Northern Territory.'

Andy was intrigued and about to ask more questions, but there was a blast of loud music, the lights dimmed and a cabaret of former TV stars began to strut their stuff. Andy shrugged at Colin and put his hand to an ear.

Colin nodded, understanding their conversation was now impossible above the noise of the music.

Veronica's sister and husband lived in an affluent North Shore suburb where expensive cars were parked in driveways and immaculate lawns and flowerbeds were maintained by professional gardening teams. Most homes had swimming pools, also cared for by regular pool maintenance men.

Although they were close to the train line, Sue and Philip both drove to the city and parked in their company car spaces, taking it in turns, depending on meetings and business appointments, to drop their two girls off at a costly private, but creative, day-care centre which had a long waiting list.

Veronica noticed the extra car parked at the curb and sighed. So there was another dinner guest. She knocked at the door rather than ring the chimes and wake the children but the door was pulled open by four-year-old Sarah jumping up and down.

'Auntie Vee, Auntie Vee.' Sarah rushed at her.

'Hey, I thought you two were supposed to be in bed. You haven't even got your nightie on. What have you been up to?'

Sue came to the door and gave Veronica a quick kiss. 'The girls are being very naughty. Wouldn't eat their dinner, wouldn't get out of the bath, wouldn't go to bed until they saw you.'

'Maybe they need a story. Is Sophie asleep?'

'Of course not. She's in there flirting with Ben. Come and meet him. I don't know where the time has gone. I haven't had time to do anything . . .'

'I hope you didn't go to any trouble,' said Veronica.

'Believe me, I didn't.' Sue tucked a stray strand of hair behind her ear and headed to the living room.

Philip and his friend were sitting on the lounge, two-year-old Sophie jumping up and down on the cushions between them. The TV was blaring, but no-one was watching. Bottles of beer were on the coffee table and the dog was eyeing the bowl of peanuts beside them. Philip waved to Veronica.

'Hey, here at last. Come and meet Ben. Say, you look great, where've you been? Cocktails with some celebrity? She works in TV,' he said to Ben.

'Kind of a work function.' She held out her hand towards Ben who struggled to his feet as Sophie clung to him. 'I'm Veronica. Sue's sister.'

'Hi. Yes, I've heard all about you.'

25

'Sorry, Philip, did I get the time confused? I thought Sue said to come late-ish.'

'That was the plan. These monkeys were supposed to be in bed. Do you want a drink, Veronica?'

'I'll wait till dinner, thanks. How about I read these two a story? C'mon, Sophie, you haven't given me a hug yet.' She peeled the younger girl off Ben who looked relieved. 'I'll see you shortly.'

'I get to choose,' squealed Sarah, dashing ahead to the bedroom as Sophie started wailing, 'Me choose . . .'

Veronica went past the kitchen. 'Sue, I'll see if I can quieten them down then I'll help you with the food, okay?'

'Thanks. When they're settled, go and talk to the boys. Nothing to do in here, I got Indian take-away.'

'Sounds good.' Veronica couldn't help noticing the smart kitchen with all its modern appliances looked as though a small army had invaded, leaving dishes and glasses and open cartons everywhere. For someone who was meticulous, a detail person and thorough in her work, Sue was unbelievably messy at home, thought Veronica. But then so was their mother, Joan, who ran an employment agency but always paid people to keep the family home tidy especially as their father, Roger, travelled a lot as a marketing executive.

As Veronica settled the girls into their adjoining beds, smoothed the covers and pulled a chair between the two beds to read them a story, it occurred to her that although her parents had never spent a lot of time with them, she and Sue never felt neglected. There were babysitters and lots of visits from their two grandmothers. Unfortunately for Sue, their mother still worked, so there were fewer visits for her daughters to enjoy.

Sue stuck her head in the door. 'You all right, girls? Now be good and quiet for Auntie Vee. Dinner won't be long.'

'We've had dinner. It was yukky,' said Sarah.

'Well, we won't get that dish again from the Yummy Tummy Shop,' said Sue. 'Poor Auntie Vee and Mummy and Daddy and his friend, we haven't had our dinner.'

Veronica glanced at her watch. It was quarter to ten. She was feeling past food. 'Sue, do you remember when our grannies used to visit, look after us? They always cooked us stuff, read stories, sewed things, didn't they?'

'God, yes. Mum loved it. When she and Dad came back the cupboards were tidy, all the ironing done, freezer full of home-baked goodies, though I think we might have worn the old dears out.' She smiled at her two daughters. 'A bit like you two. Okay, ten minutes and then lights out.'

The little girls argued with Veronica when she finished the story, but she was firm and walked out of their bedroom, shutting the door behind her, ignoring their complaints.

'Phil, I'm ready for that drink now.' Veronica moved toys off a lounge chair and sat down.

'I'll get it. What would you like?' Ben jumped to his feet as Phil went to find plates and cutlery.

Sue carried the take-away containers to the table. 'I'm not fussing with platters, we'll just help ourselves.'

'Saves washing up,' said Phil. He grinned at Ben. 'I told you this was casual, just family.'

'How about I light a candle?' Veronica took a small candelabra from a sideboard and put it on the table in a gesture to dress up the meal.

Ben was pleasant looking, with a good job. He was earnest and asked questions about her work and tried to appear interested in her brief answers. Veronica knew he was trying to make a good impression and she tried to be interested in his work but she felt they had little in common and there was simply no chemistry.

Driving home later, Veronica chided herself for not making more of an effort. Many of her contemporaries would have had at least one date with him to test the waters. What was wrong with her, she wondered. The damage from her relationship with Eddie must have affected her more than she suspected and she felt the hurt and resentment towards him resurface. Or was it something else? Veronica understood very well the pace at which Sue and Philip lived, their drive to provide for their family, but it didn't feel right. She was always glad to see them, but she always came away feeling exhausted. She didn't think that she could live in such chaos. Veronica knew that she didn't want her life to be as complicated as theirs.

The following Monday morning Veronica sat across from Andy as they shared their morning coffee prior to the production meeting.

'So how was your sister's dinner?'

'Fine. There was a fellow there who works with my brother-in-law. Don't get nervous, Andy, he wasn't my type. And by the time I'd read a story to the girls and we finally ate dinner it was past my bedtime.'

'What is your type of man, Veronica?'

'You know, Andy, I really don't know and I don't think that Sue and Philip's domestic scene helps either.'

'I loved raising my kids and all that went with it.'

'Yeah, but was it you or your wife who did the hard stuff? Did she work?'

Andy smiled. 'I concede your point. No, she stayed home. I worked long hours and by the time the kids left home and I decided that we should do things together, it was too late because she got ill.'

'I'm sorry, but you had a wonderful marriage and

you've got great kids, even if they are all over the place. You've had fun times visiting them,' said Veronica who knew how much Andy missed his late wife. 'Anyway, how was the reunion dinner? I enjoyed seeing those old TV clips.'

'It was great. I like all the industry gossip, the re-telling of the old stories.'

'I doubt I'll be going to reunions of *Our Country* and reminiscing about our days here,' said Veronica. 'Though I have a ton of stories about Andy Fitzgerald.'

'I doubt anyone would be interested. No, the early TV days were very, very different. But funny you should mention it. I met a rather interesting old chap at my table. Colin Peterson, he'd be around eighty. He told me he went on some crazy expedition to the Northern Territory to make a documentary in the 1950s.'

'What about?'

'I don't know, he was a bit vague,' said Andy thought-fully. 'Anyway, he didn't have a chance to go into details because of the noise of the music.'

'Maybe the poor old bugger doesn't remember much.'

'He wasn't an old bugger. He was very spry. Actually, I'm sorry that I didn't get a chance to talk to him more about this film expedition. My antennae sensed a story of some sort.'

Veronica shook her head. 'You and your story anten-nae. What kind of story?'

'Heading to the outback to film then was quite an undertaking. I can't recall seeing much footage taken in remote areas in those days. Newsreel grabs from a big croc attack, some first contact with a lost Aboriginal tribe. Not much else.'

'So what are you going to do about this fellow?'

'Not me. You. Your assignment, should you wish to accept it . . .' he mimicked an American accent. 'I thought you might hunt down Colin Peterson, chat him up, just see what you can find out. Charm him. You're good at that.'

Veronica sighed. 'Doesn't sound like much of a story to me.'

Andy put his fingers up on his head and waggled them.

'Yeah, right. Well, thanks for the great lead, boss.' She smiled. 'This time I think your antennae are a bit whacked, but I'll humour you and go and see this Colin Peterson. But I have my doubts . . .'

2

To COLIN, THE VOICE on the phone was soft, pleasant, friendly.

'Yes, this is Colin Peterson,' he answered. 'Who's calling please?'

Veronica introduced herself and launched into a happy, chatty, conversation. She'd found that the warm and casual approach worked best initially, as people were sometimes suspicious when getting a call from a producer at a TV network. 'I gather you met my boss Andy Fitzgerald on Saturday night. At the Pioneers' Reunion.'

'Ah, yes, from *Our Country*. Excellent show.'

'Glad you think so. We're very proud of the program. I was at the reunion dinner briefly. Saw the old film and TV clips. I'm sorry we didn't meet. Andy says you made an intriguing trip to the outback. Was that for a documentary, or just a home movie . . .?'

'My goodness, I just mentioned it in passing. I felt a bit of an imposter in such illustrious company, but I very briefly harboured a dream to get into the film industry.'

'As an actor?' Veronica knew this wasn't the case, but it made the old man chuckle.

'Goodness me, no. I had other dreams. Short lived. I spent most of my working life in the banking industry.'

'Mr Peterson, I was wondering if you'd be willing to share some of your story. I'd love to know about it. We're thinking of doing a program on the Aussie film and TV industry. It seems not many people ventured outback with a camera in the 1950s.'

There was a pause. 'I don't know if I'd have anything important to contribute.'

'But it must have been a bit of an adventure. I bet the roads were pretty rough and there wouldn't have been a lot of civilisation, would there? Who was in the party besides you?'

'Miss Anderson,' he said. 'It was such a long time ago, I'm not sure that you'd find it interesting.'

Veronica didn't like being rejected and she thought that she could overcome his reticence. Most people loved to prattle on about some small or large event in their lives, whether for a TV show or not. 'Could I meet you for a coffee, please, Mr Peterson? You just don't know what you might remember that could give me a clue, a lead for my story.'

'Oh, I'm not sure.' He sounded embarrassed.

But she heard the wavering in his voice and suspected that he might be persuaded to share his reminiscences. 'I'd love to meet you,' she said soothingly. 'You must have your own memories of TV starting in Australia, Australian movies . . .'

'I met Chips Rafferty once . . .'

Veronica pounced. 'There you go. I'd love to have a general chat about Aussie films and television, especially in the fifties. Where would you like to meet? You name the place. I love getting out of the office,' she said breezily.

'Would Kings Cross be out of your way?'

Veronica was surprised at his choice of the one-time bohemian, sleazy, dangerous, arty hangout that was now a slick and desirable residential and tourist area. 'Fabulous. The colourful Cross. Does it have any association, any memories for you?'

'Ah, well it was popular with actors . . . that's where I met lots of artists and, as you say, other colourful characters.' He sounded more enthusiastic and Veronica was sure he would begin to talk about himself when they met.

He had chosen a coffee shop in Macleay Street opposite a smart Italian restaurant. Veronica hadn't been to the Cross for some time so she took the train and enjoyed the walk from Darlinghurst Road. Although the area had changed under the 'Clean up the Cross' campaign and new boutique hotels and smart apartments had blossomed, it still had a rakish air. It felt safe in the sunshine even though strip-club touts chivvied her, but there was a sense that come the neon evening, the Cross's true lascivious, illegal and dangerous self would re-emerge as it always had.

It was early afternoon, in that period when the lunch crowds had gone and when it was too early for the cocktail and after-work wine bar set, so there was no mistaking Colin Peterson sitting alone at a table in the near-deserted coffee shop. He was as Andy had described: a round, almost cherubic face with a short, neatly clipped beard, sparse white hair and bright blue eyes. He wore a spotted bow tie and he rose with a smile as she came towards him.

'Miss Anderson?'

'Hello, Mr Peterson. I hope I haven't kept you waiting.'

'Not at all. I came early to enjoy the ambience of the Cross, even though it's changed a lot since my day.'

'You knew the Cross well?' she asked, somewhat surprised, as she sat down. It didn't fit with the conservative banking image she had imagined.

'Everyone came to Kings Cross in the old days, just to walk through, ogle the locals and feel slightly wicked on a Saturday night,' he said with a smile. 'Actually, I moved here at one stage. Lived up the road, almost opposite where the El Alamein fountain is now. It was a red-brick apartment building divided into very tiny studios and dinky flats. It was a nice building, not like some of the big old homes that were turned into illegal bedsits with too many people crammed in. Mind you, the Cross was cheap, so interesting people came to live here in the old days.'

'You mean artists, actors, bohemian types,' said Veronica as she glanced at the menu.

'And ordinary folk like me, families too. It was a community. Everyone looked out for their neighbours, regulars in the street.' He signalled to the waiter behind the cash register at the bar. 'What would you like?'

'Oh, a cappuccino. But please, let me pay, this is on *Our Country*. Would you like another coffee, something to eat?'

Colin ordered more coffee and a muffin and leaned back, making himself comfortable.

'So did you grow up in this area?' asked Veronica.

'Goodness, no,' he said. 'I originally came from Parramatta, so it was a shock to my parents when I rented a flat here. They couldn't bring themselves to tell their friends that I was living in Kings Cross.'

'So what was the appeal for you?'

'It was so different from anything I'd known. You must

remember that in the fifties, life in Sydney was conservative. We had come out of the postwar austerity and people started to have a better lifestyle, go for modern things, but it was, by today's standards, still very suburban.'

'Mum in the kitchen with a frilly apron, father knows best. Just like those old TV shows?'

'That was my mother and father. They were good people, wanted the best for me so they were pleased when I got the job in the bank. I lived at home, didn't have too far to go to work at the Bank of New South Wales at Auburn.'

'What happened to send you into cosmopolitan, bohemian Kings Cross?' asked Veronica.

There was a twinkle in his eye. 'Quite simple, really, I got a promotion but it meant a transfer to another branch of the bank.'

'Kings Cross?'

'Down the road there. It's now the Westpac. Well, initially I was in shock. I'd never seen so many foreign people, or such unusual people. And not just in the bank! At lunchtime I walked around and looked at the restaurants and eating places and finally I got up the courage to go into one of the new Italian coffee shops. I think it had the second espresso machine in Australia.'

Veronica laughed. 'How exotic!'

'It was,' he said seriously. 'But while it was so different, the Cross had the feel of a village. You soon recognised the locals, got to hear local gossip. I started buying a piece of fruit each day from a fruiterer and he and his wife knew everything about everyone. Then I discovered a French patisserie, a Greek delicatessen and a Yugoslav butcher. It was food I never knew existed. When I described it to my mother and wanted her to come here to try some of it she wouldn't have it. Said it was greasy, unhealthy and the foreigners ate bits of an animal that we wouldn't give to a dog. So I kept quiet after that.'

'What about your dad?'

'Oh, he took me aside for a quiet word about the gambling and especially the houses of ill repute . . . "If you get my drift, son," ' he mimicked.

Veronica smiled. 'Ah, the brothels. And what about the underworld, the dangerous, sinister side of the Cross that you hear about?'

'I didn't know much about that. I never went near a nightclub or any of those girly show places. Wasn't my cup of tea. But you saw prostitutes hanging around the streets. The police would round them up periodically. Sometimes you'd hear about a murder or a police raid on places.'

'Did your bank ever get held up?'

'No, thank goodness. But I was always amazed at the characters that would come in and deposit bagfuls of money. That was the legit money, I learned. The shady money never saw light of day in a bank,' he chuckled.

'And you liked it so much you moved here?' asked Veronica, trying to imagine the quiet and to her mind, rather nerdy Colin suddenly moving from his neat and tidy home where his mother did his washing, ironed his shirts and cooked his meals to the brazen madness of Kings Cross.

'Not immediately. What really got me involved in the area was the pictures.'

'Movies, you mean?'

'That's right. But not just the big commercial cinemas. I saw posters advertising all kinds of film screenings for foreign films and some local ones that looked interesting. It seemed so intriguing, so exotic. So off I went. That was a different world again,' he commented wryly.

'Why was that?' asked Veronica.

'Well, most of the movies I had seen came from Hollywood, although there were some good British ones around, too. But these movies weren't in English and the directors told the stories differently. There was more drama and yet more subtlety. It's hard to explain, but I'll never forget the first Vittorio De Sica film I went to, *The Bicycle Thief*. It is still a masterpiece. I remember how wonderful I thought Fellini was when I saw *La Strada*. Have you ever seen *The Seven Samurai*? That is one of my all time favourites. The directors in those days, they had such original ideas.'

'I suppose that there weren't many Australian films made in those days, before TV.'

'Well, surprisingly, there were a few. The fifties were a time of massive industrial unrest and I'd say the heart of it all centred around the waterside workers on the docks. They had a strong union and they fought hard for better conditions but there was an element of what my Dad called lefty, pinkos stirring.'

'Communists? Did you mix with them?'

'No, not at all. But the union made some rather interesting films that I used to go and see because I wanted to see anything Australian.'

'What kind of films?'

'They were documentaries showing the working and housing conditions of people and how social and political change could improve them, that sort of thing. They were out-and-out propaganda.'

'They don't sound like light entertainment,' said Veronica.

'That's true, but the docks area was a strong community. There were a lot of activities after hours and at lunchtimes – meetings, talks by all kinds of people, concerts, shows and such. I followed the film screenings.'

'They must've been interesting times – and people.'

Colin chuckled. 'There was a lot of stimulating debate. I met an actor there who was a famous radio voice. I was used to hearing him in the radio serials as different characters. He looked nothing like I thought he would, of course.'

'Did you like Hollywood films too?' asked Veronica.

'Oh, I loved them. Especially the musicals. At the film club that I joined we discussed them all at great length. But I was more interested in the screenplays, how the stories unfolded, came together, the characters and so on, than I was in the stars, or even the directors.'

'Ah, so you wanted to be a screenwriter?'

'I didn't imagine I ever would, of course. But I did pen a few ideas and dialogue from time to time,' Colin admitted.

'So is that why you were hired for the filming expedition?' asked Veronica, glad to be able to get back to the subject she wanted to know more about.

'I suppose so. Though I had no experience, no credits to my name. I worked in a bank. All of us who went along on the expedition kind of fell into it.' Colin suddenly smiled.

'Now I am intrigued. I want to know the whole story.' Veronica signalled to the waiter for more coffee. Colin Peterson looked more relaxed, if reflective and his blue eyes looked past her, remembering back, fifty years before.

The tram clattered to the top of William Street and seeing the big billboard advertising sign for Capstan cigarettes, Colin stepped lightly from the running board and walked down Darlinghurst Road towards his flat. Mr Hugo, an elderly man with a white goatee and jaunty hat, was walking his small dog and in a thick accent, greeted Colin. Mrs Stavros in the fruit shop had told Colin that Mr Hugo was from Romania. Everyone called him Mr Hugo as no-one could pronounce his surname.

One of the streetwalkers hovering near the corner gave him a swift smile of recognition as she watched for prospective customers. Spiro, the tout outside the entrance to a flight of steps that descended below street level to a club boasting 'Girls, Girls, Girls', nodded at Colin. He'd given up trying to persuade the young man to go downstairs and sample the delights of the topless girls' dance revue. Colin had heard it was more than just a lewd show. Illegal SP bets could be placed and alcohol was available outside legal drinking hours.

Colin popped into the continental mixed business and bought a small loaf of the dark brown bread he'd come to love. He paid for the bread as well as his dinner, which was handed to him across the counter in the lidded bowl he'd dropped off that morning. It smelled delicious, vegetables and some sort of bean in a thick rich broth. Nothing like the food his mother cooked.

Thanking Helena, the proprietor, he took his dinner back to his flat. Looking around the tiny area, Colin smiled to himself. He loved the Cross and his little home. He knew that his decision to move here had shocked his parents, especially his mother, but it all felt like such an adventure. He cooked meals for himself occasionally on his small gas stove but it was just as cheap to eat out or have food prepared for him by Helena and her husband Gustav. And while his mother would have been horrified to know he was eating strange foreign food like spaghetti, roll mops and dim sims, Colin found the food interesting and eating out gave him a reason to people-watch and enjoy the colourful parade around him at the Cross.

Tonight, however, he was eating at home, so he changed his clothes and tidied the small flat, heated his meal and broke off chunks of the bread, dipping it into the broth as Helena and Gustav had showed him. His mother would consider it ill-bred, but he wiped the bowl clean with the last bit of bread and licked his fingers with satisfaction. He turned on the radio and listened to Jack Davey's quiz show.

When it was over he sat down to work on a screenplay that he was trying to write, but felt distracted. It was only eight-thirty so he decided to go for a walk and treat himself to a coffee at Nino's, his favourite coffee shop.

The coffee house was crowded. Nino, the owner, threaded between tables, exclaiming volubly in Italian and, ignoring the liquor laws, surreptitiously poured red wine into the customers' coffee cups.

'These laws, they are ridiculous!' The large man at a table surrounded by friends, acquaintances and the curious, flung up his hands in exasperation. 'Maxim Topov should be able to drink wine where and when he wants!'

Colin, sitting alone in a corner, watched the other people in the coffee shop hover around the burly man with the loud Russian-accented voice. They appeared to hang onto his every word. To Colin, the people looked to be arty types. Some of the men had beards and wore berets. Many of the women were heavily made-up and wore flowing clothes or chic little dresses. The Russian gave out a handful of leaflets and then dramatically left the café with several people in his wake. Another man gathered up his cigarettes, paid the bill and, as he left, stuck one of the flyers onto the café noticeboard.

On his way out Colin made a point of reading it.

A Cinema Masterpiece!

*Direct from Russia! The brilliant cinematographer and filmmaker Maxim Topov will be screening his film '**Under Dark Skies**', Sunday, three pm, at the Roxy Cinema, Paddington.*

Come, hear Topov speak about his career and his exciting plans to make a film in Australia. You could be part of Topov's next masterpiece!

Admission 2/-

Colin loved films. He enjoyed the interesting ones with subtitles, as well as Hollywood movies and the few Australian films he'd seen. This Russian one intrigued him. So, on Sunday afternoon, Colin threw a long scarf his mother had knitted around his neck, which he thought gave him a more rakish air and set off for the little art-house cinema in Paddington.

There was a smallish turnout and Maxim Topov stood in front of the stage with a very large, flamboyantly dressed, alarmingly red-headed woman. The two were in deep discussion until the woman turned and marched up the aisle and took her seat in the centre of the theatre while the director disappeared into the wings. The lights dimmed save for a spotlight on the stage as Topov reappeared, parting the curtains with a flourish and announcing to the empty gods, 'I am Topov.'

There was a smattering of applause.

'Ladies and gentlemen. My dear friends. Lovers of cinema. Thank you for coming. This is truly magnificent evening. Tonight you see only one of my masterpieces. First I explain why all are here.' He paused for dramatic effect and Colin was aware that every person's attention was focused on this chunky man with the wild and woolly hair and commanding presence. Topov raised his arms above his head, his throaty, accented voice bellowing across the rows of seats as he enunciated, 'We make film . . . yes?'

There was a burst of applause.

'Australian film, yes?'

The applause was louder.

'So we are going to do this! Topov will make Australian masterpiece. I show wild Australia. Real outback, yes?' He was almost shouting. 'Next year in Melbourne comes Olympic Games. Our film will show real Australia to world.'

Colin, like most of the audience, was swept up in Topov's enthusiastic speech. He sat forward in his seat wishing he could be part of Topov's brilliant plan to make a film in outback Australia.

Topov was pacing the stage. 'So Topov needs help. You be part of great film. Topov needs investors. They can come with us – to jungle, to see wild animals, natives and film adventures never seen on screen before. Do you want to join us? Put in money?'

There was applause, slightly less enthusiastic at the mention of investing money.

Colin's mind was whirling as Topov introduced the film he was screening – a story of love, betrayal and revenge set against the background of the Russian Steppes. But as the snowy opening sequence flashed onto the screen Colin's thoughts were elsewhere. He thought of the outback of Australia – hot desert, great red rocks, large shy kangaroos, heat, dust, the remoteness of it all. He thought of the five hundred pounds that his grandmother had left him. Could he use that money to invest in Topov's film? He knew that his parents would not approve. That money was earmarked as a house deposit. However, he thought, the least I can do is meet Topov later and discuss his venture.

Colin found the film ponderous and heavy handed but assumed that was part of the Russian ethos. The Russian Steppes were not at all as Colin imagined them. He had trouble following the plot and at times he really had little idea of what was happening. Nevertheless, Colin recognised that Topov must be a creative and original director, for the film was unlike anything he had seen before.

A table and chairs had been set up in the small lobby of the cinema and Colin, who was at the head of a very small queue, introduced himself to Topov. Topov shook Colin's hand and, in turn, introduced him to the large woman with the henna hair whom Colin had seen earlier as Madame Olga Konstantinova, his business partner.

Colin found her overwhelming. She was dressed in very colourful clothes, her braided hair, swept on top of her head, was caught with an elaborate tortoiseshell comb studded with coloured stones. She wore a lot of dazzling jewellery but Colin could not assess whether it was genuine or not. His mother would have considered her flashy but even though her earrings, bracelets, rings and necklace were all large pieces, they suited her big size and personality. And while Olga's dark plum-coloured lips were full and her smile seemed friendly, her pale blue eyes, outlined in green eye shadow, were hard and calculating.

'So you are interested in films? In movie-making?' asked Topov.

'Passionate. I belong to a film society. I study films as well as watching them for enjoyment,' enthused Colin. Then he quite surprised himself by blurting, 'I'd rather like to be a film scriptwriter one day.'

'Wonderful. Olga, make a note of this. And what is your name, young man?'

'Colin Peterson. I think your idea is terrific. About the outback. All those people coming here for the Olympics. If they see the film before the Games they'll know more about the place. And when they hear the Games on the radio, they'll know what other parts of the country look like. Very good idea,' he added again.

'You know wilderness? Northern Territory? You have been there?' asked Topov with interest.

'No. I haven't been out of Sydney. But I have read a lot and seen some old Australian films shot in the bush,' said Colin.

'And so you are a scriptwriter?' asked Olga. 'Do you plan to invest in our venture?'

Put on the spot like this, some innate caution made

Colin hesitate. 'I believe I can write. And I'd love to come on this adventure . . .' The idea of handing over his only savings to the determined Olga made Colin pause.

Topov waved his arms expansively, ignoring Olga's slight frown of annoyance. 'Mr Colin, you are an Australian and a writer so you shall write our screenplay and invest in great film. We have not many Australians eager for this adventure. Here, this is Peter, he has signed on.' He indicated a tall, rangy, fair-haired man who came over at Topov's waving gesture.

'Peter is our motor mechanic and electrical technician. He is Dutch so he has little sense of humour but we forgive him that.'

Peter nodded seriously at Colin and shook his hand. 'Pleased to meet you.'

Colin was pleased to meet a fellow adventurer. 'You're new to Australia?' he asked.

'I have been working on the Snowy Mountains Hydro-Electric Scheme. I have worked hard. So now I am in need of a change.' He didn't elaborate.

Olga handed Colin a small business card on which was printed her name and an address in Darling Point. Squeezed onto the bottom was a handwritten line appearing as an afterthought: 'Executive Producer Topov Prods'.

'We shall have a meeting at my house, Wednesday at five pm. Please to be there.'

'It might be a little after five,' said Colin nervously. 'Leaving work, getting the tram, you know.'

Olga seemed indifferent and turned her attention to another person who might be a potential investor. The idea of going on this trip had now taken a firm hold in Colin's mind. Leaving work, managing expenses and assuming responsibility for writing a script were big issues yet to be tackled. Right now he was taken with the romance of the idea and the fact it could actually come to pass.

'I wonder who else is going on this trip? I hope they can get enough investment to make it work,' said Colin.

'I'm sure we shall learn more on Wednesday at Madame Olga's,' said Peter pragmatically.

The following Wednesday Peter and Colin arrived simultaneously at Madame Konstantinova's home at exclusive Darling Point.

'This place is very expensive, I think,' commented Peter as they gazed at the rambling pile of old stone set back from a lush garden with a small square of emerald lawn. Steep steps cut into sandstone wound up to the house, perched, like its more flamboyant neighbours, to capture views across the water to Point Piper.

'I got the impression Madame Olga hasn't been in Australia very long,' said Colin.

'Only a few years. I believe that she escaped from Russia with her family when she was a little girl and lived for many years in China. There, I have been told, she met her husband who made a great deal of money in that country, but when the Japanese invaded they came to Sydney with their two little daughters. I do not think that they are poor.'

'How come you know these things,' asked Colin thinking that the recent Dutch immigrant mechanic was well informed.

'Not all immigrants that come here do so with just a suitcase and the clothes on their backs. Australia is the land of opportunity and some who have come here hope to exploit that. They paint a welcoming picture but your country is conservative, indeed, oppressive,' said Peter. 'Like its mother country there is a club and you are part of it or not. Capitalism can disadvantage the poor and make the rich richer.'

The Dutchman's tone was rather grim and disapproving. But before Colin could ask more questions, their attention was taken by the gathering on the terrace where Madame Olga and Maxim Topov were hosting a small group of people, some of whom Colin recognised from the film screening and Nino's Café. The two men were swept into the circle, introductions were made and waiters passed around drinks and hors d'oeuvres on silver trays.

Colin was glad he'd worn his best jacket and tie and while he chatted he tried to take in all the expensive surroundings in order to describe them to his mother. He hoped they'd be invited indoors so he could see more. A tall, strong-looking woman was talking to Olga who waved at Colin to join them.

'You are Peterson, yes?' said Olga. 'Mr Colin. This is Miss Helen Thompson. She is business manager for the expedition. Mr Colin will be writing the script.'

'Excellent. It all sounds quite exciting. Do you have an outline or anything down on paper yet?' Helen had what Colin considered to be an aristocratic British accent. She was athletic looking, with a plain face, free of make-up and wore a grey flannel skirt with a blouse buttoned up to the neck and fastened with a cameo brooch.

'Not really. I believe this is all still in early stages. I'm anxious to know more.' Colin hesitated, not wanting to admit he hadn't actually made up his mind about the project. Helen Thompson seemed an intimidating sort of person. 'As business manager do you know exactly where we're going, how long we'll be away, the sort of things we'll be filming?' began Colin.

But before Helen could respond, Olga held up a jewelled white hand to silence them all. Her rings, sunk into fat white fingers, caught the fading sunlight. She was wearing a floor-length swirling cape made of silk and splashed with bold colours that matched the swathe of silk wound around her head, a jewelled clasp in the centre of the turban.

'You are all so eager. So charming. Topov will explain more. He works in a very unorthodox manner.' Olga smiled. 'But he is very talented. Very creative man.' She looked quite emotional at this declaration of the talents of Topov and Colin felt very uncomfortable. He turned to Helen.

'And you? Do you have family here?'

'No. I'm travelling. Looking for a bit of adventure. Life in the home counties is rather dull and the country suffered so much in the war, I rather felt I'd like to travel while my mother and father are still spry and occupied,' she answered.

'Oh, so you're not a ten-pound Pom,' said Colin lightly, trying to make a small joke. The assisted passage of British immigrants to Australia for the cost of ten pounds was regularly in the news. But his remark seemed to offend Helen.

'Certainly not. I travel at my own expense and do as I wish. This filming thing seems a good way of seeing the country that might otherwise be inaccessible.'

'Helen comes from good family,' interjected Olga. 'My family also.' She lifted a champagne glass from the tray proffered by a waiter. 'Let us drink toast to success of Topov.'

Hearing his name, Maxim Topov raised his glass. 'To great hostess and patron, Madame Olga. To all supporting great expedition to Northern Territory and to all embarking on great adventure! Salute. We are ready to make plans. You are with us or you miss out! Come, let us meet in dining room and sign names!' He turned and headed into the house.

Peter walked beside Colin as they went through the

long French doors where the pale brocaded curtains had faded from scarlet to rose in the Sydney sunlight. 'Do you suppose we sign our names in blood?' he remarked with a slight smile.

Colin thought of his savings. His late grandmother would have considered this venture a total folly and it would dismay his parents if they knew what he was contemplating. He might not see a return on his investment, despite Topov's glowing promises, but if it was a way of breaking out of the box he saw as his life, then maybe it was worth the gamble. Going to the Northern Territory sounded such an adventure, especially compared with living in Sydney and working at the bank.

'Hollywood here we come,' he said, attempting to sound jaunty as he made the biggest decision of his life.

Peter gave him an unamused glance. 'I will stick to motor repairs. This experience will be useful for me. I'm not swallowing the fairy dust of Topov.'

Colin glanced at the others in the room. What did they expect as a return on their investment? Money, the promise of a new career, being part of the Australian film industry, or an adventure, like Helen hoped?

Madame Olga, assisted by Helen, neatly laid out a pile of contracts, a large map of Australia and a receipt book. The room, with its formal decor and expensive trappings, was intimidating. There was little chatter or banter as the investors shuffled forward and committed not just their money, but also as Topov and Olga said, their passion and spirit to the enterprise.

Maybe it was the room, the champagne and the atmosphere, but Colin felt there was now no turning back. He looked around him, committing his surroundings to memory. It was a scene he could perhaps use some time later in a film – the late afternoon sunlight coming through the dusty leadlight windows, a glimpse of blue harbour through dark European trees, the hushed voices, save for Helen's brisk, ringing English accent as she filled in the paperwork for each of the investors. Madame Olga fanned herself with a document, beaming at each person as Helen handed them their formal agreement with their receipt. Topov's voice could be heard from the adjoining drawing room.

Colin was surprised at how calmly he wrote out his cheque and signed it almost with a flourish instead of his usual careful and deliberate signature. He smiled at Helen.

'In for a penny, in for a pound. One of my granny's sayings.'

'Yes,' said Helen shortly. 'I have heard the expression.'

Colin joined Peter the Dutchman in the next room. Topov stood in front of the marble fireplace as a group of people listened intently to what he was saying.

'There're a lot more of us than I thought. Do you think everyone will be coming along?' asked Colin.

Peter shook his head. 'I doubt it, these people do not look like they want to get their shoes dusty. Helen says they are non-participating investors.'

Colin took a small pastry from a plate on the dining table and suddenly saw another man he recognised. He inched around the room and when the man was alone he introduced himself.

'Hello, I recognise you. I'm Colin, I've seen you at a couple of New Realist film screenings down at the wharves.'

'Is that so? Sorry, did we meet? I talk to so many people at those meetings. I am Drago.'

'Yes, yes. The cameraman. I heard you speak at one or two of the Wharfie's Film Unit documentaries. There was one about workers' living conditions. I was interested in what you said about film being the new instrument of progress. Are you part of this project?' asked Colin with interest.

'Yes. Regretfully, there is little work for cameramen in Australia. Not much film industry, not yet TV, so when I heard Maxim Topov was planning a film, I contacted him. His idea for this film is a good one, though we don't know what is actually planned just yet.'

'So you will be the cameraman, that's exciting,' said Colin, pleased the team had an experienced hand on board. Though Drago was only in his thirties, he seemed to be very worldly and capable, like Peter the Dutchman.

Drago shrugged. 'I am not officially the cameraman. Topov likes to control the camera. I am his assistant. But I need to work and Topov is not as good as he thinks he is. Maybe he will need an experienced cameraman. This could be a big opportunity for me.'

'Yes, I'm excited to see the outback.'

'So you are coming along? What role has Topov for you?' asked Drago with a smile.

'Writer. Though I'm not very experienced,' began Colin, 'but I hope I can create something worthwhile and bring a sense of what we find to a cinema audience . . .'

Drago broke into Colin's stumbling explanation and justification of his credentials. 'Don't worry about it. Topov will tell you what he wants. He is boss. Always boss.' He glanced at Madame Olga and Helen. 'Maybe too many boss people. It will be interesting.'

The party was winding up. Topov clapped his hands.

'Topov has announcement. We have very good team coming here. We have Maxim Topov director, cinematographer.' He gave a small bow as the room politely applauded. 'We have patron, Madame Olga. We have business manager, Miss Helen. We have writer, Mr Colin. We have mechanic and driver, Mr Dutchy. We have assistant camera and second driver, Mr Drago.' Each nodded as they were briefly acknowledged. 'We take turns cooking.'

'Until we find a cook and general factotum,' broke in Helen who, it was obvious, had no intention of cooking for the camp.

'Maybe we need other man. But, big, big question is – we must find *star*,' thundered Topov. 'Trees, natives, animals, all good, but we want beautiful lady actress to be star of film!'

Drago rolled his eyes and Peter the Dutchman smiled. Olga nodded in agreement.

Helen spoke first. 'And how do we find this star?' she asked.

'Put ad in newspaper,' declared Topov. 'We make auditions.' He stabbed a finger at Drago. 'You use my Bolex camera and make film screen test.' He then pointed at Colin. 'You write scene for audition. You read with actress.'

'So is this actress being paid, or does she invest as well?' asked Helen.

'Topov make her a big star but investing is also good,' said Madame Olga.

'Topov will decide,' declared Topov. 'We meet next week. Dutchy, find vehicles. Maybe boat. Come, we talk.'

Peter nodded at Colin. 'See you next week. If you have any motor contacts, let me know.'

''Fraid not, Peter. I don't even own a car,' said Colin. He bid Topov goodbye and as his hand was gripped by the Russian's large paw, Colin asked, 'About this scene you want for the audition . . .'

'You write something sexy. Make her cry, make her laugh, make her scared. You know best paper for advertisement?'

'I think so,' said Colin.

'Then you write ad and put in paper. Say auditions on Wednesday.'

'Ah, whereabouts? How do they apply?' wondered Colin.

'Tell them Nino's Café. We take details and good ones get to screen test.' Topov turned away.

'Get a receipt from the newspaper,' Helen reminded Colin.

'Oh, right.'

The next day he lodged the advertisement, paid for it and put the receipt in his wallet. The ad appeared in a large box in the classified section of the morning newspaper.

ACTRESS FOR OUTBACK FILM

International movie director making a film in the Northern Territory seeks talented, adventurous actress. Must be prepared to travel in rough conditions for several months through outback with large experienced crew. Interviews Nino's Café, Macleay Street, Kings Cross, nine am, Wednesday. Screen test to follow.

Colin hoped he'd covered the essentials and wondered just who might respond to the ad. It seemed rather unprofessional. Didn't actors have agents? He decided to make up a few flyers, maybe he could mimeograph them at the bank and stick them up around the halls and meeting rooms at the docks where some out-of-work actors congregated. He imagined it might take some time for word to get around, but anyone could leave their details at Nino's and it would reach Topov, who treated the café as his office.

After dinner, as he was leaving his flat, he clattered down the stairs and passed Johnny the cockney, who lived below him.

'What's up, Col? You going out?'

'Hello, Johnny. Yes, I'm sticking up a few flyers. Where do you think actors and actresses might hang out? Real ones I mean, not girls from around here.'

'What d'you want with actresses? Not your cup of tea I would've thought, eh Colin, me lad,' grinned Johnny.

Colin showed Johnny the flyer and briefly explained the search for a leading lady.

'Well, I'll be blowed. A man could make a lot of use out of this if I had the time. Tell you what, come with me, I'll take you down to the theatre district. Go round the stage doors and get them to put 'em on the noticeboard backstage.'

Johnny led the way, chatting nonstop as they jumped on a tram to the city. He was a short, energetic man, about Colin's age, with a mischievous smile and cheeky personality, the sort of chap Colin's mother would describe as being able to 'charm the birds from the trees'. All Colin knew about him was that he'd come out to Australia as a ten-pound Pom and loved the place, which he confidently told Colin was 'ripe for the pickings'. He was always dressed in a shiny suit, a narrow tie and a snappy narrow-brimmed fedora hat. He seemed to turn up everywhere and he told Colin that he had a lot of fingers in a lot of pies. Johnny always had a deal he was doing or was about to do.

'So, tell me more about this film thing. Where is the Northern Territory exactly? Where are you going and for how long?'

'Well, in the north. It's the outback, way out bush. Past the black stump, Johnny,' said Colin. 'Actually I have no idea exactly where we're going.'

'You mean you're going on this caper? How's a fellow get to go, then?' asked Johnny with sudden, serious interest.

Colin rubbed his fingers together indicating money, as he'd seen Johnny do. 'You will probably have to invest in the film.'

'How much?' asked Johnny.

'Johnny, what's it matter? It's not your sort of thing.' Colin almost laughed at the idea of Johnny in his spiffy suit and hat in the bush. 'It's going to be a bit rough. You know, dirt roads, no roads, bush tracks, rivers, desert. Who knows what.'

'Listen, I want to talk to the bloke in charge. You fellows are going to need vehicles, trucks, just to get you there. Not that easy finding the right sort of transport to go to those sorts of places, but you know I've got contacts. Do you know if anything's been organised?'

'It's not up to me. You need to talk to Topov, it's his film, or Helen, the business manager. Come to the café when the auditions are on,' suggested Colin.

'I'll certainly do that. Be there with bells on. C'mon, this is our stop. Let's hit the Capitol Theatre and the Tiv and put up some of these flyers.'

Colin had laboured over his little audition scene and was feeling quite pleased with the short two hander. There was a nice speech for the actress and while he fed her lines, she could give scope to various emotions. He'd set it on the bank of a river, a scene he'd recreated from a picture on his calendar of somewhere in rural Australia where a river meandered over stones between sandy banks lined with willow trees and captioned 'On Tranquil Banks'.

He could not get to the café until his lunch break. He hurried downstairs to where Nino had given Topov the space in the basement restaurant that was closed to customers during the day. To his surprise, he found that the auditions had not even started and that Helen was just setting up a table with three chairs behind it and putting notepads in front of each chair. On one side of the table, Drago had a small tripod and a camera set up and several professional lights to take still photographs of any potential leading ladies.

'Hello, Colin. Do you have copies of the audition piece?' asked Helen.

'I dropped them into Nino's this morning on my way to work, but I only managed to do a few copies. Do you want me to get them? Where's Mr Topov?'

'He'll be along. We'll ask only those girls who have obvious talent to read,' she said.

'So how do you decide who that will be? By their experience?' asked Colin.

'What good is that? Most of them will make up their résumés,' said Helen.

'It'll be the looks,' said Drago. 'Did you put in the advertisement that only pretty girls need apply?'

At last Topov arrived, looking as if he'd slept in his clothes, rumpled hair and bleary-eyed and told Peter to bring in the applicants. Colin was amazed at the turnout. Twenty had arrived to be interviewed, including two male transvestites still in their make-up and cocktail dresses from the previous evening.

Topov dropped a large black-leather notebook on the table and called for espresso coffee. 'Topov is writing brilliant script,' he announced.

Colin blanched, wondering if he was suddenly out of a job. 'Mr Topov, I've written a scene for the leading lady. If you'd like to look at it . . .' But Topov pushed the papers back at Colin.

'Good, good. First we look at girls. Bring in first star to be.'

The women were dressed in a variety of outfits from casual to elaborate party wear. Some had never acted at all, others inflated their meagre thespian experiences. One young woman, dressed in denim jeans with turned up cuffs and a man's shirt seemed to be the most experienced and talented. But when she said she was studying method acting with another actor from New York, Topov threw his hands in the air.

'This rubbish. Crazy acting. Be a cow. Be an alligator.

Be a cloud.' He began dancing about waving his arms, in a surprisingly nimble way.

The woman scowled. 'Is that what your film is about? Cows and alligators? Count me out.' And she stomped from the room.

Topov burst into laughter. 'I like this one.'

'I don't think she's interested,' said Helen. 'Let's move on.'

Topov, Colin and Helen sat behind the table as the women continued to come forward to answer questions posed by Topov. It was an ordeal for everyone. Colin cringed as Topov challenged, taunted, teased and flirted with the women, dismissing most of them, but telling a few, 'You wait. Come back for screen test.'

It became obvious to Colin that Drago had been right. Topov only spent time with the pretty women, even when it was obvious they lacked experience or had not the faintest idea of what they would be embarking upon. One girl wanted to come back home at weekends to visit her boyfriend, another asked if she could bring her mother along. One actress wanted to be able to go back and forth for theatre auditions.

Topov continued to ignore Colin's script. When he thought a girl had some potential he leapt up and sketched a brief dramatic scenario, which proved to be mostly incomprehensible to the actress. But with Topov leaping dramatically in front of her screaming, 'Killer snake, crocodile, wild beast . . . coming to attack! What to do,' the girl quickly got the message to squeal, scream and emote. While several of the girls simply looked at Topov as if he were a madman and walked away, others flung themselves into scenes of abandon, throwing themselves around, howling and crying.

Helen sat stony faced. Drago dropped his head in his hands. Colin had no idea what to say, so tried to make notes. Finally there were no more hopeful leading ladies and Colin knew he would have to return to the bank.

'Is there anyone you want me to film?' asked Drago.

'No, they are all dragons,' declared Topov. 'We go.'

'What are we going to do about a leading lady?' asked Colin anxiously.

Topov shrugged. 'Word will spread. Someone will arrive. Let us go upstairs and have something to eat.' He called for Nino and ordered food for himself and the small entourage of fans and hopefuls who were hovering in the café.

As Colin left to go to work, Johnny scuttled into the café.

'That's the man, right?'

'Yes, but you need to speak to Helen,' said Colin, pointing at the efficient woman in the severe blouse.

'Nah. That's the man with the action. I'll talk to him.' Johnny made a beeline for Topov.

Colin walked back to the bank, digesting the extraordinary auditions. He didn't understand how anything could be achieved in Topov's unstructured, emotional and casual manner. But maybe he was too used to the ordered calmness of the bank's routine. He realised that he would have to relax and try to appreciate how these film people worked.

After work he returned to the café. Topov had left but Johnny, Drago and Peter were deep in conversation. Johnny's face was flushed and he was in high spirits. He waved to Colin. 'Hey, matey. I've organised the transport and I'm in. I'm going along. I'm going to be the cook and drive one of the vehicles. This is crazy. I love it. Come and have a drink.'

Colin was amazed. Johnny was such a town person. Colin couldn't believe that he would join such an adventure, so far from the wheeling and dealing that the young cockney loved. 'Fantastic! That's really good news. Congratulations. Is Topov downstairs? Any more girls turn up?'

'A few. Topov has gone. Helen is going through the rest of them,' said Drago. 'She said she'd call me if she needed any photos taken.'

Colin went to the basement where a waiter was beginning to set up tables and chairs for the evening. Helen sat at the desk reading the notes she'd made.

'Oh, Colin, glad you're here, you can relieve me. Not that I think we'll have any more hopefuls turn up.'

'Has anyone interesting come in since I left?'

'No. Young actresses obviously have better things to do with their time than try out for a film.'

'So what do we do about a leading lady? Maybe we'll find someone in a country town?' said Colin.

'I don't think so,' said Helen. 'I would hardly rely on rural Australia to find dramatic talent.'

'I suppose not,' said Colin doubtfully. He remembered the amateur suburban plays he'd seen with his mother, which he had thought excellent, and offered, 'What about the suburbs?'

'Really, I don't think the suburbs would supply the sort of glamour that Mr Topov is looking for.'

Colin decided to drop his suggestions. Helen was so imperious. 'Have you met the new cook?'

'I met Johnny when he and Topov discussed the transport. I hope he measures up,' said Helen.

Topov suddenly appeared in the room. 'Do not leave room. We have one more lady to see.'

Helen glanced at her watch. 'It's late. Lucky we are still here, seeing interviews began at nine am.'

'From nine am,' muttered Colin.

Topov sat at the table as a young woman came down the stairs. She had coppery curly hair, a big smile and was wearing brown capri pants cinched with a wide belt and a clinging leopard-print top that showed off her curves. Colin smiled back at her. The girl came and stood calmly in front of them as Topov frankly studied her.

'Name?' asked Helen filling in a form.

'I am Marta.' She had a soft Scandinavian accent but spoke clearly. 'I am an actress.'

'Where you have been actress?' asked Topov.

'Theatre in Denmark, some short films in Sweden. I also work in London and Paris. French theatre.' She was still smiling sweetly.

'You make a scene for us,' said Topov leaning back in his chair.

'What would you like? I can do Chekhov, Bernard Shaw . . .'

'Scriptwriter, you do with her,' said Topov waving at Colin.

'You mean, this? My scene?' Colin picked up his script feeling dreadfully nervous.

'Yes. Go stand, walk around, read,' directed Topov.

Colin handed Marta two sheets of typed paper. 'Sorry you haven't read this. It's two people on the banks of a peaceful river, when suddenly they see something scary.'

'A crocodile?' asked Marta with wide blue eyes.

'Perhaps. The girl is frightened, then excited, and then . . .'

'Read,' bellowed Topov.

Colin stood on the spot, his head down reading the lines he'd written and knew by heart. But Marta was relaxed and walked around, lifting her eyes from the page to direct her gaze at Colin, occasionally tossing her head and catching Topov's eye. When the script called for her to become fearful, she rushed at Colin and clung to him and he felt very self-conscious and knew that his face was getting red. After Marta had finished, she moved away from

Colin and stood in front of the table looking serenely at Topov and Helen.

'Dobro,' muttered Drago who had come in unnoticed. Colin sat back down.

'Script no good. Script rubbish,' announced Topov beaming, as Colin cringed. 'You,' he pointed a finger at Marta. 'You okay.'

'Would you like to give us your details?' asked Helen, pencil poised.

'Drago. Make picture of this woman. Close up, walking, doing the faces, you know.' Topov stood up as Drago began turning on his lights. 'So, you have been to Australian bush?'

'No. But I would like to.' Marta's curls bounced as she nodded and smiled.

Helen nudged Topov and murmured, 'Investing?'

Topov scratched his head and looked crestfallen. He walked to Marta and dropped an arm around her shoulders. 'You pretty lady. Good actress. Topov would like you star in his movie. But, budget, it no good. We have shoe budget.'

'Shoestring,' interjected Helen.

'But Topov will make brilliant movie, show wild Australia to the world, for Olympics. Everyone in film become famous, get rich. But for making film, we all put up money.'

'So we have shares in the picture,' said Marta brightly.

Helen stared at her.

'You have money?' asked Topov.

'If I invest and I am the star, I get a share in the returns plus living salary,' said Marta briskly.

'All investors get the same return,' said Helen.

'We make you happy,' Topov assured Marta. 'Comfortable. You will love the outback. Yes, Mr Colin?'

Colin nodded enthusiastically. 'It's a wonderful chance

to be in a film and a once-in-a-lifetime opportunity to see these places.'

'How much?' asked Marta.

'Camera ready,' said Drago.

'You do screen test, we talk money, contract after.' Topov signalled Helen and they headed back upstairs as the waiter began setting out cutlery and glasses on the tables around Drago, his camera and Marta.

'Good luck Marta,' whispered Colin as he gathered up the papers and hurried after Topov.

Everyone had dispersed and Colin headed back to his flat. He thought he might grab Johnny and go out for a drink but there was no answer to his taps on Johnny's door. So he stayed in and thought about Marta and her performance and wished he'd written a better script. But now he could see that the project was coming together with definite possibilities and he hoped that he'd be able to live up to Topov's expectations.

The next day an invitation was slipped to Colin at the bank. His hands started to shake with excitement as he read.

Madame Olga Konstantinova and Maxim Topov
invite Colin Peterson
to dinner at Prince's Restaurant, Martin Place,
this Friday at nine pm to celebrate the launch of filming
Wild Australia, *a film by Topov*

3

'PRINCE'S RESTAURANT. I'VE HEARD of it,' said Veronica. 'My granddad proposed to my grandmother over dinner there. It must have been pretty fancy. She often talked about it. Soft lights, sweet music, fine food. Very romantic.'

Colin nodded. 'Oh my, yes. I was so nervous going to the dinner Topov gave to celebrate the start of the movie. As it turned out Madame Olga was the hostess. I don't think we all quite scrubbed up to Prince's usual standard. It was black tie, very formal. Marta looked beautiful, Helen was a bit of a plain stick. She wore black and some family heirloom jewellery. Turns out she came from landed gentry. Funny, though, the person most at home was Johnny.'

'The cockney cook?'

'Yes. Turns out he had connections in restaurants

and clubland. He was into everything, worked for some very, er, colourful characters. I was surprised at how many people Johnny knew after such a short time in Australia.'

'You have very clear memories of the night it seems.'

'For an unsophisticated boy working in a bank, a dinner at Prince's was a wonderful experience. I remember the tablecloths and napkins were pale pink damask. It was all very glamorous – a last blast before heading to the bush. It also made us feel we were part of a substantial company.' He gave a chuckle. 'A week later was a different story.'

Veronica fiddled with her coffee cup, wondering if she could tell Andy there was a story here or not. Here was a cast of intriguing characters, heading into inhospitable and unknown wilderness at an interesting time. Perhaps it didn't matter about the success or not of the expedition. Maybe this was a case of the journey being more interesting than the destination. Nevertheless, she would have to find out a lot more before it would work as a story for a television program.

'What happened to the film Topov made?' she asked Colin.

'The picture was never finished, although we did shoot quite a bit of film on the trip.'

'So there was some film?'

'Yes. Several cans of it. It was sent back to Sydney for processing and safekeeping and replaced with new stock as we went along. It's probably long gone.'

'That seems a shame. It'd be interesting to see it now. Have you any idea what happened to that film footage?'

'All I know is that it was sent to Madame Olga. So many questions. You are thorough,' he smiled.

'It's my job, Colin. I trained as a journalist and I'm trying to work out how your story could fit into a program on the Australian film industry. There've always been a lot of mavericks in our film history and Topov seems to take the cake.'

'Topov was certainly larger than life,' said Colin thoughtfully. 'His background was a bit mysterious though. Sometimes we got conflicting stories. You know, I've wondered if the Topov film that I saw and was supposed to be set in Russia was actually shot there. Sometimes I'm not even sure that Topov was even a Russian.'

Veronica was planning to pay for the coffee and return to the office, but this made her pause. She knew that Andy would expect her to find out all she could before making a final judgment about the suitability of the story for *Our Country*. 'Colin, as we're here, why don't we order lunch? You might as well tell me as much as you can. I mean, you started the story, why not finish it for me?'

Colin didn't answer for a moment as he stared out at the street of smart cars and restaurants, passing people, all so far from the country he had seen so many years before. In reply, he reached for the menu and Veronica turned to a fresh page in her notebook.

'Colin, you write newspaper story. Make publicity,' ordered Topov.

Colin pulled out his diary and began to make notes. They were at Nino's. Topov, Peter, Drago and Johnny.

'What do we tell the press?' asked Colin, hoping now he'd find out some firm details about Topov's plans as well.

'We have star, we have motorcade, we announce expedition going to film wild Australia,' said Topov.

'Where's the route map?' asked Peter.

'No map. No big roads, we follow sun,' exclaimed Topov expansively. 'Bourke. We go first to Bourke.'

'Bourke? That's to the north, I think, so it's not exactly following the sun,' said Colin, but Topov missed his little attempt at humour. 'I'll contact the papers, ask them to send a photographer. Where shall we take the picture?' he asked. 'At Madame Olga's?'

'No, no. Do not mention Madame Olga to press. This is Topov Production. We go to sand dunes, place where they make films for desert. We pose in desert with motor cars. Marta in sexy clothes.'

'Where is Marta?' asked Drago.

'Helen take her for wardrobe. Buy sexy clothes.'

'How wild is the film going to be?' asked Johnny with a grin.

Topov roared. 'It be beautiful film. Beautiful scenery, beautiful animals, beautiful woman in jungle. It be beautiful success.'

'It must be nice to be so confident all the time,' said Peter tersely. 'Better we buy trucks not sexy pants. Where is Johnny getting them?'

'Johnny clever boy. He knows people,' said Topov calmly.

Topov shrugged as Peter walked away. 'Dutchy people not laugh. Always straight at your face. This is okay.'

'At least you know where you stand,' said Drago.

'Johnny good cook,' grinned Topov. 'He cook anything. You see, he cooking up good car for Topov.' He rubbed his fingers together and winked. 'Johnny good boy, he know many people, make good deal.'

They assembled on the edge of the city, at the Kurnell sand dunes. Here there were miles of rolling sandhills at the edge of a peninsula bordered by the Pacific Ocean on one side and Botany Bay on the other. Even Colin had never been there. It was a desolate place, though Captain Cook who had first landed at Botany Bay found it an acceptable and propitious landfall.

The vehicles lined up with the large sand dunes behind, looking as if they were in the middle of a desert. The press photographer and even Colin, who had no knowledge of cars, were taken aback at the strange array of vehicles. The small convoy included a 1936 Dodge, a Jeep with a canvas roof from ex-army surplus and a battered Land Rover behind which was hitched a squat round caravan that had once been canary yellow.

'This is an interesting line-up,' said the photographer. 'Could we have the young lady at the front, please.'

Marta, dressed in new khaki shorts, a low-cut blouse and a leopard-print scarf, was posed at the front of the Jeep holding a rifle. Beside her was Maxim Topov with his arm draped over a massive camera he'd had Peter and Drago manhandle out of the caravan for the photo. He announced with pride, 'This de Brie Super Parvo camera,' and directed them to set it up on a huge tripod that had a geared head with two control wheels, one on the back and the other on the left side to direct the lens.

'This must weigh a hundred pounds,' muttered Peter. 'He's not taking this contraption, is he?'

'Doesn't make for taking wildlife shots on the run,' admitted Drago grimly. 'He'll have to use the little Bolex a lot of the time, I bet. But the two cameras use different film, sixteen millimetre and thirty-five millimetre, so they won't splice together. I wonder if he knows what he's doing?'

Topov, hearing this, glared at Drago. 'Topov very clever. He use one camera for movie, little camera to make picture for TV for American market and maybe BBC. Make two productions, make twice as much money. This why Topov producer.'

Johnny climbed onto the roof of the truck and posed as if looking for wild animals. The rest of the group clustered around the other vehicles.

When the photographer was satisfied, the bulky camera was dismantled from the tripod and the photographer took down their names and a few details in his notebook. 'The office has the info you dropped in,' he said, trying to stem the flow of rhetoric from Topov. 'Let us know when you get back. I'll be very keen to hear how it goes,' he added with a sardonic smile.

The date for their departure was two weeks away. Colin's parents remained concerned that the whole expedition was an irresponsible foolishness and thought that Colin had wasted his grandmother's money. But Colin was convinced that this was his chance for a new opportunity and was excited as preparations for the trip continued. Helen told them all to pack as few clothes as possible, space being at a premium because of 'budget restraints'. They had to be fairly self-sufficient. They would mainly be camping but as their salaries would be paid to them on a regular basis, they could buy the things not provided by Topov and Helen in the various towns they passed. After discussions with Topov, Johnny was dispatched to acquire – through his contacts – tents and camping equipment.

Peter looked morose as he stirred his coffee. 'This Johnny is too clever. I think he's making money on the side out of these deals with his so-called contacts.'

'Well, if it saves us money,' said Colin.

'If the motor vehicles are anything to go by, I don't think we'll be saving money. It could cost us more.'

Drago joined them. 'The Dodge is old but strong. Have you checked the mechanics?'

Peter shrugged. 'I think these vehicles will give me a lot of trouble. I've got my tools and I think I will have to use them a lot.'

'I'm afraid I can't help. I don't know anything about cars,' said Colin.

'I will teach you,' said Peter. 'And your job? You will leave the bank?'

'Yes, I've handed in my resignation. I'm finished with the bank. Making films is my new career.'

'Perhaps you are right,' said Drago. 'This could be the start of a big change in all our lives. Despite Topov.'

Veronica and Colin had finished their coffee and Veronica was thoughtful.

'I'd like to hear more about the expedition. Did you keep a journal, do you have any photos?'

'Somewhere. I kept a journal. I suppose I could dig it out. It's nothing special. But it would be fun to read it again,' he said.

'It could trigger a few more memories and anecdotes.' She glanced at her watch. 'I should get back to the office. Can we arrange to get together again? Look at your material?'

'Yes, of course,' said Colin. 'I'm happy to help, if I can.'

'I'm sure it will. I'll look forward to more details. Oh, by the way, is there anyone else still around who was on the trip with you? Do you keep in touch with any of them?'

Colin shook his head. 'Not really. I get occasional Christmas cards from Marta, but I haven't heard from her for a bit. Everyone else was so much older than us, they would all be dead by now. Except for Johnny. He's still around, of course.'

'He is? Why do you say "of course"?'

Colin gave a small smile. 'Johnny, or John as he prefers to be called now, did very well for himself. John Cardwell, you might have heard of him?'

'The colourful racing identity? Of course I've heard of him. We wanted to do a story about him more than a year or so ago but he refused to be interviewed. He is very media shy, doesn't like journalists poking into his various business activities.' Veronica was now very intrigued. This piece of information gave the story some real legs. John Cardwell was considered by many to be one of Sydney's most notorious business leaders. While the police had never been able to pin anything on him, rumours about his illegal activities were rife. Andy would be very interested to learn of his connection with this story. 'Do you have any contact with him?'

'Good heavens, no! He moves in very different circles from me.'

'Colin, I've found all this very interesting. Let's say we meet again soon. Does any particular time suit you?'

'I'm retired and widowed, my days aren't as busy as yours,' he said. 'I'd love to tell you more about it.'

'Great. I enjoy your company,' said Veronica warmly and she meant it. Many of the stories that were pursued for *Our Country* went up dead-end streets. But sometimes they got lucky. The fact that one of Sydney's most infamous identities, who was involved in racing, gambling and a string of questionable business dealings, had been part of this strange expedition, piqued her interest. This story was worth pursuing.

Andy smoothed his hair and adjusted his shirt collar wishing he'd worn a tie. He slipped on his linen jacket and headed upstairs to answer the summons of the chairman, CEO and new owner of Network Eleven, William Rowe. Rowe had given a general address to the staff when he'd first taken over and now was slowly working his way through the heads of departments and key staff for one-on-one consultations. Rumours circulated constantly around the station about proposed changes, hirings and firings, but at this stage there had been nothing significant, although the program ratings were watched with keen interest.

William Rowe, or Big Bill, was a tall man with a ruddy weathered complexion, the result of his years in the mining industry in the remote regions of Australia. His pale eyes seemed even lighter as a result. For his age he looked very fit. He wore a tie, his jacket hung on a stand in a corner of his office. He rose and came from behind his desk to shake Andy's hand warmly and his hand was surprisingly smooth and soft.

'Andy, nice to see you again. Take a seat. Coffee? Tea?'

Andy perched on the small sofa, Rowe sat in the deep armchair, a small coffee table between them. Andy knew that Rowe had inquired about staff names and the way people preferred to be addressed. He had asked staff their opinion of their various bosses and had taken a big interest in every department including the creative and technical people – which was unusual for an executive running a network. Andy was slightly bemused at Rowe's friendly remark, as though they were old friends, when in fact he'd never spoken to him.

'I'm fine, thanks.' He waited.

Rowe leaned forward, his hands clasped between his knees. 'Andy, as I'm sure you're aware, I'm chatting to people like yourself who are responsible for the output of this station. I'm trying to identify how we can lift our game. I'm not being critical of specific people or programs – at this stage – but trying to see where we can drag up the numbers, shift the focus and emphasis. I'm interested to hear your ideas, your thoughts.'

'I didn't come prepared with any ideas off the top of my head, though I'm happy to put some thoughts on paper. Obviously the first issue that always comes up is money,' said Andy candidly. 'Having a budget that allows us to travel, get the best people and facilities makes a difference. But *Our Country* has become pretty adept at making the most of what we have.'

'It's a fine program. Hits that middle demographic solidly. Very consistent.' Rowe paused.

'But always room for improvement?' said Andy wishing the conversation was less vague.

'Of course, every show would like to increase its audience share. My concern is that a lot of the programming of the station is a bit – comfortable. I'd rather we became less the favourite slipper and hit somewhere between the stiletto and the Doc Marten.'

Andy's heart sank. 'Younger? Trendier?'

'More relevant, shall we say. You have good, on-the-ball staff?'

'They are. Especially my senior producer, Veronica Anderson. She's young, intelligent, sensitive. Good nose for a story.'

'Attractive? Be good on camera?' asked Rowe.

'She's very attractive, gets on well with people, smart interviewer. As you know, we have a studio host but essentially the stories in *Our Country* are told with only an occasional presenter or reporter. We let the story and its subjects tell it so we see it through their eyes. No personal interpretations or interjections. The art of the neutral interrogator is a lost artform these days, every journo wants to be talent, a personality,' Andy observed.

Rowe looked thoughtful. 'Your show's appeal is to the middle aged, middle class, isn't it? Any ideas how we could get a younger generation interested as well?'

Andy took a breath and kept his voice even. 'Horses for courses. Our research has found that as kids mature they tend to watch what their parents always watched – if it's still on air. Maybe we need an innovative program for the youth market but without shifting the demographic focus of the entire network. If it ain't broke . . .' He paused.

'I take your point,' said Rowe with a smile. 'Now, from

a technical point of view, can you tell me where your program could cut costs and what you'd like in an ideal world? Not right this minute, but you could work with me on this one, Andy, to our mutual benefit. I'll leave that with you.' He rose, signalling that the brief meeting was over.

Andy frantically tried to think of some imperative that would swing support for their show without simply asking for more money.

'Mr Rowe. I'm very proud of *Our Country* and I know viewers feel the same. It's more than an interesting, entertaining, quirky look at our people and our country. It's reaffirming who we are, our heritage, history and future for Aussies and newcomers. In this global village where we are all linked for better or worse, as the pressures of globalisation, politics, the economy and climate change affect us all, we need to cling to our culture, our stories. It gives us a sense of family, of belonging, no matter what our heritage. *Our Country* is just that – a look at who we are, where we've come from and how we might create a future we all desire.' Andy drew a breath. 'It's in the stories of everyday people that we find the heartland. Politicians, corporate leaders, experts can say what they want. What people want to hear are personal revelations they can all relate to. To hear and see things in our country they might not have the opportunity to do or share. But it gives them a sense of understanding the land, the narrative of people getting on with their lives, albeit under different or unusual circumstances.' Andy shrugged. 'Basically people are interested in other people. More so than in the superficial doings of so-called celebrities.' He smiled. 'I rest my case.'

Rowe studied the executive producer, whom he knew had a long and respected career in television. 'Andy, I've taken on this network as a business. And it doesn't matter whether you're making steel or TV shows, if you don't succeed, you'll sink. I'm not heartless, so I hope I can improve the fortunes of this station and everyone working here. But I cannot indulge the arty, cultural warriors who argue that what we do is un-Australian.'

'You mean making our own programs costs more than bringing in US or UK shows,' broke in Andy, 'but surely there is a balance and audiences in my experience have always supported us. And I do feel we have an obligation to tell our own stories.'

Rowe opened the door. 'I'm a businessman and you're a producer and a passionate one.' He shook Andy's hand. 'I hope we can make it work for both of us. Thanks for your time, Andy.'

Back at his desk Andy felt angry and worried about the future of *Our Country*. He rang Veronica and asked her to pop into his office.

'I was just coming in to see you.' Veronica said. 'I've met with Colin Peterson.'

'And?'

'Debatable. Interesting, but requires work.' She saw Andy wasn't paying full attention and seemed distracted. 'What's up?'

'I've had my consultation with William Rowe. All very charming and we're in this together, but I can't stem the disquiet I feel over our new leader.'

'And owner, don't forget. Big Bill can jolly well do whatever he wants to,' said Veronica. 'Why the concern?'

'I think he's doing what others have tried before – go for the younger audience, dumb us down.'

'Not again! The top women's magazines tried that and failed. There's one channel that's already got the youth market tied up. So how's all this going to affect us?' asked Veronica knowing their show appealed to a mature audience.

'I'm supposed to come up with ideas, a plan. Let

me sleep on it. I'd value any input from you, of course. Might throw it open to the team, too. But back to the moment – what did Colin Peterson have to say?'

Veronica quickly ran through the gist of her conversation with Colin and Andy looked thoughtful.

'Do you get the feeling there's more to this tale?'

Veronica nodded. 'Yes, I do. It's such a bizarre story, crazy-sounding characters, you can't help wondering about the group dynamics, especially in what must have been rugged conditions.'

'Humour me, pick away at it while we're thinking of other things to entertain the under thirties set,' said Andy.

'Hey, that's me! I'm not thirty for four months,' Veronica reminded him.

Andy stared at Veronica. She was so capable, so easy to get along with, her sense of humour and her ability to handle any office drama made him forget her age. 'Well then, you can throw some of those young ideas into the production meeting, see what people come up with.'

'Andy, *Our Country* isn't about superficial celebrity stuff. Everyone working on the show respects what it's all about. I think we should take the opposite tack. Go harder, dig deeper, refuse to do shallow.'

Andy grinned. 'That's what I like about you, Veronica. You're a bit of a rebel at heart. Dig away to your heart's content.'

'We could dig up some interesting players. Like John Cardwell.'

'I wonder what that slippery fellow got up to with your expedition?' asked Andy. 'Have you talked to him?'

'Not yet. I'm waiting till I hear more details from Colin. Seems in those days he was Johnny, the young cockney cook cum contact man. The guy who knew someone who could get anything . . . at a good price.'

Andy smiled. 'Is that where Cardwell started? And

now he owns a string of racehorses, blocks of flats, a casino and a nightclub. Well, they're the legit business dealings, right?'

'Yep. But if rumours are to be believed you can add a couple of brothels and money laundering. Wasn't he called the robber baron of Surry Hills? This story is definitely looking up.'

It was Friday evening and Veronica was meeting two friends for a drink and dinner. She'd been looking forward to catching up with Gordon, an international air steward who was an old school friend and his partner, Brad, a graphic designer. It had been a while since she'd seen them and she was looking forward to the evening as they were such good company and made her laugh. But as she was dressing, she had a call from her sister.

'Vee, I hate to do this to you . . . Can you help us out?'

'What's up?' Veronica recognised the frantic tone in her sister's voice. It wasn't panic as in an emergency, it was the breathless, overrun, can't cope, all too much desperation.

'The babysitter let us down . . . again. Philip has a really important dinner this evening . . . Do you think . . .? Could you . . .? Are you free?'

Veronica loved her sister but she found her trying at times. She just took on too much. Everyday was jammed juggling work, children, her husband's career and their busy lifestyle. 'Well, if you're really desperate. I was meeting Gordon and Brad for dinner. Haven't seen them in so long . . .'

'Bring them over here. We'll get in gourmet take-away. The girls won't be any trouble once they've had dinner.'

'It doesn't make for much social interaction,' sighed Veronica. 'I'll call the boys and run it past them.'

'That's okay, Veronica. We'll come over and help entertain the angels and bring dinner with us,' said Gordon. 'I haven't seen Sue's girls since they were tiny. What shall we bring?'

'Absolutely nothing. Sue has everything that has ever appeared in an ad on TV plus half the local store. But sweet of you to think of it. The girls will enjoy flirting with you and Brad. And Sue will provide dinner.'

'We'll read them a story. It'll be a nice change to have a touch of domesticity,' said Gordon. 'What time is bedtime? We'll come early to help tuck them in.'

'Anytime after six-thirty,' said Veronica, adding, 'until midnight.' She hoped the girls would settle down at a reasonable hour so she could gossip with Gordon and Brad.

'I've made up the spare bed. You are a sweetie.' Sue kissed Veronica and hugged the girls who were glued to a DVD. 'You do exactly what Auntie Vee tells you.'

'You look lovely, Sue,' said Veronica, eyeing her sister's expensive dinner dress.

Philip put his jacket on. 'Thanks Vee, this will be a boring evening, but if it helps the career, gotta do it, right?'

Sophie and Sarah were bathed and in their pyjamas. Dinner was a quarter eaten. Veronica had tried to make a game of the meal, bribed them and threatened that they wouldn't have time with Gordon and Brad if dinner wasn't eaten. Sophie had cried, spilled the remains of her spaghetti in her lap and had to be washed and changed. When Veronica brought her back to the table she found that Sarah had left her dinner and the table and was in front of the TV.

'Sarah, I said no television or DVDs until you'd finished dinner. Come on, back to the table,' said Veronica firmly.

'I don't like the table. I want to eat here.'

'No food in the living room,' said Veronica firmly as

Sarah knelt in front of the coffee table, pushing the magazines to one side. 'You don't learn manners eating in front of the TV.'

'I don't want to eat dinner. I don't like it.'

'Me too,' echoed Sophie. 'Ice-cream.'

'No ice-cream till your dinner is finished and you sit nicely at the table. If you do and you're good, Gordon and Brad will bring you something nice.'

Too late. The doorbell rang.

The girls squealed and jumped as the boys came in, kissed Veronica and teased the girls.

'What's all this?' said Gordon as he picked up Sarah. 'You haven't finished your dinner. My goodness, that's no good.'

Brad inspected a messy plate. 'Is this one of Veronica's gourmet delicacies?' he asked wrinkling his nose.

'It's spasgetti,' said Sophie.

'Yum, it looks good,' said Gordon, giving Brad a warning look. 'Come on we'll watch you finish dinner while Veronica does drinks for us all.'

The girls adored the two visitors but, trying to keep them at the table, let alone making them eat, was impossible so Gordon and Brad gave up.

'Okay, story time.'

'Yaaay,' squealed Sarah, racing for a book.

'No, not out here. This is quiet time. Brushing teeth, into bed and sit quietly and Uncle Gordon will read you a story.'

'Later. I want to watch *The Simpsons*.'

'No way!' exclaimed Gordon. 'Look, Brad has a lovely book, let's go and read *Possum Magic*.'

The boys battled on with the girls as Veronica cleaned up the mess.

'I need a drink,' said Brad, coming into the kitchen. 'I've capitulated. They're watching a video game thing on their computer. I can't believe that a four year old has her own computer. Where's the wine? Good lord, the fridge is absolutely chock full of food. There's enough here to feed an army. How would they ever get through so much? Why did she get take-away?'

'Sue buys everything at once, when she has the chance. I think a lot of it gets thrown away. What's Sophie doing?'

'Helping Sarah win the war of the worlds in some dungeon,' said Gordon as he joined them. 'You know what I said about an evening of domesticity? I've changed my mind. Spare me from children. This place is bedlam.' He wrinkled his nose. 'Doesn't Sue have a cleaning lady? They must be able to afford it. The girls' room is buried in dirty laundry, toys and I hate to think what else.'

'I'm sorry, Gordon. Yes, they have a lady a couple of times a week, but I don't think that she's much good. Sue's always saying that she'll get someone else, when she's got a moment to look.'

'Well, I hope your kids don't turn out like this. Marry someone very rich so you don't have to work or can have a live-in housemaid. Let's warm up the goulash,' said Gordon.

There were a few more squabbles because the girls wanted to be with Gordon and Brad but the boys were surprisingly firm and made the girls stay in their beds with a book while the grown-ups ate dinner. 'It's how I handle passengers who over-indulge,' explained Gordon. 'I can be quite the bossy boots.'

With Sophie and Sarah finally asleep, Veronica caught up on news and gossip and talked about her job.

'I love my job, I love my boss – in a fatherly way – and I think the show is really good. I just hate the idea that the new CEO might want to dumb us down,' she said.

'Why don't you go overseas, take leave? You need a change in your life,' said Brad.

'I couldn't leave them at a time like this! And it's no fun travelling by yourself. And there could possibly be a lot of changes in my professional life if Andy decides, or is told, to reposition our show.'

'And what about your personal life?' asked Gordon. 'I'm getting worried about you. No social life, no lover, no interests. What's wrong with you?'

Veronica was unoffended and laughed. 'Nothing, I hope. It's hard to meet the right people. I don't have time to hang out in bars and clubs. Don't like it much, anyway.'

'Are you over Eddie?' asked Brad hesitantly.

'Oh, ages ago. No idea where he is or what he's doing. And you know, it doesn't matter. I'm not interested anymore.'

'Thank goodness for that,' said Gordon briskly. 'Well, it's time we left. I have a flight tomorrow and I need my sleep.'

'Thanks so much for coming over. I'm sorry it was such a madhouse. The girls are at that demanding age.'

'Don't make excuses. The whole family needs a dose of discipline,' said Gordon crisply.

After the boys left Veronica fell asleep on the sofa in front of a cable movie. When she woke it was after midnight. She checked the girls and got into the guest bed. On opening the closet to hang up her shirt she shook her head at its crammed contents. Sue had bought clothes at a designer sale that she'd yet to wear. Tags hung from them and, looking at the slashed prices, Veronica could see they were bargains, but if Sue wasn't wearing them and she had so many clothes anyway, surely this was an unnecessary indulgence.

Veronica was asleep when she dimly heard her sister and Philip come home. They'd obviously had a few drinks and they made no effort to keep their voices low as they sat in their living room for a nightcap. Sue's burst of laughter startled Veronica into wakefulness. She got out of bed, pulled on the cotton robe Sue had left behind the door for guests and padded downstairs.

'You obviously had a good time.'

'Hey, Vee, have a brandy. Help you sleep,' said Philip.

'No, thanks, I was doing pretty well, sleeping,' said Veronica. 'I'll get some water. How was the evening?'

'Very interesting,' said Sue. 'Were the girls good?'

'They're so sweet, but getting them to go to bed and making them stay there is tricky,' said Veronica. 'So, how do I interpret "interesting" evening? Good? Bad? Boring?'

'Kind of exciting, actually. We might have some news in a few days.' Sue smiled at Philip. 'Shall we tell her?'

'Nothing's confirmed, but sure, she's your sister.'

'Tell me what?' asked Veronica now very curious. Philip was looking rather self-satisfied.

'Philip's boss is giving him a promotion and sending him to Melbourne.'

'Really? What about your job?'

Sue shrugged. 'I can transfer to a Melbourne firm which has connections with my law firm.'

'And you feel good about being in Melbourne? It's a lovely city, but different from Sydney. Do you know people there?'

'Not really, but Melbourne people socialise at home, at dinner parties and so you network and meet people in your own milieu,' said Sue. 'And of course the promotion means a lot more money.'

'What will you do with this house?'

Philip got up to pour himself another brandy.

Sue waited till he was out of earshot and said quietly, 'We had to take out a second mortgage as things have been a bit tough lately, so if we can rent this house it will help cover the mortgage. Philip wants to sell it, but I can't bear the idea of not having a home here in Sydney.'

'Oh, I see. Well, the promotion sounds good,' said Veronica, suddenly thinking about Sue's closet of unworn clothes and wondering how she paid for them. 'When will you move?'

'About a month. I have to go down and find a place to rent and suss out my job prospects.'

'Okay. I'm going back to bed. I have an early call in the morning so if it's okay I'll just mosey out the door at six-thirty,' said Veronica giving her sister a quick kiss. It was a bit of a white lie but she couldn't face the breakfast chaos of Sue and Philip getting themselves and the girls ready for the day.

'That is early. Thanks again, Vee. Did you see Gordon and his pal?'

'Yes, we had a lovely chat – once the girls were in bed.'

'You'll be off the hook when we move to Melbourne. No more babysitting,' said Philip, downing his drink.

'I'll miss you. And the girls,' said Veronica.

'Oh, we'll be backwards and forwards and of course you'll come down. And I'm sure Mum and Dad will come and visit a lot. Anyway, it's exciting to think about it. New horizons.'

'I hope things work out the way you want. Maybe it's time you kicked back and relaxed and enjoyed the girls.'

'Oh, I definitely want to work. I'd go nuts being a housewife. Besides if I take a break from my career, I'll have no money and we need the extra income.'

Veronica was surprised at the enthusiasm her parents showed at Sue's news when she went to see them on the weekend.

'We'll miss the girls, of course. They grow up so quickly. But Sue can send videos and we'll talk on Skype,' said Joan.

'Easier to hop on a plane,' said Roger. 'I might be able to work in a business trip or two down there. This promotion will be great for Philip's career.'

'You'll have to line up some stories in Melbourne, Vee,' said her mother.

'We don't create the stories or where they're set, Mum. They come to us and we follow along and see where the characters lead us. Like writing a book, but it's all true.'

'I never believe half of what I see on TV,' said her mother. 'Especially those tabloid shows.'

'Then you shouldn't watch them, Mum,' said Veronica.

Roger raised his glass. 'Let's make a toast to this new venture. This is a special bottle from my cellar.' He poured the wine and sniffed it appreciatively. '2004 merlot. Excellent little red. Perfect for this occasion.'

On Monday, Veronica mentioned Philip's pending promotion to Andy over their first cup of coffee of the day.

'I know that you'll miss them all, Veronica. But if a break in Melbourne is what you'd like, to catch up with them, that can be arranged.'

'Thanks, but it's not just that. I have to say that when I see how Sue and Philip's careers dominate their lives, I feel sad for their girls. I hope I don't turn out like that.'

'That's not what you want?' asked Andy calmly.

'No. Of course not.' Veronica paused. 'They're my family and I love them, but I don't want to end up like them.'

He glanced at his watch. 'C'mon, show time.' He paused. 'Veronica, you're a bright girl, talented and sensitive. Concentrate on your own life. And anytime you want an ear to listen, I'm here.'

'Thanks, Andy. You're a good friend.'

She gathered up her papers, made herself a cup of tea,

settled herself at her desk and looked over the notes she'd made with Colin Peterson as she picked up the phone to ring him.

'Hi, Colin. I was wondering if I could ask you a few more questions,' said Veronica. 'I'm trying to get the story in my head, as it happened. How did you feel when you finally set off on this great adventure?'

Colin was surprised that everyone was on time and ready to go when they assembled outside Madame Olga's mansion at Darling Point in the dawn light. It augured well for the trip, he thought. He gazed at his fellow travellers.

Topov strode among them, dressed in what appeared to be a new outfit of large khaki Bombay shorts held up by a leather belt with an elaborate buckle. Glasses hung around his neck as well as his director's eyepiece, which was on a length of leather and tucked into his top pocket. He carried an ancient straw hat and wore boots that looked to be more suitable for snow than dust. Topov waved his arms a lot and kept checking on the last-minute loading of the cars. Peter and Drago ignored him.

'Keep camera ready on top. Put in number one car. Topov can shoot quickly.'

'There won't be anything to film yet, for a while,' said Drago.

'Where is map? Topov keep map, show way to Northern Territory.'

'Won't we need a map to get to Bourke first?' asked Colin. 'We have to know which highway to take.'

'We need to be on the road,' said Helen, glancing at her watch. She was sensibly dressed in cotton slacks and a short-sleeved shirt and carried a large notebook.

Johnny lit a cigarette. 'Who's carrying the food? And who's going with me?'

Johnny, Drago and Peter were the drivers. Topov, who assured them that he was an excellent driver, preferred to be in the lead car and navigate. 'I see shots, we stop.'

Colin thought it strange that they'd be filming random things that caught Topov's fancy. From the books he had read he was envisioning a large crew carefully setting up cameras and directing proceedings. 'Is this how it's always done?' he asked Drago.

'Shoot from the hip and run seems to be Topov's idea, which is okay for some sequences. But I'm sure you'll see the Hollywood-style director extravaganza before we finish,' said Drago with a grin that was almost a grimace.

They set off. Johnny drove the Land Rover with Topov and Helen, who kept a wary eye on the little caravan they were towing. Drago drove the Jeep. Peter, Marta and Colin followed in the Dodge. There was little traffic as the convoy drove west towards the Blue Mountains.

'Goodbye, Sydney. Goodbye, Sydney Harbour. I don't suppose we'll see as much water again for a long time,' said Peter.

'It is a beautiful city,' Marta observed. 'So . . . unspoiled. I don't mean clean or not built up, but untouched. These Australians are very fortunate people.'

'Untouched by war, you mean,' said Peter looking at her. 'Sweden was neutral. I don't expect that you saw very much of the war. You didn't see what I did.'

'I saw enough. Where were you in the war?'

'I was with the Dutch Resistance. Some of my family were killed in the war. After it was finished I wanted to get as far away as I could, so came to Australia. I worked on the Snowy River Scheme. Why are you here?'

Marta glanced back at Colin. 'Europe is old and dying. I wanted to see the new world. Do as I wish.'

'You must have a lot of stories, Peter,' said Colin.

'We have a long drive. Okay, I will tell you my story, sometime. And you must do the same.'

'I don't have anything exciting to tell. I've never travelled. Until now,' said Colin. 'So this trip is a first for me.'

'For all of us it will be new,' said Marta. 'I wonder how we will be when it is all over.'

The day was long. They crossed over the Great Dividing Range and Colin explained that it was called the Blue Mountains because from a distance the range looked a hazy blue. They parked at the scenic lookout of Echo Point with the craggy peaks known as the Three Sisters on one side, the deep valleys below. It had been cool and cloudy and as they stood there the mid-morning mist floated away. Golden shafts of sunlight stabbed the sinister gloom and the sharp clear call of a bird reverberated.

'I've seen grander mountains. But this is very magnificent,' said Peter.

'It needs snow,' said Marta.

'Shall I take a shot, Topov?' asked Drago.

The director shook his head. 'No. It is beautiful but not exciting. We go to jungle.' He turned back to the Land Rover.

Colin decided to travel for a while in the Jeep with Drago. By late afternoon they were travelling through open countryside, past paddocks filled with sheep.

'We're out in the country now,' said Colin. 'Haven't seen another car or town for ages.' He glanced at his map. 'But it looks like we still have a way to go to Bourke. We'll have to stop somewhere. Like Dubbo.'

'I hope Topov doesn't want to film anything. It's going to be dark. And where are we staying?'

'Let's ask him. They've stopped.' Colin pointed up ahead to where the Land Rover had pulled over. The Dodge was some distance behind them. As they pulled to the side of the bitumen road they saw Topov studying a map. Helen was striding ahead, stretching her legs. Johnny was smoking a cigarette.

'Is there a problem?' Drago asked.

Topov took off his hat and rubbed his head, stabbing at the map with a finger. 'Here, is town. Topov want coffee. Where coffee place?' He looked around accusingly.

'What town?' asked Colin.

'Red star here means town. Here must be town. You say we go Bourke way.'

'Not in one day, Mr Topov,' said Colin.

'Here, look on map. B-O-U-R-K-E. Here, Sydney.' He measured with the tip of his finger. 'Is just finger between.'

'On paper. But in Australia there are long distances between places,' said Colin.

'Well, there ain't nothing out here,' said Johnny. 'Let's drive on, it's hard to tell distances.'

Drago looked at the map and the stretch of empty road disappearing towards the horizon as far as they could see. 'No towns out there.'

Helen walked back to them. 'There's no point in standing around. Let's continue. We'll get coffee when we arrive in Dubbo.'

'I hope they drink coffee in Dubbo,' said Colin quietly to Drago. 'Australians drink tea. You don't see coffee much outside Kings Cross.'

Drago rolled his eyes. 'I hope Johnny packed some coffee or Topov will go crazy.'

Two hours later they stopped at a café in a small country town but the waitress shook her head when Topov ordered coffee. Topov went red in the face and shouted at her, which sent the girl scuttling into the kitchen and the rest of the group looking embarrassed.

A woman appeared from the kitchen with a bottle of Camp Coffee Essence, a black sticky liquid she assured him tasted 'quite nice with condensed milk'.

'What is condensed milk?'

'It's thick, sweet, tinned milk.'

'Okay. Bring me cup of condensed milk, I pour this black sludge in it.'

They travelled on much more slowly than they had expected because of the caravan and the poor road. It was now dark, the headlights illuminating a stretch of road lined with the occasional ghostly silver eucalyptus tree. In the three cars, all had fallen silent. The day had seemed endless and they all felt that they were travelling into a void. They were tired and uncomfortable.

Their packed lunch had long gone and all were hungry, each thinking of what they would like to eat when suddenly the Jeep ground to a halt. A quick inspection by Peter revealed that it had run out of petrol. It was refilled from the petrol can in the Land Rover.

'Why it is empty? I hope it's not leaking,' snapped Peter looking at Johnny, who shrugged.

'It doesn't have as big a fuel tank as the others. We should have filled up when we stopped for coffee,' said Johnny.

While Peter was filling up the tank some of the petrol spilt and when Johnny went to reach for a cigarette Colin stilled his hand. Johnny put the packet back in his pocket after exclaiming in some very ripe language.

'Watch your language, please, Johnny,' snapped Helen.

They had barely travelled another two miles when the Dodge's engine began to make a pinging noise. Peter slowed down and pulled over.

'Trouble?' asked Colin, who'd joined the Dodge after the last stop.

'Sounds like it. I'll have a look.'

'Can you tell what the matter is?' asked Colin anxiously.

'Could be a small thing. Could be a gasket. It will need a part. This car needs a big overhaul.' Peter glared at Johnny. 'Not such a good vehicle for a long journey.'

'So what do we do? How much further to where we're staying?' asked Marta, shivering in her shorts and top.

'How far is the next town?' asked Johnny.

Helen got the map from the Land Rover and woke Topov who was snoring in the back seat.

By the beam of the torch they peered at the map spread on the bonnet. 'We're not far from Dubbo,' said Colin. 'But I doubt there'll be anything open this late.'

'Might be best to wait till daylight and get to a garage. I don't think it is a good idea to travel in the dark in case the engine gets worse,' said Peter.

Topov ambled to the group and hearing this announced, 'We camp. Go in bush and make fire. Make food, put up tent.'

There were sighs and grumbles.

'We're all tired and hungry. This is the best thing to do,' agreed Helen.

They pulled into the dirt and under Peter's direction began unloading tents and the other camping gear. Marta took a torch and walked further from the road into the bushes looking for kindling. In a minute there was a shriek and she hopped and squealed, dropping the torch.

Colin raced over. 'What's up?'

Marta pointed at a bush. 'Over there. A snake!'

Colin nervously swung the beam of his torch at a small shrub.

'Get a stick, kill it!' Marta grabbed a branch lying on the ground and handed it to Colin.

'Be careful picking thinks up in the dark.' Cautiously he poked the stick at the bush, then leapt back.

A small rodent with a long tail darted away.

'It's only a bush rat of some kind. You'd better not go into the scrub alone in future. Take Helen or someone with you so you can look out for each other.'

Marta wrinkled her nose. 'Helen wouldn't like that. She is a very snobbish person, you know.'

Colin wanted to agree that he found Helen very intimidating but said comfortingly, 'Oh, she'll settle down once we're all roughing it.'

At the fire Topov announced, 'Topov has caravan. It is my house. My office.'

'Where are the rest of us going to sleep?' demanded Marta.

'We've got tents but I'm happy to sleep in the car,' said Drago. 'Let's get some food going.'

The discussion went to and fro. Drago and Peter began putting up the tents and Colin continued collecting wood for a fire.

'Be careful there aren't spiders or snakes under the bigger pieces,' Marta reminded him.

'Helen, you know how to put up a tent?' called Peter, anxious to get on with things and end the talk.

'I do not.'

'Then you will have to learn,' said Peter. 'We'll make a rule that everyone has to put up their own tent.'

'I'll need a lesson I'm afraid,' said Colin.

'Topov make rules,' said Topov who felt he was losing control of the situation as the activity swirled around him, everyone now anxious to get settled.

'Why bother with tents,' said Johnny. 'I'll just sleep in a sleeping bag.'

'Good idea,' said Drago.

Peter began to swear under his breath in Dutch then turned to Johnny. 'There aren't enough tent pegs or guy ropes. Who sold these to you?'

'It was a good deal, army surplus. They're good enough for fighting men,' answered Johnny. 'Look, we can pick up what we need tomorrow. There won't be a problem.'

'Oh shut up, Johnny,' said Marta. 'Where is the food? You're the cook.'

Tinned soup and toast made over the fire and a hot pot of real coffee helped everyone's temper, although, not surprisingly, Helen preferred tea. Topov announced that he would now retire for the night and closed the caravan door behind him. Drago and Peter were the first to roll into their sleeping bags while Helen and Marta were sharing the best tent. Drago had shown Colin how to put up his tent and he gladly settled inside. Only Johnny remained in a collapsible chair by the fire, staring thoughtfully into the dwindling flames.

In the small hours when the fire had become warm ashes, not even a cattle truck rattling south along the Mitchell Highway disturbed the exhausted travellers camped by the side of the road, miles from their destination, while, unseen, cattle chewed quietly in a paddock beside them.

4

THE SECURITY IN THE small but ultra-modern building in the city initially surprised Veronica. There were surveillance cameras, a buzzer and speaker for entry into the building and another set of doors into the reception area. Thick carpet, the security guard next to the elevator and dark tinted glass doors at the entrance gave no clue as to what lay beyond. As she noticed the heavy gold frames around pictures of thoroughbred horses, she realised that someone like John Cardwell would take precautions.

She thought back to their research about him when they'd wanted to include him in a story on the racing industry and recalled tales of gold bullion under beds, a horse-swapping swindle in Hong Kong – blamed on the trainer – and offshore casinos with high-roller rooms frequented by celebrities, corporate executives and Saudi princes. But Cardwell had refused to be interviewed, no-one would speak about him and there were scant press cuttings or photographs of the elusive businessman.

The receptionist was a stern looking, middle aged woman, conservatively but elegantly dressed. 'Please take a seat. Mr Cardwell has made an exception to see you. As you know he doesn't give interviews, but you did say this was just a five minute conversation?' she asked pointedly.

'That's right. It's not a story about Mr Cardwell, but some people he once knew. I thought he might be able to help throw a bit of light on them,' said Veronica reassuringly.

The receptionist didn't look convinced. 'This is very unusual for him. He's making a few moments between appointments for you.'

'Thank you. I shan't keep him,' said Veronica. She'd been amazed he'd actually agreed to see her in the first place. 'Does he work every day? He must have tremendous energy.' Like Colin, he must be at least eighty, she thought.

A few moments later Veronica entered a wood-panelled lift with a mirror on one wall and she wondered if there was a camera behind it, then admonished herself for feeling paranoid. She glided to the third floor where Cardwell's personal assistant, a pretty young woman, was waiting as the doors opened. She escorted Veronica down a carpeted hallway, slid a security card into the door and ushered Veronica into an anteroom with closed carved-wood doors.

'I'll announce you in a moment or two. Would you care for anything?'

'Thank you, no,' said Veronica taking a seat on a small sofa. 'I don't want to hold Mr Cardwell up.'

There was a buzz, the girl reappeared, motioned to Veronica and opened the wooden doors.

The office was expansive with heavy furniture and wide windows that overlooked the Botanic Gardens. Behind a solid desk sat a man with thinning white hair and glasses, dressed, in contrast to the room, in casual pants and a golf shirt. He stood up and nodded to her, holding out his hand across the desk.

'Hello. Now what's all this about? Why is anyone interested in a non-event that happened fifty years ago?'

Veronica was tempted to ask why, if it was such a non-event, was he prepared to see her, but instead said, 'It seems such an adventurous expedition with such an interesting group of people wanting to film the outback at a time when travelling there couldn't have been easy.'

'That it wasn't. Go on.' He waved at her to sit as he leaned back in his chair behind his desk and clasped his hands, waiting.

'I gather the film was never completed, but could you tell me anything that you can remember about that time?'

'No. The whole episode fell apart in Darwin and we went our own ways. I never expected to hear about it again and I don't want to relive it with the media, even *Our Country*. But what brought it to your attention?'

'A chance meeting with Colin Peterson. He was the only Aussie in the group apart from yourself and Marta. Colin doesn't think anyone else from the expedition is still alive.'

'Colin and Marta and I were the youngest, so I assume everyone else has gone to God by now,' said Cardwell.

'Yes, Topov must have long died. How old was he when you met him?'

Cardwell narrowed his eyes. 'You don't know very much about Maxim Topov?'

'Only what Colin has told me. What are your memories of him?'

'As I said before, Miss Anderson, I don't give out interviews to the media. Colin was very naïve and the project came to nothing. I suggest that you look for a more entertaining story to explore.' He rose and held out his hand to end the conversation.

His abruptness surprised Veronica. While she knew that he was media shy and this was an episode in his life that he either wanted to forget or didn't consider the least bit important, why had he agreed to meet her?

'Thank you for seeing me, Mr Cardwell. I had hoped that you would like to help me more, but I realise how busy you are.' Veronica strode across the room and grasped the brass door handle but the doors wouldn't budge. She glanced back at the old man. Smiling broadly now, he touched a button on his desk and there was a click and the doors opened.

Veronica appeared at Andy's office door. 'Can I come in? I've just seen Cardwell.'

'I know. Pull up a chair.' Andy looked grim. 'So tell me what transpired.'

'Not a lot. The place is like Fort Knox. He's very different from the impression I'd built up of the cheeky cockney cook with connections, though the good contacts must still be there. Cardwell's outfit smells of serious money. He must have called in a designer to do the office.'

'His wife. She is old money. That was a cause for speculation too. Why would a classy well-bred, rich, if plain-looking, woman, who had her pick of the best, marry such a rough diamond?'

'He probably had a charming silver tongue. Now he

just seems grumpy. And frankly I wouldn't want to get on the wrong side of him.'

'Yes. Well, we should discuss that.'

'Don't you want to hear what he had to say?' she asked.

'Did he give you anything of interest?'

'No. Andy, what are you holding back?' asked Veronica.

'I had a call from Mr Cardwell. He was pretty quick off the mark. He was not amused at our digging into his past, as he put it.'

'What? I went to great pains to say it wasn't about him. It was about the trip and that it was for a story about the Australian film industry!' exclaimed Veronica.

Andy lifted his hands in resignation. 'He thought it a pointless exercise for a story – though I don't need him to tell me my job. He felt it was an invasion of his privacy and that anyone still living might well have faulty memories and he would prefer we didn't pursue such a non-story. There was a veiled threat of his going to Big Bill, our new leader.'

'That's outrageous,' said Veronica. 'Why is the old man reacting so badly?'

'I don't know. Now, tell me everything that happened.'

Andy listened carefully to Veronica's account of her brief conversation with John Cardwell. 'Hmm. Not much there. So, why all the threats? Is it just that he doesn't like media attention, or is there something more?'

Veronica grimaced. 'Mr Cardwell's threat has stirred you up.'

'Yep. Give your friend Colin another call and see what else he can tell you, especially what happened to cause the party to break up in Darwin.'

'I suspect the disintegration could have started before then,' commented Veronica.

'Ah, yes, Darwin,' said Colin in answer to Veronica's question when she called him to ask what had happened.

'A lot happened on the way, so by the time we finally arrived, things were pretty tense. We ended up staying there quite some time.'

'Colin, do you think you could meet me again at the coffee shop at the Cross? I'd love to hear more about the journey.'

'Yes, I guess so, if you're still enjoying it.'

Later that day Veronica and Colin settled themselves into the corner of the coffee shop in the Cross and Veronica began to ask questions about the extraordinary trip that Colin had undertaken.

'Tell me, Colin, had you formed any opinion of your travelling companions by now?'

'They were all so different. Topov, well he was the centre of our little world, although sometimes I thought that perhaps he was a bit crazy. Johnny, I already knew him, although I must say that the way he took to the outback life surprised us. Peter was quiet and taciturn and Drago was a great cameraman, but he was always frustrated by Topov's directions. Helen was always very superior. And Marta. She was wonderful and very talented. Do you know, she put on a one-woman show in Darwin? Played to packed houses. The locals had never seen such a performance. Of course this was right towards the end and we'd all got to know each other a lot better by then.'

It was a week into the expedition and a sort of routine had been adopted which included stops, excursions and general disruption usually initiated by Topov. The change in the country from scattered rural towns and farms to cattle stations and remote settlements with hours on the road where they rarely passed another vehicle was a shock to the party. Once they left Bourke they seemed to be heading into nowhere land as Peter called it. They had all been unprepared for the great distances. Topov accused Colin of not explaining this.

'Too much time gone. No action. No film.' Then he glanced at the red dirt dunes, clumps of spinifex and the stark silhouette of a dead tree beside the road and called a halt. 'We make picture with Marta. She lost. No water.'

'What is this, a drama or a documentary?' asked Drago.

'Colin, write something. We make docu-drama. Drago, put up big camera.'

They had taken shots of Marta, alone, driving the Jeep with its top off. Topov now wanted her to drive the Jeep through the sandy soil, leaving tyre tracks that headed towards the deserted horizon shimmering in the heat, the dead tree to one side, the blue cupola of sky above. It took several takes, with Colin and Johnny sweeping away the tyre tracks each time to leave unmarked sand. Drago then took shots with the small camera from the Land Rover as Johnny drove it beside the Jeep over the bumpy trail.

'Drive slowly, this is a shaky tracking shot,' complained Drago to Johnny as he steadied his arm on the back seat of the Land Rover to film.

Then Topov had them set up the big camera and told Marta to drive towards him and stop in front of it. From behind the camera he called out directions. 'You stop, stand up, look ahead. Look frighten. Look worried.' Topov turned to Colin. 'What she see, Mr Australia?'

'Oh. Goodness. Um, a kangaroo? A storm? An Aborigine?' suggested Colin.

'Good, good. Now we must find, kangaroo, storm, Aborigine. We do close-up,' said Topov.

Everyone laughed until they realised he was serious.

They set off again with Helen studying the map and trying to work out where they might camp that night. She had taken the map away from Topov who had no

97

navigational skills at all. They had stocked up on more supplies in Bourke but with no way of keeping food cold, they had to rely on tinned foodstuffs, rice and potatoes and hoped to supplement their supplies as they came to other towns along the route. They realised that water could be a problem and so Johnny bought several jerry cans for water as well as others which would hold the petrol. They tied as many as they could to the roofs of the Dodge and the Land Rover.

'I think we should camp anywhere we can before dark,' sighed Helen. 'Really, this is frightfully boring scenery. I do hope things pick up when we get into the Northern Territory.'

As they drove across the flat gibber plains, Topov became excited by the rocks they passed and stopped the cars.

'Many fossils here. This place would tell great old story,' said Topov.

'How do you know about fossils?' asked Colin.

Topov put several stones in his pocket. 'My father great geologist. Teach me many things.'

As they came closer to Tibooburra they saw strange granite rock formations. Several camels wandered across the track. Topov insisted on stopping to examine the rock formations, which looked like the detritus of some massive eruption aeons before. 'You film camels,' he told Drago. 'Wonderful rocks,' he exclaimed. 'I take picture.'

'Will we stop for supplies in Tibooburra?' asked Helen.

'No,' said Topov. 'Next town close, get food there.'

After Tibooburra they pressed slowly on to Innamincka. But they were shocked when they arrived. Topov couldn't understand how a place could be named on the map and then turn out to be a ghost town, but in Innamincka everything had shut down. There was a closed pub and thousands of empty bottles in a great dump next to it. Their idea of purchasing more food was now impossible. That night they camped near Cooper Creek eking a supper from their dwindling supplies.

'I feel like a character out of Dickens,' muttered Helen, lifting her spoon out of the pannikin of watery soup. 'Dry bread and gruel.'

'We were supposed to be stocking up along the way. How was I to know everyone has left the countryside and turned out the lights,' muttered Johnny. 'There's nothing wrong with soup and toast.'

'I'm accustomed to slightly better fare,' snapped Helen.

Colin couldn't help noticing the contrast between Johnny's cockney twang and Helen's upper-crust vowels. 'I'm sure we'll be able to get supplies in Birdsville,' he said, trying to keep the peace.

Peter was silent as he wolfed down his food. It had been a stressful day's drive with yet another breakdown. He'd made repairs as best he could but was concerned about the old Dodge surviving the rough unsurfaced track. He had complained enough to Johnny about the poor choice of vehicles and he just hoped he could keep them going until they got to a town with a repair shop. The responsibility of keeping the vehicles functioning in this remote country made him more morose each day.

Topov appeared oblivious to the mutterings in the camp. He got up and said to Drago. 'Camera, please. I go take sunset picture. Very beautiful.'

Drago gritted his teeth but said nothing. He was getting used to Topov's demands to use the Bolex camera. Topov would just take it and walk off, not allowing Drago to have any input into the shots he was taking.

Drago took the camera, checked it and adjusted the settings. At first he'd let Topov set the aperture but after a brief discussion with the director, he'd quickly ascertained that they had very different ideas when it came to using the camera. Drago liked to use natural light, setting the stop low to overexpose the film to create a look of shimmering heat, while Topov used a standard exposure for everything regardless of the prevailing light. With a choice of three lenses, Drago liked to experiment, whereas Topov used only the wide-angle lens and talked about his studio days with the big thirty-five millimetre cameras, a lighting cameraman, a grip and two assistants. He did a lot of striding around looking through his director's lens pretending not to notice as Drago readjusted the camera settings.

'Well, we have no control over the natural light here,' said Drago. 'But it can work to our advantage.' Quietly he decided that where possible he would double up on scenes Topov wanted to film, knowing that his would look better and if it made the finished product better and saleable, that would help them all.

Topov was gone some time and the light was fading. Colin and Drago walked down to the great serene sweep of water, euphemistically called a creek. Drago hoped that Topov had taken shots of the flocks of birds swooping low over the water on their way back to their roosts in the trees along the river bank. After the harsh and flat country they had been travelling through this expanse of water was a refreshing change.

'This place is quite famous, sadly so. Burke and Wills were explorers who wanted to cross the continent from south to north, but they died here,' said Colin who'd been reading his little book about central Australia.

'They were lost?'

'No, they ran out of provisions. It's said they died of arrogance because they refused help from the local Aboriginal tribes. They thought they were superior, even out here when they were starving to death. The third member of the party survived because he accepted help from the Aborigines.'

Drago gave Colin a small smile. 'Perhaps there is a lesson for us.'

They reached the edge of the water but couldn't see Topov. As they walked further through the gnarled coolibah trees they caught sight of him. He had put the camera to one side and was scrabbling among the roots and rocks at the edge of the creek. When they called to him, he rinsed his hands in the creek, straightened up and picked up the camera.

'Tomorrow we send Johnny to catch fish for breakfast,' he announced.

'That's a good idea,' said Colin. 'Maybe we can all have a go. It'd be fun.'

'You got some good shots? The birds coming in?' asked Drago.

Topov shrugged. 'So-so. Not so exciting.'

'It's good to have some scenic cutaway shots,' said Drago.

'Sure, sure. You do postcard pictures. Topov make exciting film.'

'I think Drago likes taking the pretty pictures of the scenery,' said Colin, but neither of the other men answered him as they all trudged back to the camp where everyone else was settling down for the night.

By the time Colin woke up, the sun had risen and the shriek of the birds made sleep impossible. The campfire had been reignited and the billy was nearly bubbling. He presumed Drago had headed out to take his early morning pictures of this tranquil setting and as he sat by the fire he spotted Marta coming from her tent wearing a bright red swimsuit that showed off her shapely figure.

She smiled at him. 'Coming for a swim?'

'Great idea.'

For the first time in what now seemed an eternity since they'd left Sydney, there was a sense of enjoyment and a spirit of adventure. Marta and Colin swam and floated in the water of the creek while further downstream Johnny flung in a fishing line with furious energy while Drago wandered off into the distance.

When Colin and Marta returned to the camp, Helen and Peter were sitting by the fire talking as the smell of toast gave the scene a comforting sense of normalcy, almost bonhomie. When Johnny triumphantly returned with a fish to throw into the pan over the fire with a can of tomatoes and the last of the onions, spirits lifted again. Everyone was in a good mood as they packed up and set out for, what they hoped was, the metropolis of Birdsville.

But within a day, the buoyant mood changed to dismay as the rough dirt track they were following led them along the fringes of the Simpson Desert. Suddenly the red dirt ruts they'd been driving over became sliding drifts of orange sand obliterating the road in places. Rolling dunes studded with grey-green spinifex were the only landmarks.

Drago commented to Colin, 'It all looks the same. How easy it'd be to get lost out here.'

'There's no shade. Nowhere to get water,' said Marta.

'Or food,' added Drago. 'There's not much of anything left.'

'We all thought we'd be going through towns with shops,' said Marta.

'Let's hope we can buy things in Birdsville,' said Colin.

Topov, however, was revelling in this adventure. He called a halt and decided they'd take more film of the desolate setting and had Marta collapse beside the Jeep then flounder through the sand. 'For your story,' he said to Colin, who looked perplexed.

There was no shade but Peter, seeing a spindly small

skeleton of a tree, took a tarpaulin and flung it over the top braches, turning the stunted dead tree into an abstract umbrella. The others settled under the shade and shared a meagre lunch of tinned beef and very stale bread as Topov, Marta and Drago conferred on the filming sequence. Johnny and Peter were directed to set up the big camera. Drago would be 'second unit' with the Bolex.

Colin stood with Marta, holding a large black umbrella that Helen had produced from the caravan. He shared his water with her and handed her his clean handkerchief to mop her face as her make-up ran in the heat.

She sighed and shook her head. 'Why are we doing this, Colin?'

'For the adventure,' he grinned. 'And, hopefully, to make money.'

'What do you think of Topov's film? It's crazy. There is no story. What are you writing?'

Colin was uncomfortable. While he agreed with Marta, he didn't want her to think he was incompetent. 'Oh, I know it seems disjointed, but when we get to the real outback with the wildlife and Aborigines, there'll be more exciting scenes.'

Marta gave him a shocked look. 'The real outback? What is that?' she asked, pointing at the endless waves of sand rolling towards the horizon.

Colin had to chuckle. 'Yes, it's pretty empty isn't it? Yet Aborigines can live in places like this.'

'I wish I could meet some,' sighed Marta.

'Marta!' roared Topov and she rolled her eyes, as he added, 'On set.'

Drago, with a bandanna tied around his forehead to keep the sweat from running into his eyes, took the shots that Topov requested of Marta slumped next to the Jeep which, supposedly, had broken down leaving the heroine stranded in the desert.

But when it came to the scene where Marta staggered down a sand dune, Topov wanted Drago to film it from the Jeep. 'Topov drive. You take picture, Marta beside Jeep in sand.'

Marta, looking and feeling exhausted, waded down the slope of the sand dune next to the track, followed by the Jeep with Topov driving and Drago filming from the driver's side of the back seat. Topov was screaming instructions to Drago while he waved his arms at Marta, so he didn't see the sudden build-up of sand blown across the already sandy track. The Jeep ploughed into the deep sand and slewed, then spun, then, as Topov wildly struggled with the wheel, it tilted and rolled onto its side in a thick bank of sand.

Fortunately it fell onto the empty passenger side slamming Topov and Drago across the seats. Drago curled into a ball, hugging the camera to his body to protect it. Topov was bleeding from his shoulder and a small cut on the side of his face, which was flushed and furious. He started shouting at Johnny about the stupid car he had bought.

The group under the tree leapt up and raced to the Jeep, pulling the two men free. Marta sat down in the sand and put her face in her hands. Drago was dazed, still clutching the camera to his chest and Peter had to prise his fingers open to release his grip on the little Bolex. Helen was more concerned about the state of the Jeep.

'We will all have to fit into the other vehicles if we can't get it going again. This could cost a lot of money!'

Colin helped Marta to her feet and led her to the caravan. 'Do you want to lie down?'

'Just some water. I thought it was going to roll on me before it fell the other way. Topov is a mad driver. I'm never, ever getting into a car with him.'

'You won't have to. Johnny and Drago are furious with him too.'

'Can it be fixed?' she asked worriedly, holding onto Colin's arm.

'I'm sure Peter will be able to get it going,' said Colin, though he was worried also.

With the help of the Land Rover, Peter got the Jeep righted but it took several hours to get the engine running again. Drago spent the time tenderly checking and cleaning the camera. A cheer went up as the Jeep finally coughed to life and even Topov looked pleased.

'See, no problem. Dutchy good mechanic. We go now.'

The rest of the day's trip was slow not only because of the bad track but also because all the drivers were now very cautious. At their camp that night everyone was subdued and tired and the rationed food and water made them all realise the seriousness of their predicament. The next day they left after sunrise, crawling through a caked landscape of split earth and flat-topped jump-ups beside dry creek beds and scorched rocks.

'This scenery is like the ruddy moon,' declared Johnny.

Then suddenly before them was a mob of red kangaroos led by several large males.

'Don't hit one,' shouted Colin to Peter as the 'roos raced across the track. 'They'll smash the car to smithereens.'

In the Land Rover Topov was beaming. 'Quick, quick! Dinner,' he cried. 'Where's gun?'

Drago had reached for the Bolex and filmed a few quick shots from the window, but by the time they'd stopped and Johnny had the rifle loaded, the 'roos were standing up watching them impassively, out of range.

'Do we go after them?' asked Johnny.

'In what? The ground is stony and rough, we don't want another accident. We'd have to unhitch the Land Rover. Let's wait till we get to Birdsville,' said Helen.

The gibber plain of flinty stones shook the vehicles and the passengers so much that Johnny complained that his back teeth were rattling out of his head. But it took more of a toll on the little caravan bouncing behind the Land Rover and finally one of its tyres blew out. As Peter began to change it, Topov leaned back in his seat and slept, the two women sat in the cars with the doors open and Johnny paced up and down smoking a cigarette, one of his remaining few. Colin helped Peter by passing tools.

'Dust and shaking, very bad for these cameras,' muttered Drago as he checked them.

'This spare tyre is rubbish,' said Peter. 'I hope it lasts until Birdsville.'

The next day they were all shocked as Birdsville came into view.

'Is this it? This isn't a town,' snapped Helen as they drove towards the tiny settlement.

The pub with its broad tin roof glinting in the sun stood out beside several smaller buildings in the dusty street.

As the convoy limped into town Colin pointed, 'Look, someone is waving at us!'

Outside the rambling old building that had 'Inland Mission Hospital' painted above the door, stood the sister-in-charge, a vision in a crisply starched white uniform and veil.

'It is angel,' cried Topov, clapping his hands.

Sister Graden welcomed them cheerily and broke the news that the supply truck hadn't yet arrived from Marree so there were no provisions available to buy at the moment. 'But you'll get a good feed at the pub.'

Johnny got out of the Land Rover and headed to the bar for a drink and cigarettes. Sister Graden was sympathetic to their predicament but said her own supplies were low and she had several patients to care for and suggested they see what they could get from the pub in the way of food to see them through to Boulia, the next place with a general store.

'How do you manage here?' asked Marta. 'When do supplies come?'

'Tom brings the mail truck through from Marree every couple of weeks, except in the wet, but we manage.'

The travellers trudged into the pub where two stockmen at the bar were already in conversation with Johnny. Marta and Helen were directed to the ladies' lounge, a small, pokey, dusty room where the handwritten menu offered limited Meals and Refreshments. They ordered steak sandwiches and chips.

'I couldn't eat another baked bean,' said Helen. 'I think I'd better supervise the food purchases next time.'

In the bar Topov grandly explained to the bemused bushmen and the bartender that, 'We make film of outback. Where is exciting place? No more desert.'

'It can get pretty exciting around here on occasion,' drawled one of the stockmen.

'You still got some bad country to cover if you're heading north-west,' added the other.

'But is nothing, nothing out there,' declared Topov. 'All empty. No good for film. We go to Northern Territory.'

'Plenty of action in the Territory, all right. But it's not empty out there,' said the other drover, inclining his head towards the doorway. 'No way, mate.' The two stockmen grinned at each other.

'Phsst. What is? Out there?' demanded Topov. 'We see nothing.'

'You weren't looking, mate. Wildlife galore, thousands of emus, camels and birds. Why do ya think this place is called Birdsville?'

'You want to get off the track, go look for the wildlife, eh, Topov?' teased Johnny. 'You can take one of these fellows' horses.'

'You joke, Johnny. You wait to see Northern Territory. Big jungle, big river, plenty wild things.'

'You going to Rum Jungle?' asked one of the stockmen with interest. 'We hear there're Japs living there still, hiding from the war they think is still going on.'

'Bulldust. No Japs ever got to Australia. Anyway, it's full of uranium. They're digging it up to make bombs,' said his mate.

Topov was instantly curious. 'They make mining in jungle?'

'Yeah, there's work going at this new place, Batchelor. I thought droving was hard work, I don't want to know about heavy machinery jobs. Too bloody noisy, give me a few head of cattle and a horse any day,' said the stockman, knocking back the last of his beer.

Helen poked her head through the door. 'Topov, are you eating? Come and join us, the steak sandwiches are pretty good, even if they are a bit tough. It will make a nice change.'

They ate their fill, the men opting for large slabs of steak with 'all the trimmings' – a fried egg, slices of tinned beetroot, fried onions and soggy potato chips. Gravy or tomato sauce was mopped up with slabs of damper.

'You learn this damper. Is Australian bread,' Topov told Johnny.

'We have a camp oven. Do you use one to make it?' Colin asked the bartender.

'Talk to Gloria. She's the cook,' he said. 'She's out the back.'

Johnny and Colin found Gloria throwing wood into a blazing wood stove in the lean-to open air kitchen. Gloria was part Aboriginal, plump and stoic. When Colin and Johnny asked about making damper, she gave a bit of a smile and nodded, showing them how to throw the flour, salt, baking powder and water together, kneading it lightly before putting it into a pan dusted with flour. She slammed the heavy lid on the cast iron pan and pushed it into the oven. 'Good with cocky's joy.'

'What's that?' asked Johnny.

Gloria reached for a sticky green tin labelled Golden Syrup.

'Ah, yes. That'd be good,' said Colin. 'Put it on the shopping list.'

'Yeah and where's the bloody shop?' muttered Johnny as they left. 'We'll come back later, to try the damper, okay?' he said to Gloria.

They left Birdsville the next day with what supplies they'd been able to scrape together to buy, plus a few extras given to them by the publican. They had refilled their jerry cans with water and petrol. Gloria, who kindly made them a few dampers, gave them a tin of golden syrup from the pub's storeroom.

Her parting advice had been, 'Plenny lizard, emu, bird. You hunt, plenny good tucker.'

So Johnny tucked the butt of the rifle between the seats of the Jeep, ready to grab it should they see any game. Helen was seated beside him.

'I'm quite a good shot,' commented Helen. 'If we see anything, let me have first crack.'

Johnny was irritated. 'Oh, I suppose you went pheasant shooting on Daddy's estate, did you?'

'Yes, actually,' she answered calmly.

'What's that?' Peter squinted out of the Dodge to the glare of the western horizon.

'A small tower. Look, there's an old fence. Do you suppose it's a building of some kind?' asked Marta.

'Would be good wouldn't it,' said Colin. 'It's sunset, we need a place to stop soon.'

'Turn in, let's have a look,' said Marta as Peter slowed and studied the indentations in the loose red sand that had once been a track.

'I'll wait for the others. Maybe best not to take all the vehicles up there till we know what's there.'

When the others caught up they conferred and waited while Peter drove the Dodge slowly along the winding ruts.

'It's a windmill,' exclaimed Marta. 'Oh, look, there's a stone farmhouse.'

'Maybe we'll have some company for tonight,' said Peter.

'No,' said Colin, 'I don't think there's anyone there. It looks abandoned.'

'Let's see what's inside,' said Marta.

'Be careful of snakes and things,' warned Colin.

They wandered along the verandah, peering into the rooms. They were empty except for a few pieces of old furniture that were covered in dust and animal droppings – a table, broken chairs, a bed with bare wire springs.

'Look at the old stove and chimney. It's a wood burning stove that probably works,' said Marta. 'Be nice to have a fire going in this. We could cook dinner here. Let's get the others.'

Peter drove back to the road leaving Colin and Marta to explore. Beside the windmill was an old water tank atop a small tower. Colin turned the rusting wheel at the base of the pipe and was suddenly hit with a rush of brown stained water. He jumped back as Marta laughed.

'Phew, it stinks. It's putrid. Must be something dead in the tank, I suppose,' he said.

'You smell awful,' said Marta sniffing his hair.

Her face was close to his and her hair brushed his cheek. He felt himself tingle and wished he didn't smell so bad.

'Let's explore and see what's over the rise there.' He took her hand and they walked through the loose dirt and up a small rise studded with spinifex grass and clumps of grey coarse bushes.

'Oh, dear.' Marta's hand flew to her mouth as they saw three graves, each surrounded by rusting iron fences. One was small and its border appeared to be an iron baby's cot. Quietly they stood to read the sad headstones.

'A father and his two children. One just a baby,' said Colin. 'They all died within three years of each other. I wonder what happened to the woman.'

'How terrible to die out here and be alone like this,' said Marta. 'I hate this emptiness.' She gazed around the land, deserted as far as she could see. 'This is a lonely country.'

They stood in silence still holding hands.

'Look over there,' said Colin. 'In the dip, the grass and plants are quite green. Do you think that's where the water is coming from?'

They walked several hundred yards and found that it was a water soak which looked to be a natural well. Colin bent down and cupped his hand in the water and tasted it. It was quite cool and earthy. 'I suppose we could boil this up if we strained it through a cloth.' He splashed himself to wash away the tank water. 'It's certainly a lot fresher.'

The rest of the group wandered around the forlorn homestead and finally Topov agreed that they would stay there the night.

'We light fire. We have rum. We make party,' he announced.

Colin wondered if Topov was trying to inject a little cheer into the tired and cranky travellers who had followed him into this desolate country.

Drago and Peter built a campfire in the front yard and set the chairs around it while Colin and Marta helped Johnny get the old wood stove going. They soon had a stew, made from the steak and vegetables they'd bought in Birdsville, bubbling in the camp oven on top of the stove and Gloria's damper and golden syrup ready for dessert.

The billy was set on the campfire to boil for tea. They carried out the old table and Topov put out their enamel mugs and set up a bar.

As darkness fell, bringing the chill of a desert night, they rugged up and sat around the fire enjoying the rum. Helen preferred her tea but Marta accepted a small toddy of rum and pulled her chair close to Colin.

'Look at those stars. Trillions of them,' said Colin. 'You don't see the sky clear like this in the city.'

'It's beautiful. Like diamonds,' said Marta. 'It makes you feel less lonely.'

'I couldn't live in a place like this,' shuddered Helen.

'Wonder what happened to the lady of the house after her family died,' said Colin. 'We found some old graves over that way.'

'Graves! That's sad,' said Helen.

By the time they'd eaten their dinner everyone declared it had been one of the better meals of the journey.

'I'm sleeping on the verandah,' announced Drago, dragging his sleeping bag up the steps. 'A roof and a floor, what luxury.'

'I might sleep in the kitchen, stoke the fire up,' said Johnny. 'We've got porridge and powdered milk with golden syrup for breakfast.'

Colin helped Marta put up the tent for herself and Helen. Topov was having another rum and telling Peter about a filming experience in Russia. Peter sat staring into the fire holding his drink and not speaking.

'Are you putting up your tent?' Marta asked Colin.

'No, I think I'll share the verandah with Drago. It's easier.'

Topov was the last to go to bed. He had started singing to himself, quietly at first but soon his singing grew more lusty until Drago and Johnny shouted at him to be quiet. His gait was unsteady as he headed to the caravan.

It was after midnight, the ground cold and the air still. Everyone was asleep. Suddenly there came a cry, a howl. Colin, a light sleeper, sat up. Whatever it was it could be some distance away as sound carried far in the clear night. The cry came again and Helen scrambled out of her tent.

'What's that? Who's there?'

'It's nothing, Helen. It's a long way away,' whispered Colin from the verandah. 'Probably some animal, maybe a dingo.'

'I don't like it. I'm not staying out here to be eaten by wild animals.' With that she pulled a blanket and a pillow from the tent and marched to the caravan. 'I'm sleeping in there on the other bunk. And locking the door.'

Marta scrambled out of the tent. 'What is it?'

Colin got up and went to her. 'It's all right, Marta. It's probably a wild dog. You know, a dingo. I've never heard one before.'

'Get Johnny's gun,' she said.

'Go to sleep. There's nothing dangerous out here,' mumbled Drago.

'He's right,' whispered Colin. 'Go back to sleep.'

'I don't like being out here on my own. I'm coming on the verandah too.' She grabbed her sleeping bag and followed Colin back onto the creaking wooden verandah, put her bag close to his and wiggled into it, pulling it up to her nose.

Colin smiled at her. 'You look snug. I'll bring you tea in bed in the morning.'

Colin was up early and took a bucket to the spring at the little soak hole and carried it back to the stove. Johnny had the fire stoked up and roaring.

'I'm bathing in hot water this morning,' said Colin cheerfully.

Helen appeared with her hat draped in a fine veil. 'The flies drive me mad.'

Everyone was now resigned to living with the small black bush flies that glued themselves to clothes and sought the corners of eyes, mouths and nose, but they all hated them.

'And how did you sleep, Helen?' asked Johnny with a faint grin.

'There is no need to smirk, thank you. I took the other bunk and felt far safer than out here on the ground with wild dogs. Apart from Topov's snoring, I slept well.'

Topov appeared looking rumpled, complained of a headache and demanded coffee. Without consulting him, Drago took a few pictures of the deserted homestead and the graves before they left. Topov, if he noticed, made no comment. Marta and Colin travelled with Peter, as usual.

'You're very quiet, Peter, did you not sleep well?' asked Marta.

'Only when the silly old man stopped singing,' he said dourly.

'He was telling you some long story,' said Colin.

'A fairy story,' said Peter.

'What do you mean, Peter?' asked Marta.

'I don't believe anything he says. I think he is all bull-shit.' He bit his lip and clearly didn't want to discuss it anymore.

Their water and petrol were low. Johnny joked they might have to run the cars on rum and everyone's water was rationed. They fervently hoped that they would have no trouble getting water when they got to Boulia.

The Land Rover was in the lead and Johnny squinted at the road ahead. 'Dust. Hope it's not one of those crazy dust storms, tornado things you hear about.' He pulled over to confer with the others as they came alongside. 'Lookit that. What do you make of that big red cloud. A storm?' he asked.

'Could be a willy willy. I've heard about them,' said

Colin. 'But they're normally a big pillar or column of dust whirling in the sky.'

'What do we do?' asked Marta. 'Where to go? It's a huge cloud.'

'Let's pull off the road,' said Peter. 'Maybe get out the tents and anything that we can cover ourselves with. It's moving slowly.'

They all worked feverishly to cover the vehicles with tents and tarpaulins, anchoring them as best they could.

'As soon as it gets closer, get inside, put handkerchiefs, cloths, shirts, hats, over your faces,' said Drago.

'Cover cameras,' instructed Topov.

They waited and in a short time the great dust cloud hovering above the road was revealed to be dust churned by a large mob of cattle. The beasts plodded along, seemingly at their own pace and whim. As they drew closer two men at the head of the herd rode over to investigate the strange convoy battened down beside the track. The filmmakers swiftly flung off their dust protectors and Topov called for the small camera to capture the passing cattle.

Peter hailed the riders. 'Hoy there, where're you going?'

'Moving five hundred head of fats for market. We're taking it slow, keep up their condition. Not much water about this season,' said one of the men.

'Where you blokes headed?' asked the other drover.

Both of the drovers were suddenly riveted by the sight of Marta emerging from a car in her shorts and tight blouse with a bright lipstick smile. While Topov and Drago were busy with the camera, Helen explained they were a filming expedition.

'Not much out here to film. Where else you going?'

'Up north,' said Colin. 'Darwin and the wilds.'

'Ah, the Top End. Plenty up there. We was there in the war before shipping out with the army.'

'Are these your cattle?' asked Marta.

One of the men, still mounted, yanked off his battered hat as he addressed Marta. 'Cripes, no. Me and me mate Bill, here, we're just droving. Suits us fine.'

'Do you go to the city much?' she asked. 'It's so lonely out here.'

'Don't have much time for cities. We like our freedom,' he answered.

Bill, his face shadowed by his low-brimmed hat, commented, 'We had our share of excitement in the war, thanks. New Guinea. Now we get our fun by droving.'

'Is there any water, wells, or anything coming up?' asked Helen.

One waved an arm. 'Two miles west, there's a bore . . . It's a hot spring. Bloody hot. So be careful. But good enough to boil up for drinking water and throw in the radiator of your cars.'

'Thanks for that. It's marked, is it?' asked Peter.

'Yeah, there's a bit of a signpost. We'll be pushing on then. Good luck with your trip,' said the other drover, glancing over to where Drago was walking slowly behind some cattle holding the Bolex close to the ground, following the cattle's feet.

As they watched, the two young veterans headed down the track with their cattle. Johnny sighed. 'That's a lot of beef.'

'Such handsome young men. Imagine, they've been to war and now they choose this solitary, uninteresting work,' said Marta. 'Such a waste of their lives. Do they not have wives, children?'

'If they have, they're stuck at home,' said Johnny.

Colin was thoughtful. 'This is what appeals to Australian men . . . going bush, being your own boss, sleeping under the stars, being self-sufficient. Living with the rhythm of the seasons. Well, that's what people in the city think, but they would never do it themselves.'

'But now you're doing it, Colin,' said Marta seeing the sudden embarrassment on Colin's face. 'These country men, they would wilt like flowers in the city.'

'Come on, let's hit the road,' said Drago as Topov headed to the Land Rover. Drago looked cheerful, pleased at the shots he'd captured. Topov had been wary of the large cattle and stayed back, happy to allow Drago to get in close.

The country was still gibber strewn, studded with coarse grey saltbush and canegrass, the track just two grooves, corrugated from the churn of tyres, horses and the tread of cattle. It meandered between ruts gouged by the rush of the wet that spread over the channel country surrounding Boulia. But the group were all feeling happier. They'd found the bore and replenished their water.

Suddenly they came to a line of sandhills. They were long, low and undulating, distorting the perspective of sky and horizon. There were no peaks and troughs and the spindly bushes keeping a toehold in the shifting sand, were stunted by the force of wind that rushed unchecked across the open land. Nothing rose between them and the horizon. There were no shadows, only bright light. The dunes in the foreground were dusty red, paling to silver. Some had patches of thick yellow and grey green herbage. There was no sense of distance, no hint of anything beyond.

At first the travellers became excited at their initial glimpse of what appeared to be cliffs rising from sparkling waters. When the elusive sight came no closer they realised it was only a mirage that glinted between sand and sky. As the light changed so did the sandhills, their contours and colours becoming soft or flint hard.

'Beautiful, but a harsh place to be lost,' commented Marta.

A dust storm had recently passed through and as well as burying the track in parts, it muffled all sound. There were no birds, no trees, no semblance of anything having ever lived here. The glare of the setting sun burned into their eyes, forcing the drivers to squint.

Johnny was in the lead now driving the Dodge and whether it was a sudden lack of attention, tiredness or frustration, he ploughed too fast into a bank of sand. In seconds the vehicle was bogged, sunk in the dribbling sand that seemed intent on burying the heavy car. They all piled out of their vehicles and in dismay studied the Dodge that appeared to have settled in comfortably for an extended rest in the desert.

They tried to dig it out with their one small shovel but the sand poured in as quickly as it was dug out. When Topov insisted on getting behind the wheel to try and drive the Dodge out, the wheels dug in even more deeply.

'We need sheets of iron, or something to put under the wheels,' said Peter.

'Why don't we get some of the bushes, lay them under the tyres,' suggested Drago.

It was hot work and though it looked like the matting of chopped spinifex and grass might do the job, the Dodge remained firmly in place.

'Let's try to pull her out with the Land Rover,' said Peter. 'We just have to be careful it doesn't get stuck too.'

'How far away is Boulia to go and get help?' asked Johnny.

'Too far for the moment. And I don't think that they would send out a tow truck,' said Helen sarcastically. 'We'll have to do the best we can.'

As the day dwindled it seemed they'd never extricate the Dodge. Over a cup of billy tea they discussed the options. Topov glared at them all, obviously fed up with the whole situation and he grabbed the Bolex and the rifle and strode away. 'I take picture. Lost people in desert. Maybe Topov hunt food.'

There was a bit of muttering at his arrogance and unhelpfulness, but most of them were glad he'd stopped giving ineffectual directions and advice.

'He might be the one needing to be rescued,' muttered Peter.

The Land Rover strained, but it just didn't have the oomph to do the job. Johnny slumped dejectedly over the wheel. Everyone had been pushing, pulling or digging and they all fell by the wayside, panting and dejected.

'This is looking to be a bit serious,' Johnny commented to Colin.

'The rule is – stay by the car. Everyone knows that. Topov is crazy to set off out there. Do you think we should look for him?' worried Colin as he sat in the shade of the caravan.

'Sod him,' said Johnny, stalking off to talk to Peter.

Marta slid beside Colin and slipped her hand into his. 'I'm scared.'

'It will be all right. If the worst comes to the worst, some of us will have to drive into Boulia in the Land Rover and get help.'

'You told me people die out here.'

'We're supposed to be on a main road . . . well,' he smiled, 'a track between outposts. Someone must come along. People live out there somewhere.' He swung an arm at the desolate surroundings.

'Why would they? You mean Aborigines?'

'I suppose so, though I think they're nomadic. But there are far-flung cattle stations around. Those two ex-diggers we met, where were their cattle from? Who are they working for?'

Marta shook her head. 'I can't imagine. You would have to be desperate, crazy, running away from a crime, to live out here.'

Colin was thoughtful. 'Yes. It's lonely. Must be tough.

But I'm beginning to think I've had some of the nicest times of my life on this trip.'

Marta cocked her head and gave a coquettish smile. 'Really? Like what?'

Colin hesitated, then grinned. 'Swimming in the creek with you, sitting round the campfire, looking at the stars, just talking to you. It's been nice. When I look back on all this, I'll remember being with you. Seeing you cry at the graves, how you slogged on through all those things Topov had you do . . . I'd love to see you really act, Marta.'

She smiled at him. 'Me too. I am quite good you know. But I am used to performing the classics in a refined theatre . . . This is . . . nonsense.' Quickly she added, 'I don't mean you. It's Topov . . . He makes it up as he goes along. But, sometimes, surprisingly, what seems silly at the time can look quite different on the screen. Editors are the gods. Provided the cinematographer has got it right.'

'Drago seems to know what he's doing,' said Colin.

'He does. But it's frustrating for him being relegated to second fiddle unless Topov allows him to film something.'

'Topov is the boss – director, producer, cameraman . . .' Colin sighed.

'Yes, I know, but who knows what will come out of this? We haven't even got to the Northern Territory yet.'

Colin hadn't let go her hand. 'Marta, whatever does happen, will we still be friends afterwards? See each other?'

She looked at him, a big smile replacing her fears. 'I hope so. Who knows?' Then the smile faded. 'I've seen things change, when your life seemed so safe. And then . . .' she shrugged. 'Live for the minute is perhaps the best way, eh?'

At her words Colin flung his normal propriety to one side and leaning forward, impulsively kissed her. It was a quick, spontaneous kiss, but he was unprepared for the effect it had on him. Marta, too, seemed surprised for she suddenly grabbed his head, pulling his face close to hers, and kissed him strongly and quickly before breathlessly moving away.

'We must be careful. Do not fall in love with me, Colin.'

Such a thought hadn't occurred to Colin. He hadn't planned to kiss her and certainly didn't consider falling in love. Marta was a fantasy, an unreachable creature. But in this moment when she'd seemed vulnerable he'd seized the chance, shocked by his daring.

'It's just where we are, I suppose,' he said softly.

Marta snuggled against him. 'It's this country. So terrifying because it's so big, so . . . unknown. It makes me feel like an ant. It's beautiful but you feel you can be swallowed up.' She clicked her fingers. 'Like that.'

There was shouting and they turned to see Topov coming over the rise, the gun over one shoulder, the camera under his arm, dragging something behind him.

He strode from the dune, singing and laughing. 'Here is Topov! Big hunter!'

'What is it? What's he got?'

They all hurried towards him as he walked back to the cars dragging a large bird.

'What is it? An emu?'

'Looks more like a turkey of some kind.'

'We didn't hear the gun,' said Johnny. 'Did you fall over it?'

'If it died of natural causes, I'm not eating it,' sniffed Helen.

'You take picture of Topov,' he instructed Drago. 'Still photo, for publicity.' He struck a pose with the large gangly bird, the rifle and the camera, looking pleased with himself and breaking into self-congratulatory chuckles.

When the photo was taken, everyone asked questions and examined the scrawny long-necked bird with its mottled brown wings. At that moment there was the sound of an engine and a large truck roared into sight. Everyone cheered.

'Thank God,' sighed Marta.

The truck stopped and a beefy man in a torn shirt got out followed by an Aborigine in old trousers held up by a leather belt. Both were grinning broadly.

'Hey, Topov! The great white hunter. Greetings!' boomed the big man. The Aborigine slapped his leg and chuckled. The driver took off his battered hat and shook Topov's hand, then grinned at the group, who were speechless. 'G'day. I'm Fred. Found this dopey bugger wandering around out there trying to shoot anything that moved.'

'Did you shoot that bird?' asked Marta.

Topov handed the bird to Fred. 'We play little joke.'

'He wanted to raz you blokes up a bit so I loaned him my bustard.' He looked at the Dodge. 'Bogged, eh?'

'Yes. We have tried everything,' said Peter, annoyed at Topov for showing off by pretending to be the big hunter when the party was in serious difficulties. 'We have more pressing things on our mind than jokes.'

Fred crouched down and looked at the Dodge's wheels. 'We should be able to yank you out.' He snapped his fingers at the Aborigine. 'Wally, go and get the cable. We'll pull these bastards out of the sand with the truck, okay?'

'Yeah, boss.' Wally hurried to the truck.

'That'll do the trick. Thanks a lot, Fred,' said Peter.

'Very kind of you,' added Helen. 'Do you live around here?'

'Ah, down the track a bit. I gather from Topov that you're a bit low on grub. Can you hang out till Boulia?'

'Is there a property, a farm, a station, between here and there?' asked Helen.

'There is,' he said slowly.

'Then we ask for provision, food, from them. We pay,' said Topov.

Fred scratched his head. 'Don't know that Mac and his missus will have much to spare. Been a bit of a tough season. They're heading out themselves to stock up on tucker. Help a bloke in a crisis of course, but they only get supplies every six months and it's that time again. When the wet comes you can be stranded on your place for months.'

'But we pay,' insisted Topov.

Helen looked annoyed. 'He doesn't get it,' she said to no-one in particular.

'Shopping every six months! I couldn't begin to think of managing that,' said Marta.

'We're down to basic rations,' added Johnny. 'What're you doing with that bustard? Are they good to eat?'

'Stringy. But you're welcome to it. That's Wally's dinner. But he can go and get himself something else. Once we have you outta this mess we'll send him off for a goanna or something. Maybe he can find you some eggs, bit of bush tucker, eh?'

'Yeah, boss. That right boss,' agreed Wally.

Fred and Wally connected the cable to the Land Rover and the truck, turned on the engines of the vehicles so that the Dodge was eventually pulled out of the sand while Topov filmed the action. Everyone thanked Fred profusely.

Fred handed around his waterbag in the way of a celebration. 'Save your water. Wally knows where to get more. Enjoy the old bustard. You know how to cook it, right?'

Johnny raised an eyebrow. 'Stew it? Roast it on the fire?'

'Chop it up, throw it in the pot with a couple of stones.

When the stones are soft, chuck out the bird and eat the stones!' Roaring with laughter he gave them a wave, then shouted at Wally who swung himself onto the back of the truck and they drove away, a cloud of dust soon obliterating them.

The party drove as far as they could before dusk, trying to make up the distance, but they had to make one last camp before Boulia.

The bustard dinner was not a great success.

Topov spat bones into the campfire. 'Johnny, this shit. You buy food at farm.'

'He can't,' snapped Drago, 'Because they can't be giving or selling food to every lost and disorganised outfit that passes the gate.'

'I think Johnny did the best he could with an old bird,' said Colin.

'At least there's wildlife out there,' said Marta.

'I think you have to be an Aborigine to find it and catch it,' said Helen.

Marta stretched languorously, causing Colin to catch his breath and look away. 'I just hope we get to sleep in a comfortable bed soon.'

Helen didn't say anything but scraped her plate into the fire. She was still sleeping in the caravan and neither she nor Topov ever made any mention about this arrangement. Secretly Colin was hoping they could all spend an evening in a country pub with hot water. Even a lumpy mattress would be a welcome change from the hard ground.

When they arrived in Boulia, Helen went to the bank while everyone headed straight to the pub for a cold beer. She returned looking grim and drew Topov to one side and they had a heated discussion before Helen strode back into the pub.

'Enjoy your drink. We won't be staying here. There's

a bit of cleared land where we can camp, but I can't get any money to buy provisions.'

Before she could finish there was a clamour of protest.

Helen held up her hand. 'It seems that we forgot that it's Saturday afternoon and the bank is shut. We can't get any money.'

'If we didn't have such rubbish vehicles we wouldn't have broken down and wasted time,' said Peter angrily.

'You're the business manager, Helen,' added Drago. 'We need cash with us. Where's the money?'

'We were told it wasn't safe to carry too much cash. But the locals won't cash a cheque for a lot of strangers passing through.'

Colin and Marta looked at each other. 'Very disappointing,' said Colin.

That night there was no communal gathering around the fire as Peter, Drago and Johnny returned to the pub and Colin and Marta pooled their resources and went to the local Waitis Café. Topov and Helen were already in camp when the others returned.

In the early hours of the morning Colin felt a soft nudge on his shoulder and found Marta bending over him.

'What is it?' he whispered.

'There's something strange out there. I got up to go to the toilet and when I came back I saw, over there, a strange light.'

'Not the moon?'

'No. Though it was big and round. It shimmered and moved around.'

'Not a car headlight?'

She shook her head vehemently. 'No. It was in the sky. But low. Very weird. I am frightened.'

Colin sat up. 'There's nothing there now. Just a few stars.'

'It didn't go out, it suddenly moved very fast, away,

over there,' pointed Marta. 'You do believe me, Colin?' She was shaking, her eyes wide and shocked.

'Of course. Come on, I'll take you back to your tent.'

'I don't want to be by myself. Bring your sleeping bag, put it in where Helen slept,' insisted Marta.

'Sleep in your tent?' He was about to say what will people think, but threw caution to the wind. 'All right. I'm sure it was nothing to worry about.'

'Do you think it was a spaceship?' Marta held his small pillow as Colin picked up his sleeping bag.

'I don't think so.'

'I wish you'd seen it,' she said.

'We'll keep the flap open. You go to sleep and I'll keep watch. If it comes back I'd love to see it.'

But he soon felt sleepy and after glancing over at Marta, who was now asleep, breathing evenly, her hair splayed across her pillow, he turned on his side and tried to watch the patch of empty sky through the tiny tent entrance.

Colin and Marta were first up and had the fire going and the billy boiling before Helen joined them.

Johnny emerged looking bleary eyed and Marta told him about the odd ball of light she'd seen. He looked skeptical and announced he was going to walk into town. 'I'll bring back some bread and eggs and stuff.'

'How are you going to pay for it?' asked Colin.

To his shock, Johnny pulled a wad of notes from his pocket. 'I played cards with a couple of the lads in the bar. I did very nicely.' He winked and downed his mug of tea and set off for town.

After their first hearty breakfast for weeks, everyone was grateful to Johnny and in a cheerful mood as they packed up, ready to head for the Stuart Highway.

'Hey, Marta, you know what you saw last night?' said Johnny as he stowed the kitchen pans. 'Man in the store said it was something called the Min Min lights. Turns up every so often.'

'What's that?' asked Colin.

Johnny shrugged. 'No-one knows . . . Could be space people, though he said the Abos reckon it's some sort of spirit.'

'Is it good luck?' asked Marta.

'We'll find out, eh, won't we,' said Johnny.

5

VERONICA HAD STARTED HER second muffin and her third cup of coffee. She knew that she was having too much caffeine, but Colin was so absorbed in telling his story that she didn't want to break the spell. She also knew that at some stage she would have to get Colin to tell it on camera, but for now she was happy to sit and listen so that she could understand the whole extraordinary chain of events.

Cities recalled, homes in far-off countries, the stresses of urban life, all peeled away like layers of an onion the further the group journeyed. Priorities were basic. The enforced paring down of daily rituals to work and relationships suddenly made life simple in comparison to the lives they'd left behind. What had gone before, just a few weeks previously, was on hold.

Caught in the limbo of the journey, the pressures were different, the awareness of their surroundings shifted. While they had known that there was this other part of Australia over the mountains dividing the coast from the great sheep and cattle stations and rolling countryside – the dead heart – none of them had ever really considered what it might be like. Now they had found that it was not a landscape that embraced them or belonged to them. It challenged them.

The further away they travelled from their previous existences, the less they thought about them. Their world turned inwards. They fed off each other with laughter, frustrations, small irritations and loud disagreements as they hiccuped forward. They were still unsure of where they were going, knowing they were following a vague dream, a rubbery vision dictated by a man for whom they sometimes had contempt, who they sometimes joked about, who was sometimes infuriating, but who they still wanted to believe, so that his dream would also be theirs.

'I'm feeling a little excited that we are getting somewhere,' Marta said to Colin, as they sat together, fingers linked in the back of the Dodge. Peter was driving and Johnny was in the front beside him, having let Topov take the wheel of the Land Rover.

'Helen says the Stuart Highway looks to be a decent road,' said Johnny.

'On paper, maybe. As we've learned that doesn't mean much,' said Peter.

But when they reached the Stuart Highway they realised it was a much better stretch of road than the rough tracks they'd been on. They all came to a halt where Topov and Helen were poring over the map, which they had spread on the bonnet of the Land Rover.

As the others gathered around and began arguing, Helen rapped on the bonnet and said, 'We need to discuss this.'

'No talk. We go north,' said Topov.

'No,' said Helen. 'We go south to Alice Springs. We're very close already.'

'Alice Springs is the heart of Australia,' said Colin timidly. He'd always hoped to go there. Darwin was a bit of a mystery, he'd never heard of anything exotic there but the Alice, he knew, in the very centre of the country was special. 'Surely there'll be great things to film.'

'Yeah, what's in Darwin?' asked Drago.

'Darwin exciting place. More wild places past Darwin. What is called Arnhem Land,' said Topov firmly.

'Arnhem Land? What's that?' asked Marta. It was the first time she'd heard this place mentioned.

'What's there?' asked Peter.

Topov spread his arms. 'This place very beautiful. Jungle, water, native people, crocodile, exciting place. We make film no people ever see before. This Topov dream.'

'Might be your ruddy dream, mate,' said Johnny, 'but it's out in no-man's-land. What's wrong with Alice Springs? We're really close to it, maybe only an hour or two away and Darwin's still days off. I could stand a bit of civilisation.'

Topov shook his head. 'We go that way. Darwin, Arnhem Land.'

'Let's take a vote,' suggested Marta. 'Alice Springs. Sounds good and civilised.'

'Topov not film civilisation. Topov film wild Australia,' said the director firmly and stubbornly. 'Darwin good place. We go Top End.'

'We'll have to get some money pretty quickly to go anywhere,' said Helen.

'We get money soon,' insisted Topov. 'We find bank.'

'So where's the next stop if we don't go to Alice Springs?' asked Drago. 'Where is there a bank?'

Helen studied the map. 'The next place would be Tennant Creek. On the way to Darwin. But Alice Springs is so much closer. It would be much more sensible to head there.'

Johnny pulled a coin from his pocket. 'What say we flip a coin? Heads to Darwin, tails to Alice.'

'The great Aussie tradition,' grinned Colin. 'Heads or tails.'

Johnny tossed the coin in the air as everyone stood back waiting for it to land. But swiftly and with surprising ease, Topov stepped forward, snatched the coin while it was still in the air and put it in his pocket.

'We go to Darwin. Topov say.' He yanked open the door of the Land Rover.

'We could argue about this for the next hour,' said Helen. 'It's six of one and half a dozen of the other, I suppose.' And with that, she folded the map. 'Topov might be right. This is what he wants to do, it's what he's talked about, in his own way. I don't see that we have any option, seeing none of us knows any better.'

No-one could argue with her logic, but there were disgruntled and disappointed comments.

'What do you think, Colin?' asked Marta as they returned to their car.

He shrugged. 'Like everyone else, I don't know enough about either place. But it's probably going to be the only chance I ever get to go to the far north of Australia. I suppose we could always come back via Alice Springs.'

'Let's hope we find a bank quickly and get some money,' said Marta.

'Blimey, in for a penny in for a quid,' said Johnny philosophically.

They drove north along the highway, heading towards Tennant Creek where they could stock up on food and water and, perhaps, glean some information about this mysterious Arnhem Land where Topov was determined to take them. But a sight that pulled them up and had them scrambling for cameras was a formation of rocks on either side of the highway that, according to the name on the map, were the Devil's Marbles.

'We must go and see it,' said Colin.

'Blimey,' said Johnny. 'You can't miss seeing them. They're enormous.'

Topov was particularly excited as they bumped off the road into the stretch of shallow valley where huge rounded granite rocks were scattered like a giant's marbles, abandoned in the middle of some casual game. What stunned them most of all was the sight of boulders, bigger than a small house, precariously balanced on top of each other.

'I'm scared to go close,' said Marta. 'They might roll on us.'

'They've been here for centuries and centuries, I'd say,' said Colin.

'How could they get like that?' exclaimed Helen.

Topov folded his arms and gazed around. 'This space people. They do this.' He pointed a pretend ray gun. 'Zap zap. Alien people come here.'

'Ah, so speaks the geologist,' commented Peter. 'But they are amazing.'

'We must film this,' said Drago.

Topov began waving his arms. 'Marta, you must be in picture to show huge size. Drago, set up big camera.' Topov whipped out the director's lens from his pocket and began striding about looking for camera angles. 'Yes, we put camera here. Little camera walk around for shots.'

Drago didn't move but looked at the sky and the huge valley scattered with the stones. 'Wouldn't it be better to set the camera there, to get the light on the rocks?'

'Of course. Anyone knows that.' Topov strode away.

The rest of the group had taken off on foot to explore the weird landscape. Johnny took a penknife from his pocket which he normally used for peeling potatoes and scratched the surface of one of the rocks.

'You're not carving your initials into that, are you,' chastised Helen.

'Just checking it's not some precious mineral. I bet you before we leave here Topov will have chunks of these rocks in his pockets.'

Helen inclined her head as if to agree, but only said, 'Let's get on with this stopover, we still have to get into town.'

But once they started wandering among the towering rock balls and boulders, everyone, even Helen, became fascinated and the further into the valley they explored the more they were impressed by the enormous scale of the boulders.

'These are so big, yet they look like they are balanced on a pinhead. How do you suppose they got here?' Marta asked Colin.

'Peter and Drago reckon it's probably to do with volcanic activity and then weather and erosion have carved them. Look, some of them have split neatly in half.'

'Like giant gold grapes,' said Marta. 'It's incredible. You almost feel like agreeing with Topov that aliens had something to do with this.'

'Like the Min Min lights?' Colin smiled. 'I think Topov was only teasing us about the aliens.'

Marta remained quite serious. 'This is a strange country. Mysterious, magical, scary. It looks empty but it's full of . . . spirits, whispers, ghosts, strange beings . . . Who knows?'

'So you shouldn't feel lonely out here.'

She took his hand. 'I don't want to be alone. How can people take off and explore and travel in this continent on their own? Can you imagine travelling out here by yourself?'

'Many do. And some die,' said Colin. 'The first explorers became heroes, even when they died. Now who knows how many cattlemen, swaggies, wanderers have disappeared out here and no-one has found them?'

'That's awful.' She snuggled against him. 'You could call and call for help in the outback and no-one would ever hear you.'

'Except the birds. The birds of prey, in a great silent sky.' He held her for a moment. 'But in my story a black-fellow would suddenly appear from around one of these magic stones and lead us to water.'

Now Marta smiled. 'I like your stories.'

Drago had his camera out and was taking photos of Johnny posing, crouching beneath boulders as if holding them up like Atlas.

'Drago! The camera! Roll camera!' bellowed Topov.

Drago cursed beneath his breath and returned to where Topov was standing next to the big camera. 'This not good angle. Look, sun going down over there, we need camera this side.'

Drago gritted his teeth. 'I told you that.' Muttering in Croatian he began repositioning the heavy tripod and camera to capture the sinking sun.

'It's going to look stunning,' said Marta.

'It'll be dark before they get what they want,' said Johnny as Topov sent Marta off to pose by two particularly enormous egg-like rocks perched side by side with another heavy rock atop them. 'I'm starting a fire.'

'We'll have to camp here,' said Peter. 'But I think that the sunrise should be pretty spectacular as well.'

'So will the night sky,' said Colin.

'All right everyone, let's drive the vehicles off the road to where we're camping,' directed Helen.

They found a clearing where the surrounding rocks stood guard and sheltered them and everyone agreed that despite the cold this would be a night to sleep beneath the stars. Johnny took the axe to break up some wood to make a big bonfire. To one side of it he built a smaller cooking fire. Colin helped him by collecting spinifex and other kindling and thought how quickly Johnny had adapted to bush ways.

All fell silent as the sunset began to turn the sky an opalescent firey red and orange. The rocks however seemed to blaze with an internal light, looking as though they were burning hot. From amber to gold to deep sienna they throbbed with light and Topov and Drago were ecstatic, each in his own way.

Topov did a small dance, his tiny feet bouncing daintily beneath the bulk of his body while Drago concentrated on adjusting the focus and camera angles to capture the sunset lighting the strange rocks with Marta, a tiny silhouette, between them. Colin stood beside him making notes.

'I suppose Topov will take credit for what you're doing,' said Colin in a rare moment of perception.

Drago straightened and lifted his face from the eyepiece. 'I know he will, but it's important we capture these scenes and that they be correct. Or we have no film.' He shrugged, 'No film, no money.'

As he bent to the camera a flock of brilliant small finches exploded like a burst of thousands of coloured gems, flashing between the rocks.

With dinner finished, everyone gathered around the fire in the twilight awaiting the show of stars in the clear night sky.

'We have to walk away from the firelight to see them properly,' said Peter later as the sky changed from indigo to velvet black.

'I'll watch from my swag, thanks,' said Johnny.

Helen yawned. 'Wake me if there's anything unusual. I've seen enough. I'll take a peek at sunrise.' She headed to the caravan.

'She's never been up by sunrise,' Colin whispered to Marta.

'Wake me if there's anything good,' said Marta heading for her tent. 'I'm tired too.' She glanced at her watch. 'I cannot believe I am going to bed this early. In Europe I stayed up till the small hours. At sunrise I was just going home!'

Topov sat nursing his rum. After the elation of his sunset dance he now seemed morose, deep in thought. The others ignored him as they readied themselves for bed.

Suddenly Topov pointed at Drago. 'Drago! You did not get good shot of sunset.'

'Yes I did. I changed the position of the camera,' he said pointedly.

Topov's face went purple. 'You say Topov put camera in wrong position! No, Drago! You listen to Topov. Topov is director. Topov make film.'

'Then go ahead. If we did everything you said the film will not be any good. I am the film cameraman. You brought me on this trip because you know Drago is a film cameraman. Not Topov,' shouted Drago.

'Cameraman do what director say,' bellowed Topov.

Colin looked at Peter who inclined his head as if to say, let's move away. Colin moved and as Peter stood up, Drago eyed him.

'This is between Topov and me.'

Peter nodded understandingly. 'We're going to look at the stars. C'mon, Colin.'

Colin grabbed his jumper and a torch from his chair and followed Peter who strode away from the fire.

'Leave them to it. This has been brewing for a long time.'

'Topov has had quite a few rums, will he get aggressive?' worried Colin.

'Yes. But he's all hot air and shouting. So is Drago. Yugoslav emotion. Topov will go to sleep before he gets physical. Let's explore. Do you know astronomy?'

'No. Do you? Here, let me go first, I have a torch.'

'No. It's better to see by the stars, get your eyes accustomed, turn out the torch,' said Peter.

Colin did so and in a few moments realised he could see more around him in the silvery light than by following the small yellow pool of torchlight. Peter climbed over flat rocks, past large boulders, around some of the massive boulders until they were on a slight rise and could see the chessboard of giant marbles placed around them. He sat down and leaned against a large rock. Colin joined him.

'I was half expecting you to lean back and push that rock away,' Colin said. 'They seem so lightly balanced that a push from a finger could dislodge them.'

They settled themselves and sat in silence. Peter lit a cigarette as they gazed at the brilliant constellations.

'You know these? Orion's belt . . .'

'I call that one the saucepan. And of course, the Southern Cross. Even I can recognise that, but in the city you can't see a night sky like this,' said Colin.

'I used to look at the stars a lot when I was sleeping out, hiding in the forests and around farms in the war,' said Peter.

'When you were in the Resistance? Was it to keep your bearings?' asked Colin.

'No. For companionship. I was mostly on my own on reconnaissance or carrying messages. You never knew who to trust, even so called friendly farmers, so I kept to myself. It was a lonely time.'

Colin nodded. This helped to explain why Peter was

still very reserved and solitary. 'And here, in Australia, do you have any family?'

'I have no family.'

'So what will you do after this trip? I mean, why did you come along with Topov?' asked Colin.

'Why did you?'

Colin was silent a minute. 'I thought it was a chance to get into the film business. Scriptwriting. But that's looking less likely. I think now that it was an excuse. I just wanted an adventure to break the routine of my life.'

'You've certainly done that. Will you go back to your life? The same job? The same safety?' asked Peter.

'I don't know. I guess I have to see how this play ends.' Colin smiled in the darkness.

'The final curtain might be interesting. To see if Topov pulls the rabbit out of the hat.'

'You think he's a bit of a magician? He has a way of springing things on you. He seems a lucky person. Lands on his feet when he should be flat on his face,' said Colin.

Peter didn't smile at Colin's description. 'Topov is the actor amongst us. I don't believe he is who he says he is.'

'He's not Maxim Topov? Who do you think he is?' asked Colin, quite shocked.

'Who knows? The name is immaterial. I don't think he's Russian, I don't believe he's a famous director and he doesn't seem to know much about cameras and film.'

'Well, I agree Drago seems to know a lot more about cinematography . . . But Topov is the reason we all came along! Madame Olga would know about him, surely, or she wouldn't have helped him. She's put up money too. And he seems really committed to make this film,' added Colin. 'We have to give him a chance.'

In the darkness he couldn't make out Peter's expression

but he felt the Dutchman was smiling, which was a rare occurrence.

'You're right Colin. I'm trained to be suspicious of people's motives. We're here, we've all invested in this project in some way – money, time, effort. We all want this to work. We shall see what tomorrow morning and those that follow bring.' He stood up and started to climb back through the rocks.

Colin was thoughtful and realised that the taciturn Dutchman still really hadn't revealed anything of substance about himself. But his doubts about Topov seemed a bit extreme. In the dwindling moonlight the rocks looked soft, spongy, as if a strong breeze would send them blowing away like tumbleweeds. A light cloud suddenly obscured the stars. Colin had started following Peter who suddenly stopped.

'I don't recall seeing that rock formation. Did we come this way?'

Colin hadn't been paying attention. 'I'm not sure.' Suddenly he felt they were surrounded by forbidding shapes that were blocking their way, closing in on them and silently observing them.

Peter looked up at the sky. 'Can't see the stars. We could walk around here for hours. Best we wait till daylight.'

'You have matches. If we light a fire, the others might see us.'

'It will keep us warm.'

By torchlight they gathered enough wood to make a small fire and huddled into a crevice in front of it. With their jumpers tight around them, they tried to sleep.

The next morning, at first light, Colin and Peter easily found their way back to the camp. It appeared that no-one, apart from Topov and Helen, had slept well that night. The ground had been hard and the night chilly. But at dawn

everyone forgot their discomfort as they watched, mesmerised, the sun glowing as it rose over the strange rock-strewn
scene, changing it from harsh outlines to soft pink and lav-
ender that then hardened to diamond sharp brilliance.

Drago tried to capture as much of the exquisite scene
as he could, moving the bulky camera with Johnny's help
to the best positions. A sleepy Topov emerged from the
caravan and, as the fire was stoked under the billy, Helen
also stepped out looking businesslike and purposeful.

'We must move on, this has delayed us.'

No-one answered her as everyone was discussing
Colin and Peter's night among the rocks.

'It was a bit spooky,' said Colin. 'And at first we didn't
sleep well as there was all this scuttling about.'

'Lizards. Lots of strange little ones in the rocks,' said
Peter. 'And the tracks of quite a big one.'

'Should we see if we can find it? Goanna over the
coals for breakfast?' suggested Johnny.

'I'll toast the stale bread, thanks,' said Marta.

Topov plonked himself in a chair to await a mug of
coffee. 'Drago did good. Do like Topov say.'

Everyone ignored the comment.

They were still south of Tennant Creek when later that
morning, they came across a group of Aboriginal people
walking beside the road. The men wore torn shorts, the
women faded and ragged dresses. All were barefoot and
carried string bags. They looked scruffy and unhealthy.
They stared sullenly at the cars as the group pulled over.
Topov greeted them heartily but they simply stared at him.

'Maybe they don't understand his accent. You talk to
them, Colin,' said Helen.

Colin stepped forward and introduced himself, then
asked, 'Where are you from?'

One of the men jerked his head to where a single track
wound westwards.

'Is there a town, a settlement, over there?'

'Camp,' muttered the man. 'Where you go?'

'Darwin. Is it far to Tennant Creek?'

The man shrugged. 'Little bit long way.'

'Ask him if we can go see their camp,' said Drago.

'Can we drive to your camp? Are many people there?'

The man shrugged again and said something to the others. Another man shook his head.

Topov butted in. 'We make moving picture. We take pictures, okay?' He lifted the Bolex.

At this one of the younger women, who despite the dust and dirt might have been considered pretty with her large dark eyes and matted curls, stuck out her hand saying, 'Two bob.'

'She wants money! Like heck,' said Johnny.

'Let's go,' said Marta.

But Topov would not be deflected. 'Drago and me take Jeep, go look. Colin, you come. Do talk.'

As they returned to the vehicles the Aborigines silently headed off the road, walking slowly into the scrubby landscape. They took no notice as the Jeep followed them. Within a mile Colin saw the glint of sun on tin and figures moving about but as the Jeep drew near, the Aborigines stood and stared. There was one building, merely sheets of iron nailed to rough-hewn posts. Its floor had tattered blankets spread on the dirt. The solitary wall was made of sheets of iron tacked together to act as a wind break. Other sheets of corrugated iron were bent over the ground forming small shelters where one or two adults could sit. Other humpies in the camp were made of branches and bark.

Scattered around were the remains of several campfires and a lot of rubbish and bottles. Emaciated dogs scratched about or lay in the dirt. Everyone was partly clad in an assortment of cast-offs. The women sitting outside their bark shelters wore strips of skirts, their bare breasts hung, wrung dry and their ribs were etched on their shrinking skin.

Everyone looked dejected, unhealthy and filthy. A few pans, a kerosene tin with wire as a handle, lay beside the fire, but there were no other amenities of any kind.

'This is terrible. Horrible,' said Drago. 'We can't film this.'

'Poor people,' said Topov. 'Yes, take picture. We show world Aborigines worse than peasant.'

Colin was embarrassed and shocked. If he had thought about it at all, he had imagined Aborigines as still strong tribal people or settled in missions. Reluctantly Drago filmed the depressing scene from a distance, using the telephoto lens, but nobody seemed to notice or care. When he had finished filming they turned the Jeep around and followed the tracks back to the others.

Closer to town they saw a mission and paused. It was surrounded by a fence with barbed wire on top and inside there was a neat church and a row of what looked to be dormitory buildings. Aboriginal children were lined up outside them and were being addressed by two nuns. The children looked clean and well cared for. Despite the surrounds being treeless and bare, creating a seemingly soulless place, it was certainly better than the camp they'd seen.

'That's why there were no children in that camp,' said Colin softly.

'Good idea church to look after children,' said Topov.

'I suppose they think it will help the children,' said Colin.

'It's better than that dismal camp. They live like dogs there,' said Drago.

'What are we going to find in Arnhem Land?' wondered Colin.

'People stay wild. More better,' said Topov.

'I hope so,' said Drago vehemently.

Tennant Creek was what they'd come to expect of outback towns – a wide dusty street, some pubs, a few buildings and scattered houses, but Topov became hugely enthusiastic the moment he spotted the mine heads that edged the town.

Anticipating some money from the bank, everyone booked into one of the town's hotels and luxuriated in a hot bath, a bed with a mattress and hearty country cooking. The hotel was, by Helen and Marta's standards, not the cleanest but it was a welcome change from camping. After they had all freshened up, Helen went to the bank, the men hit the bar, while Colin and Marta walked up Battery Hill to look at one of the ore crushing plants. Topov disappeared.

When they got back Colin and Marta sat outside the hotel on a bench having a glass of beer and Helen, looking annoyed and flushed, joined them.

'Women are second-class people in this country,' said Marta. 'I'm glad you've joined us Helen. The ladies' lounge is awful.'

'I suppose I might as well have a gin and tonic seeing as we're all in a mess now.' She sighed and sat down.

'What's wrong, Helen?' asked Marta. 'Is there a problem with the money?'

'You might say so. It hasn't come through.'

'Why not? Madame Olga was supposed to send it. Why hasn't she sent it? What are we going to do?' said Marta with some heat. 'Where is the money we put up?'

'I just telephoned her, reverse charges and she says it will be in Darwin when we get there. That doesn't help us here.'

'We didn't think we had to pay our own expenses,' said Marta. 'That wasn't part of the arrangement.' She looked as though she didn't know whether to cry or throw something.

'It will get sorted out. It's hard for me as business manager, of course,' said Helen. 'I don't know how we'll get to Darwin without any money.'

'Maybe we should be leaving in the middle of the night,' said Marta darkly.

'Please don't say anything to the others just yet. Let's see what happens,' said Helen. 'I don't appreciate being left in the lurch like this.'

Topov didn't reappear until dark and then, having eschewed a hotel room, he disappeared into the caravan parked behind the hotel. When Topov and Helen walked into the hotel together, Colin, Marta and Johnny were seated in the hotel dining room, a basic but clean establishment. Topov was clearly in an expansive mood, jovial and loud, but as Helen rested her hand on his arm and whispered something, he brushed her aside and strode into the bar where a few men were drinking.

The barmaid, a sharp-eyed, sun-weathered woman, began pulling beers when Topov announced that he was buying drinks for everyone. He introduced himself to the two stockmen and a truck driver delivering cattle to the town of Katherine and waved to the other men in the room.

Helen joined the others in the dining room and Marta asked, 'Why is he so generous? How is it that he can buy drinks for strangers when we can't buy food and petrol for us?'

'I don't believe it. He seems to be one of those people that get hit in the rear end by rainbows,' muttered Helen. 'He spent the afternoon fossicking for gold. You know that he fancies himself as an amateur geologist.'

'Did he find something?' asked Marta, her eyes wide.

'Yes. A nugget of gold, which he says he sold to some fellow from the mine.'

'Did you see it?'

'No, but he showed me some money. The problem now is to stop him spending it all.'

'Let's get him out of the bar,' said Marta firmly. 'We'll help you.'

By the time Colin went back to the bar, Topov had engaged another three strangers in conversation about finding a 'good place to make film'. Marta signalled Johnny to come over and she quickly explained the situation. Johnny, who was enjoying one of Topov's free drinks, understood at once what Marta was saying and he slapped Topov on the back.

'Hey, what's this? You struck gold?'

Everyone in the bar went quiet and all looked at Topov.

'Topov know rocks. I look at river, I look at hill. Topov knows where to find gold. I find big piece.'

'So where is it?' asked Drago.

'Topov sell! I make good money. We all drink to celebrate. Friends, you drink,' he exclaimed, dropping his arm around one of the stockmen who pulled away in shock. Topov threw some more notes on the bar but before the barmaid could swoop Johnny and Colin had their hands on the money.

'This is for petrol. Supplies. No more drinks,' said Johnny.

'This money belongs to Topov. I say we drink.'

'You want to share some of that cash? You can share it with us,' said Johnny, 'We're owed expenses.'

Topov's face darkened as they led him from the bar. 'Topov find gold. Topov get more gold. Plenty gold in rocks.'

'We're not here to mine for gold,' said Helen.

'Can you just pick it up off the ground?' asked Johnny, suddenly interested.

'If it was that easy we'd all be out there,' called the barmaid after them. 'I reckon he's having you on. Did ya see the nugget?'

Topov was incensed by her insinuation. 'She think I tell lies. You talk to mine manager. Topov great geologist.'

Outside the hotel, Helen insisted that Topov settle their bill right away.

'We want to leave early in the morning.' She held out her hand. 'Give me the cash. I'm the business manager, I'll look after it.'

Topov reluctantly handed over a wad of money.

'How many ounces of gold was it?' asked Johnny.

Topov shrugged. 'Enough.' And stomped towards his caravan.

Everyone was subdued at breakfast after the drama of the previous evening.

'Where's Topov?' asked Colin.

'He's having a shower upstairs,' said Helen. She pulled out some money and said to Johnny, 'Let's go to the store for food supplies, fill up the jerry cans with petrol and get some water. We've got to make this money last until Darwin.'

'Those blokes in the bar suggested that we should stop in Katherine. See the gorge. Sounds pretty spectacular,' said Colin.

Helen shrugged. 'There's scenery and there're things that are more anthropological. We've yet to see any traditional Aborigines, any real wildlife or the jungle that Topov wants.'

'I say we take a side trip to this gorge,' said Drago. 'I want to take photographs. Let's vote.'

Everyone raised their hand.

'So long as it doesn't waste time, money or energy,' said Helen.

'Oh, it's sure to do all of that.' Marta smiled.

Topov was annoyed that a decision had been made without him. 'We see big gorge, better place near Darwin,' he said gruffly.

'Maybe. But we have to drive right through Katherine and we don't want to miss something magic,' soothed Helen.

'Well, Katherine ain't any metropolis either,' drawled Johnny as they came into the outback town past the meatworks and a couple of pubs, one of which had a glaring pseudo-Aboriginal mural of boomerangs and kangaroos on its walls.

'I'm so tired of cattle country,' said Marta. 'It's scruffy land and you hardly see a house or a cow. Where are the forests?'

'These cattle stations here are half the size of European nations,' said Drago.

'I think we have to drive off this so-called road to get an idea of the scale,' added Peter.

'The stock feed isn't lush like Europe, but the cattle are tough and spread widely,' said Colin. 'You need a lot of acres to feed one beast.'

'It would be great to see it from the air,' said Johnny. 'You blokes need to get a plane to film it and get the real idea of the size.'

'Where we get plane?' asked Topov, his eyes alight.

'You mean, where do we get the money to hire a plane?' asked Helen, instantly pouring cold water on the idea.

They camped at the edge of the town for the night and Johnny turned out a respectable meal for them, as they all had turned up their noses at the local greasy spoon café in town.

'We're here to see this gorge,' said Marta. 'So how do we get there?'

Colin spoke up, pleased to be the one with the

information. 'I had a chat to the garage man when we filled up. He's got a small boat and he said he'd be willing to loan it to us to go down the gorge. Said it's quite something to see.'

'Johnny, why we no bring boat?' demanded Topov.

Johnny threw up his hands and Drago stepped in.

'You saw the land we've come through, the bleeding caravan is bad enough, can you imagine bringing a *boat* as well?'

'Seems you have something arranged, Colin. Let's talk to the man tomorrow,' said Peter.

It was a small, old boat, but despite its heavy construction it had a broad beam and was sturdy. They could all fit into it and the engine sounded healthy. Peter took the tiller, Topov sat in the bow with the Bolex and Drago had a small stills camera ready. The others settled into the little open boat as it chugged away from the makeshift landing towards the giant red cliffs which towered over the stretch of turquoise water.

'The colours! Magnificent, yes?' said Topov. He lifted his arm in a gesture of approval as if he were personally responsible for the stunning palette.

The linked gorges were still and peaceful, the stretch of calm water protected by ancient gold and red walls. Trickles of wet-season waterfalls, ferns, and small rock outcrops and overhangs sheltering caves marked the jagged cliff face. In the sky above, large birds swooped and shrieked.

Peter steered the boat close to the cliffs of the gorge then out to the centre before taking a right-hand turn under another row of cliffs. Here they could see that further along the river narrowed and at the bottom of the sheer cliffs were low flat rocks and shallow pools.

'We could go ashore and walk around there,' suggested Colin.

'We'll have to be careful where we leave the boat,' replied Drago. 'We don't want it to drift.'

'There looks to be some caves up there,' said Peter, shading his eyes.

'It's so hot and still in here, it's like an oven,' Marta exclaimed. 'I want to jump in the water.'

'Sounds like a great idea, but let's wait till we're ashore and we can check it out,' said Colin.

Topov shaded his eyes and looked up at the cliffs. 'Good view from top. How we get up there?'

'You're joking, mate,' said Johnny.

They pulled in to a large flat rock in a scoop of water. A metal spike had been jammed into the rock as a mooring and they tied the boat up after scrambling ashore. The rocks were like scattered loose leaves of a large book that had been dropped from the sky, a story yet to be read by these travellers. The group stepped along them to the shallow end of the waterway where a trickle of a waterfall fell down the iron-red cliff face into a pool.

'Let's swim!' cried Marta peeling off her shirt and shorts to reveal her red swimmers. Helen had also worn her swimsuit as had Colin, but the others swam in their shorts. Like children they frolicked under the gaze of their chaperone, Topov, who held the Bolex and refused to come in.

'Take a shot of the wild natives,' called Johnny, splashing the water. He was not a good swimmer, but the water was shallow so he paddled about contentedly.

'Let's swim out into the main channel, this water is too warm,' said Colin, pulling Marta's arm and they swam to find the narrow cool currents in the middle of the watercourse. Drago, however, decided to join Topov and take some photographs of this idyllic place. He stood on the rocks looking through the lens of the camera.

Suddenly he shouted. 'There's a crocodile!'

'Oh my God!' Marta started churning through the water.

Colin froze, so frightened he couldn't move. He closed his eyes and waited for the crunch of jaws to grab him. Drago and Johnny, who had stayed close to shore, pulled Marta to safety and Peter quickly followed.

'Colin, swim, hurry,' screamed Marta.

Remembering that he had been told that sharks were attracted by thrashing in the water and thinking that the same might be true of crocodiles, Colin tried to creep through the water with as little noise as possible. Then he saw it. A brown shadow, about three feet long, that glided towards him, its horny snout nosing unconcernedly through the water. Colin stopped swimming as the reptile kept going on past him. He turned back to the stunned group on the rocks.

'Look there's another one! Up there on the ledge,' shouted Johnny. 'Blimey, the bastards are everywhere.'

'But they're not taking much notice of us,' said Drago, taking photos of the reptiles that seemed to surround the party.

Colin got out of the water and looked to where Marta was pointing at one of the sunning crocodiles. 'These crocs don't look very big,' he said. 'You'd think that if they were dangerous, the bloke in the garage would have said something about them. Maybe they aren't the man-eating variety.'

'Well, I'm not going back in there,' declared Marta.

Topov had clambered around the rocks and was heading back to the boat, when he called to Drago.

'Look! Aborigine art!' He was pointing up the cliff face where, in an open cave, they could see the ochre daubs of several figures and what looked to be the stick figure of a man with a crocodile head which had been painted onto the rocks.

'How the hell did they get up there to do those paintings?' asked Johnny.

'I think they must have climbed down from the top,' said Peter.

Drago took some still pictures and because he was able to see the paintings more clearly through the telephoto lens, he passed the camera around for them to all have a closer look. They were quiet, gazing up at this hidden gallery in the magnificent gorge.

'This is more of what I hoped to see,' whispered Marta to Colin.

He slipped his arm around her waist. 'Me too.' He spoke softly as if in a church.

Topov eyed them sternly but said nothing. Colin dropped his arm from Marta's body.

Johnny whistled as he drove the Jeep. Colin was deep in thought, scribbling in his notebook.

'Hope you can read your handwriting, even the good roads are pretty bad,' said Johnny. 'What're you writing? Your diary?'

'I'm supposed to be writing the script of our film, so I make as many notes as I can. I've no idea how it's all going to come together.'

'You really think we're going to end up with a proper film? That people'll want to see?' said Johnny sarcastically.

'Well, how many people would love to see a place like Katherine Gorge and never get out here?' countered Colin. 'So long as Drago backs up Topov I think we'll get some sort of mileage out of the film. And we haven't got to this Arnhem Land yet, either.' He decided not to mention Peter's doubts about Topov as in the bright light of day the Dutchman's comments seemed the musings of a negative and dour man.

'Yeah, matey, you might be right. I see a lot of opportunities out here. I think Topov does too,' said Johnny.

'For films?'

'Ah, more than that. People are just beginning to scratch the surface of Australia.'

'All the more reason then that a film about this unknown part of the country could be of interest,' said Colin. 'Maybe Topov is right about the interest and the Aborigines and whatever Arnhem Land has in it.'

'Takes money to exploit a place,' said Johnny. 'More than what you and I have in our kick.'

'Sometimes it also just takes a bit of luck too,' added Colin.

Johnny glanced over at Colin and grinned. 'You don't sound like a bloke from the bank. But that's what can happen to a fellow. A bit of luck can be the start of a whole new life. Or you can blow it in a night. That's the gamble, ain't it now?'

'I'm not a gambler,' said Colin.

'Well, that's where you and I are different. Like Topov and his gold nugget – he threw the lot on the bar to big-note himself.'

'I wish I could be like that – easy come, easy go,' said Colin. He wrote quickly in his notebook. 'Maybe I have to learn to take a risk now and then.'

'You've made a good start by coming along on this little jaunt.' And Johnny burst into laughter.

6

THE ROAD STRETCHED AHEAD of them, flat and straight, like an arrow to the horizon as they got closer to Darwin.

In the far distance a small dust cloud rolled along towards them so Topov called a halt. They pulled over, got out to stretch their legs and light a small fire to boil the billy. They'd learned now not to make a huge blaze and hang the billy over it, but rather light a small fire and stand the billy to one side letting the breeze blow the flames against it so it could boil quickly.

They were sipping their tea in the sparse, token shade of a gum tree as the dust cloud now formed into the shape of three horses. The bushman in the lead was followed by another horse. They saw the slight figure of an Aboriginal child riding it, leading a third horse loaded with bags. As the riders came closer they could see that the man was rangy, long legged and sat comfortably in the saddle. He dismounted, tilted back his well-worn hat that looked like part of his body and smiled at the group.

'Ah, smoko. Mind if I join you?' He had the air of a man very much at home with himself and his surroundings. There was a chorus of welcome.

'Not at all.'

'Please.'

'You're very welcome.'

'What is smoko? You have cigarettes?' asked Topov who smoked on occasion, generally when other people provided the cigarette. He was also a keen cigar smoker when they were offered.

'I roll me own, mate. You're welcome to the makings.' The visitor handed Topov a small leather pouch of tobacco and papers and nodded to the party. 'I'm Len Buchanan. Where you people headed?'

'Arnhem Land,' said Topov quickly.

'First we have to go into Darwin,' Helen corrected him.

'We make film in Arnhem Land,' said Topov.

'A film? Like at the pictures? Go on.' Len looked impressed. 'That's some undertaking.'

'Mug of tea?' asked Helen.

'You bet. Thanks.'

'And what about your little friend?' asked Colin.

The child on the horse was still mounted, the hat shading the face, wearing an old blue shirt and shorts, but riding barefoot. Large brown eyes stared shyly at the group, but it was the little once-yellow caravan that attracted most attention.

'C'mon, cobber, hop down. Get the waterbag, give them horses a drink as well as yourself.'

The child slid down and went to the packhorse for the canvas and leather waterbag. Everyone was curious about the child but no-one liked to ask.

'Where are you going, Len?' asked Marta.

'We're heading back to the station. Had to take a mob of cattle in to Katherine, then go north to see a man about some brumbies.'

'Just the two of you?' asked Colin.

'We managed the cattle all right, they were a quiet mob. But I'll need another hand if we go back to pick up the brumbies. They're crazy buggers.'

'What is brumby?' asked Topov.

'Wild horses,' said Colin.

'Are they any good? I mean can anyone just go and round them up?' asked Helen curiously.

Len retrieved the tobacco pouch and pulled out a plug of tobacco before answering. 'You're a Pommy, eh? Know something about horses?' he asked non-commitally.

'We have horses at home. I ride,' said Helen shortly.

'She rides to the hounds chasing poor bloody foxes, right Helen?' said Johnny with a grin.

Helen shot him a sharp glance, refusing to rise to Johnny's bait. 'Horses for courses,' she said with a thin smile.

'Nothing wrong with getting rid of a few bloody foxes, mate,' said Len. 'Damn pests.' He grinned at Helen. 'And it was you English people that brought 'em into the country down south. And bleeding rabbits.'

Topov had made a rough sort of cigarette and he lit up, the straggling shreds of tobacco flaring from the end of it. 'Wild horses, you go chase wild horses? Be exciting thing, I think.'

'Can be,' said Len, expertly rolling a smooth cigarette, licking the paper and sealing it single handed. 'But I wouldn't think of filming it, if I were you sport. You'd never keep up. You have to be a really good horseman for that sort of thing.'

'Where did the cattle come from?' Johnny asked Len.

'Out the back of our station. Well, the joint where I work,' said Len.

'What station is that?' asked Colin.

'Brolga Springs. Beautiful place. Wish it was mine. I muster for 'em. Do a bit of this and that in between my real job.'

'What is your real job?' asked Marta, quite fascinated by the visitor.

'I shoot buffalo and crocs. Sell the hides in Darwin. Some of 'em end up in Paris. Handbags and shoes,' he grinned.

'Really! I love crocodile shoes,' sighed Marta.

'You seem to like dangerous work,' said Helen.

'Life in the Territory, love. You do what you have to so's to make a quid, right?'

'That's why we're here,' said Peter dourly.

'What action you got in your film?' Len asked.

Drago glanced at Topov who was examining the soggy remains of his cigarette. 'Not a lot. Marta throwing herself down sandhills, cars bogged. Some nice scenery.'

'Scenery? You want scenery, you've come to the right place all right. Be sure to go to Arnhem Land, it's magic. Unbelievable in the wet. Like an inland sea. But she's a ripper anytime. Bird life, the fish, the escarpment, the Abo stuff.' He shook his head. 'It's brilliant bloody country. But it's good cattle country here. Very pretty river, nice lagoons.' He turned to where the child was squatting in the dust, holding the horses' reins. 'Bird? Waterhole, pretty good one, isn't it? Good swimming hole.'

The child's face lit up with a big smile. 'Yeah, good waterhole, good fishing one.'

'It's a great little place, nice and flat, few paperbarks for shade, good swimming hole. Comes off the big river.'

'Any crocodiles?' asked Johnny.

'Nah. Blacks have a good camp there. They get well looked after by the missus at Brolga Springs.'

'Maybe a good place to film?' asked Drago.

156

'Depends what you're after. For someone like me it's a good station, nice people and for the station blacks, a decent life. Good tucker, good rations, kids have a little school.' He wagged his finger at the child. 'You should be in school.'

'No way, boss. No like school. Horses more better.'

'So who is our little visitor here?' asked Marta. 'Come and say hello.' She held out her arms, but the child was suddenly shy.

'This is my little horsebreaker. Doris, get over here. Quick, quick. Say proper hello.'

Scuffing feet, head down, avoiding eye contact, the child shuffled over and stood next to Len, who straightened up from where he'd been crouched.

'Take your hat off. This is Doris.'

'It's a girl. I thought it was a boy,' exclaimed Marta.

A mass of thick curls sprang free from under Doris's hat and the full view of her thickly lashed large dark eyes and her smiling cupid's bow mouth gave no doubt that the slim, elfin-like child was a girl.

'Doris hangs around me like a bad smell,' said Len fondly. 'But she's a natural with horses so I take her with me on occasion when I can't get another offsider.'

'Well, I never,' said Helen studying the little girl. 'She's what, five, six years old?'

'Nearly eight. Just a slip of a thing.'

'You should be in school,' said Helen firmly. 'How will she get on in the world if she can't read and write?'

'The missus does her best with them,' said Len, 'But Doris will never leave the station anyway. She's already picked out to marry one of the old men.'

'What? That's disgusting!' exclaimed Marta.

'Ah, it'll be a few years before she's allowed to go off with him. That's how it is. Tribal custom, it's the way it is for them,' added Len.

Topov looked at Helen. 'We go this place. See people, see landscape.'

'Topov we have to get to Darwin!' said Helen.

'Where is this station? Can we camp there?' asked Drago who was enchanted by the little girl. 'She'd be great to shoot.'

At this the girl and Len reacted in shock.

Drago laughed. 'Shoot. It's an expression for taking pictures. We shoot film.' He looked at the girl whose eyes were wide. 'No gun, no bang, bang.'

The girl broke into giggles and Len chuckled. 'Had me going there for a minute.'

Topov stood up. 'We make little girl big star.'

'What about me?' laughed Marta.

'If you want to head for Brolga Springs,' Len pointed west, 'there's a track that goes out there, slower going than this road.' He eyed the caravan. 'That thing looks like it might make it.'

'It's been good, better than the Dodge,' said Peter.

Doris tugged at Len's arm, pointing at the caravan and whispered in his ear.

'She's never seen a yellow house on wheels before,' he said. 'Can she have a look?'

'I'll take her over,' said Marta and held out her hand. The little girl followed, curiosity overcoming her shyness. 'But we can't go in. It's not really my place. But we can look at the outside.'

'Can we just show up at this station place unannounced and camp there for the night?' asked Colin.

'Bush hospitality, sport. She'll be right. You all look pretty self-sufficient.'

There was a silence as everyone glanced at each other. Finally Johnny spoke up.

'We're a bit skint, matey. Our money got held up, which is why we're heading for Darwin so we can replenish supplies. You said the fishing was good, maybe we could catch some fish?'

Len waved an arm. 'Hey, that's not a problem. We'll send some of the hunters out. I'll take me gun, we'll get some bush tucker in no time flat. And there's always damper and stew in the oven at the Big House. Missus is on her own as the boss is away, so I think she'll enjoy meeting you all.'

Len drew a mud map in the dust describing how to get to Brolga Springs and estimating they'd be there by late afternoon if they left now.

Topov stared at the marks scratched by the stick in the red dirt. 'This map no good.'

'It's all right, Topov, we can figure it out,' said Peter. 'We go back the way we came for a few miles and then we turn left off the track at the burnt tree stump by the little dry gully.'

Topov just stared at him as if he were speaking a foreign language.

'Listen, why don't you take Doris with you? She can direct you. She'd love to ride in a car,' suggested Len.

'What about the horses?' asked Helen. 'Can I help? I could ride one of them for a bit.'

'You look a bit keen.' Len eyed her trousers and solid shoes. 'Give it a go if you want. Get a hat and tell me if the going's too tough.'

He spoke to Doris who immediately jumped up and ran to the little caravan.

'Jeez, you can't go in that fella, matey,' said Len.

Topov pulled the little caravan door open. 'She go in house on wheels.' He smiled and lifted the wide-eyed girl into the caravan.

Doris sat on one of the tiny beds and gazed around. 'No touch all this. No touch door,' Topov admonished.

She nodded her head.

'Will she be all right in there?' asked Helen.

'You won't be going very fast, so she'll be okay,' said Len. 'Get her out when you get to the turn off and need directions. See ya back at Brolga, Doris. Okay?'

In the warm glow of the afternoon light they rolled towards the homestead buildings that were surrounded by trees, a windmill and stockyards. Waiting by the gate were Len and Helen, both still mounted. Doris, now sitting beside Marta in the front of the Land Rover, leaned over and waved, shouting excitedly.

'Pull over there, I'll show you where to camp later,' said Len. 'Come and meet Mrs Johns. Doris, get back here.'

As the girl ran to the horse, Helen, looking dusty but pleased with herself, slid from the saddle and rubbed her back. 'I'm a bit stiff. Been a while since I had a long ride.'

'You did good,' said Len gruffly.

'We're not very respectable to meet anyone,' said Marta looking at their well-worn clothes and unwashed faces.

'Ah, the missus knows how it is travelling out here.'

They walked to the homestead with its high-pitched tin roof and wide screened verandahs. Len whipped off his hat as a small, middle aged woman came towards them, smiling warmly.

'Hello, hello. Welcome. I'm Annabel Johns. Len has told me you're on a filming trip. How interesting.'

Topov was the first to greet her, taking her hand and bending over it with a kiss. 'Beautiful lady, so kind.' He straightened and with a flourish added, 'I am Topov. Maxim Topov.'

Helen who had already met Mrs Johns introduced everyone else.

'Lovely to meet you all. Would you like to refresh yourselves and meet for a cool drink on the verandah? Len will show you where the amenities are,' she said.

The basic wash house constructed for the station-hands had cold showers but plenty of water so everyone was feeling refreshed and cheerful as they gathered later on the verandah of the homestead where a table was set up with jugs of cordial and bottles of beer.

'This is very kind of you,' said Marta.

'We don't see a lot of visitors. And with my husband away, Len thought I'd enjoy meeting you all. Now, do please tell me more about your project.'

Len had tidied up and looked a different man with a clean shirt and slicked back hair. He hovered in the background, rolling a cigarette and sipping a glass of beer. Mrs Johns listened attentively to Topov's extravagant description of their film plans, with Helen interrupting periodically to clarify a point.

'Well, I think that's a wonderful idea,' said Mrs Johns. 'Few people really have any idea of how the native people live – their dancing, hunting and riding skills. Of course, their ways are very different from ours, but my husband swears by them as stockmen. Isn't that so, Len?'

Len nodded. 'Yep. They're natural horsemen and bushmen. Their bush ways don't always seem right to white people but that's how they've always been. And no matter what you think of their customs you can't say that they don't know this land and how to survive in it better than white men ever will.'

'Could you explain some of those customs to us?' asked Marta.

'Ah, not my place to do that,' said Len.

Mrs Johns clapped her hands. 'Len, why don't you go and talk to Samson and Joe and the rest of the boys. See if they'll put on a corroboree for these people that they could film.' She turned to the group. 'They are wonderful dancers and they sing and tell stories that are quite dramatic. It's very colourful.'

Len put down his glass. 'I'll go and ask. They can be funny about what they do in front of us. Specially women.'

'Can I come with you? Perhaps I can explain to them what we're doing,' said Helen.

Len looked doubtful but he didn't know how to rebuff Helen who stood up, attempting to smooth her crumpled skirt as she stepped off the verandah.

'We'll take the ute,' said Len. 'The camp's down near the creek.'

Topov sprang to his feet and followed them.

'I do hope your lady friend is prepared to visit the blacks' camp,' said Annabel. 'She's seems a rather high-class sort of person. Has she been out here very long?'

'Long enough,' said Peter. 'Despite her airs and graces I don't think Helen gets shocked very easily.'

'This is a bit different,' said Mrs Johns.

'Could you explain a bit about this corroboree?' asked Drago. 'It's a dance?'

'Oh, it's a shame that you can't talk to my husband about these things. He's very knowledgeable. It's like a celebration, for an important event – anything from a funeral or initiation ceremony to something like a good hunting trip, or any occasion. There's a lot of important rituals we aren't privy to. But they seem to make up dances about anything. They're wonderful mimics. I've seen them do a corroboree about things that happen around here. I swear you can pick the people they mimic, including myself. And of course the way they imitate animals is wonderful. Their stories are very special. My husband says I should try to get them explained and put them down in a book, but, really, who'd be interested?'

'What sort of stories?' asked Colin.

Mrs Johns smiled. 'My goodness, they have a story about everything and anything. Why kingfishers have blue feathers, why rocks are in a certain place, how the stars came to be, why rivers go where they do, why the emu has a long neck and legs. Doris knows lots of them. I think she likes to tell me legends to pass the time and get her out of doing schoolwork.'

'Who does Doris belong to?' asked Marta.

Mrs Johns sighed. 'She's what they call a little bit mix-up child. Her father was a white stockman who has moved on. Her mother is very young so her grandmother looks after her, but all the tribe feel responsible for her well-being, even though she's a half-caste. And I have to say, I keep an eye on her myself. I can't agree with the welfare people just snatching the light-skinned children, though some of them are well looked after. Her grandmother is a smart old thing and hid Doris when the welfare people came out to this station.'

'So are you teaching Doris to read and write? Len mentioned a school,' said Helen.

'Oh, it's very informal. Not all of the children want to do my little lessons. But Doris, she's always asking me questions, but she's equally curious about her traditional lore.' Annabel straightened up, 'Now, if you are going to stay overnight, can I direct you to the best place to camp?' She turned to Marta. 'My dear, of course you and Helen are welcome to stay in the Big House here. We have beds along the sleep-out on the other side of the house.'

'A bed! How wonderful, thank you so much,' said Marta.

There was an area that was used for rough camping near several large trees. Hessian sacks stitched together were suspended on poles to provide a rough awning. Under it were old chairs, several upturned logs worn to smooth seats and a fire circle, ringed with stones, held the remains of many fires. Further away, a primitive toilet, a seat over a hole in the ground, was surrounded by a few sheets of tin and screened by more hessian sacks. A forty-four gallon drum of water stood in the shade and several waterbags were hung from a branch of a tree in the shade to keep the water cool.

'There could be excellent filming opportunities, if Topov and Helen don't frighten the natives,' said Drago.

By the time Topov, Len and Helen returned from the Aboriginal camp, the filmmakers' vehicles were parked close to the campsite, bedding rolled out, extra chairs and a table set up and a campfire was burning brightly with a large blackened teapot swinging over it from an iron tripod. As the women were sleeping in the Big House, none of the men had bothered to pitch a tent as the weather was fine.

'What did they say?' asked Colin. He was feeling quite excited at the thought of seeing a genuine Aboriginal ceremony. 'Are they going to dress up?'

'Undress. Naked,' declared Topov. 'Big dance tomorrow night. All day making ready.'

'At night? What'll we do about lighting?' said Drago. 'A campfire won't be bright enough to film by.'

'You think of something. You fix,' said Topov airily as he fell into a chair. 'Johnny, where is rum?'

Len strolled over and glanced at the sky and Topov's rum. 'Sun's not down yet. By the way, the blacks aren't allowed any grog. Now, I was going to suggest we go catch dinner. You might like to film one of the boys bringing down a 'roo, spearing a fish.' He looked questioningly at Drago and Peter but it was Johnny who jumped up. 'I'll be in that.'

'If there's any shooting I'd like a crack at it,' announced Helen.

'Not shooting,' said Len. 'Doing it the old way, with spears.'

They broke into two groups. Topov insisted that Marta go with the fishing party in her red swimming costume to film a sequence at the river. Helen chose to rest in the caravan parked near a tree. Colin and Peter took the Land Rover with young Doris between them in the front seat to show them around the property. She pointed out where the ceremonial dancing ground was, but shook her curly head when Colin asked if she danced too.

'No good place for Doris. Grown-up business.' Mischievously she put her fingers to her lips.

Peter, who was rarely effusive leaned back and stretched his arms. 'My God, look at this country . . . it goes on forever.' They had parked on a rise and before them stretched rich green and brown country with a small river twisting through it and ragged ranges on the horizon. Shining lagoons fringed with lush plants dotted the foreground. 'It is beautiful but . . . empty. Why do these people live in such an empty, lonely land? It is not for me.'

'It seems some of the stations that run a lot of cattle must do pretty well,' said Colin.

'It is too quiet. Even the native people live around the white people. I would not like to be lost out there. Inhospitable country,' said Peter.

Doris, young as she was, had grasped the sense of what they were saying and she touched Colin's arm and pointed to the distance. 'Doris home. Longa time walkabout. My people take Doris special place.'

'Out there? You walkabout out there? What special place?' Colin asked the young girl, wondering what she meant by 'home'. As far as he could see, the land stretched away to the horizon in a vast empty wilderness of soft muted blues, grey-greens and rusty red. The splash of river, the wetlands, the patch of dry earth, an occasional tree and the distant ranges looked as untouched as when it had been created.

Peter started the Land Rover and Colin patted Doris's hand wishing Drago had been with them to capture the expression on her beautiful little face with his camera.

They arrived at the river to find Topov wading into the shallows, shouting at Marta who was posed lying on a rock. Above her stood Samson, a tall thin Aborigine with blue-black skin whose sinuous body was taut, poised, ready to throw a spear.

'Topov, you're frightening the fish!' exclaimed Marta.

'We pick up fish shot after. You lie down.'

Samson lowered the spear. 'Fish all gone. No good hunt 'em.' He made to leave.

Drago lowered his camera and waved at the Land Rover. 'Bring Doris over here, let's get some pictures of her.'

Marta sat up and the little girl scampered over and sat with her on the rock. They started talking as Topov waded from the river.

'Colin, you write story of how little girl help Marta find fish.'

'Ah, right.' Colin joined Marta and Doris and squatted on the rock as Doris talked about the big fish that lived in deep holes along the bank. She took Marta by the hand and entered the water to show her how the women went searching for roots of plants and waterlilies, using their toes to find them in the muddy shallows.

Drago, noticing Samson walk further downstream, picked up the Bolex and followed him. From near a tree on the bank Samson pulled out what appeared to be a long piece of bark but as he pushed it into the water Drago realised that it was a very shallow canoe. He was amazed that anyone could balance on it let alone manoeuvre it.

Samson glided past the pandanus trees, their labyrinth of arched roots making a toehold in the river and stopped. Not a ripple from the canoe broke the surface as he stood, still and silent, spear poised until, with a sudden movement that caught Drago by surprise, he thrust the spear deep into the water, teetering but not losing his balance on the tiny leaf-like bark canoe beneath his feet. When he lifted the spear, a fat silver fish wiggled frantically on the end of the prong. He stroked the canoe to shore, flung the spear and fish on the ground.

'How you cook this fish?' asked Drago.

Samson picked up the still-quivering fish and handed it to him. 'Cook 'im in fire. Good tucker.'

Doris and Marta had a pile of rhizomes that Marta had tied in her shirt as she and Doris squeezed into the Land Rover with Colin and Peter. Approaching the camp they passed a group of women out gathering food and Doris became excited, calling to them. Shyly the women halted and Doris jumped out, pulling Marta by the hand and chattering to them.

'She wants you to go with them,' said Colin.

'All right. I suppose I'll see you later,' laughed Marta. Dressed in a pair of shorts over her red swimsuit and old canvas sandshoes and a hat, Marta gamely followed the women with little Doris bouncing beside her. Colin watched them weave through the tall grass and couldn't help but notice that while the women walked with ease and grace, they did so very swiftly. He hoped Marta could keep up.

'Where's Marta?' asked Helen, as the others returned to the camp. She looked hot and bothered.

'You should go for a swim at the river, it's beautiful,' said Colin.

'And we have dinner,' announced Drago dragging the fish from the car.

'Marta's gone with the native women. Do you want to catch up with them and dig for food?' suggested Peter. His normally dour expression had a slight gleam of mirth in his eyes.

'I believe I can make myself useful in other ways.' Helen turned on her heel. 'Topov! What have you filmed?'

That evening Mrs Johns sent freshly baked bread, a tub of butter and a boiled fruitcake to the visitors. Samson, who'd assumed the role of guardian angel, showed them how to cook the fish wrapped in paperbark and sprinkled it with several leaves that gave the fish a tangy citrus-like aroma. The bulbs and roots that Marta had collected were baked in the hot ashes and spread with butter. It was all followed by billy tea and fruitcake and voted one of their best ever meals.

After dinner as they sat in a ring around the campfire, a group from the Aboriginal camp silently appeared to sit in the shadows. Doris quietly came and curled up next to Marta and Drago took photographs of her, the copper highlights in her hair lit by the glow of the fire. Len also appeared and, together with Samson, slowly negotiated plans for the corroboree the following night.

'Y'see, they can only do certain dances, show you certain things. Lots of their ceremonies are taboo for whites and for women to see,' explained Len.

Colin was deeply interested. 'But they tell a story? These people have no written language so they act out their history in dance, is that right?'

'Yep. And a lot of singing. The songs, chants even more so.' Len scratched his head. 'It's how they read the country, their land, their law, their customs, ownership, ever since they can remember, way, way back. Right, Samson?'

The tall Aborigine nodded. 'Yeah, boss. We sing 'em stories, we sing our country, we keep 'im strong. Alive. And paint up them pictures good.'

'You mean the cave paintings?' asked Marta.

'They're not just in caves, there're carvings on rocks and they do a lot of drawings in the sand too. Keeping the stories going,' said Len.

'It's so interesting,' said Marta to Colin.

'What is the story they'll do for us tomorrow night?' asked Colin. 'Can I write it down?'

'Just watch and listen, mate,' advised Len. 'Some of the ceremonies, like initiation for the boys, can go on for weeks.'

Topov was in his element. He leaned back sipping rum out of his tea mug. 'Topov film native ceremony. This good, very good.'

'Yes, thank you, Len, for your help,' said Helen.

'S'orright,' he said modestly. 'Y'know a lot of these old ceremonies could die out. You talk to the young Abos in Alice and Darwin and they don't always know the old stories, or want to. Not a lot of the stations are like this one, let the stockmen take off for ceremonies and stuff. And the missions . . . they try to wipe the old ways out. Make the kids modern.'

Samson frowned. 'Mission people want piccaninnies. Welfare man take 'em piccaninnies.'

'What do you mean by *take*?' asked Helen.

Len looked at her. 'Half-caste kids with light skin are taken away by the protection people to be assimilated into white society. They're being "saved" by the missions. To my mind it's just a way of training them up to be bloody domestics for the white stations and breeding the black out of them.'

'But what we saw at the blacks' camp, back before Tennant Creek you couldn't let children live in those conditions,' said Drago.

'Maybe not,' replied Len. 'But not all Abos are bad parents, they just do things different to us. Some families hide their kids, rub charcoal on them to make their skin dark. But they get found and taken anyway.' He glanced at the silent, listening faces at the perimeter of the fire. 'I'll be off then. Can I walk you ladies to the Big House? See the rest of you in the morning. It'll be a big day. The paint 'em up for the corroboree will start early. See ya.'

After Len, Helen and Marta disappeared into the night, they left behind a quiet group at the fire.

Topov was the first to speak. 'What does one do for little black children? Is not easy, eh?'

Practical Drago broke the spell. 'Topov, this ceremony. There's going to be singing and music with this dancing . . . We need to run sound.'

So far they had shot film that had no sound because synchronising sound with vision in these conditions was difficult. Topov had evidently planned that this would not be a problem because they could overlay a soundtrack with Marta later on, as she was an experienced actress. However, there was no way they could recreate the Aboriginal music, singing and sound effects of the corroboree. They had to use a sound system.

Topov, for once, was thoughtful. 'Who will do sound?'

'Do we have the gear?' asked Drago. 'I said we'd need to bring it.'

'Topov knows this,' he snapped. 'Recorder in caravan. Peter. He know machinery, he do sound.'

'What? I'm a mechanic not a movie person,' Peter expostulated.

'Calm down, friend. It is simple once you understand. It runs on torch batteries,' said Drago. 'If it is portable.'

'You mean we could've done sound recording all this time!' exclaimed Johnny.

'Marta actress. We dub later,' said Topov.

The tape recorder was brand new, had never been out of its box.

'What else do you have in that caravan?' demanded Johnny.

Topov ignored him, tossing the box to Peter. 'You make sound for tribal people.'

'I'll help you,' said Drago.

'Let me check it out first,' said Peter curtly.

Colin produced his notebook. 'I'll need to know what you're recording to match it up with the filmed sequences.'

The following morning Len arrived back with Marta and Helen, who both said how they had enjoyed their night of relative comfort.

'The blacks are starting to put paint on to get ready for the big show. Figured you might like to film them doing it. It's quite a performance in itself,' said Len.

'Is that them singing down by the river?' asked Marta.

'Yep. The initiated men are chanting.' As Helen rose, he said apologetically, 'Sorry, love, women taboo. You're not supposed to see this. Same as the men can't look at what the women are doing before they dance.'

Topov pointed at Colin, Drago and Peter. 'You go film. Topov come later.'

'Should we be filming it, if it's taboo?' asked Colin.

'Topov does not care. Just get pictures.'

'I'm going fishing then,' announced Johnny.

'Maybe we should see what the women are doing,' Marta said to Helen.

'I'm really not all that interested.' Helen retreated to the caravan.

Colin and Marta exchanged a look and Marta clamped a hat on her head and went off to the camp to find Doris and the women. She was quite intrigued by the women's activities. Later, as Marta sat with Colin eating their dinner, he quietly told her of the amazing scenes of the men preparing for the corroboree.

'You know, some of the men cut themselves so that they bleed and they use the blood as glue to stick on feathers as well as paint. They use ochres and clays as well and the designs are magnificent. There's such a ritual to everything. Drago was beside himself filming it all. I think he was glad Topov wasn't there.'

'How did Peter go with the sound?'

'Great. Though it was a bit touch-and-go when he played back something to see if it was properly recorded and the men got upset and quite scared to hear their voices coming back at them. But after a few moments they thought it was a big joke.'

Annabel and Len joined them as the sun was setting and they could hear that the singing had begun.

'I brought along some camp stools, these things can go on all night,' Annabel said as they walked to the Aboriginal camp.

The ceremonial ground had been brushed clean with branches and some of the other stationhands joined the small party as they settled in for the show. Johnny and Peter had driven the three vehicles through the trees and parked them so that the headlights would help illuminate the dancers. Topov had ordered the cumbersome tripod and big camera to be set up and directed Drago to move among the dancers and film them using the smaller, more portable Bolex. Peter sat on the ground holding the microphone of the tape recorder.

Slowly some of the young women with babies and children and frail old people settled in behind them, though the children soon wiggled their way to the front.

The old men who had daubed their bodies with clay designs, filed in singing and chanting to a beat pounded on clapsticks and boomerangs. Behind them appeared the dancers. The men – wearing only small loincloths, paint, feathers and headbands – were already stirring a dust cloud that swirled around their stamping feet. The energy, the powerful imagery, the sinuous movements accompanied by stamping and high-pitched chanting, combined with the thudding sticks and the pulsating sound of two didgeridoos was hypnotic.

To Colin, the body paintings – ochres and dramatic

white pipe clay in dots, waving lines and intricate scrolls studded with feathers – looked like living, writhing masterpieces. He tried to draw some of the patterns in his notebook but hated to take his eyes away from the dancing for a moment.

Marta studied the dancers' faces, the expressions and the body movements and began to follow the story. 'Look, he's the hunter and that man is a crocodile and there . . . Look at the birds.'

Annabel leaned over and told them. 'This is the brolga dance. Have you seen our brolgas, the beautiful grey birds with long legs and necks? This is how they dance when they're courting.'

The story had now moved to a lagoon and one of the dancers, paddling in a make-believe canoe, was being trailed by a sliding crocodile. Several of the children cried out, warning the hunter. But it was the flock of beautiful and majestic brolgas that came to the hunter's rescue by chasing away the crocodile.

And then on the edge of the make-believe lagoon, the women dancers suddenly appeared. The phalanx of women, their pendulous breasts swaying, their arms swinging as they looked down at the ground, didn't have the lithe lightness of the men but their strong voices, heavily painted faces and hair matted with white powder created a chorus to match theirs.

Topov was beside himself. He swayed and clapped and, as the dance reached its crescendo, he leapt to his feet and, to the onlookers' amazement, he joined the line of men, stamping and chanting. What shocked the filmmakers was not his audacity at involving himself in something so culturally foreign, but the fact that despite his weight he moved with such agility and rhythm that he imitated the hopping and stepping line of men.

It didn't last long. There was a shriek of approval

from all the audience, the kids jumped up and down and clapped, but soon Topov was out of breath and triumphantly returned to his seat.

For everyone present, time seemed to have disappeared as they were swept away in the power and magic of the dance. The firelight sparking into the night sky, the gleam from the car headlights on the shining black bodies, gave them all, for a moment, a sense that they were peeking into another dimension where millennia had passed and that this was how it had always been.

When there was a lull in the proceedings Annabel leaned over and said, 'No matter how often I'm privileged to witness these events I feel I'm watching something so unique, so special.'

'It's wonderful. I hope this dance never dies out,' said Marta.

'Ah, that is a question for the future, isn't it? I'm very proud our blacks can live here and keep up the old ways,' said Annabel Johns getting up. 'If you'll excuse me, I have to be up early. I hope you have enjoyed the evening. They'll go on for quite some time yet, but they won't be offended if you leave.'

They thanked her and watched her drive back to the Big House.

'You have to be a special type of woman to live out here,' said Marta.

'It's certainly isolated,' agreed Helen. 'One would crave decent company.'

'We're very lucky to have seen this, just the same,' said Marta.

'It's something I'll never forget,' added Colin.

'Len, can you escort us back to the homestead? I'm looking forward to a comfortable bed again.' With that Helen rose and she and Marta, accompanied by Len, walked into the darkness.

The following morning they packed up and said good-bye and thank you to Annabel. As they drove through the homestead gate, they saw Len and Doris saddling their horses. Everyone stopped to shake Len's hand and thank him for his help and kindness. Marta called Doris over and gave her a hug.

'You're a gorgeous little girl, Doris. I hope your life will be a happy one.'

'You pretty lady,' said Doris staring at Marta.

Impulsively Marta took off a thin etched, silver bracelet with a small silver charm of a star from her wrist and handed it to Doris who quickly put it on her arm. 'It's too big. Here, wear it like this.' Marta twisted the bracelet and snapped it twice around Doris's wrist. Doris held out her little arm and admired the adornment, looking immensely pleased.

Len pulled off his hat and shook hands with them all. 'Good luck with the rest of your trip. Sorry I can't be of more help along the way. Man's gotta job to do.'

'You've been extremely helpful. Given us a chance to get some wonderful footage,' said Helen graciously.

Topov waved regally from the Land Rover. 'We send you invitation to premiere!'

'Right, yeah, thanks,' laughed Len.

After dinner on what was to be their last camp before Darwin, Colin and Marta walked away from the campfire together.

'We'll be in Darwin tomorrow, if nothing goes wrong. It will be strange being in civilisation again,' said Colin. 'I like the peace of being in the wide open spaces.'

'Me also. Except for the discomfort. If we had better places to stay, even better tents and beds and proper equipment, I would like it more,' said Marta. 'But only for a short time. I couldn't live so far from everything. My mind would starve.'

'You're used to an audience, the bright lights,' said Colin. 'I've done more thinking out here than ever before in my life.'

'What are you thinking, Colin?' asked Marta, leaning close to him, her voice husky.

'About you, of course,' he said quickly. 'But also about my life, my family . . . my future. All this.' He waved at the starry sky, a hill with a tree silhouetted against the moon. 'It makes you feel insignificant in the big plan of life. But it also makes me feel big. I mean big-hearted, you can dream big dreams, that there's a bigger world out there. I now think cities make you feel small, cramp your mind.'

'Because out here life is reduced to being very simple. Food, shelter, stillness,' said Marta. 'And it makes you face who you are. There isn't much pretence in a place like this. There's nowhere to hide.'

'You mean from each other? It's interesting how we all get on, know each other's faults, annoy each other, but help one another. I wouldn't know these people so well in a city.'

'And that can be a good thing and a bad thing,' agreed Marta. 'The fact is we have to rely on each other to get us through so we all get something out of Topov's crazy dream. I won't care if I never see any of these people again once we are done. Except you.'

'Oh, Marta. That's what I've been thinking too,' said Colin in a rush of emotion. He put his arms around her and held her tight.

She wound her arms around his neck and lifted her face to be kissed. Colin sighed and pressed his mouth to hers. Then he sighed again. 'Oh, Marta. I wish we were really alone. How romantic this would be.'

'We can be alone in Darwin. Everyone will be busy there. We can do things together.' She smiled coquettishly at him.

'Like a nice dinner? Once we get our money,' said Colin.

Marta snuggled against him. 'We can be together without spending money.'

'Oh.' The knowledge of the invitation she was proposing, aroused him and he kissed her passionately, feeling the curves of her body press into him.

Marta drew away. 'Let's wait till Darwin. We can be together then.'

7

VERONICA HAD PUT TIME aside to have lunch with Colin. She knew he enjoyed these meetings and she was anxious to know what had happened to the filmmakers in Darwin. She was especially interested in finding out if Colin knew how the cheeky cockney kid Johnny had transformed into the rich and notorious businessman now known as John Cardwell.

'Hi Colin, it's Veronica here. I was wondering if you're free for lunch sometime?'

Colin drew a long breath. 'I'm sorry, Veronica, I can't meet you again. Let's just forget it. I really don't want to talk about this whole episode anymore. It was just a wild goose chase.'

'What? Why ever not? It's a fantastic story. We're really quite keen to pursue it.'

'Please don't, Veronica.'

Veronica paused, quite shocked. What had brought about this sudden shift in Colin's thinking? Then she realised. 'Colin, how long is it since you've seen Johnny, John Cardwell?'

'I haven't seen him in many, many years. I've told you that already, we just don't move in the same circles. I'm sorry, Veronica, I must go now.'

'Colin, just one last thing, I know that you haven't seen John Cardwell, but have you spoken to him recently? Did he ring you?'

The silence on the end of the phone told her all she needed to know. No wonder Cardwell had wanted to see her. He wanted to know who her source was.

'Whatever happened in Darwin? Were you happy? Did it change your life?' persisted Veronica, fishing hard.

But Colin just answered softly, 'Goodbye.'

Andy rubbed his chin. 'Mmm, more and more interesting. It would appear that Cardwell is trying to stop us digging. But why? It makes me want to know more.'

'Yes. Me too. I can't believe that I was so stupid not to get some of Colin's story on film. But it never occurred to me that he would stop talking, he so clearly enjoyed relating the events. But without Colin, we only have a few clues. Everything seems to hinge on what happened in Darwin,' said Veronica. 'I've looked online to see if I can find anything in the local papers, but only newspapers till 1954 are available that way. The rest of them are still on microfilm.'

'So that's your next move, right?' said Andy.

'Prise open your wallet, boss. I'm heading to Darwin to see if I can pick up the trail,' Veronica replied.

Andy looked concerned and gave her a rueful smile. 'Ordinarily, I'd say go for it, even though the story's still a bit of a long shot, but I've been summoned to a meeting with Big Bill. Economic constraint seems to be the buzz-word around here.'

'Oh. Would there be any point in my taking off before the ground gets cut from under us? Do you really think our budget will be slashed? Or worse . . .?' She couldn't bring herself to even think that the program might be axed. Apart from how it would affect her and the rest of the team, it would break Andy's heart. He'd poured so much of himself into *Our Country*.

'I'd hate to have to haul you back and frankly I'd have a hard time justifying the trip on such tenuous leads. I don't think our new leader would appreciate the fact we're chasing a story based on your gut instinct and my antennae.'

'And the fact that, for some unknown reason, one of the country's most notorious characters has tried to squash the story about this funny little filming expedition by putting the hard word on you and scaring off my source,' added Veronica. 'When's the meeting?'

'Tomorrow at ten.'

'So we put everything on hold for twenty-four hours.'

'You don't give up easily, do you?' Andy smiled. 'By the way, since there seems to be only one other person we can still talk to, did you get Marta's last name?'

'No. Colin loved talking about her. But stupidly I didn't ask him what it was before he was frightened off.'

'Mmm. Depending on the outcome of the meeting with our new fearless leader, I might call my old pal Jim Winchester at the *Darwin Daily* and see if he can find anything.'

'Andy, it's our story! If we can't afford to go to Darwin and pursue it then we have to drop it,' said Veronica.

Andy looked at her, knowing Veronica would never let a story go if she could help it. 'Okay. Let's see what tomorrow brings.'

*

William Rowe greeted Andy courteously if less effusively than their last meeting and Andy took his businesslike manner as meaning bad news. He sat opposite the man behind the desk while he signed some papers.

Rowe looked up and took off his glasses. 'I've done a lot of work since I saw you last, Andy. Reading reports and press clippings, watching shows, interviewing staff, wandering around the station, watching shows go to air, chatting to the folk in control rooms and in various departments. Interesting to hear in-house opinions.'

'As opposed to viewers'?' said Andy.

'That too. I've seen the market research reports. I often find it fruitful to talk to the barber and the lady in the supermarket as well.'

'I imagine you have quite an across-the-board overview then,' said Andy carefully.

'You might say that. I think I've identified where our weak spots are, where talent and programming are letting us down. And I see where we could improve and boost shows that have perhaps not met their full potential.'

'Well, I guess we all have a view on that, even if biased,' said Andy with a small smile.

'I won't beat about the bush, or country,' Rowe said with a slight grin at his word association. 'While the emphasis on demographics has to change, as I mentioned in our previous meeting . . .'

'Younger,' said Andy.

'The twenties and thirties, yes. Younger but not silly. There are enough idiot shows out there for hormone-hyped, boozed blokes and wild-girl audiences. It's actually come as a pleasant surprise to discover there are a lot of bright, articulate, motivated young people under thirty – and forty come to that – who, apart from sport, soaps and dramas, don't have shows that interest them very much at all.'

Andy felt he should speak up for his program. 'We have a pretty solid youthful audience. How to attract new ones, well, that's the question, isn't it?' He was thinking positively, assuming *Our Country* was being considered in this new push for audiences.

'That is your challenge. You and your team, Andy. I have to admit, I was rather surprised at the solid ratings of your show even though it's tucked away there on Wednesday nights.'

'The comfortable old shoe?' remarked Andy, remembering their previous talk.

'Quite. But I'm seeing the potential for a bit of spit and polish. A makeover. Well, not quite as drastic as that. But I think there's a good chance we can boost the ratings and prestige of the station by giving you guys a bit of a push.'

'A push? Not a heave-ho?' quizzed Andy.

William Rowe roared with laughter. 'Come on. Would I axe a show with your numbers? Of course not.'

'It's been done before,' said Andy quietly. 'With other solid shows.'

Rowe ignored his comment. 'Here's what I think we should do. Your program has the potential to strike a nerve at a time when we need to unite families and promote our own country – in a friendly, easy-going Aussie way. No sappy, hand-on-your-heart stuff, but an acknowledgment that we live in a bloody lucky place that's unique and pretty amazing but most of us have no idea what's beyond our back fence, be it city, bush or desert. How many of us have seen the west coast, the north, the centre, the Victorian coast, the Adelaide Hills, inner Sydney, you name it.'

'I couldn't agree more. How do we sell stories on places and not make it a travel show, for example? Please don't say a cooking show.'

Rowe chuckled. 'No, that's been done to death, hasn't

it. Look, with a bit more ammunition you could expand on the stories you do, find a bit more meat, delve a bit deeper, spend time on stories so they're not superficial.'

'I like the sound of that.'

'And get a new presenter or two.'

Andy's enthusiasm cooled. 'Ah, we've tended to keep the presenters in the background, just introducing stories in the studio rather than flying in and doing bits to camera.'

'That's because those two presenters you have are dills,' said Rowe forthrightly. 'Lightweight. Fluff balls. Pretty people who can read an autocue. We'll move them to morning TV. We want someone who's real. Gets in and gets their hands dirty, is on top of and involved with the story. Someone that people – young people – can relate to.' He leaned back in his seat.

Andy stared at him. 'You have someone in mind?'

'I do.' Rowe smiled. 'You said yourself Veronica Anderson would be great on camera.'

'Oh. Yes. She's clever and intelligent. But she's always veered away from being a front person.'

'I realise that. I spoke to the film crews, they have a lot of respect for her. She's a good journo, a smart producer and nice young woman. Perfect. And she's got a job that a heap of gals would love.'

'Veronica is a natural and has a good story instinct. She's rare. You can't teach that,' said Andy hastily.

'Oh, I know that. Anyone who's good at what they do usually makes it look easy. But we want young people to imagine that they can do it too, even if they can't. Everyone who watches medical shows, detective shows, enjoys them vicariously and imagines that they are in the shoes of the professionals. Why can't this be the same idea? That's the beauty of it.'

'Mmm. I see what you're getting at. That's putting a lot on Veronica's shoulders.'

'Let's see how a couple of shows go. She won't be on her own. She'll have a good team backing her.'

'Phew. Bit of a tall order.' But Andy was thinking fast. He could see what Rowe was after and while Veronica might rebel at first, it could be the saving of the show. A bigger budget, more scope . . . 'I'll talk to Veronica, as well as the rest of the team. It's a collaborative show.'

'You're the EP. If you think you can deliver what I've proposed, I give it the green light. Are you working on a story that could kick this off?'

'Quite possibly. Requires a trip to Darwin and the Top End for Veronica.'

'There you go. I've also decided that if your team thinks that it can deliver, I'll make *Our Country* the flagship program for Sunday nights. Are you fine with that?'

'Ah, I guess so,' said Andy, feeling rather dazed. 'Sunday night – we're up against the big current affairs guns, *60 Minutes* and the like. Many have tried . . .'

'And done it. I believe we have the right combination. A fresh new approach. Just get your new star onto that story. Whatever it takes,' said William Rowe.

Andy leaned across the desk to shake Rowe's hand. 'This is a challenge but a great opportunity. Thanks.'

Andy called Veronica into his office and uncharacteristically shut the door. He started by telling her, 'You can go to Darwin.'

'Really! Fantastic. So our budget isn't being cut?'

'Nope. The reverse.'

'We have *more* money to play with?'

He smiled. 'Rowe has a new idea for the program, to increase viewers, boost our profile. And a changed time-slot. Sunday night. Prime time.'

'Whaaat?' She narrowed her eyes. 'And what's the price? There has to be a catch.'

Andy outlined Rowe's idea, talking faster as Veronica started shaking her head. 'Look, it doesn't make a heap of difference. You just do what you do – dig, research, travel, interview people, talk things through with me, direct the crew. But you just do it all on camera. Show the inner workings.'

'You're crazy. I spend hours on the phone, I sit in archives, I spend hours chatting with someone to get maybe one lead, I write copious notes. Watching paint dry is more exciting.'

'Not if the boring bits are edited out. Listen, it's worth a shot. You can't let everyone else on the team down.'

'I'll look like an egomaniac. I'm not talent. I'm a slogger doing my job. And half the time a story doesn't work out. It's not like an Agatha Christie novel.'

'And that's life, that's the business. Let people see that. The frustrations, the dead ends, the way people misrepresent things. The media gets a bad rap, you can show the balance. You're dedicated, you're good at what you do, you're part of a team – we'll be sure and show that – and you have a winning personality.'

Veronica stared at him, then burst out laughing. 'Andy. That's total rubbish. Don't try and bullshit me.'

He shrugged. 'All right. Just be yourself. You can be a pain in the backside at times too. Especially when you think you're right.'

'I don't know . . . It's so invasive. My privacy will be gone. People will know who I am. That's going to make my job harder.'

'Veronica, give it a shot. One program. The crazy expedition – it's perfect, some backstory, history, the outback setting, those characters . . .'

'They're mostly dead and the ones who are still alive won't talk to us!'

'Try getting that on film.'

'Ugh, foot-in-the-door stuff. I don't want to appear on camera having doors slammed in my face.'

'Be smart then. Think around it. Look, go to Darwin. See what you can find out. Especially anything about Marta. And John Cardwell's involvement. There's a challenge. You've started unravelling this story, now you have the blessing and the budget to keep going. You can't say no.'

Veronica shrugged. 'I hate the whole idea of people watching me go about my job.'

'Yeah, every teenage girl in Australia is going to want to be Veronica Anderson when she grows up.'

She threw a pencil at him and, as she got up said, 'You sell it to the rest of the team. Make sure they know it's not my idea and I'm not happy.' She stomped out.

Stepping off the plane in Darwin, Veronica made a mental note to get aerial shots of the approach to the city. She was astounded at the freighters and tankers lined up in the blue bay. The high rises and new complexes around the harbour surprised her too. This was not the sleepy, casual city she'd imagined. Even from the air it looked bustling, energetic, in the grip of a huge boom. She was travelling alone as she'd persuaded Andy to let her hire a cameraman in Darwin when she needed one.

'I'm sure that our affiliate station up there will be able to arrange something. Trust me to set up shots as needed and allow him free range to accompany me when I'm actually doing something interesting so he won't be hanging around while I do the boring research. Y'know this is doubling my workload, slotting myself into the story as well,' she moaned.

Her serviced apartment in the Mantra was nicer than a hotel, she decided, with a view over the Esplanade to the sea and within walking distance of the CBD and restaurants.

It was steamy and humid, as she expected, which was a nice change from the rain in Sydney. As she always did in a new city, she headed out to walk a few blocks, find some lunch and get a feel for the place.

There were backpackers and tourists everywhere, local office workers on their lunch breaks were casually dressed and all seemed young. The population seemed to be made up of a mixture of races that reminded her of Broome. Darwin was typical of the north with its proximity to Indonesia. It was a place with a history of intermarriage between Asians, Europeans, Aborigines and all combinations in between, which had produced attractive and interesting-looking people. There was a definite buzz in the air.

The choice of where to eat with the variety of cuisines on offer was bewildering. She opted for 'Asian-fusion' and discovered it was a modern take on popular Indonesian, Malay and local seafood delicacies. She wrote a note to include the food as a sidebar in the story. Then crossed it out. Too travel reporterish. There were always pictures of the reporter eating somewhere flash. And who looked good sucking a crab leg?

She sipped a glass of white wine while waiting for her meal, breaking a rule not to drink at lunchtime when working and looked at the notes she'd made on the plane. She didn't have much to go on. Colin had mentioned that Marta had done a one-woman show. There might have been some publicity about it. And Topov sounded colourful enough to get a run in the local paper, especially in the 1950s. She wondered if they ever made it to Arnhem Land. Damn Colin and John Cardwell, she thought. She needed more information.

Andy had given her the phone number of his friend Jim, on the local newspaper and her next call would be to the chief-of-staff at the local TV affiliate to book a crew. She was still uncomfortable with the new thrust of the show and worried that it would inhibit her usual routine. Perhaps, she thought, this whole idea would go away as quickly as it had been whipped up. But she really hoped that she could find out more about Topov's expedition and turn it into a good story, especially with Cardwell's involvement in it. Like Andy, her story nose was twitching. How to explain that to a TV audience, she suddenly thought with wry amusement.

After lunch, using the street directory she had picked up from her serviced apartment, she set off to the Darwin Archives in Cavenagh Street. She explained her request to the receptionist who rang through for an archivist. Collette, softly spoken, calm and courteous, was understanding and helped her observe the protocols of registering and signing in.

'I know you media people are always under pressure. Not like other researchers and academics who come in with more time up their sleeve,' she said with a smile.

'I'm sorry. I just arrived in town and I thought I'd start here researching my story, but you're right, I am under pressure,' said Veronica with a smile.

'Well, tell me a little more about what you're after. Perhaps I can make some suggestions.'

Collette listened attentively as Veronica outlined the story that Colin had told her, omitting any reference to John Cardwell.

'What an intriguing story. Is there a particular reason you want to follow this up after all these years?' asked Collette.

Veronica smiled. 'You're very smart. The story started out as a nostalgic look at the early days of our film and

TV industry but it's kind of grown into a more interesting one as I've learned details about the expedition.'

'I won't probe further,' said Collette diplomatically. 'Now, we can search for filming expeditions. There could be journals, letters and references in oral histories. But obviously the newspaper files would be the first place to start. You can read the newspapers online up until 1954, so you just missed out. From 1955 onwards you'd have to go to the Territory Library in Parliament House and trawl through the microfilm.'

'Yes, I know. That's one of the reasons why I had to come to Darwin. I'm also heading into the newspaper to look up my boss's old pal, to see if he can help and then I'll have to put a day aside to go through the microfilm.'

'If you wouldn't mind filling in some paperwork and giving me as many names and details as you can and leaving it with me I might be able to find some relevant material for you. Names of people, places they visited, anything you can think of . . . You never know what we might turn up.'

'That would be wonderful.' Veronica paused and gritted her teeth. 'I hate to ask this, but as this is for a TV story and I'm filming much of my research as I go along, could I film a short segment with you in here? It could promote the archives and perhaps encourage people to donate material. I find it embarrassing but for the moment I'm the focal point of the story – until I find out something more exciting.'

Collette smiled. 'I'll have to organise the required permission but I'm sure it would be fine. And as you say, if it encourages people to donate family papers and special documents that would be helpful. It's tragic what treasures families throw out when their relatives pass on. We have some very important historical documents but some of the family histories of life in the early days in the Territory are quite fascinating, as well.'

'You're very kind, thanks so much for your help,' said Veronica taking her card from her wallet.

'My pleasure. I'll be interested to know what you find out. Here's my card. Let me know when you want to film.'

Veronica had made an appointment with Jim Winchester, Andy's old journo friend whom she'd met at the Pioneers' Reunion. Although he was officially retired, he still worked as a sub-editor, part-time, on the *Darwin Daily*

'Well, hello again, Jim. Andy sends his best wishes.'

'Thanks. I've been looking forward to hearing from you. Here, sit down in this cubicle they call an office. Can I get you something?'

'No, thank you. You're subbing the paper?'

'Only the news section. And I only work three days a week. Came out of retirement as I was bored. How can I help? Any leads yet?'

'Not yet, I've just arrived in Darwin. It seems to be a very energetic place, not the laidback lazy tropical town I was expecting.'

'Those days are long gone. Tell me how I can help you, Veronica. I feel something of a proprietary interest in this story as I was there at its birth, so to speak.'

'Yes, of course. Had you met Colin before that evening?'

'No. Seemed nice enough from our brief meeting. Has he been helpful?'

'Very. Until a certain heavyweight leaned on him and he's clammed up. Scared off.'

'That's interesting,' mused Jim. 'Can I ask who that might be? Confidentially, of course.'

'John Cardwell.'

The older news man raised his eyebrows. 'That *is* interesting. He has his fingers in a lot of pies, I believe.'

'Really? Like what?' asked Veronica. 'Up here in the north, you mean?'

'The far north, into Asia, the rumour has it. He came through town a few months back, which didn't go unnoticed.'

'He has casino interests in Asia, doesn't he?'

'Yep. But this time he was seen in the company of some resource high flyers from Saudi Arabia.'

'Oil people?'

'Yes, but of course they are also interested in good horse flesh.'

'So what happened?'

'Nothing, as far as I am aware. It's hard to get past the suits and wall of silence that surround the man. Very private fellow. And with his money he can make sure the screen around his activities stays in place.'

'He must have very loyal retainers. Or he pays them well,' said Veronica.

'Or else they are no longer employed. Which can also be interpreted as disappearing,' Jim said grimly. 'Mind you, there's as much myth as substance around John Cardwell and he probably perpetuates a lot of it to confuse people.'

'I can understand why Colin got scared off,' said Veronica. 'But why? What does Colin know?'

'And the connection between our meek and mild failed screenwriter and one of Australia's most colourful businessmen is?'

Veronica hesitated, then decided to trust Andy's friend. He might prove a helpful ally. 'Cardwell was one of the people on the filming expedition with Colin back in the fifties.'

He let out a low whistle. 'Then this story is certainly

worth pursuing. Definitely got legs. But I suppose you're still scratching the surface, eh? How can I help?'

'I'm not sure. Any contacts you can think of that might be worth talking to. And a suggestion of a good place for dinner?' Veronica then ran through what she knew and the advice she'd been given by Collette at the archives.

Jim nodded. 'The NT Library should be useful but the research will take some time. I know a couple of old timers who might be worth talking to. Just to give you some background on those times in the fifties. They were pretty rough and ready days back then and I assume you'll need a few talking heads for a bit of nostalgia.'

'You bet. That'd be great.' Veronica shook her head. 'I need as much help as I can get. Your good friend Andy has come up – thanks to our new CEO – with a change in the format of the show.'

'What was wrong with it? Why do new execs feel they have to reinvent the wheel?'

'Because they can, I suppose. Anyway, Andy has gone along with it as we've been given a bigger budget, hence my being here. But the uncomfortable thing is that I have to be on camera, which I loathe. I'm racking my brains to figure out ways to illustrate what I'm doing because digging into a story can be a pretty boring slog.'

'Yeah, reading files and papers doesn't make for riveting TV,' agreed Jim. 'You definitely need Bonza and Reggie.'

'Bonza?' laughed Veronica. 'Who are these men?'

'Bonza is an old croc shooter who describes everything as bonza. Or beaudy,' Jim chuckled. 'Reg is an Aboriginal tour guide. They'll give you some local colour even if it's got nothing to do with the core of the story.'

'Great. I rang the chief-of-staff at Network Eleven, Darwin. The head camera guy is out of town on a story so he's trying to get me a cameraman. But I'll be okay with a stringer if he can't. Where do I find Bonza and Reggie?'

'I'll put the word out via the pub. They have no fixed abode connected to a phone,' said Jim.

'Thanks heaps. Can I buy you a drink sometime as a thank you?' she asked.

'You can do that. But I'll talk to my old girl and see if we can rustle up some friends for a barbecue one night. And bring along anyone you care to. Do you have friends in Darwin?'

'No. Just you,' said Veronica.

Jim looked flattered. 'I'll call your mobile when I've made contact.'

When Veronica received a call from Dougie, the junior cameraman from the TV station telling her that he was available, she asked him to come over and meet her at the Mantra.

Dougie was in his early twenties and eager to work with her. 'I think *Our Country* is a fantastic show. I've often thought there are some stories around here that'd be worth doing.'

'Well, why didn't you put them up to your boss?' asked Veronica.

Dougie looked uncomfortable. 'Ah, who'd listen to me? I'm told to just point the camera and keep my mouth shut.'

Veronica nodded. 'Yeah, it's a tough business. But you've got to just keep hammering away, Dougie. One day someone smart will listen. Now, let me explain what I'm doing.'

Veronica didn't want Dougie to know that this was a new concept, so that when the time came to unveil the 'new look' program, no-one would have any idea how the show had been changed. With this in mind, she outlined her idea that he should just follow her around while she researched her story.

'Okay. Sounds easy enough. You tell me what you want and I'll do it. You're the producer,' said Dougie sounding relieved that he didn't have to make decisions. 'Okay so we have the two blokes, Bonza and Reggie, I've heard of them. Then there's you in the archives and the newspaper office. What else?'

'Ah, I suppose we need some overview scenes of Darwin. How about you take me on a tour and we pick up shots of me wandering around the places in Darwin you think people would want to see.'

'Yeah. Cullen Bay, that's cool. What about the terrific aquarium or the Crocoseum? Get you in the cage. It's the big new thing to do here. And there's Mindil markets tomorrow night and Parap markets on Saturday morning. And the harbour . . .'

'Whoa. Sounds like you have your finger on the pulse. Terrific,' said Veronica.

She devoted the next day to the sights of Darwin with Dougie. She drew the line at the new tourist attraction of a wildlife complex where large 'retired' crocodiles had their own private domain and two people at a time could get into a protective glass cage and be lowered into the water for a very close encounter.

'C'mon, Veronica, get in the cage, it'll look great,' said Dougie.

'No way. Film that couple in their swimsuits,' said Veronica, as a pair who were obviously on their honeymoon got into the cage, which was lowered into the water. 'Have you noticed the gouges and teeth marks on the outside of the cage? But you're right, this is a novel attraction in the centre of the CBD. Perhaps I could go as far as holding a snake or lizard.'

Veronica loved the colonial-style buildings along the seafront and the bustling restaurants at the wharf. Then they headed over to Cullen Bay with its expensive new high rise apartments and cluster of eateries facing the sweep of the bay.

'This is a great place for dinner, expensive though, sixty dollars for a mud crab meal,' said Dougie. 'I'd rather eat at the markets. We'll do that tonight. It's become an institution. Started out as a casual thing. Locals used to go to the beach to watch the sunset, bring a picnic and there were a few stalls and now there are hundreds. It's huge.'

That evening as their taxi followed the stream of traffic past the big casino it seemed that everyone in Darwin was heading to Mindil Beach. They got out near a forest of thick trees covered in vines and walked to a beach fringed by palm trees. Already people were setting up chairs and picnics while the walkway was lined on both sides with colourful stalls. The lights, decorations, inviting cooking smells and mix of people looked, to Veronica, like a mini international gathering. There were musicians, tarot card readers, massages, cooking, crafts, art, gifts and children's play and entertainment areas.

'This is incredible. Best market I've ever seen and what a setting,' she told Dougie. 'I see what you mean about the food. Everything looks fabulous.'

'I go for the Asian stuff, but there's everything – Greek, to African . . . you name it,' said Dougie. 'Maybe you'd like a buffalo burger, or crocodile kebabs? Will I take some shots of you wandering through all this? Then we'll set up for the sunset.'

'Go for it, Dougie. I'm going to look around.'

Veronica bought a selection of foods, including the crocodile kebabs, which were delicious and a bottle of beer for herself and Dougie, who'd chosen a barramundi stir fry for his dinner. Sitting on the sand she ate from a paper plate as Dougie filmed the great red ball of the sun sinking into the Timor Sea.

The next day Veronica dropped her notes into Collette

at the archives, listing as many names, places and details as she could remember from what Colin had told her. Then, with Dougie in tow, she headed to her appointment at the library.

Parliament House, which housed the library, was a spectacular new white building adjacent to Government House and the Supreme Court, with views across the harbour. After passing through the security check Veronica and Dougie took the lift to the well-appointed library. Veronica explained to one of the librarians that she'd come to do some research and that she had been given permission to film her scrolling through the microfilm. When she located the microfilm section and started to look through the old papers, Dougie peered over her shoulder so as to get a close-up of the screen.

'Amazing old stuff. Wish I'd been up here in the old days, bit like the wild west,' he said.

'Yes, a bit of a frontier by the looks of it. Pretty rugged country once you left Darwin. And it's close to Asia – you can practically see Indonesia. Makes you realise how near our northern neighbours are,' said Veronica.

'My granddad talks about the war, reckons there were a lot more Japanese midget subs that came close to shore than they know about,' said Dougie. 'Well, I'll leave you to it. Let me know how you get on, Veronica. Been nice working with you, if there's nothing else you want me for right now.'

Veronica pulled her attention away from the screen. 'Aren't you going to be working with me anymore, Dougie? That's a shame, you've been great.'

'Thanks. Yeah, the chief camera guy comes back tomorrow. I hope I can get out on some of the trips he gets to do, sometime. I've only been up in a chopper once. Loved it.'

'Good luck, Dougie. I'm not sure what else I have to film around here. Sorry it's not been so exciting for you.'

'My turn'll come. Eddie moves around a lot.'

'Eddie? The chief guy is Eddie? Eddie who?' asked Veronica, her heart sinking.

'Eddie Jarman. Used to work in Sydney, done a lot of documentaries. Do you know him?'

Veronica turned back to the computer screen to hide her confusion. 'Yes, I know him. See ya, Dougie.'

'Right. Well, see you then. Let me know what you want done with this footage or when you want to look at it and edit it.'

'Yep. Thanks, Dougie.'

Dougie glanced back at Veronica as he left. She suddenly seemed very occupied at the computer and yet slightly distracted.

Damn you, Andy, she cursed under her breath. Surely he knew Eddie was up here. She was shocked at the unexpected news that her ex-boyfriend and colleague was working in Darwin. Why hadn't Andy told her? Veronica sat still, her eyes closed, trying to calm herself and sort out how she felt about seeing him again. I'm over you, Eddie, she told herself firmly. So why was she feeling so rattled? Perhaps he was married or in a stable relationship, if Eddie knew what that was, which would keep some distance between them.

But creeping into her mind came memories of the fun they'd had together and the great working relationship they'd had – before they'd fallen in love and slept together. Or was that the other way around? She couldn't help smiling as she thought about their trip to Norfolk Island when they'd become more than professional colleagues.

Well, maybe the story would fizzle out and she wouldn't need a cameraman. When this ridiculous idea came to her, she realised that she wasn't concentrating – skimming images on the microfilm were just whizzing past her eyes.

She decided to take a break and rang Andy.

'If you tell me you knew Eddie was working up here and didn't warn me, I'll wring your neck,' she said as soon as he answered the phone.

'Veronica? Is that you? How nice to hear from you. How're things going in Darwin? Is it hot? Have you caught up with Jim?'

'Andy! You damn-well knew he was here! Why didn't you tell me?' she shouted.

'What difference would it have made?' he asked calmly.

Veronica was silent for a moment. 'Well, I might have been prepared.'

'So how is he? How's the research going?'

'I haven't seen Eddie. He's been out on a job. I've had a young kid who's been great. In fact, I might ask to use him and not Eddie.'

'That's up to the head of the camera department. Who happens to be Eddie, I understand. How was Jim?'

'Nice. Helpful. Does he know about me and Eddie?'

'No, of course not. Why should he? Look, Eddie's a great cameraman and you said you're over him, so what's the big drama, Veronica?' asked Andy.

'Men. You're hopeless. I am over him. It's just, well, a surprise. And I have nothing new to report. I'll have to spend quite a few more hours poring over the newspaper records. But I'm going to meet a couple of outback characters, friends of Jim's.'

'Great. You can trust Jim. I wouldn't go into too many details with anyone else about Cardwell though,' said Andy.

'If I've got a cameraman in tow, like Eddie, it'll be hard to keep things quiet,' said Veronica.

'I suppose so,' said Andy. 'But be careful.'

'Around Eddie? That I can guarantee,' said Veronica. 'But Darwin is interesting. Must have been a wild place in the old days.'

'See if you can get some archive footage of Darwin in the fifties. Go out bush a bit. Try to capture what it must have been like for those innocents making that film and dealing with the loneliness and isolation of the outback after Europe. The landscape won't have changed too much.'

'I'll wait until I have something to go on,' said Veronica. 'I'll keep you posted.'

Veronica again sat at the computer in the library till her eyes ached and she thought that she couldn't look at another page of print. She felt as though she'd sat through hours of news footage as images and headlines of 1955 Darwin rolled past. There was so much to get through, especially as she wasn't sure what she was looking for, so she had refined her search to just the entertainment pages when suddenly a classified advertisement jumped out at her – 'European Actress to Star in Famous Plays'. The words 'European' and 'Plays' were unusual compared with the rest of the stories she'd been reading. Holding her breath she enlarged the ad.

Famous Swedish actress Marta Johanssen will star in a one-woman show performing scenes from playwright Henrik Ibsen's *A Doll's House* and *Ghosts*, as well as scenes from Shakespeare and other classics. The Outdoor Theatre, Darwin . . .

'Hallelujah,' breathed Veronica, skimming through the ad looking for any photographs. She went through the papers for the following week to find, at last, a grainy photograph and small write-up.

Success for One-Woman Show
Miss Marta Johanssen has extended her series of dramatic performances at The Outdoor Theatre

for another two weeks, due to popular demand. The attractive Swedish actress is starring in a film documentary to promote the Northern Territory prior to next year's Olympic Games in Melbourne. Following on the success earlier this year of *Jedda*, Australia's first colour feature film set in Outback Australia and starring Aboriginal actors, the exposure of the north at the cinema could soon make it a popular destination for foreign travellers. Miss Johanssen has taken time off from this venture to entertain audiences in Darwin with her superb acting.

Veronica studied the face of the actress with her curly hair, broad jaw and large smile. She looked fun, Veronica thought, with a strong face that seemed to reveal a bubbly personality. And now she had her last name. Veronica continued to scan the papers but there were no further write-ups of Marta's show.

Leaving Parliament House she rang Andy as she started to walk back into town.

'Pay dirt. It's Marta Johanssen. She did a one-woman show which was extended as it was apparently quite popular.'

'A one-woman show, eh? Curious. I wonder why. And nothing else about any of them? Any pictures?'

'Just a portrait of Marta. She looks cute.'

'What's your next move?'

'I'm heading back to the archives as I have a message from Collette to say that she's found something.'

'Okay. Keep me posted. And say hi to Jim for me.'

'I will. He and his wife have invited me to dinner tomorrow night.'

*

Collette greeted her warmly. 'Your story has me quite intrigued, I have to confess. I've been doing some searching. How did you get on at the library?'

'Two references to Marta putting on a one-woman show.' She handed Collette the photocopies.

'Hmm. We might have something on this, as well. People tend to collect programs and playbills. Anyway, come and see what I've dug up.'

'This is very kind of you,' said Veronica.

Collette directed her to a table in the reading room and handed her a pair of white cotton gloves.

'It's a policy. While this isn't an old document, it's a bit fragile because it's been kept in poor conditions, but I thought you might find it interesting.'

She laid a journal in front of Veronica and opened it at a bookmarked page. 'It's the diary, well, journal, kept by a Mrs Annabel Johns who lived for a number of years on a station called Brolga Springs.'

'They stopped there! Colin said that's where they saw the corroboree. What does she say? Does she mention the group?'

'She does.'

Veronica was excited. This was corroborative evidence of Colin's story.

Annabel Johns had neat handwriting and she'd kept a journal of daily events at Brolga Springs. Some entries weren't relevant, dealing with food supplies, rations, stock details, work she'd given to certain staff, what mail had arrived but the arrival of Topov's group had given her some entertainment and she'd written about it in detail.

Len Buchanan met some weary travellers on the Stuart and suggested that they come in and camp for a couple of nights. I was introduced to a very unusual group led by a rather loud and overbearing Russian gentleman, a Mr Topov. They are making a film about the outback and I don't think they have yet had much luck, so I had Len and Samson round up some of the blacks from the camp to do a corroboree for them. I think it made quite an impression on them as most of the visitors were foreigners. One of them, an actress, a pretty young woman, took a great fancy to little Doris, as did the Yugoslav man who took many photographs of her. Doris was very impressed with an old yellow caravan they were towing. They said that they're heading to Arnhem Land but I don't know how successful they'll be as they seem rather inexperienced in dealing with our conditions. I also had the feeling not all of them were in agreement with Mr Topov, though there was a quite capable woman in the party, a well-bred Englishwoman who seemed rather out of place. However, I do hope they manage to put together some sort of film. I can't help but wonder how much longer before the Aborigines die out and there will be little record of their ceremonies and their culture.

'She was prescient in a way, don't you think?' said Collette. 'By the 1960s there was a lot of change. And it's changing again, now, though not the way Mrs Johns imagined. Mr Topov sounds a difficult man, doesn't he? Now, let me see if we have any reference to Marta's stage show.'

While Collette went to her desk, Veronica used another computer and, on the off chance Marta had made a name for herself, googled Marta Johanssen. To her surprise, there were several results for Marta. One came from Sydney's *Daily Telegraph* and showed a photo of the expedition group taken at the sandhills at Kurnell prior to their departure. There was the Dodge, the Jeep, the Land Rover, the caravan and the group posed around them, just as Colin had described it. Veronica peered at the faces trying to see if they looked the way she'd imagined them. Marta, curvy in shorts, hand on hips looked flirtatious. Johnny, perched on top of the Land Rover, was too far away to make out any resemblance to the older John Cardwell she'd met. She almost laughed out loud at the sight of Topov. He was just as she'd imagined. Colin was still recognisable even with a shock of dark hair.

The second hit was the announcement of the stage show in the Darwin newspaper, which she had already found, but then, a couple of years later, there was a picture of Marta 'heading for Hollywood' and an article from the Sydney *Sun* newspaper.

The Australian-based actress Marta Johanssen, well known for her stage appearances at the Elizabethan Theatre and for her appearances in TV commercials, has landed a small part in a Hollywood film. The film in which she will play a war time European spy for the British Secret Service, will be shot in Los Angeles and Italy. Miss Johanssen, who now has a Los Angeles agent, hopes to continue to work in Hollywood films. Miss Johanssen added, that she would always consider Australia to be her second home.

'Well, well,' said Veronica. 'Did Marta make the big time after all, I wonder? I've never heard of her, but she could have changed her name. And did she do it with Topov? And what happened to her friendship with Colin?'

'The more you find out, the more questions you have,' said Collette, who'd returned and was peering over Veronica's shoulder. 'Here, I found this.' She opened a folder and delicately handed Veronica a leaflet.

It was a flyer for Marta's show. Apart from listing times and ticket prices it didn't say much more than the newspaper ad.

'Oh, look here,' said Veronica. In small letters was printed, 'Produced by Colin Peterson'. 'Well, they were still together, here in Darwin. Where were the others I wonder?'

The back of the flyer listed Marta's show business credentials from Europe. 'It looks quite impressive. I suppose Darwin would have been pleased to have someone of her calibre here.'

'Actually a lot of entertainers and troupes travelled round Australia in those days,' said Collette. 'So you have some more clues. What do you do next?'

'Eventually, I'd like to try to find Marta and I hope that she'll talk to me, but for now I'd like to go to Brolga Springs. May I use your computer a moment longer, please?'

Quickly Veronica googled Brolga Springs NT to discover the word brolga was a popular trademark in tourism. But as she scrolled down, she found that there, in accommodation/adventure tours, was Brolga Springs Station. 'Wow, it's a commercial enterprise now.'

'Check the newspaper reviews and articles linked to it,' said Collette.

They both read the write-ups and looked at the photographs of the station, which now comprised of a large homestead, donga accommodation and safari-style tents. There was also a dining and entertainment area and a variety of tours and activities. A smiling young husband and wife were the hosts who promised visitors a true 'Eco/indigenous Aussie experience'.

'It's owned by an Aboriginal corporation,' read Collette. 'That's happening a lot as land goes back to the traditional owners. A lot of ventures have failed but this one looks very successful.'

'Maybe because it's got a great young couple in charge,' said Veronica. 'Look at their background, they've both grown up on stations. They're running an indigenous training program for the staff and have included cultural activities with local community people. All under one roof, plus it's a commercial cattle enterprise. Now that's a good story.' Veronica leaned back. 'I have to go there. By the way, what's a donga?'

'It's like a cabin, except you can lift up the sides, so that it's open and lets the breeze through. I wonder what happened to Mrs Johns?' Collette added.

'I'm sure I can find out when I get there. Unless the end of her journal gives us some clue.'

'Would you like a coffee before you start on the journal, Veronica? You have a bit of reading to do.' Collette smiled.

Veronica found Annabel Johns' journal an interesting record of her time at Brolga Springs, filled with the dramas of injuries, deaths, cattle musters, wet-season isolation and humorous interludes with her Aboriginal domestic staff, but it didn't give Veronica much material for her story. Her husband seemed to be away more than not and when he was at the station he was gone at dawn and returned at dusk. Annabel didn't have children so Doris seemed to be her companion, friend and surrogate child.

But at the end of the diary Veronica felt saddened as she read of the death of Annabel's husband in a riding accident during a flood. Mrs Johns had to sell up and move south as she found the property impossible to manage by herself. She wrote of her struggle to find a solution for Doris. She was sure that without her protection, the light-skinned child would be taken away to the missions to be trained as a domestic. Faced with this prospect, she consulted Doris's mother and grandmother and they decided that the best thing for the intelligent little girl would be for her to have a good education. Annabel

Johns then approached the mission nuns and explained the situation and they managed to get Doris enrolled in a convent school down south.

There was a postscript, evidently written a few years later. It seemed that the new owner of the station was a businessman from Brisbane who didn't live on the property. He put in a manager with instructions to double the carrying capacity of the station by introducing new breeds. He was not interested in the locals or their customs and the tribal families splintered and drifted away.

'Oh, how sad,' said Veronica.

'Yet, look how it's turned around. I think Annabel Johns would be pleased to see how Brolga Springs is being run today,' said Collette when Veronica told her how the journal ended.

'Perhaps. When I get out there I hope I can get a feel for its history as well as what's happening today,' said Veronica. 'Collette, I can't thank you enough, this has been such a breakthrough.'

'You're welcome. And have you finished going through the newspaper files? Will you do that?'

'I guess so. I've no idea how long they all stayed in Darwin. Right now I'm interested in Brolga Springs. At least it will give me some good vision.' And at that thought she sighed. 'I have to talk to the TV station about a cameraman.'

'Good luck, Veronica. If I can be of any more help, do let me know. And I'd love to hear how you get on,' said Collette warmly.

'I'll keep in touch. I owe you a coffee, lunch, really,' promised Veronica.

Back in her apartment, Veronica poured herself a drink and phoned Murphy, the chief-of-staff at the Darwin TV station.

'Ah, yes, Andy spoke to me. Was Dougie okay? Sorry our head camera guy was out of town,' said Murphy.

'Dougie was great – polite, quick and took directions, as well as thinking for himself,' said Veronica quickly.

'Good, good. Some of the young blokes can be a bit on the slow side.'

'In fact, I'd quite like to keep using him. Keep the continuity going,' said Veronica.

'Ah, you need more stuff? What did you have in mind?' asked Murphy cautiously.

'Actually I'm planning to go out of town. Head out towards Katherine and go to Brolga Springs Station.'

'Aw, that could be difficult. We need Dougie on call for the city stuff. He hasn't done a big assignment out of town.'

'Oh, I wouldn't say this was a big job, a few scenics, touristy stuff,' cut in Veronica.

But Murphy wouldn't buy it. 'Nope. No can do. You need someone who knows the area. I can't send a new kid out with gear, a vehicle. He's just not experienced enough. No, Eddie Jarman is the guy for the job. He used to work at Eleven in Sydney, surely you know of him?'

'Yes, I know him.'

'Then why quibble? Why would you want anyone else? He's an ace cameraman. And if you're worried about him being a city slicker, don't. He's become a real Territorian. But if you have a need to get out into that kind of country, he'd probably be the first to suggest you take a local with you.' When Veronica didn't answer immediately, Murphy asked, 'What did you have in mind to shoot?'

'I'm not sure. But some local knowledge would be helpful.' She was clutching at a straw. The idea of going anywhere alone with Eddie was unnerving her, but a third person, some kind of guide, suddenly seemed a good idea.

'Yes, yes. A guide, a local, would be excellent. Do you have anyone in mind?'

'Are you looking at any indigenous stuff, or what? Andy said you weren't doing anything fluffy, not a touristy piece.'

'Absolutely not. I'd like someone who could fill in some of the gaps in the history of Brolga Springs between the fifties and the present. And some local cultural knowledge, some contacts with indigenous people, any old timers . . . That'd be great.'

'Jamie McIntosh. He's your man.'

'Great, great,' said Veronica.

'Don't you want to know about him?'

'I trust your judgment, Murphy. Yes, sure, fill me in,' said Veronica, simply relieved there'd be someone else coming along to ease the tension of working with Eddie again.

'He works for National Parks as a ranger and as an environmentalist and sits on the board of some community groups. Does media, radio, the occasional TV show, so he knows the kind of stuff you want. And he's local, educated and articulate. He's also pretty handy when it comes to boats, cars, crocs.'

'That's nice to know. He sounds perfect.'

'I'll give him a call. And why don't you have a talk with Eddie. Tell him what you're after. Catch up on old times?'

She took a deep breath. 'Sure. Tomorrow morning?'

'Come in after the production meeting, say nine-thirty am?'

'Fine. Could you tell Eddie that I'll be coming in to see him, please?'

'Roger. And how long are you going to steal my chief camera guy for?'

'Oh, I have no idea. Let me speak to Eddie and this Jamie. I'll let you know.'

'We'll need to fix up the roster, you know how it is.' Murphy hung up.

Veronica finished her drink as her mobile rang.

'Hi Veronica, it's Jim. You still on for dinner tomorrow night?'

'Yes, I'm looking forward to it.'

'Anyone you want to bring along, feel free.'

'No, thanks. It'll just be me. What can I bring?'

'Don't worry about it, love. Say, Reg and Bonza, the two blokes I told you about?'

'Oh, yes, right. Are they willing to be interviewed?'

'They'd like to meet you. So I invited them along tomorrow night. They're a blast. Is that okay?' asked Jim.

'Why, yes, I guess so. If it's okay with your wife,' said Veronica.

'She's sweet. She's used to people just turning up.'

'That's nice,' said Veronica.

'Yep. I reckon there'll be a few people who might be able to help you. Oh, and I invited a couple of blokes from the TV station, including the head camera guy, Eddie. He's made a bit of a name for himself since moving here. Says he knows you. So you can catch up. Righto?'

'Terrific. Looking forward to it. Thanks for going to the trouble.' Veronica tried to sound upbeat.

'I'll text you the address. See you round seven.'

Veronica sat on her balcony, feeling the shift in temperature as the heat of the day faded and a slight breeze came in from the ocean. She still felt sticky and hot and decided to have a shower. She shut the doors, turned on the air conditioning and ordered room service. Suddenly she felt tired. The thought of seeing Eddie again was stressing her more than it should. She admonished herself. She'd walked out on Eddie, not that he seemed to care, particularly as he had someone waiting in the wings. But she'd been hurt and while she had moved on in her life, professionally, there'd never been any passion since Eddie. She knew that there was no way she would ever let herself be swept away by Eddie again. But seeing him was going to be difficult.

8

VERONICA STOOD AT THE reception desk at the TV station gazing at the photographs of the local on-air staff as well as the glossy pin-ups of the national network stars. A young girl appeared and led her to the camera department. She was dressed in punk black tights and a ripped top. She wore goth-like eye make-up and carried a clipboard, her self important manner screaming, I work in teevee . . .

'I'm Heidi. Can I help?'

'I'm looking for Mr Jarman.'

'Oh, Eddie. He's so cute. He's through there.'

With Veronica in tow, Heidi pointed out things of interest as they wove around the back of the studio. 'That's the main studio. Where they do the news and stuff. And in there are the OB vans and things, for when they cover sports matches and stuff. Now, down here, is the camera department. They're back here 'cause of all their equipment and stuff.'

'I understand,' said Veronica.

The girl gave her a sideways glance. 'Are you a model or something?'

'Goodness, no. I'm a producer.' Veronica didn't know whether to be flattered or not.

'Really? I'd like to do that sort of stuff. Are you going for a job? I didn't know there were any vacancies. Will you be able to find your way out?'

'I think so,' said Veronica.

The girl stuck her head through the doorway, 'Hey, Eddie, you've got a visitor.'

'Thanks, Heidi.'

Eddie came to the doorway and grinned at Veronica. 'She's a hoot, isn't she? All that "stuff". Say, you're looking great.' He leaned over and kissed her cheek. Veronica felt herself stiffen and didn't lean towards him, but he appeared not to notice and took her arm. 'Come into our quarters. Want a cuppa?'

'Don't go to any trouble.'

He led her into the small tea room. 'No trouble. Want a cold drink instead?'

'Just a cool water if you have it.' She sat down. 'I see that the technicians are still at the top of the totem pole.'

'Yeah, great little shithole isn't it? I'm the big banana here and there's no way I want to be in carpet land with the execs. What are you doing up here in Darwin? Hey, you won Dougie's heart. He thought you were great.' He handed her a bottle of water from the fridge, took out a Coke for himself and sat at the table.

'Dougie is a nice kid. Keen and helpful.'

'Andy told me you're hunting down some story that might or might not go anywhere. Must have something going for it if you've come all this way.'

'How do you like it up here?' asked Veronica, changing the subject.

'Suits me. I travel a lot. Getting up to Bali regularly to surf is a real plus and I like being my own boss.' He took a swallow of Coke. 'How are you doing, Vee?' he asked. His tone was concerned, caring almost.

As if you care, thought Veronica. 'Good. Same old, same old. The show is doing well.'

'I mean you.'

'I know. And I'm fine. Look, Eddie, if this is uncomfortable, I'm really happy to work with young Dougie,' began Veronica.

'Hey! Who's uncomfortable? Not me. Listen, I dig working with you. And I'd like to again. Water under the bridge, okay? Or are you still pissed off at me?'

For a moment she wanted to slap his cocky handsome face but she gritted her teeth and smiled. 'Don't flatter yourself. In fact I should thank you. You did me a big favour taking off with – whatever her name was. You and I were never meant to be together, Eddie.'

'That's for sure. But heck, we were a good working team. So where are we going?' He was all business as he folded his arms on the table and leaned on them. 'I'm all ears. We're heading inland? How long you reckon?'

Veronica adopted the same professional attitude. 'Couldn't say. Depends what we find at Brolga Springs. You ever been there?'

'Nah. But one of the travel shows did a story on it a year or so ago. It sounds a good set-up for tourists and they've got some indigenous training program running. The couple who manage it are apparently terrific.'

'Yes, Vicki and Rick Hodge. Locals, not city people,' said Veronica. 'I read up on it.'

'Well, that's a story always worth updating, even if you don't get anything else out of it. You only have to

213

scratch the surface here in the Territory and you fall over a story,' said Eddie cheerfully. 'Helps if you have a local to show you around. You contacted the Hodges about borrowing one of their local boys?'

'Actually, I've organised a well-known environmentalist to come with us, Jamie McIntosh. Do you know him?'

Eddie gave a short whistle. 'You've got a top-notch bloke there. He knows his stuff, very well regarded. Very media friendly. He's often used on TV as a spokesman for the environment. Quite well known as an expert, so he's a good choice. So what are we doing?'

Veronica matter of factly gave him the bare bones of the story and what she was after.

'Eddie, you should know I'm not a front-of-camera person. It makes me very uncomfortable . . .'

'I see your point. Don't worry, I won't take any fat bum shots.' He laughed. 'I couldn't take a bad angle of you if I tried. So when do we set off? How long do you intend being away?'

'I'm really not sure. Travel there and back and two or three days at Brolga Springs.'

'Sounds fair enough, but I'll need a day or so to get square here. Sort vehicles and gear, make sure the others know what to do.'

'That's fine. I'll check in with you tomorrow.'

'You still got the same mobile number?' he asked.

Veronica stood up. 'Yes, I do. I'm staying at the Mantra. Talk soon.'

She retraced her steps, wishing she wasn't so unnerved by the fact he had kept her phone number.

'Veronica, it's Jim at the *Daily*. Reg and Bonza. They'll be at dinner tonight. You could film them tomorrow sometime, but you'll get better stories after a few beers at the barbie.'

'You've already asked Eddie to come, so I'll get him to bring a camera,' said Veronica.

'Yes, with those two, I'd grab 'em while they're in town,' said Jim.

She rang Eddie and ran the idea of filming at the barbecue past him.

'Bloody good idea, might not all be useable but it will give you a bit of local colour. We'd better get some release forms for them just in case. I'll stick some in my bag. So I can't get too pissed if this is a work assignment,' he laughed.

'Only for a short while, I expect.'

'Right. Get in early. See you there. Unless you want me to pick you up?'

'I'm fine, thanks. See you about seven-thirty,' she said quickly.

Jim's home was in a residential suburb of bright green lawns without fences, scarlet bougainvillea and cyclone-proof, airy houses. The smoke from the large brick barbecue built in the back garden was curling and the smell of frying onion infused the night air. Coloured lights were strung around the outdoor deck and a group had settled themselves in comfortable cane chairs and lounges. A knot of men in a semicircle before the barbecue, beers in hand, were laughing heartily. The chatter of the women and clatter of plates came from the kitchen. The front door was open so Veronica headed towards it.

'Hi. I'm Veronica. Can I leave this somewhere?' She put the cakebox she was carrying on a sideboard and a bottle of wine beside it.

'You didn't have to bring a thing, Veronica. But how

lovely of you. Ooh, cheesecake, wonderful.' The smiling woman held out her hand. 'I'm Jim's wife, Mary.'

'This is very kind of you. It's quite a party,' said Veronica, hoping that Mary hadn't gone to all this trouble especially for her.

'Oh, just friends and neighbours, a few of Jim's pals he wants you to meet. Oh, and your friend Eddie is here.'

'What's he filming?' asked one of the other women. 'I'm Pam, this is Alison.'

'I hope you don't mind. It's just a bit of background colour and hopefully a short chat with Reg and Bonza for a story I'm doing.'

'Short chat! Those two can talk for hours,' said Pam.

'And be careful, they'll pull your leg,' added Alison.

'Can I help with anything?' asked Veronica looking around at the plates of food, bowls of salad and piles of bread.

'Of course not. You go and do what you have to do. We'll sit down for a chat when you're ready,' said Mary.

'Looking forward to it,' said Veronica, taking an immediate liking to Jim's friendly wife.

'Take a wine with you,' added Pam, handing her a glass.

Jim called Veronica over to the barbecue.

'Come and meet my mates. Now, here she is. Veronica, this Bonza and this is Reggie.'

She shook hands with the two men. Bonza was a wiry, wizened man in his late seventies who looked as though the sun had tanned his skin to match the worn crinkled leather hat he was wearing. He was dressed in a tight T-shirt and wore a heavy gold chain with a large shark or croc tooth suspended from it. His hand was calloused and he gave Veronica a direct, but friendly, stare. Reg, probably a bit younger, was dressed in a blue cotton shirt and jeans held up by a leather belt with a fancy silver buckle. He had smooth dark skin and a shy smile.

'So you're up here working on a TV story, are you?' said Bonza. 'What's it about?'

'A bit about the north in the fifties, the characters, what life on a station was like back then. If I were going to make a TV documentary back then, what do you reckon I'd put in it?'

Bonza threw back his head and roared. 'Bloody everything. Not that a lot of us would've wanted to be on camera back then, eh Reg?'

'Wasn't TV back then was there? Just as well, eh, Bonza?' laughed Reg.

'Ain't that the bloody truth eh.' He winked at Veronica, 'I wouldn't want a lot of my life on TV.'

'Were they good times, better times back then?' asked Veronica.

'Ah, they were bonza days, that's for sure.' He sighed and took a large mouthful of beer.

Eddie joined them, camera tucked under his arm. 'G'day fellas, hi Veronica. Mind if I film you standing there chatting while you're having a bit of a yarn?' He lifted the camera onto his shoulder as Jim and two others turned and busied themselves at the barbecue where the sausages were cooking.

Bonza shrugged and Reg shifted his posture, uncomfortable in the presence of the camera, but they continued to smile.

'Tell her about your job,' prompted Reg.

'Which one?' asked Bonza. 'Me proper one or me secret one?'

Eddie turned the camera light on, brightly illuminating the two men and started filming.

'Your secret job, of course,' said Veronica.

'Ah, I'm sort of retired now, y'see. Officially I was

a contractor, a mechanic with a bit of engineering know how. So I moved around a lot in the sixties. Learned a few tricks from people like Reg here . . .'

Reg held up his hand. 'Leave me out of it, I never did nothing wrong.'

'You blokes never had to have a licence, but,' said Bonza.

'A licence for what?' asked Veronica.

'Killing crocs. It was open slather for years and I got pretty good at catching 'em and tanning the skins. Even stuffing them. Then after seventy-three, I think it was, it was illegal to kill the bastards. But I managed to knock off a few here and there. Had a nice little business going.'

'Among other things,' said Reg.

'We won't go into that,' said Bonza.

'What did you do with the crocodiles?' asked Veronica as Eddie swung the camera to her.

'People still wanted the skins and, of course, the meat was bonza eating. 'Specially when you got one with eggs in it. There was quite a business in trophy crocs, even stuffed little blokes were popular.'

'And now?'

'Yeah, well there's a lot of old croc hunters calling themselves conservationists and breeding them. But I reckon we should still be able to cull the buggers. Too many of 'em. Some of those big old rogue crocs cause a lot of trouble. You be careful where you swim, sweetheart,' warned Bonza.

Reg nodded. 'There've been a couple of little kids taken in some of the communities and the crocs are turning up where you wouldn't normally expect them,' he said. 'Aboriginal people can hunt them as their right, but not whitefellas, unless they get a permit.'

'But if it's your Dreaming ancestor, totem or something, you shouldn't take 'em out,' said Bonza with a bit of a nod at Reg.

'There's talk of introducing big game hunting,' said Reg. 'But unless they can take the head or skin home, hunters aren't so keen.'

'So what are you doing, Reg?' asked Veronica.

'I'm a tour guide. I take people out spotting crocs on the river at night. Barra fishing, camping, that sorta thing.'

Bonza nudged Veronica. 'He'd make a lot more money if he took tourists out shooting and marauding feral camels and crocs. Foreigners would pay up to fifty grand for the safari package if they could get a big croc to show off back home.'

'Is there much illegal croc hunting going on now?' asked Veronica.

In reply Bonza looked at Eddie and ran a hand across his throat. 'That'll do, eh mate.'

'If I stop filming, I'll expect a really good story from you,' said Eddie turning off the camera.

Bonza gave a hearty laugh. 'Jeez, that won't be hard. I had some wild days.' He looked at Reg. 'Do you remember when I was sorta on the wanted list? Got caught with all those bloody crocs? Y'know where they ended up?'

Reg held his hands over his face.

Bonza downed his beer and leaned towards Veronica. 'Listen to this. I got all these stuffed bloody crocs, little fellas, some skins, teeth, few trophy items. And the damned cops are after me. Knew a great lady who ran a station by herself. I had a few pals there who worked for her, who used to get me permission to put me boat in the river and in return I'd leave a dozen or so barra fillets inside the kitchen door. So this day I call in but nobody's home. You bonza beaudy. So I stash my gear and the crocs in the house, for safekeeping like.'

Reg, who's heard this story before, can't help laughing. 'Tell Veronica where you stashed them.'

In a stage whisper Bonza said, 'In the bloody roof.

I got up the manhole over the bedroom. I left the lot up there and, ya know, I never did get back to get them. Far as I know they're still there!'

'It must have smelled,' said Veronica.

'Hey, don't insult me, I know how to stuff a croc, tan a hide,' said Bonza indignantly.

''Cept the eyeballs and teeth fall out,' said Reg.

'Well, that's age, you can't help a bit of wear and tear, same as you,' said Bonza. 'This story your doing . . . Where do you plan to go to from here, Veronica?'

'A place called Brolga Springs. I hear it's great for tourists and there's an indigenous training program and some cultural exchange, as well,' said Veronica brightly.

Bonza and Reg exchanged a look. 'Sounds good on paper,' said Bonza. 'Been a few changes out there.'

'You know the place?'

'Yes, way back.' Bonza shook his head. 'But it's been two steps forward and five back.'

'What do you mean?' asked Veronica.

'Used to be a bonza cattle station, but now, well, you check it out. I reckon all that tourist stuff just spoilt it, but they call it progress,' said Bonza shortly. 'Now if you want a really good story, why don't you get onto some of the illegal croc hunters? The skins go up to Asia, a boat picks 'em up every fortnight. They come back as handbags and shoes to Sydney tourist shops. Bonza business,' he laughed.

'And I s'pose you know them?' Veronica asked Reg.

Reg lifted his hands. 'I don't know anything about this. I'm not hearing this conversation.'

Bonza put a finger to the side of his nose. 'Seeing as it's illegal – as long as faces aren't seen and it's night, what the heck. Give your film a bit of action, eh?'

'Where are the skins collected?'

'Up the coast a bit.'

Veronica nodded her head. 'There are a lot of stories up here.'

'Always has been, luv. Bonza bloody country. Makes the wild west look tame as a fat cat,' declared Bonza.

Reg smiled at her. 'If you want the more legit side of tourism up here, I'm your man.' He handed her his card.

'Aw, come off it, Reg. You haven't been as pure as the driven snow all your life,' said Bonza with a grin.

Reg looked at his arm. 'Nope. Been black as the ace of spades as long as I can remember.'

They both laughed.

Later, after dinner, as the men sat around yarning and the women, back in the kitchen, cleaned up, Veronica spotted Jim at the bar and went over to him.

'Thanks for this evening, Jim. It's been huge fun. Mary is lovely. She went to so much trouble.'

'She enjoys a bit of a bash and the other women always bring stuff. So, has it been helpful?'

'Extremely interesting. I was told Bonza was a bit of a leg puller, but he's given me a few ideas for stories. Is he on the up and up?'

'He bullshits a lot, but, yeah, he used to have pretty sticky fingers. I don't know how much he does now.'

'Reg is a nice man,' added Veronica.

'Yeah, kinda balances the story. He's had a rough time of it. Stolen from his family as a kid, by the time he figured out where he came from they'd all gone. He was pretty bitter, drank, got into a bit of strife. He joined the church, got married, got into a training scheme,' said Jim. 'Made a good life for himself.'

'So he's showing tourists around? A cultural tour is it?'

'Oh no. Reg knows Arnhem Land really well, but he mainly works with the big game fishing people and the helicopter joy flights.'

Veronica pulled Reg's card from her pocket and read,

'Discover Darwin and the near North. Reg Sculthorpe, Tour Guide.'

Eddie wandered over to her and said, 'Illegal croc hunting still goes on, I'm sure. Could be a bit dangerous, but hey, never scared us off in the past.'

'I don't think so,' she replied. 'It's illegal and I don't want to be involved in anything that could compromise the program. Doesn't really have anything to do with the story I'm after, anyway.'

'No, I guess not. So I certainly wouldn't mention it to Jamie the ranger guy that's coming with us.'

Veronica thanked Jim again for the evening. 'I'm just going to say goodnight to Mary and make a quiet exit. I'll be in touch.'

The next afternoon, as Veronica was contemplating her meagre wardrobe and wondering if she'd brought the right clothes to be heading to a remote station with the possibility of camping out for a couple of days, the phone rang and Jamie McIntosh introduced himself.

He was softly spoken and polite but he didn't waste time with smalltalk and pleasantries.

'We want to get away as soon as possible after daylight, it's a long drive. I'm just checking you have the right gear for this. You'll need boots, or sturdy trainers, socks, hat, fly veil if flies bother you, sunblock, a shirt with long sleeves, a warm jumper for night, long pants to protect your legs, sunglasses. Maybe a small backpack to carry water and camera or whatever you need if we're walking a lot in the day. Your personal stuff.'

Veronica got the feeling he was trying to tell her to bring just the essentials.

'Thanks. I might be short on one or two items, any suggestions where to get them?'

'There's a big camping store in Mitchell Street. Has clothes, everything you'll need. Are you allergic to anything? Food, insects?'

'Not that I know of,' said Veronica.

'Good. Perhaps as we drive you could fill me in on the background to this story, what you're hoping to find and so on.'

'Of course. Eddie is picking us both up in the morning.'

'Good. He has a decent four-wheel drive. It'll do the trick as it's geared for water and bogs and just about anything that comes along. We'll share the driving.'

'You know Eddie?' asked Veronica.

'Oh, he's been the cameraman on a few jobs I've done. He's very professional. And pretty creative, not like some of the news guys.'

'Yes, I know. I worked with Eddie in Sydney,' said Veronica.

'Did you? Well, that makes it easier when you know how someone works.'

She was tempted to discuss the job with Jamie but figured they'd work it out as they went along. He was coming as a field advisor with local knowledge, able to arrange permits and deal with the elders if needed. Yet he also had front-of-camera experience, which would be good. He could do a lot of the talking so that she didn't have to be on camera too much.

'We'll pick you up outside your hotel about six tomorrow morning.'

'Thank you, Jamie. And thanks for helping us on this,' said Veronica.

'You're welcome. It's my job.'

Later Veronica walked along the Esplanade and noticed an elegant restaurant in an old colonial building where people were eating in its garden. She decided she might treat herself when they came back from the bush trip. Meanwhile, she ordered a meal in a small Asian restaurant and rang her mother.

'Vee, hello dear. Where are you again?'

'I'm in Darwin, Mum. But I'm heading out to the wilds tomorrow morning. An old station that's now some big tourist venture.'

'Whatever for? Are you on holidays?'

'No, it's the story I told you about. About those people who went outback filming in the fifties. I'm trying to retrace some of their adventure.'

'Really? That sounds interesting. Is it far away?'

'Actually, yes. It's in the middle of nowhere, we have to stay out there.'

'Goodness me, Vee, do be careful.'

'I'll be fine. We have a special guide and official person with us.' She decided not to mention Eddie. Her parents had never really liked him. Too flash by half, her mother had sniffed.

'I thought you had a promotion and didn't have to go rushing about the country like some junior reporter,' said her mother.

'Mother, people pay hundreds of dollars a night, and more, to stay at this place. It's very luxurious.'

'Doesn't sound like my idea of a holiday. Well, do be careful. Oh, your father wants a word.'

'Where are you? What's all this about Darwin?'

'We're heading for the outback, Dad. Going to a fancy tourist cattle station.'

'I see. When are you coming back? Your sister has found a place in Melbourne and hopes you can go down.'

'And help her unpack? Dad, I have no idea when I'll be back and I'm really busy at work for the next few weeks. Tell Sue I'll call her and will go down as soon as I'm free.'

'All right, dear. Are you having a good time up there? Not too rugged?'

'No, Dad, though I might be about to have a bit of an adventurous time. Makes a change from Sydney.'

'Sorry you can't come over for Sunday lunch. Your mother has some new friends. They bore me rigid. All right, all right. Take care, Vee. Bye.'

She could imagine her mother digging her father in the ribs for criticising her new friends. Poor Dad, he hated having to be charming to women he didn't know and hoped he'd never see again. Gazing around the tropical scene, taking in the smells and feeling the soft air, her family and her sister's suburban dramas suddenly seemed far away. Tomorrow a whole new landscape beckoned. It was going to be a lot of togetherness for the next week. She hoped Jamie McIntosh would be easy to get on with and would share a beer and a joke.

Veronica felt a bit silly in her new outfit as she waited in the lobby the next morning. She'd gone a bit crazy in the enormous camping and disposal store and had taken a liking to a range of clothing designed for tropical wear, a non-pretentious but stylish safari look. She wore greyish green shorts that were loose and comfortable, a jacket shirt with plenty of pockets, a singlet top underneath and tough canvas boots and carried a bush hat that she'd scrunched up a few times so that it didn't look brand new.

She watched as the dusty four-wheel drive came into the driveway. It had gear roped on top and 'Australian National Network' written on the side. The man in the passenger seat jumped out as she struggled with her bag and the glass door of the lobby.

'Let me.' He scooped up her bag and held out his hand. 'I'm Jamie.' Before she could answer he opened the front door of the car and helped her step up into the seat next to Eddie.

'Morning. My, you're looking the part,' commented Eddie with an approving grin as Jamie put her bag in the crowded rear and got into the back seat next to the camera. Eddie, like the good cameraman he was, always kept a camera handy in case he drove past something worth a shot.

Veronica turned to Jamie. 'Sorry, would you prefer to sit here in front?' It was her first good look at him and she was momentarily silenced by how handsome he was – brown skin, dark thick hair, finely sculptured nose and mouth, high cheek bones and vivid hazel-flecked eyes. She knew Eddie was watching her, gauging her reaction with slight amusement.

If Jamie noticed her staring he didn't react. He was probably used to it, she thought. He was around the same age as Eddie, though slimmer and looked a lot fitter.

'You're the tourist, take in the sights,' he said pleasantly. 'I'm going to get a bit more shut-eye. Let me know when you want to trade places, Eddie.'

'I'll be right for a couple of hours. Maybe switch at the roadhouse.'

'Right.' Jamie pulled his worn, well-shaped bush hat over his face and leaned his head back on the seat.

'So what did you make of Bonza?' asked Eddie.

'Colourful. But I think Reg is the more interesting character. He fits in better with our story.'

'Your group wouldn't have come across an Aborigine like him back in the fifties,' said Eddie.

'No. Which, based on the descriptions that Colin gave, makes the comparison interesting.'

'So have you filmed this Colin person, relating all this?' asked Eddie.

'Not yet,' said Veronica shortly. 'There's also an interesting woman who was in the expedition who's still alive. She was an actress. I think she lives overseas, we just have to find her.'

'This trip to Brolga Springs sounds a bit of a wild goose chase, but what the heck. Does me good to get outta town,' said Eddie.

'Do you miss Sydney?' asked Veronica.

'Nah.'

He didn't elaborate so she didn't ask about friends, girlfriends or his trips to Bali. None of her business now anyway.

When Eddie pulled into a roadhouse that served as a pub, petrol station and fast food outlet, Veronica found that she had dozed off. They ate egg and bacon rolls washed down with unpleasant coffee. Jamie handed her a large bottle of water.

'It's a good idea to drink plenty of water in this climate.'

It was now Eddie's turn to doze in the back seat. Jamie took the wheel, pushed a CD into the player and turned back onto the highway. The powerful sounds of the Aboriginal group Yothu Yindi drifted through the car.

'Their voices are wonderful. I love listening to them in Sydney, but here it seems more appropriate,' said Veronica as the red earth and stands of acacias and mulga trees swept past against a background of distant ranges stark under the blue sky.

'That's because they're singing about their country,' said Jamie quietly. 'East Arnhem Land. You been there?'

'No, but I want to . . . It sounds magic.'

'You can't miss Kakadu,' he said. 'Lot of tourists prefer Litchfield Park, which is great, well planned and set up for visitors. But I prefer the wild country. Can I ask what the story is that you're chasing in the Territory?'

'Well, I found out that a group of people came to the Northern Territory in the mid-fifties to make a film and I'm trying to find out what happened to them and to film some of the places that I know they saw. The film group were headed to Arnhem Land, but I don't know if they ever got there. The whole expedition fell apart in Darwin.'

'Do you know what happened?'

'That I don't know. I'm still unravelling the story.'

'What are you hoping to find here at Brolga Springs?' he asked.

Veronica couldn't make out Jamie's expression behind his dark glasses. While he was polite and friendly there was a reserve about him like a sheet of glass mounted between them.

'I know that the party stayed at Brolga Springs and filmed a corroboree there, according to Colin, my main contact. Anyway, I found out what's become of Brolga Springs today and so the contrast is valuable. Colin said it was pretty basic and isolated when they called in, but it was very beautiful country.'

'That it is. So they stayed at Brolga Springs? Well, it certainly would've changed, you're quite right. It's taken a while for the tourists to get out there. And even now it's for the more adventurous.'

'Do you know Brolga Springs, then?'

'Yes, I certainly do. As a matter of fact I know the Hodges well and I go there quite often. They've done a terrific job.'

'It sounds like it. I suppose other properties will start copying them.'

'A few have,' said Jamie. 'But they haven't been as successful. Rick and Vicki Hodge are born and bred Territorians. Their hearts and souls are here and the local people, including the traditional people, respect them.'

'What's happened to the other stations that haven't been successful?' asked Veronica.

'Ah, it goes back a long time. Once the Aboriginal people were dispossessed, kids taken away and tribal people lost the right to their land to do ceremonies, hunt, care for it, as they always had, the whole system broke down. Places where they'd been born and worked and lived with their families were taken over, leased by big corporations from down south or overseas as tax write-offs. White managers were put in, none of them local or necessarily experienced, so often the places were mismanaged. A lot of the cattle stations were run down, went bankrupt, but the big bosses in the cities down south didn't care as it was a tax loss.

'Then came change. There was a push for Aborigines to control and run stations and some have been very successful. Local indigenous people were hired to run them and training for the young people was introduced and often there was sophisticated tourism marketing and promotion. In a way some of them have been too successful, or else they've taken their eye off the ball.'

He paused and Veronica waited. 'The neighbouring place, three hundred Ks to the west of Brolga Springs, was doing well, so well that the corporation sold its lease a few months ago to one of the biggest hotel chains in the world. It fired the indigenous trainees, but kept a couple of token traditional people as "cultural guides", added a health and wellness spa and it's now losing everything that made it the special place that people wanted to see.'

Veronica heard the tension in his voice and realised this was a subject he felt strongly about. 'What made it special? What did it lose?'

'You mean apart from its spirit, its dreaming, its heart?' He gave a wry smile. 'You can't create five-star-plus luxury accommodation for spoiled, old, rich tourists without carving into the landscape. Wheelchair access to art sites that now have cement steps built and wire fences around them for security.'

'Is it true that Aboriginal rock art paintings and carvings have been vandalised, chopped up and stolen?'

'Yep.'

'It's catch twenty-two, isn't it,' said Veronica thought-fully. 'When something is precious, interesting, of great cultural significance, everyone wants a piece of it but as a result, its original importance is lost.'

'Y'know these people you're following, when they came through in the fifties, they might have seen examples of an almost pristine Aboriginal culture.'

'They may not have realised that,' said Veronica.

'Exactly.' Jamie waved a hand out of the window towards the expanse of seemingly empty landscape. 'Isn't it nice to think that out there are untouched landmarks, ancient tools, totems, art that depicts life and history and Dreaming along with sacred sites, significant places that are meaningful and spiritual. A living cultural heritage that's been unchanged for thousands of years.'

'But it's like the pyramids and tombs, the Sistine Chapel, the Roman roads, Pompeii – you have to be able to see tangible evidence of the past to appreciate how it was.'

'*Was*!' Jamie reacted. 'This isn't a culture that *was*, it's a culture that's still with us now, despite all the attacks, the despoiling, the dismissal of it as an inferior civilisa-tion, it still survives.'

'And will it continue to survive?' asked Veronica.

He gave a slight smile and didn't answer.

'Can you say all that again, on camera?' she asked.

'You need to talk to my mother,' he said finally. 'She's knowledgeable and also something of an activist. She's a teacher but she sits on a couple of boards dealing with these issues.'

Eddie woke and stretched. 'Are we there yet?' He looked out the window. 'Veronica, why don't we take a couple of shots of this. If you lose the road, the landscape is just as it was when your group drove through.'

'Good idea. I'd like to stretch my legs, anyway.'

The turn off to Brolga Springs was well marked and the dirt road, suitable for small tour buses, was quite different from the road Colin had described. The country was rugged with flat-top ochre jump ups and dark green gorges where a hint of a waterfall glinted. They glimpsed heavy-set Brahman cattle among trees to the side of the road and then they spotted the first fence. Soon there was a gate marked by two carved wooden brolgas supporting a tree trunk arch with the words 'Brolga Springs' burned into it. Then they passed landscaped trees and bushes, artfully placed boulders and parked by a fence was an ancient bull catcher that looked as though it had been gored and rolled many times over.

'I bet visitors take their picture in that old thing,' remarked Eddie.

'Don't think it's driveable anymore, but it's the real deal,' said Jamie. 'Tourists can buy gear at the store, hats, boots, croc-teeth hatbands and belts, souvenirs, if they're looking for that sort of thing.'

They passed neat wooden signs pointing to the homestead, the bunkhouse, the Sunset Bar and barbecue, toilets and 'The Springs Dining Room'. Jamie swung past the gravel parking lot filled with dusty four-wheel drives, campervans and a nine-person troop carrier and stopped in front of a log building that was marked 'Reception and Office'.

'It's quite elaborate,' said Veronica, slightly disappointed. The building like all the others looked new and not like the old-style homestead and cattle station she'd imagined.

Jamie sensed her reaction. 'There's more to it than this. Like I said, once you open to tourists you have to cater for them.'

Behind the reception desk they were greeted by an

attractive Aboriginal girl in a black and white uniform with a red insignia of a brolga with 'Brolga Springs' printed underneath it. An Aboriginal man in a matching T-shirt and black pants could be seen at a computer in the office behind her.

'Hello. You must be Miss Anderson. Hi, Jamie. And you're Eddie Jarman?'

'That's right. Are Rick or Vicki Hodge about?' asked Veronica.

'They're out of contact at present. They suggested that you get comfortable in your accommodation and they'll meet you later at the Sunset Bar for a drink. But if there's anything you want to do in the meantime, like going to the lagoon, or horseriding.' She handed them a brochure. 'This might give you a few ideas.'

'Where are we staying?' asked Eddie.

'We have you in the Castle Cabins or, if you prefer, the Castle Tents are very comfortable. They face the river.'

'What river is that?' asked Eddie.

The girl smiled. 'It's a creek really, though it can get pretty full in the wet. Comes down from the gorge. Rick has it stocked with fish. There are canoes if you want to go for a paddle and a fish.'

'Thanks but it's a bit hot for me right now. Think I'll wait for it to get cooler before I walk around and get the feel for the place,' said Veronica.

'Very well. I'll have one of the boys drive you over to your cabin and he'll be happy to take you in the buggy for a look around.' She pointed to one side where several all-terrain vehicles, like golf buggies with large wheels, were parked.

'I have a few things to do. Shall we meet round five-thirty in the bar?' suggested Jamie.

'Sounds good. Am I taking the car with me?' asked Eddie.

'Yes, follow Roly in the buggy. You can park by the cabin and walk or take one of the buggies further afield. There's a pool, a hot-spring bathing area, picnic place, all kinds of facilities.'

'They've thought of everything,' said Eddie.

Veronica's cabin was airy with large push-out shutters, all fly screened, a polished wood floor and a tiny verandah with a view towards a distant lagoon. There was a small shower and toilet, a comfortable bed with a mosquito net above it and a large fan in the middle of the room. It was simply but tastefully furnished with no unnecessary frills. She splashed water on her face, took off her shoes and sat on the bed.

What would Colin make of this she wondered? It sure beat the rough camping Marta and Helen must have endured on their trip here. But how unspoiled it must have been then. She wondered if the original homestead was still standing. All the buildings she'd seen so far looked to be only a few years old.

Roly appeared in the buggy at three pm as she'd arranged and she grabbed her hat, sunglasses and camera, and got in beside him.

'Okay, give me the tour,' said Veronica.

The young Aborigine looked confused. 'We have many tours . . .'

'No, I meant just drive me around. I'll take one of the tours tomorrow. Which do you recommend?'

'Oh, we have the bush tucker tour, the ladies like that one. As well as finding bush foods you can learn how to make dilly bags or baskets and find out about bush medicine. There's fishing, riding, canoeing, swimming in the springs and hiking up the gorge to see the rock art. The men like to go with the stockmen when they bring in cattle, or get a killer – a beast that they butcher for station meat. A lot to do here.'

'That certainly sounds like a full schedule. How long have you been here?' asked Veronica.

'About nine months. I'm in the training program. There's a term of twelve weeks and a TAFE instructor comes out here to teach us how to look after the tourists.'

'Where are you from?'

'I was in Darwin, but I originally come from Katherine. This is my first job,' he added proudly.

Roly looked to be around nineteen or twenty. 'What were you doing before this?' asked Veronica.

'Ah, nothing much. Didn't finish high school and just hung around. Then I met Rick and he talked me and some other blokes into doing this course.'

'Do you like this? Do you see yourself moving up in hospitality or tourism?'

He shook his head. 'More money in the mining jobs. Reckon I might head out that way when I can.'

'Oh, I see,' said Veronica. 'I guess its not too exciting driving the buggy around and looking after visitors.'

He shrugged. 'No, it's okay. The rules are strict here. No drinking on the station, no cards, y'know, gambling. Got to look clean all the time. And the money is put in the bank for you.'

'Well, that's not a bad thing. Will you finish your program here?'

He gave her a huge and disarming smile. 'Yep. Sure. But you can make a lot more money in mining.'

There were around thirty people in the bar when Veronica went in at sunset after her tour of the complex with Roly. She was surrounded by foreign accents, young backpackers and older retirees. Eddie was at the bar with a couple she assumed to be Rick and Vicki Hodge. Rick was dressed in a blue shirt embroidered with the Brolga Springs logo and mud-stained moleskin pants. Vicki was in a simple cotton dress but had added sparkly earrings.

Vicki turned to Veronica and with a smile said, 'Welcome. Great to meet you. I'm Vicki Hodge. Been hearing all about you from Eddie. And we're big fans of *Our Country*. This is Rick.'

Rick shook her hand with a firm calloused grip and his big smile extended to his warm blue eyes. ''Scuse my outfit, still on duty. Been out with a group of visitors at the gorge. Glad you got here. We're keen to help you any way we can. Now, a drink?'

'A white wine please. How was your afternoon, Eddie?'

'Amazing. Two of the trainees took me out to get dinner.'

As everyone laughed, Veronica raised an eyebrow. 'You took the camera of course?'

'Of course.' Eddie downed his beer and pushed it towards the bartender for a refill. The pretty girl, a backpacker, thought Veronica, refilled it quickly.

'Where's Jamie?' she asked.

'Dunno. Haven't seen him,' said Eddie. 'He's in one of the tents. Probably crashed.'

'No, he's around, he'll be here soon,' said Vicki. 'Now, tell us, how can we help with your show? Eddie says you're here about the old days but you're interested in what we're doing here today. Of course, we're keen to show that too,' said Vicki candidly. 'I mean, we always like publicity but I know your show isn't into travel fluff stuff. But we'd really like to promote our indigenous program.'

'No, the second. Indeed. It's nice to have a positive story,' said Veronica. 'Is this the first group to go through the program?'

'Yes. It's taken a while to get it up and running. Lots of reasons,' said Rick. 'It's not one of those things you can just push out there and let it run on its own. Needs constant supervision, guidance, hand holding and adjusting to cultural issues.'

'And lack of them,' added Vicki. 'Many of these kids have never had any serious connection with their culture. Been brought up in the towns, because they lost contact with the land when their families were broken up. Often they find it hard to fit into both worlds, neither of which they know properly.'

'Listen, I'm going to go and clean up. We thought we'd throw some steaks on the barbie at our joint as we're slightly away from all this. We have two little kids. Suit you guys?' said Rick.

'Wonderful,' sighed Veronica who could see a country and western band setting up in the outdoor area.

'Have another drink on the house and I'll get one of the lads to fetch you,' said Vicki.

Veronica watched the two of them stop and chat to a customer, speak quietly to a staff member, talk to the chef putting food on the buffet, check the bar and make a quiet exit.

Eddie had watched them leave also. 'Reckon this'd be a twenty-four seven job for those guys.'

'Yeah. This isn't quite what I expected.'

Eddie took a swig of his beer, eyeing the blonde backpacker at the end of the bar. 'Been fifty-plus years, Vee. ''Course it's going to change.'

The use of her pet family nickname unsettled her for a moment. 'God, what I'd give to talk to Topov, to all of them, about their time here, brief as it was. Anyway, I hope Jamie comes soon. I want to work out what we do tomorrow. So what'd you shoot this afternoon?'

Eddie chuckled. 'Two trainees. Reckon they'd be more at home in a video games parlour. But there was an old fella, a local elder, who knew the ropes, trying to get them to hunt down a steer. The trainees were scared stiff. They had rifles but I was more worried about them shooting each other, or us, rather than the bloody beast. The old man finally brought it down. Bloody magnificent. They strung it up from a tree branch and he showed them how to butcher it. The boys were better with a knife than a gun.'

'That's not our dinner is it?' said Veronica.

'Nope. Meat needs to be hung a bit longer than that.'

One of the backpackers came up and parked herself beside Eddie and introduced herself with a smile. 'I am Joseline. I like very much your country.'

Veronica tapped Eddie on the shoulder. 'We're expected for dinner.'

'Hey, one drink and I'll be over. Get one of the kids to take you. I'll be there in twenty minutes.'

Veronica stared at Eddie, a hundred flashbacks buzzing through her mind. 'Eddie, we are working. I want you over at Rick's place. Make whatever arrangements you want for after dinner, but you will be there, understood?' She turned to the pretty blonde and lifted her finger. 'He is working and he will walk out of here now. Okay?'

The girl lifted her shoulders. 'I do not care. Whatever he wishes.'

'No. It's not what he wishes. It's what I am telling him. I am his boss.' Veronica turned on her heel and walked out of the bar as the blonde girl pretended to quiver.

'She is scary boss.'

'Yeah. She is.' Eddie finished his beer. 'See you back here at closing time.'

'Maybe,' said the blonde.

'Whatever,' sighed Eddie, hurrying after Veronica.

Rick and Vicki's house was lit with soft lights and candles. The low hum of the generator powering the station houses could be heard on the night air. It was a comfortable family home with a pile of shoes and boots at the door, along with jackets and hats on a rack. A country music CD was playing and a small girl was rolling on a sofa with a puppy. A boy, about seven, got up and came to greet them.

'Hello. I'm Toby. Mum said to come out to the patio.'

Rick, Vicki, Jamie and another young woman were gathered at the barbecue. Vicki handed Veronica a glass of white wine and gave Eddie a beer.

'This is Sandra, she's working with us as a nanny and cook for a year. A change from life in Sydney.'

Sandra smiled. 'I sometimes think Toby and Natalie look after me. Nice to meet you.'

'We're teaching her to ride,' explained Toby.

'I'd like to learn properly too, one day. There must be some fantastic places to ride around here,' said Veronica.

'There certainly are,' said Rick. 'You could go out early in the morning. There's a quiet old stockhorse you could use.'

'Oh. I'm not sure,' said Veronica. 'What about you, Eddie? We'd need to take the camera.'

'I'm happy to go with you,' said Jamie. 'Eddie could meet us at the gorge pool. Roly can drive you up, Eddie. I'll take Veronica a different way by horse. You'll both get a good feel for the place. Then I thought you might like to see the original homestead,' he said. 'Up to you, I'm sure you both have ideas.'

'Not at all. I'm in your hands. And Rick's and Vicki's,' said Veronica and was about to ask Eddie his opinion when she thought, blow him, I'm making the decisions. She turned to Jamie and said, 'Actually, I'd love it. If you're sure you can manage a novice horsewoman.'

'Calico will look after you,' grinned Rick. 'That's the horse.'

Sandra smiled at Veronica. 'It's time I put the children

to bed. See you later, enjoy the ride. Vicki, the salad and garlic bread are all done. See you later, Jamie, perhaps next time you're down you can bring your Billy as well, so that he can play with these two.'

Veronica turned to Eddie and said, 'Sandra seems to be a very nice girl.'

Eddie knew she was telling him to keep his hands off and he grinned. 'I have a date later with one of the backpackers.'

'We can shoot the old homestead tomorrow. I'm so glad it survived. How far is it from here? Couldn't it be incorporated into this station?' asked Veronica.

'It would be a nice tourist attraction wouldn't it?' said Eddie.

'That was the original idea, but people went in, camped and trashed the place. It's not in good enough nick to be a show place or a museum and it's too remote to keep someone there to look after it, so it's fenced off and we don't publicise it,' said Rick.

It was a relaxing evening. After dinner they filmed an interview with Rick and Vicki sitting together on the lounge giving a brief history of Brolga Springs and of themselves and how they'd grown up on stations like this one and how they'd come to see that its future was going to be brightest through the development of tourism.

As arranged, at first light the next day, Jamie tapped on Veronica's door and handed her a pair of riding boots. 'As Vicki promised. I have a backpack with me so if you don't mind skipping breakfast we can set out and have a snack up at the gorge.'

'Fine,' said Veronica who was hanging out for a coffee, but pulled on the comfortable old boots and grabbed her hat and sunglasses. She'd already smothered her face in tinted sunblock.

'I brought the horses up, so we can walk out from

here. Saves going down to the stables.' Jamie pointed to the two stockhorses tethered to the railing that fenced in the patch of lawn around the cabins.

'Don't be nervous, just relax. Calico will follow my horse. Let him have his head when it gets steep. Enjoy the view,' said Jamie helping her into the saddle.

It was quiet. A few early morning risers were walking towards the shower block from the camping area and some of the staff were already at work in the kitchen. By the time they'd left the complex of buildings and yards and were on a sandy dirt track through low scrub, Veronica was starting to relax and enjoy the rhythm of the walking horse and the clear crisp air.

In the pearly pre-dawn light they wound through open land and skirted the small creek and lagoon where colourful canoes rested on the glassy water. A flock of screeching parrots skimmed past them and further away the dark shapes of the cattle stood quietly.

'How many cattle are on here?' she asked Jamie.

'Only about eight thousand head. Country's too rugged. Better for tourists Rick thinks.'

'It's certainly beautiful.'

'There's a small rise, want to try a gentle canter?'

'Lead on,' said Veronica gamely.

She was exhilarated and feeling more confident as they sped up the rise of the hill, but then she saw the steeper track leading towards the peak of a small sloping mesa. 'Is that where we're going?'

'Yep, the track winds around, so let your horse find his way, he knows where we're headed. Let's go, then we'll make it for sunrise.'

The sky was already running pink and gold as the horses stepped out smartly, Jamie in the lead. Veronica kept her eyes on the ground, worried where the horse was going, but it clearly knew its way. When they came out at the top she caught her breath as she saw the view spread below her. They reined in the horses.

'I should have brought my camera.' As far as she could see the landscape of rocky outcrops, grey and green trees, thick in patches, sparse in others, spread beneath her. The waterway and lagoon glinted in the first rays of the sun. But most breathtaking was the rock face beside them where a dancing trickle of a waterfall slid down into a broad, palm-fringed pool below.

Jamie swung off his horse and helped her dismount. 'Take a seat on one of those flat rocks, almost purpose built and take in the sunrise. I'll grab us a snack.'

Eating a sandwich, sipping a mug of tea from the Thermos and watching the sun rapidly rise and light the scene around them, Veronica didn't speak. It was too beautiful for words. Jamie sat quietly, contemplating the scene, his back to her as the horses nibbled tufts of spiky grass. Finally he stood up.

'We'd better pack up and head down. There're some sweet biscuits if you want one.'

'Okay. This air has given me an appetite,' she smiled.

He put the sandwich wrapping and Thermos in his backpack and slung it on his shoulder, taking a final look at the view. But before he slid on his dark glasses, Veronica caught something in his expression, a sadness almost.

'I'm very glad I've seen this. Thanks for bringing me.'

He nodded. 'It's not normally on the agenda. It's a special place for me. I thought you might get a sense of how this country speaks to you,' he said softly.

'You seem to really love this place. Where did you grow up?' asked Veronica suddenly.

'Melbourne. My mother was a teacher and my father was a professor of ancient history. He has retired and they both live in Darwin now.' He gave a slight smile.

'Mum likes to tease him and say that there's more ancient history out here than in Europe.'

'And that didn't interest your father, but it does you,' said Veronica with a sudden flash of insight.

'Yes. I got my degree in Melbourne and then had a stint in Canberra in the public service. Couldn't stand the bureaucracy so I headed to Darwin.' He walked to the horses and untied the reins from the spindly tree sprouting from a rock crevice. 'Enough about me. C'mon, let's mount up. You can have a swim in the pool and hopefully Eddie will be there.'

'I hope Roly managed to drag him out.'

Towards the bottom of the rise, the track wound through a cool forest of trees and then they came out on a grassy verge that led around to the pool at the base of the small cliffs they'd just descended. There was a truck parked and Roly was squatting next to it, smoking a cigarette. Eddie was at the pool with the camera on his shoulder. At Veronica's call he swung around to film the riders moving towards him.

'Pretty spot,' commented Eddie. 'I've done everything I can. You need anything else here?'

'How about some scenes of Jamie and me swimming?'

'No, you go ahead,' said Jamie. 'Roly and I will hang around.'

It was hot and Veronica was glad Jamie had told her to wear her swimsuit. As he tethered the horses she went to the truck and pulled off her clothes and boots, then picked her way to the pool and slipped into the refreshing water.

'Wow, this is wonderful.'

'Roly says it's a natural spring. You can drink the water,' said Eddie. 'Swim out into the middle by the little waterfall. Must run a gusher in the wet.'

As she paddled around, Veronica noticed the exquisite

ferns and plants clinging to the rock face and a small bird chasing a large moth-like butterfly.

'That's enough. I'm coming in.' Eddie put the camera on the seat of the truck and stripped down to his trunks and plunged in. 'Ah, that's better. Clears the head.'

Veronica gazed at his body, once familiar to her but now somewhat heavier. 'So how was last night?'

'Those girls at the bar had me drinking some crazy cocktail. Should've stuck to beer. But this is good. Just as well we're early, there's a big group coming out for a picnic later.'

Sitting on a rock to dry out, Veronica asked Jamie to tell her the names of the plants and describe how the area changed in the wet season.

After a while he glanced at his watch. 'We'd better move on to the old homestead. This is where we'll be following the original road, well, track, that your mob would've come in on. You still up to riding? Roly can bring Eddie in the truck along behind us.'

It was flatter country now and, with the surrounding range and small mesas, she felt a greater sense of isolation as though they were hemmed in by the enormity of the landscape. It was haunting and lonely. They arrived suddenly at a new barbed wire fence and a large locked gate with a 'No Trespassing' sign. Jamie got out, pulled a key from his pocket and unlocked the padlock, leaving the gate open as they rode through.

Veronica had the feeling she was seeing what Topov and the others had seen as they were led to Mrs Johns' homestead by Len Buchanan. How pleased Helen and Marta must have been to have a shower and a bed to sleep in. But the sight that now greeted Veronica tore at her heart.

What remained of the original wooden fence was nearly buried in the sandy soil. The old garden was now a patchy brown graveyard of tree skeletons and empty flowerbeds. The stone blocks of the main house were still there but the wooden part of the structure was splintered and sagging from the effort of trying to hold up the rusting roof. What windows were left were fringed with the tattered remnants of torn flyscreens. Piles of wood and corrugated iron were all that remained of the outbuildings. In the midst of rubble, a brilliant red-flowered vine clung to a lone brick chimney. But what wrung Veronica's heart more than the neglect or the passage of time, was the silence of abandonment and the sense of loss.

She turned to Jamie as he dismounted. 'Thank goodness Mrs Johns can't see this.'

'It would be hard for anyone who knew this homestead as it was to see it dying, slowly, like this,' agreed Jamie. 'Places like this show the futility of trying to outlast the land.'

'Can we look around inside?' Veronica slid off her horse.

'I'll show you where to step. There are a lot of rotten boards in the house.'

In the dim interior where the roof still held, some of the old furniture remained and it smelled musty and dank.

'Do you suppose ghosts are here?' asked Veronica, speaking softly.

'There are no ghosts or spirits here. They've long gone to their proper place,' said Jamie. 'This wasn't a grand place, but it was comfortable and there was a big verandah. Over there, on the other side of the yard, were quarters for the men, further down towards the creek there was the Aboriginal camp and somewhere over in that direction was the little schoolhouse.' He squinted as he pointed.

'How come you know this place so well?' asked Veronica. 'Is it part of the National Parks?'

'No. It's still part of the Brolga Springs lease.' Jamie hesitated, then said, 'I've been told many stories about this place, so it feels like part of my history too.'

'But you grew up in Melbourne.'

Jamie paused. 'My mother was born here. Lived here till she was ten.'

Veronica studied him, a premonition stirring in her. She saw his features, his skin colour, the reserved character that she couldn't put her finger on.

He continued, 'My mother, Doris, was a protégé of Mrs Johns. After Mr Johns died she didn't want my mother to be sent to a mission so she arranged for her to go to school in Melbourne.'

Veronica stared at him, murmuring 'Doris . . .'

Jamie went on. 'Mrs Johns continued to make provisions for Mum's education. She died just when Mum was accepted into uni. Mum said she was so proud of her.'

'Jamie, you are not going to believe this, but Colin remembers her. He told me about Doris. Did you know about this connection when you were contacted to help us?' asked Veronica.

'No. I didn't but I put a few things together. I know that Mum has a bracelet that she told me was given to her by a beautiful woman more than fifty years ago and I've read Mrs Johns' journals in the archives.'

'My God. I don't know what to say,' said Veronica.

'You'll need to speak to Mum, I reckon.'

'Would she be willing to be interviewed?' asked Veronica.

Jamie gave a short laugh. 'Try and stop her talking. She's a fierce little person though. She's been quite involved in indigenous rights for years.'

'I'm overwhelmed. But Jamie, you're now involved in what I'm doing.'

He shook his head. 'Not really, I'm just a small part

of the puzzle. I think there's a lot more you have to find out that has nothing to do with me.'

Eddie, who had stopped to film on the way and Roly drove up in the truck. Eddie jumped out with the camera.

'Well, this is more like it. Amazing old place. I got some great shots coming in. Where do I start? Is it safe to go inside?'

'Jamie will show you,' said Veronica. 'He knows the place well.' She watched the lean figure of Jamie, his blue shirt sleeves rolled up over his brown arms, his hat pulled low over his sunglasses, his boots silent in the dust, as he walked slowly over to Eddie.

9

VERONICA WAS SEEING THE land through new eyes. After seeing how interested she'd been in the old homestead, Jamie McIntosh offered to take her to the station cemetery. As they drove he told her some of the stories his mother had told him.

'As a kid I loved the Dreaming Stories, the legends of my mother's country, which her grandmother told her. But it wasn't till I came here and saw the country for myself that they made sense.' He pointed to the landscape. 'Those red rocks, the gullies that run wild in the wet, those trees, the birds and lizards and little marsupials that I know are out there, well, what's left of them, make me feel connected to this country because I know their stories and my mother was born here. I tell the stories to my son too.'

'Have you brought him out here?'

'Oh, yes. My mother insisted we do his smoking ceremony before he turned one. He's nearly seven years old so its significance is starting to mean more to him now. The ceremony is a rite that cleanses the child, makes him strong and healthy and connects him to his belonging place. Billy often asks when he's coming back to his country for a visit.'

'And his mother?'

A shadow passed over Jamie's face. 'Janine – my wife – died suddenly.'

'Oh. I'm sorry. That must be hard for you. How do you manage?' Veronica didn't want to probe but she couldn't help feeling curious.

'Family. Billy's got more aunties, uncles, doting grandparents, cousins and friends than you can poke a stick at,' he said with a smile.

'And he lives with you? Who looks after him when you come away like this?' asked Veronica.

'I have a house that is a bit elastic. It stretches to accommodate whoever is around. And my parents live just a few houses away. They moved to Darwin when Janine was killed in a car crash. Billy was just a toddler. He was in the car too. Came through unscathed.'

'I can't imagine how hard that must have been.'

'Yes. It was.' He was quiet for a moment. 'My family have been wonderful. I don't think Dad saw his retirement being in Darwin but he loves his grandson, too.'

'Your mother sounds pretty special,' said Veronica.

'She is. She's had an amazing life when you consider she was born in a blacks' camp out here.'

'Strange how life can twist and take unexpected turns,' said Veronica, thinking of Jamie's wife. 'Fate, I suppose.'

'And luck and perseverance and sheer hard work, like mother becoming a teacher in Melbourne.'

'You said she is very active politically, as well?'

'That came later. She was nominated for an award

and a magazine journalist wrote a feature on her and she talked about being born out here and that prompted Mum to make the journey back to Brolga Springs. She found it in a terrible state of decay.'

'That must have upset her. How old were you then?'

'I was about five, but I have some memories of Mum's journey because she was so moved, I guess. I hadn't seen my mother cry before. She came home to Melbourne and started the long painful process of tracing whatever relatives she could find.'

'How did she go – finding them?'

He gave a slow smile. 'I'll let her tell you that story.'

He drove through a stand of eucalypts and stopped. Ahead was a small clearing, several headstones in its centre. Rusting iron stakes and a wall of trees separated this space from the rest of its surroundings. It was a small country, silent in its aloneness. Jamie turned off the engine of the four-wheel drive and they sat quietly for a moment.

He turned to her. 'Do you want to go and see it?'

'Yes, will it be okay?'

Jamie smiled. 'I don't see anyone around to object.'

As he helped her down from the vehicle the heat slammed down on her and she almost staggered.

He took her elbow. 'Put your hat on.'

Veronica put on her hat and sunglasses. 'There's not a breath of air here.' She glanced up at the motionless leaves, hanging limply.

The dried leaves and small twigs crunched under their feet.

'The silence, it's eerie,' she said softly.

'We're far from anything. In the old days you would've heard the echoes from the station, cattle and the people at the camp. But I would prefer to be buried here rather than in a crowded cemetery near a busy highway in a city.'

'But this place – it feels so lonely, so neglected. Who

would ever come here?' asked Veronica as they walked towards the biggest grave, marked by an elaborate marble headstone and small iron picket fence.

Jamie didn't answer as she bent over to read the inscription on the bronze plaque:

Here lies Anthony Augustine Johns, 1885–1956
Master of Brolga Springs.
Beloved husband to Annabel. A friend to all.
'The Best Boss in the Territory.'
Behind shadows standeth God.

Jamie touched her arm and pointed to a smaller, modest white marble plaque beside it, saying. 'Her ashes were sent up here from Melbourne. Mum said Annabel always wanted to return to Brolga Springs.'

Veronica read aloud;

Annabel Johns, 1890–1964
Mistress of Brolga Springs.
Beloved wife of Anthony Johns.
At peace at last.

'She had no children. Your mother must have been like a daughter.'

He nodded. 'Mum'll tell you the full story. But Mrs Johns sounds like a great woman, I wish I'd known her.' He glanced at Veronica. 'I hope you don't mind but I rang Mum yesterday and told her that you were here and what you were doing. She said she'd be happy to talk to you. She remembers that group coming through, especially the woman who gave her a silver bracelet.'

'Yes, that's right,' said Veronica, feeling rather elated that Colin's story was coming together.

He gave her a quizzical look. 'Mum still has it.'

'Really! That's wonderful to have a tangible link between then and now.'

Veronica walked around the tiny cemetery. 'Who else is buried here?'

'A couple of men who were killed in accidents over the years, old Paddy the cook who worked on the station forever and didn't have any family that anyone knew about and two of the old black stockmen.'

'They didn't have any links with their people? No traditional ceremony when they died or anything?'

'Mum told me they considered Brolga Springs to be their home, so this is where they wanted to be buried. They'd lost their family links.'

'Colin told me that your mother was good with horses when she was a little girl,' Veronica said as they completed the circuit of the cemetery.

Jamie nodded enthusiastically. 'She's amazing, just has a natural gift with them. Wherever she's lived she's managed to keep a horse. She keeps some outside Darwin and spends most weekends working them and riding. She taught Billy to ride,' he added proudly.

'What a woman of contrasts. I look forward to meeting her,' said Veronica, thinking Doris was really a story on her own.

The secrets and stories of those long gone but who rested here, seemed to linger in the whisper of the leaves and the gentle sway of shadows. Who was left to celebrate their lives, to mourn and miss those buried in this lonely place? The solitude of the setting, and the reverence and respect shown by Jamie to them made her pause.

'I'm glad your mother knows something about this place, the people buried here and what it must have been like when Brolga Springs Homestead was the centre of a bustling cattle station. Now it seems so sad. Let's go, please.'

Jamie nodded and she turned to him as he held the car door for her. 'I just feel that I'm intruding,' she said softly.

He smiled. 'I understand why you feel that way. There are some places I'd hate to see tramped over by tourists.'

'Thank you for showing me.'

Driving back to the new homestead they talked about their careers and first jobs.

'How do you find working for *Our Country*?' he asked. 'It's one of the better shows on TV.'

'I agree. And my boss is lovely. Internal politics, egos, and now a new direction for the show keep life interesting.'

He heard the uncertainty in her voice. 'But?'

Veronica had to laugh and relaxed. 'They want to change the format and have a front person, not a presenter but a hands-on person who does the stories . . . Which is why Eddie is tailing me. I'm the one. I hate it.'

'Ah, I understand. Must be a bit restricting.'

'The good thing is I'm the producer so I can still call the shots. Say,' she smiled at him, 'you're good talent, how about you talk a bit on camera?'

'Only if I have to, I like my privacy too.'

'Were you a shy boy at school? What interested you in this job?'

Jamie made Veronica laugh as he recounted how uncomfortable he was when he started university and studied economics. 'I quickly discovered that I'm an outdoors person and that I'd never be happy in a desk job. My parents were both understanding and Mum suggested that I do an environmental science course. Dad helped me get a position in the public service in Canberra but breaking down statistics and talking to engineers about problems with river degradation, water flows and salinity drove me crazy. But once I got out and started actually looking at the land, talking to long-time farmers and indigenous custodians I saw a different picture.'

'It seems strange to talk about water when it's so dry out here,' said Veronica, looking around at the raw red rocks, the ochre earth and the plume of orange dust churning behind them.

'You should be here in the wet season. Tremendous time. Wonderful storms, torrential rain, the rivers flood and the birdlife is spectacular. Only trouble is you can't drive anywhere.'

'So what happens to all the water that floods over the land, heads down the rivers?' asked Veronica. 'Is it going to waste?'

'No way. That's how Mother Nature designed it,' said Jamie emphatically. 'The wetlands need it, the ocean needs it. People don't seem to like wetlands. They like the word but a wetland is a swamp and they don't like swamps, so they cut them open, dry them out, expose the soil to the air and then any water that touches it turns into acid or evaporates. I feel quite passionate about it. Water is this country's most precious commodity. Anyone who touches a river, who tries to control any aspect of it, should first understand what a river does. You'll understand better if you visit Kakadu and see the billabongs and wetlands.'

'I'm intending to go there,' said Veronica firmly, although, as yet, she had no idea how it would fit in with her story. She turned to him. 'Say, I could do a great documentary on water in the outback, with your help!' Veronica realised that Jamie was not only charismatic, he was knowledgeable and passionate and would look great on television.

'But it's not the story you came to do,' he reminded her. 'Another time perhaps.'

When they parted company at the TV station back in Darwin, Jamie handed her a bit of paper.

'Here's my phone number and Mum's and her address.

There's a bit of a party at her place on Saturday for lunch. It's Mum and Dad's fortieth wedding anniversary. We'd love you both to come.' He looked at Eddie who was unloading his camera gear. 'Hope you don't mind, but we'd prefer you not to film anything. It's just a family social occasion, okay? Mum is happy to be interviewed on camera later. But please come anyway.'

'Fine by me, mate. Anyway, sorry, I can't make it. I have plans for Saturday,' said Eddie.

'Do you want me to pick you up then, Veronica?' asked Jamie.

'No, please don't trouble yourself. I'll grab a taxi. I'm looking forward to meeting your mother.'

'Just casual,' said Jamie and left them with a wave.

'He knows what he's talking about. I suggest you take him along if you plan to go to Kakadu,' said Eddie.

'Of course. He's our entrée into off-limit communities and his local knowledge is invaluable.'

'You going to try and get him on camera?'

'When it's appropriate,' said Veronica.

Eddie gave a wry smile. 'Be careful, he can charm birds out of trees. Don't be swayed because he's good looking and sensitive. He has an agenda too. So keep your journalist smarts sharpened.'

'Thanks for the advice, Eddie. If you might recall, I've never let personal emotions interfere with a story,' she said tartly.

'You can say that again,' said Eddie.

The taxi driver was chatty and cheerful. 'Yep, I was here during Cyclone Tracy. Now there's a story that's never been fully told,' he said confidentially. He pointed to the new buildings along the waterfront. 'Look at those complexes and high rises, I don't know how they'll stand up to a cyclone. Won't catch me living in a glass tower, thanks. So you a friend of Doris McIntosh's, love?'

'You know her?' asked Veronica in surprise, as she'd only given him the address, no name.

'Yeah, she's a very smart lady. And nice too. A very good ad for her people. They need more like her.'

'Her people? So she's more Aboriginal than white? Is that how she's seen?' asked Veronica.

'Well, of course, she's light skinned, half-caste they used to call them, though that's not a PC word now. She's a nice, respectable lady, her husband is a great bloke too, but she's strong and she speaks out. And good on her, I say.' He chuckled. 'Mind you, I wouldn't want to be on the wrong side of Doris's opinion. She calls a spade a bloody shovel.'

The house was how Veronica imagined old tropical homes were, even though she could tell by the slope of the conical roof that it was a new cyclone-proof design. The simple structure with open breezeways, louvre windows and a lush overgrown garden, had an easy-living ambience. Veronica could imagine lazy afternoons in a hammock and she noticed flame torches in the garden for night-time. The garden had been planted with easy maintenance in mind but the drooping coral bougainvilleas and frangipani flowers scattered on the small patch of lawn created a dramatic effect. As she walked up the gravel pathway, Jamie, with a slim young boy following him, came out to meet her.

'Glad you found us okay.'

'I didn't even need to give an address, I should've just said take me to Doris McIntosh's house. The driver knew your mum lived here,' laughed Veronica.

'I'm not surprised. Darwin's not such a big place. Now, Billy, this is Miss Anderson. This is my son, Billy,' said Jamie proudly as the boy shyly shook Veronica's hand.

The child was lighter skinned than his father and had huge melting brown eyes and a big smile that turned up at the corners giving his mouth a mischievous twist.

'Please, call me Veronica. If that's okay with your dad.'

Billy looked to Jamie who nodded. 'If you say so, Veronica it is. Lead the way. What've you brought? There was no need,' he said, taking the paper carry bag she offered to him.

'Just some fresh fruit and chocolates.'

'Ooh, chocolates,' said Billy.

'They're for Nana, not you,' said Jamie firmly.

Billy skipped ahead calling out, 'She's here!'

'What delightful manners,' said Veronica. 'He's a beautiful boy.'

'He takes after his mother. Now he's on his best behaviour of course,' said Jamie fondly.

She could hear laughter and voices and Jamie led her through the house to a back garden where a large group was gathered. Veronica's fleeting impression of the house was its coolness, coloured cushions, rugs on polished wooden floors and a great profusion of books, pictures and carvings. A woman came through the door, but with the bright light behind her Veronica couldn't make out her features, just an erect figure with a halo of backlit curls.

'Veronica, lovely to meet you, I believe we have a lot to talk about. First off, come and have a cold drink, meet the clan.' She clasped Veronica's hand and led her outside.

'Don't overwhelm her all at once, Mum.'

'Only way to get to know our mob, just dive in,' said Doris.

Veronica felt suddenly rather shy as all eyes turned to her with friendly interest. Doris drew her towards a straight-backed, tall man with a shock of greying hair.

'This is my husband, Alistair.'

'Well, Veronica, it's a pleasure to meet you. Jamie tells us you're working on a very interesting project.'

Veronica almost smiled at the strong Scottish burr in Alistair McIntosh's voice. 'Yes, he's been so helpful. I nearly fell over when he told me that the little Doris from Brolga Springs that I'd heard about from my source, Colin, was his mother.'

'We'll talk about little Doris later,' said Jamie's mother, taking Veronica's hand. 'Come and meet the family.'

The family consisted of Jamie's two sisters, Margaret and Janet and their husbands and children. There was also his Aunt Charlotte, who was visiting from Scotland and appeared to be the family matriarch. Then there were a series of cousins and nieces and nephews belonging to both the Scottish and Australian branches of the family that had Veronica quite confused. Between the fair-skinned, red-headed Scots and the mixture of other races on Doris's side the gathering looked like a melting pot of the UN. But the unifying force was undoubtedly Doris. Children rushed to her, clinging to her as she moved around giving a pat to a head, a tug of an arm, a quick word with a promise to spend more time with them later. She also radiated a firmness and Veronica was sure that Doris would brook no nonsense.

Most of the men congregated around the barbecue, while the children played and the women all seemed to have a job to do organising the food. She watched Jamie move easily among them all, the fondness and humour between them very evident. There was an attractive fenced swimming pool and she wondered why the children weren't in it until Margaret handed her a fresh lime juice with a sprig of mint and explained, 'Lunch won't be long, well that's the plan at the minute. The children have been told to wait and be sociable before eating, then they can play in the pool.'

The drink was refreshing and Veronica noticed how the children were passing around plates of nibbles. Some of the older girls were setting the long table for the adults and a smaller one near it was set for the youngest children. Several of the children were talking with the adults and from what she could hear, the conversations were about school, football and friends.

Jamie joined her and effortlessly guided her around the group, so she drifted in and out of conversations without feeling awkward. There was a lot of laughter and teasing and she wanted to sit down and spend time with every person present.

'I just get interested in a conversation and you move me on,' she whispered to Jamie as he took her over to sit with Aunt Charlotte.

'That way you can't get bored,' he said with a wink. 'Don't worry, I'm keeping an eye on you and I'll rescue you when I think you need it.'

'I can manage just fine, thanks,' said Veronica.

'Charlotte is a challenge,' he warned.

Aunt Charlotte patted a cushion beside her and Veronica sat down on the wicker lounge.

'So how do you know our Jamie?' she began.

Veronica sketched out the details of her TV assignment, her scant knowledge of Doris's story as a child and how she had been told that Jamie would be a very helpful guide.

'He's more than that. Your story'd be far and away a better one if you spent a wee bit of time with the lad. He's a wise one. But a quiet one. Now tell me about yourself.'

Charlotte was insistent. She probed Veronica about her marital status, asked if she liked children, whether she had travelled and expressed astonishment that she had not been to Scotland. With this sort of interrogation, Veronica was grateful when she saw Jamie ploughing towards her even though everyone wanted a word with him as he passed.

'Excuse me, Auntie, I'm stealing Veronica, we're about to eat.'

'You win,' said Veronica as he steered her away. 'Is Charlotte that probing with everyone?'

'Afraid so. Very upfront is Auntie. My father is so much the opposite. It's like pulling teeth to get information of a personal nature from him.'

'Charlotte must frighten off your lady friends,' said Veronica.

'I don't plan to introduce any lady friends, should they come along,' he countered. 'Now we'll eat, which is a lengthy process, but I promise after lunch, you and my mum will have time together. Just the two of you.'

'I'm having fun, so whatever suits everyone,' said Veronica. She really was enjoying herself.

Billy took Veronica's hand and led her to the table. 'Sit here, near me. Dad told me to look after you,' he whispered.

Jamie's older sister Margaret sat on one side, and beside Margaret sat her daughter Anastasia, a pretty young teenager. On her other side was Billy and next to him Alistair, then Travis, one of Jamie's younger cousins. The conversation was lively.

'We don't all live in Darwin. We're just here for Mum and Dad's wedding anniversary,' said Margaret.

'But there's always someone visiting us,' said Billy.

'That's because this is a fun place. Much more than Melbourne,' said Anastasia. 'A lot of exciting things to do here.'

'Then how come you didn't go in the cage of death?' said Travis and everyone laughed.

'I'm with you, Anastasia,' said Veronica. 'I refused to get in the cage with the crocs.'

'My dad said he was going to show you crocodiles in the wild if you go to Arnhem Land,' Billy said to Veronica.

'Really? I'm not sure I'm really thrilled about that,' she said.

Billy was serious. 'My dad will look after you. Sometimes he's a ranger but sometimes he's a hunter. You'll be safe with him.'

'I didn't think crocs could be hunted, though I know they're multiplying out of hand,' said Veronica.

'Parts of the country are still traditional lands so we could hunt because of mother,' said Margaret calmly. 'But there are no crocs at Brolga Springs. Any crocs Jamie hunts are nuisances which are captured and sent to croc farms.'

Veronica stared at the sophisticated Melbourne woman and her attractive daughter. 'You're such an interesting lot. It's easy to forget that you have a connection with two cultures. Your family is so cosmopolitan, your life in Melbourne sounds so interesting. If you don't mind my asking, how involved are you with your mother's culture?'

'It's been a slow process,' said Margaret.

'And we're all still learning,' added Anastasia. 'Billy knows more than us, 'cause he's up here. That's why we like coming. Once a year Nana and Jamie take us back to our country.'

'It means a lot to Mum because she lost her connection with her birthplace and all her family as a kid, even though in many ways it was an advantage. She'd never have got the education she did, or met Dad and travelled, or done what she has if she'd been left in a mission or on an outstation,' said Margaret. 'But now, being able to piece the story together, find some kin and know where she's come from, where she belongs, means a lot to her.'

The young people listening, nodded. Alistair leaned across the table.

'Veronica, my wife's one of thousands who were

dispossessed. She recognises the advantages as well as the disadvantages. That's why she works so hard to help those who didn't have her opportunities.'

'You must be very proud of her,' said Veronica.

'We all are,' said Alistair, glancing down the table to where Doris sat at the head with Jamie on her right. 'She's a teacher by profession but, unlike me, she's a born teacher of life as well. What she is passing on to this family, these children, everyone she meets, is of inestimable value. A great gift. But it's hard won.'

'Don't underestimate yourself, Dad,' said Margaret. 'You're pretty special too.'

Veronica could only silently agree. Here was a man with a string of academic achievements and degrees, who, as she'd learned from Charlotte, came from a well-to-do Scottish family with a privileged upbringing but had been happily married for forty years to a part Aboriginal woman whose childhood couldn't have been more different from his.

Alistair gave Veronica a charming smile and lifted his glass of red wine. 'I do not regret a moment of the past forty years. Life with our beloved Doris has never been dull.'

Veronica returned the toast and glanced down the table and caught Jamie's eye. As if knowing what had transpired between her and his father, he too, lifted his glass of wine in a small salute.

As the courses of food kept appearing on the table, everyone taking turns serving, Billy tapped Veronica on the shoulder.

''Scuse me, Veronica. Dad says would you mind changing places so you can talk to some of the others.' He helped pull out her chair, confiding, 'They all want to talk to you.'

'That's because I work in television,' whispered Veronica and Billy looked shocked.

'No, it's not. We don't watch much TV and we can't get many stations here anyway. No, they like you.'

'Oh. Well, thank you,' said Veronica, feeling chastened.

The meal was finally over. They'd all lingered over coffee and fruit and suddenly everyone was clearing the table and a babble of laughter drifted from the kitchen as many hands helped with the clearing up. Jamie led Veronica through the house to Doris's study, where she was sitting at her desk with a cup of coffee.

'Make yourself comfortable. Do you want anything, more coffee, a drink?'

'I couldn't eat another thing, thank you. I feel guilty – I'm being waited on hand and foot and I haven't lifted a finger.'

'You're our guest. And besides, all my children like to catch up on news over the dishes. We don't all come together too often, so you've caught us on a hectic weekend.'

'Happy anniversary. I hope I haven't intruded on the family gathering.'

'Heavens, not at all. But we frequently have intruders, as you put it. With such a large family who all get on, we feel it quite acceptable to foist any number of strange friends and associates in to it,' said Doris cheerfully.

'Everyone does seem very close,' said Veronica.

'Family means a lot to me,' said Doris softly. 'Having lost mine for most of my life.'

'So you have traced some of your relatives from Brolga Springs?' asked Veronica.

'I did, eventually. And I still have an auntie out there who knew my mother and told me what happened.'

'Where's your auntie?' asked Veronica.

'She's in Katherine. There are people there she knows and it's still close to her country. I take her out to the old place when I go there. She might be a stooped, old, uneducated black lady, but she draws great strength and energy from being on her land. As I do. And she holds knowledge, so it's right that it be passed on. I try to teach Jamie the little knowledge I have.'

'And his sisters?'

'They respect their heritage but they've grown up in a white world. It makes me sad sometimes that they have no lore, no country to call their own. I have no claim to my country either. I was born under a tree on Brolga Springs to a young girl, fathered by a white man who never saw me. There was another white man who cared for me when I was a kid. I used to wish he was my father. He worked on the station a few months each year. He used to take me out mustering, let me work with the horses. That's when I met that group of white people.'

'You were with Len Buchanan,' said Veronica.

Doris nodded. 'I'd never seen so many white people all at once, and they seemed so different from the people who came to the station. I couldn't keep my eyes off the lady with the curly red hair and she smiled so nicely at me and took an interest. I can't describe how I felt about her. I suppose it was like how you'd feel if a character in a fairytale suddenly appeared.'

Veronica opened her handbag and pulled out one of the photos she'd printed out at the archives. 'Is this her?'

Doris took one look at the picture and nodded emphatically. 'Oh, yes it is. How did you get this? This is how I've always remembered her.' She lay down the picture and pulled open a drawer, took out a small silver bracelet and laid it on the desk. 'She gave me this. I wore it for years.'

Veronica picked it up and examined the filigree work on the chain and the small star charm that hung from it.

Doris sighed. 'Whenever I looked at the stars, I thought of her, imagining that she was up there watching over me. It helped me through some lonely times. I didn't even know her name.'

'It's Marta. And we think she's still alive. Somewhere in America we believe.'

For once Doris was at a loss for words. Then she smiled. 'Well, well.'

She seemed quite affected, so Veronica asked Doris to tell her what happened to her after Mr Johns died.

'The missus, as I knew her, struggled on. But for a white woman alone out there, it was tough. I suspect she was taken advantage of with some cattle deals so one day she took me aside and told me I had to go. My mother and grandmother raised me and I wanted to stay with them but the missus said I'd be taken without her there to protect me, because I was light skinned.'

'Had the welfare men been out to Brolga Springs?' asked Veronica.

'Yes. I remember the kerfuffle when a black car and truck came and everyone was shouting and running and my grandmother rushed up to the house and she and Mrs Johns rubbed soot from the kitchen fire all over me and made me hide in the pantry. Mrs Johns told the white men to go down to the camp and made me be quiet till they'd gone.'

Doris shook her head. 'I was very lucky. Anyway, eventually Mrs Johns made me dress up nicely and pack a little port with my things in it – my writing and spelling books and my clothes. She tied some money in a handkerchief and pinned it inside my dress in case I needed it. And she drove me to the mission. She had a long talk with the mother superior. I was so scared and upset.'

'But you were sent away from the mission?'

'After a couple of weeks, yes. Mrs Johns had organised it. The nuns took away my money but I had hidden my precious things, so when I was told I was being sent away to school I took them without the nuns knowing and I jumped in that mail truck – I didn't know where it was going. Mrs Johns had arranged everything.'

'What were your precious things? The bracelet?'

'Yes. And a photograph and a Bible. When I got to the mission I found Mrs Johns had slipped them in my bag.' Doris smiled. 'I kept those too. Through thick and thin.' She reached into the drawer again and slid a small leather Bible towards Veronica and a photograph. Veronica opened the Bible and saw in the flyleaf written in a copperplate hand – 'Annabel Johns'.

'And this photo?' Veronica studied the round-faced woman with her hair neatly coiled on top of her head. 'Is it the missus?'

'It is. I thought you'd like to see it.'

'It's so intriguing to suddenly put faces to the names,' said Veronica.

'And to know the names. May I get a copy of this picture of . . . Marta?' asked Doris.

'Of course. If we find her I'll let you know straight away. I'm sure she'll remember you.'

Doris didn't answer but sat fingering the paper print of the picture of Marta and the framed picture of Annabel Johns.

'So you did well at school?' prompted Veronica.

Doris straightened up. 'Yes, I did. I was sent to boarding school in Melbourne and Mrs Johns came to visit regularly and my reports were sent to her. She always introduced me as her protégé.'

'You never went back to Brolga Springs?'

'Not for a long, long time. By then I was eighteen and Mrs Johns was in poor health. She asked me to travel with her on a sentimental journey and she paid for me to fly to Darwin – my first time on a plane. Len Buchanan drove us down to Brolga Springs. I had no idea how she found him.'

'Was he pleased to see you?'

'Yes. He seemed happy enough. He was married and breeding and training horses, so we talked about horses. It was very upsetting for the missus to see the changes to the station, not all good. All the Aboriginal people had left so I had no way of finding my family.'

'But you did, eventually?'

'Not for many years until there was an understanding of what terrible wrongs had been wrought on Aboriginal families, which was one of the reasons I became active in trying to help fund and set up groups to help reunite families. Initially it was a needle in a haystack situation but as the awareness of what we now call the stolen generations grew, more efficient linkup programs were established. Everyone wants to know where they came from, who their parents were and what their origins are. Black, white or brindle. It's why family is so important to us now.'

Veronica was silent, thinking of her own family. She'd never tried, never wanted to know about distant relatives. While her immediate family was a small unit, Veronica had to admit there were not the closeknit ties in her family as there were in Jamie's. She'd watched the interaction between his relations, the behaviour of the children who were now playing in the pool as their chores were done. No-one wanted to watch TV or a DVD – Margaret had told her such things were regarded as special treats, not used as babysitters.

'Doris, just being with your family today has made me realise I don't appreciate my own family enough.' Veronica didn't want to say she thought her own sister's kids were spoilt and would not grow up with the same ethos as Doris's family.

Doris reached out and held her hand. 'I hear that a lot. When you've lost family, you realise how precious it is. For when there is trouble and sadness, family will always stand up for you. Now, what else can I tell you that might help you with your show?'

'I'm not sure. I'm a bit on overload,' confessed Veronica. 'Obviously the scenario I'd love would be to see you and Marta reunited, but, whether that's possible . . . Who knows?'

'Step by step, Veronica. Things will unfold. I get the sense there's more to this story than you realise. Or perhaps you do?' She smiled.

'Yes, I feel that too. I suspect that there are stories within stories. You. Jamie. Brolga Springs and whatever it was that drew those people to follow Topov out into the wilderness to a dream of a magic land . . .' Veronica sighed. 'I'm a bit confused. The journalist in me is being subsumed by other emotions and that's not very professional.'

'Surely being professional is following your instincts, is it not?' said Doris. 'Against all the expected and obvious leads you know there is some other little track to follow.'

'That's how I've generally operated,' admitted Veronica. 'My cameraman reminded me to not let my emotions get in the way of a good story.'

'Be truthful, be honest in your dealings with people, trust and take risks and you'll be all right. I have sense you have a high degree of integrity. Jamie is cautious, but he knows far more than he realises, so don't push him. Work with him.'

'Jamie seems the one in your family most connected to his Aboriginal heritage,' commented Veronica.

'That's because he's on the ground – literally,' said Doris candidly. 'He's in the landscape. To understand the essence of what all this is about . . . that film mob that followed the big fat bearded man into the wilderness, the connection country has to the heart of Aboriginal and white people like Mrs Johns and any number of men and women, white and black, who have lived and worked in the outback, you have to get a feeling for the land itself. For Aboriginal people it has deep spiritual meaning. To the grey nomads, people who, in their later years, sell the family home and get in caravans and four-wheel drives and spend time travelling around the "real" Australia, they get a sense of what this ancient continent and its first people are all about. You can only do that by being there.'

Veronica was nodding in agreement. 'Yes, I've seen a lot of Australia, but I realise that the outback is quite special.'

'Then spend time with someone who loves his country, in every sense and you might get closer to the core of what you're chasing,' advised Doris.

'I wish I could have filmed all of this,' sighed Veronica. 'You put things in perspective.'

Doris had a twinkle in her eye as she straightened up and put the bracelet, photo and Bible back in her desk drawer. 'My dear, I'm a professional too. I didn't get people to listen to me or sway a meeting without a little bit of a performance here and there. We can do this again. You might have different questions next time. Good luck and I'm sure we'll be seeing you again. The door to this house is always open.'

Jamie offered to drive Veronica back to her hotel, but she insisted on calling a taxi. Billy waited out the front of the house and when he saw the car arrive, he rushed in and told her it was there.

'When are you coming to visit again?' Billy asked, as he and Jamie walked her to the taxi.

'Soon, I hope. It's been lovely meeting you all,' said Veronica and she meant it.

'Come and see our house next time. We live over there,' said Billy pointing diagonally across the road. 'I've got a pet joey and a wompo you can feed.'

'What's a wompo?' asked Veronica.

'A sugar glider,' explained Jamie. 'The animals will go back into the wild eventually. They were injured and we picked them up last time we were out in Jawoyn country. They're well on the mend now. Thanks for coming, I hope it was helpful.'

'More than you know. Thanks, Jamie. I'll be in touch. See you, Billy.'

'So long, Veronica.' He took his dad's hand as the taxi pulled away. Looking back, Veronica saw Jamie drop his arm around his son's shoulders as they walked back into the house.

That evening she rang Sue.

'Hi, Sis, how're things going down there in chilly Melbourne? It's a balmy twenty-five here,' said Veronica cheerfully.

'Well, lucky you,' said Sue. 'It's cold and wet, though it's been nice. But trying to get settled is a nightmare. I hate moving. When can you come and help me?'

'Sorry, Sue, I'm in Darwin. Not sure when I'll have a break from this story. I thought you'd be unpacked by now.'

'We're still in a temp house. Can't find a house with a double garage and a nice garden close to town and close to a good gym. And as for finding a decent nanny . . . it's all too hard. The girls are so bored, too.'

'Why on earth are they bored?'

'The DVD isn't hooked up properly and their favourite toys aren't unpacked.'

'Take them to the park, feed the ducks, go for a walk,' said Veronica.

There was a short silence. 'That's all very well Vee, but I have a hairdresser's appointment, we have to go to a dinner party tonight and I can't find a babysitter.'

'Sue, your life sounds terrible,' said Veronica facetiously.

'It's wearing me down and Philip doesn't help – he's working such long hours in this new job trying to make a good impression and I'm starting my new job soon. I asked Mum to come down but of course she's too busy.'

'You need to simplify your life. Downsize, have some quality time with your kids,' said Veronica, thinking of Jamie's family.

'When you have a family, you can give me advice,' said Sue briskly. 'So when are you coming home and what are you doing again?'

'Oh, just a story. I'm enjoying the north though. Darwin is very buzzy and the outback is stunning.'

'Not my cup of tea. Well, I'd better run. Call us when you can come down. Hopefully we'll be in a house by then.'

'Sure. Good luck with it all, Sue. I'm sure you'll manage.'

Veronica felt sad for her sister and herself. She loved her sister and wished that they had a closer relationship. But Sue's life was her world and she wasn't really interested in what was happening to Veronica. Veronica couldn't remember the last time they'd had fun and a few laughs together, just the two of them.

After the lovely day, Veronica felt restless. She wasn't hungry so she didn't want to go out to dinner. She decided to settle down with a book she'd brought to read on the plane but hadn't opened.

The ringing phone startled her.

'Veronica, sorry to bother you.'

She sat up. 'Not at all, Jamie. Thanks again for introducing me to your mother and family. It was a lovely lunch.'

'Glad you enjoyed it. Mum is looking forward to talking with you more. I was just wondering if you might like to come with Billy and me tomorrow. We're going out to Litchfield National Park for the day. It's one and a half thousand acres on the Tabletop Range with lots of different habitats: monsoon forests, waterfalls, gorges and caves, termite mounds. It's only about an hour and a half drive but we'll be gone all day. We can swim in one of the falls and take a picnic.'

'It sounds wonderful, I'd love to see it.'

'Ask Eddie if he'd like to come along, there's some spectacular scenery.'

'I'll ask him. I think he had a big date tonight so I'll see if he's up to it. It's probably not country that fits in with my story, but handy to have on film, I guess.'

'Just come for a relaxing Sunday, take a day off from your work,' said Jamie amiably.

'You're right. I'll tell Eddie that, too. So what time?'

Eddie wasn't enthusiastic. 'I've been there. I can't see that it has anything to do with your story and if my plans for tonight fall into place I won't be up for it tomorrow, anyway.'

'That's okay. I'm looking forward to it,' said Veronica.

'I bet you are.'

Veronica felt a shiver go through her as she recognised the belligerent tone of Eddie's voice. 'What do you mean?'

'C'mon. He's a good-looking bloke, nice enough, but you can't take him home to mother, eh?'

'Eddie, are you referring to Jamie?' She wished she hadn't got into this conversation. 'He's a colleague, just trying to be helpful.'

'Come off it, Veronica. I saw the way you looked at him. You've never slept with a black man, have you?'

'Eddie, I'm going to hang up the phone now. I know you're a liar and a cheat and now I know that you're a racist bigot. Maybe you've spent too much time with your redneck friends. I'm glad I left you,' she said with some heat.

'I left you, sweetheart. Well, have a nice day skinny-dipping in the cascades.'

'Eddie, I'm not going to work with you again if you don't apologise and please, never speak to me like this again.'

'There you go, madam on your high horse. You can boss around the coloured help, honey, but not me. I quit.'

Veronica couldn't believe the conversation. She knew that Eddie was selfish and could be spiteful at times, but even she found it hard to believe this present attitude. Then she realised, Eddie resented her as his boss. Her giving him orders that night at Brolga Springs must have really rankled with him. Clearly he was now saying anything to make working with her impossible. She was furious with him. He was such a professional but he obviously wanted out. What a chauvinist, she thought. Well, if that's what he wants I'll call Murphy at the station tomorrow and get Dougie reassigned. You're not going to ruin this story, Mr Jarman, she told herself firmly.

It was a glorious morning. Veronica loved the balmy sunrise with a hint of the warm day ahead. She sat on her balcony with a cup of tea and watched palm fronds shine and stir in the first breezy breaths of the day.

She pushed the memory of Eddie from her mind and decided to enjoy the day and the company of Jamie and Billy. She'd looked up Litchfield National Park on the internet and it looked spectacular.

'Did you bring your swimmers?' Billy asked as she got into Jamie's car.

'I'm wearing it. Where are we going to swim? Nowhere near crocodiles I hope.'

Billy laughed. 'No way! Where are we going first, Dad?'

'Do you have a preference, Veronica? It's probably best to have a swim in the middle of the day when it's hot.'

'Good idea. But I'm happy to go along with whatever you suggest. You're the ranger, you must know the area well.'

'He does. He knows shortcuts and secret spots,' said Billy. 'Don't you, Dad? We go places tourists never go.'

'Ah, local knowledge, that's great,' said Veronica with a smile.

'It's not so secret. It's just that we like the tourists to follow the paths and use the facilities as that's safer than people ploughing off the track on their own,' said Jamie.

Jamie and Billy proved to be entertaining and interesting tour guides as they stopped at some of the popular sites. Veronica was fascinated by the remains of an old tin mine and by Blyth Homestead, which was a basic single room ringed by an open verandah with a sandstone floor.

'It was settled around 1928 by a family who had to be very self sufficient,' said Jamie. 'They must have supplemented their income with tin mining and cattle but they grew everything themselves.'

'Must have been a close-knit family,' said Veronica. 'It makes you realise how tough the pioneers had to be.'

Billy's favourite place was the huge area of densely packed termite mounds which he said looked like 'an ant city'.

'Notice how they're all facing the same direction – a north–south alignment,' said Jamie. 'That's so they can control the temperature in their mounds.'

'These mounds must be over four metres high,' said Veronica, quite fascinated.

'Further down the road we can stop and walk for a bit and I'll show you some mounds that look like red dirt sculptures that'd beat the work of any contemporary artist,' said Jamie. 'We have fun deciding what or who they look like.'

Along the way Jamie and Billy talked about the animals and plants that lived in different habitats. 'I'm bringing Sugar back out here to let her go when she's big enough,' said Billy.

'Ah, your sugar glider,' said Veronica. 'And what about your baby kangaroo?'

'He's not ready to be set free yet,' said Billy firmly.

'You mean you're not ready,' said Jamie. 'He'll have to go sometime, matey.'

'On the way to the cemetery you said something about what animals are left . . . What did you mean?'

'Don't get me started,' said Jamie. 'Australia is losing animals at an alarming rate. And by losing I mean they're extinct.'

'With diseases? Introduced pests? Development? Out-of-control bushfires?' asked Veronica.

'All of that but what's worrying is that the mammal population is dying out in untouched remote areas.'

'Dad says it's feral cats,' said Billy.

'They are a disaster, we don't know they're there half the time. Unlike mining. We certainly shouldn't be allowing full-on development like that till we know what we might lose and see if we can rescue at least some remaining species and put controls and programs in place,' said Jamie.

'That's part of my dad's job,' said Billy proudly.

They swam in pools of clear water, the steep cliffs of a gorge carved by the force of water over aeons towering above them. As they swam, Jamie pointed out where the elusive bats lived and named the birds peculiar to this area. They sat on a warm flat rock and ate the sandwiches and fruit Jamie had brought along, washed down with water. It was simple, easy and well, comfortable was the word that sprang to Veronica's mind.

Their final stop was at the mysterious Lost City. They drove along a rough, thickly forested track to where massive sandstone blocks and pillars were standing as if they were the remains of an ancient civilisation.

'How did they get like that?' asked Billy.

'Who knows? Maybe the Romans settled here secretly,' teased Jamie.

'This is like coming across some anthropological site,' said Veronica. 'It's eerie.'

As the sun began to set on the way back to Darwin, Veronica sighed. 'This has been such a wonderful day. We crammed so much in. I'm so glad I've seen all those places. Thank you both so much.'

Billy was chuffed and bounced in the back seat. 'Dad knows heaps more good places, don't you, Dad? When are we going camping again?' He touched Veronica on the shoulder as he told her, 'We have to go out into our country and do men's business and ceremonies.'

'Billy, that's wonderful. You're very lucky, aren't you, that you do all the same stuff as the other boys at school but you also learn about your nana's culture.'

'I think football is still number one on the agenda,' said Jamie.

The lights of Darwin were glittering in the twilight when Jamie shifted in his seat and turned to Billy.

'What say we ask Veronica to stay for dinner. You could make your speciality.'

'Yes! Can you come, Veronica? Then you could meet my joey.'

'Well, it depends. What's your speciality, Billy?'

'He makes a mean pizza,' said Jamie.

'You got me,' said Veronica.

Like Doris's house, Jamie's home evoked old-style Darwin but it was much smaller. It was surprisingly neat without the clutter of books, memorabilia, art and collectables Doris and Alistair had accumulated over forty years of marriage. Billy tugged at Veronica, asking her to come out the back and see his pets while Jamie began to organise things in the kitchen.

Veronica was entranced with the tiny joey, which was sleeping in a cut-down pillowslip on a coathanger in the laundry. Billy picked him up and handed him to Veronica. The joey immediately gave her an affectionate lick with its sticky tongue.

'That's a kiss,' said Billy.

'Come on, mate, wash your hands and start getting that pizza going,' said Jamie as he handed Veronica a glass of white wine. 'I noticed you drank white, is this okay?'

'Heaven,' she sighed, as she sat in one of the old rattan chairs on the small patio.

Jamie hit a switch and the garden was bathed in a soft glow. Billy raced around with a long match taper and lit several fat candles.

'That's pretty,' she said.

'It's for the mozzies,' said Billy as he went inside.

'Is he okay in the kitchen?' she asked.

'Oh yes, it's ready-made dough he rolls out and plonks the tomato paste on and whatever else he can find. They're, er, creative pizzas,' Jamie grinned.

'He's so independent.'

'He's had to be in some ways. Not that he ever lacks for family around him. But I want him to be able to look after himself in town and in the bush. Mum's taught him to ride, Dad wants to teach him to shoot, my sisters teach him manners and stuff and I'm trying to keep him in touch with his heritage. Easy stages, though. It's his choice how far he wants to go with learning traditional stuff.'

'I think it's wonderful. Who taught you, Jamie? Your mother?'

'Some. I'm still learning, too. But the elders, the old men, they've taken me under their wing.' He gave her a direct stare. 'Does that make you uncomfortable?'

'No, why should it?'

'I mightn't look very Aboriginal, but my heart is. A lot of white Australians aren't sure how to handle someone like me even if they're three-quarters white, as in my case.'

'I thought since reconciliation and the reports about the stolen generations and myriad other issues that we'd come past that,' said Veronica. But then she remembered her unpleasant conversation with Eddie and realised that not everyone thought the way she did.

'You're a journalist, Veronica. You know that it's the land claims, compensation claims, mining settlements and royalties being paid to traditional owners selling off their country that's causing conflict,' said Jamie. 'And there are arguments between indigenous people over what's the best use for their land.'

'Where do you stand on the mining issue?' asked Veronica bluntly.

'Well, that's a very broad question,' he said calmly. 'We have to develop some of the resource riches we have in the ground, but it's where and how and who gets the profits. Kakadu for example, should be carefully protected from contamination from uranium mining.'

'And the Great Barrier Reef and Ningaloo Reef and the Kimberley should be carefully protected, too,' said Veronica.

'Exactly,' said Jamie. 'I'm trying to look at all sides. Looking at Australia from an environmental standpoint, we can't keep going entirely the way we are. I want Billy to be able to see what I've seen, to be able to know that the last beautiful ancient landscapes of Australia will be there for his great-grandchildren.' He put down his wine with a rueful grin. 'I'd better go and see how the chef is doing.'

'Can I help?'

'Oh, maybe with the salad shortly. Enjoy your wine.'

The pizza was in the oven. Billy set the table while Veronica made a salad and Jamie dug among his CDs looking for some local music he thought Veronica might like to hear.

Over dinner Jamie asked about Veronica's childhood and Billy asked if she had lots of brothers and sisters. They talked about Arnhem Land and how she could work it into her film.

Billy was very proud of his pizza which was a smiling red face: half a pineapple ring for the smile, tomato circles for eyes with slices of olives as the pupils, strips of green peppers for eyebrows, two slices of olives made the nose and melting mozzarella formed the hair.

'Excellent, Billy,' said Veronica. 'Very creative.'

Jamie asked Billy to clear the table as he went to refill their wine glasses.

'What's for dessert?' Jamie asked.

'Surprise,' said Billy.

Veronica watched the father and son and their easy but respectful camaraderie and couldn't help comparing Jamie's family with the chaotic life of her sister. Billy produced bowls of ice-cream sprinkled with hundreds and thousands and slices of banana.

'Perfect,' announced Veronica. 'But I insist on washing up.'

'Thanks,' said Billy. 'But we have a machine.'

After the dishes were in the dishwasher, Jamie made coffee while Billy went to his room. As they finished their coffee he emerged in his pyjamas with a book.

'I'm going to bed. Goodnight, Veronica.' He unselfconsciously gave her a kiss and hugged his father.

'Teeth?' asked Jamie. When Billy had left he said, 'It's been a big day, he's tired. And school tomorrow.'

'Jamie, I have to say, he's extraordinary,' said Veronica. Billy seemed too good to be true.

'Ah, we have our moments. But he has so many women keeping him in line. Makes my job easy.'

'He hasn't watched TV or been near a computer. Does he have one in his room?'

'God, no. We share the computer, I like to monitor that.'

'Well, he's a credit to you.'

'Thanks, Veronica. He's a good little mate. I enjoy him. It's just a shame that his mother can't see him.'

'It's very sad about her. What happened?' Veronica hadn't liked to ask about Jamie's wife, but now that the subject was raised, she felt she could.

'Janine was killed in a car accident, not long after we arrived in the Territory. She was coming back from the shops and another car ran into her. We were both so excited when I got the job up here. Darwin seemed such an adventure after growing up in Melbourne and working in Canberra. We met at uni and we were both passionate about the environment, so this seemed a wonderful way to do something practical. Her parents were pretty cut up about her death, naturally enough, but they understood that I wanted to stay here. They visit as often as they can to see Billy. They are great people and love Darwin. They're of Greek heritage, so they fit right into this multicultural city.'

'It's great that Billy has such wonderful family around him,' said Veronica. 'Jamie, I've had an unforgettable day but I have to say I'm weary too. I'm not used to climbing up gorges. Thanks so much. Call me a taxi and I'll head home.'

'Nonsense. I've only had two wines, I'll drive you. I'll just ring Mum and ask her to pop in as I'll be gone a short while, in case Billy needs anything.'

When they pulled up at the Mantra Jamie jumped from the four-wheel drive, still muddy from their trek into the Lost City and opened Veronica's car door for her before she could open it herself.

'Thank you, thank you,' said Veronica.

'Sleep well. Let me know how you get on and if you need me to arrange anything if you're going to Arnhem Land and when.'

'I will. Thanks, Jamie.'

He gave a smile and small wave and leapt back in the car but he didn't pull away until she was inside the lobby.

The next morning Veronica called Andy and discussed the row she'd had with Eddie.

'Oh dear, Veronica. That's too bad. I hoped Eddie might have matured or calmed down since being up there. I guess he just resents your authority, but he is a good cameraman.'

'Y' know, Andy, I'm the boss, this story's my responsibility and if Eddie can't cope with that, then blow him. I can use young Dougie. I was happy with what he shot.'

'You'd better talk to Murphy. Now, I've been on the case tracking down Marta.'

'Go Andy!'

'Don't get too excited. She did a bit of modelling in Sydney as well as acting. I've put out feelers among the old casting agents who're still around. And you remember my pal Alec Blair. You met him at the Pioneers' Reunion?'

'Ah, yes. TV director. Advertising?'

'Right. I'm having lunch with him today so I'll take along the picture of Marta you sent me. Alec has a memory like an elephant, especially for pretty girls. He might give me some leads on other people or agencies to chase up.'

'Okay, let me know. Doris would love to make contact with her.'

'So how is little Doris?'

'A feisty, smart and amazing woman. A terrific family. I loved them.'

Andy caught a wistful note in her voice. 'And? She remembered Marta?'

'Oh yes. I thought it was strange enough that Jamie McIntosh is Doris's son, but that Doris has kept the bracelet Marta gave her all those years ago is touching.'

'Women never part with jewellery,' said Andy.

'C'mon, it was one of three very special things she owned.'

'Well, keep me in the loop. Where to next?'

'I'm going back to the library for a bit more trawling and maybe back to the archives, too. You never know, something useful might turn up.'

'Anything else?'

'I'm interviewing Doris on camera in a day or so.'

It was an uncomfortable meeting with Murphy, the chief-of-staff, but he allowed Veronica to use Dougie again as her cameraman.

'It's no reflection on Eddie's work,' Veronica reassured Murphy. 'It's just that it's been a difficult personal relationship.'

'If I'd known the history I might have avoided teaming you up. I thought you'd worked together before, not been in a relationship.'

'These things happen,' said Veronica.

'Yeah, tell me about it,' he said.

Back at the library and having exhausted the entertainment pages and finding no more references to Marta, Veronica decided to continue looking in the general section of the papers of 1955 to see if she could find anything else relevant. In the hushed atmosphere Veronica hunched over the microfilm reader. As she scrolled through, she saw a banner headline that stilled her hand and made her gasp out loud:

FOREIGN FILMMAKER KILLED BY CROC!

Quickly she took in the gist of the story, her heart beating.

European film producer Maxim Topov, who has been making a documentary on outback Australia, was taken by a crocodile in Arnhem Land near the South Alligator River. Mr Topov, who is believed to be Russian, had left his companions to film at sunset and did not return. His possessions were found but his body was not recovered. Professional crocodile shooter Len Buchanan said there had been reports from Aborigines in the area of a rogue croc. Police are investigating. Said District Officer Sergeant O'Hara, 'Travellers, especially foreigners, need to be better educated about the threats to their safety from crocodiles and not camp near their known habitats.' Mr Topov's companions have returned to Darwin. The authorities plan to notify Mr Topov's friends and family in Sydney. A hunting party has been dispatched from Darwin to locate the croc.

My God, when John Cardwell said things fell apart in Darwin he wasn't joking, thought Veronica. She couldn't believe it. She looked at the date of the story. It had happened only a couple of weeks after Marta's performance had finished. Poor Topov. She thought of the photo she'd seen of him, with his wild hair and rotund figure. From Colin's description, he'd seemed so much larger than life. What a terrible thing to have happened.

Veronica hurried outside, her finger on Andy's number in her mobile phone.

10

EMERGING INTO BRIGHT SUNSHINE on the manicured lawn outside Parliament House, Veronica headed for the shade of a tree as she told Andy the shocking news about Topov's death.

He let out a low whistle. 'That puts a different slant on things, doesn't it?'

'Do we still have a story to tell?' asked Veronica.

'I think so. We never expected to find Topov living after all this time, anyway. I wonder why Colin didn't tell us about this right away?' mused Andy. 'Is there something odd about the secrecy?'

'I don't know, Andy. Perhaps he wanted to surprise me. I'm so tempted to go back to Colin and try again,' said Veronica.

'You might not have to, I've had a bit of luck with Alec.

I took the picture of Marta to lunch and he recognised her. Couldn't remember her name but he always remembers a pretty face. She was in a couple of ads he did.'

'Really! Does he know what happened to her?'

'The last he knew she was still around in Australia in the late fifties and she'd been doing some acting – stage mainly as her accent was a handicap for film – but he remembers that there was a bit of a write-up in the paper about her going to Hollywood to play a foreign spy in some war film.'

'Yes, I've found a reference to that, too. Did he know any more?'

'No. But Alec said we should contact SAG – the Screen Actors' Guild – in the US as she'd have to have been a member.'

'Good one. Doris would adore to see her again if we can find her.'

'I'll see what I can find out from SAG. What's your next move?'

'I'm going to see what we can dig up in the files about Topov's death. There must be a report on it somewhere.'

'Let's hope. Good luck, Veronica. Talk to you later.'

It was Collette at the archives who suggested Veronica look at the death files.

'Here are the files for 1953 to 1959,' said Collette as Veronica settled herself at a table in the archives' reading room. 'You could expect to find police findings and reports, witness accounts. There could also be correspondence exchanged with the family of the victim,' she added helpfully.

'Okay. I'll see what's in here. Thanks, Collette.'

'I'll get you a coffee before you start looking, if you like,' offered Collette with a smile.

'You've been so helpful, I'm very grateful,' said Veronica.

'I'm as interested as you are, now, to find out what happened,' said Collette.

Two hours later Veronica rang Dougie. 'Can you come over to the archives and shoot a sequence with Collette and myself please, Dougie? We're looking at old police records.'

'How are we going to make that look interesting for TV?' he asked.

'Collette can be the star of this segment,' she answered.

So Dougie filmed Collette reading and discussing the file she'd found on the death of Maxim Topov with Veronica.

According to the police report, the authorities in Darwin had been notified by the group of travellers that one of their party, Mr Maxim Topov, had gone missing after going out late one afternoon and had not returned that evening or the following morning. The group were filmmakers and Topov had been making small forays from their camp to film the area. Others in the group had been helping Mr Len Buchanan, a well-known crocodile hunter, to hunt the crocodiles known to frequent that part of the South Alligator River. The party had been camped above Wild Man's Crossing, a small stone weir used by horses and cars to cross the river and some of Mr Topov's possessions, a knapsack and food, were found near it.

During the wet season, the flow from the river covers the crossing making it dangerous or impossible to cross, but at the time of year Mr Topov disappeared, the water was shallow, making it easy to cross on foot, but also providing easy access for crocodiles. Next to the crossing was a clearing used by locals to launch small boats. It was regarded as a dangerous place to stop because crocodiles were known to wait along the banks.

'So the police theory was that when Topov was filming either along the bank or as he went over the crossing he was nabbed by a croc,' said Veronica.

Collette nodded. 'Even today the crossing is a well known croc habitat, although it's become a popular tourist spot and the local Aborigines run indigenous river cruises from there.'

'Is there anything else you can tell me? Was there any follow-up? Was anyone else in the area? What happened to his possessions? Were there any other investigations?' asked Veronica.

Collette scanned the notes. 'A policeman visited the scene some time later, but no remains of Topov were ever found. Brief statements were taken from his party when they arrived back in Darwin, all corroborating the details. They're attached here. Basically they told the police when he hadn't returned late the next morning and they went looking for him. They found his personal effects and also croc mudslides along the bank. The policeman found evidence that someone had been on the opposite side of the crossing, but that was several days later so it might not have been Topov at all.' She looked at Veronica. 'It's a beautiful but treacherous place. It is named after an old prospector who ran cattle and was a buffalo shooter and a friend of the local Aborigines. We've got a file on Wild Man Johnson in here.'

'It sounds an intriguing place. I'll have to go there now and film it. I wonder what Topov was trying to film?' said Veronica.

'I don't think you'll ever know that. But you'll need a permit because once you cross from the Kakadu side of the river to the other side you're in Arnhem Land.'

'Yes. I understand. I'm working with Jamie McIntosh, I believe he can help me there.'

'Ah, then you'll be all right.' Collette flipped to the last page of the file. 'There's one last statement here. Apparently all Mr Topov's personal possessions were handed over to his business partner, Olga Konstantinova.'

Collette closed the file. 'That's it. It was a long time ago. I don't know that you'll find out anymore.'

Veronica knew her friend at the archives was right, unless, of course, they could speak with Marta. But she wanted badly to see the country that had so attracted Topov and which had killed him.

Dougie went back to the television station and Veronica ate lunch in a restaurant in the middle of town, marvelling at the variety of delicious food. As she walked through the CBD afterwards she spotted an art gallery with a poster in the window for an Arnhem Art Exhibition. She went in and was immediately transported to a world unlike any other she'd ever seen. The vibrancy and energy of the colours, the sense of place, affected her quite unexpectedly. While the style was what she could only think of as Aboriginal abstract, she could see the ranges and the strange jump-up rock formations, the rivers and the billabongs. What she'd thought of as traditional Aboriginal art with its distinctive dots and patterns was nothing like this. In these paintings pinks, purples, yellows, greens and blues were used in a strong and confident manner. As she studied them further, she saw stylised interpretations of birds, crocodiles and people. Some of the other paintings were more muted, dreamy images of the landscape as if seen through mist, or soft light, or perhaps, memory.

The woman staffing the gallery came over to her. 'Can I help you? Or are you just looking?'

'Just looking. This is amazing work, so different. Where's it from?' asked Veronica.

'Several centres in Arnhem Land, as well as Roper River, a community at Ngukurr, Yolngu and there are several small family groups who work out of their settlements. Stunning, isn't it?'

'Yes. I love these.' She picked up a multicoloured, finely woven basket from a display.

'The Yolngu are master weavers. They dye strips of pandanus leaves to weave into all kinds of practical and pretty things. Look at these bead-like necklaces – they're made from seeds, fish vertebrae and shells.'

Veronica bought a necklace for herself and a set of beautiful placemats for Sue and a basket for her mother. She really longed to buy a painting, but was so overwhelmed by all the different styles she'd seen, she decided to ask Jamie's advice.

'How's it going?' he asked, when she rang him. His voice was warm, which made Veronica feel it was more a personal than a professional question.

'I've got some very surprising news.' She filled him in on the death of Topov.

Jamie let out a deep breath. 'Tragic. Where was he taken?'

'At a place called Wild Man's Crossing.'

'I know it. South Alligator River. It's probably even more dangerous now than it was then because of the recent increase in crocodile numbers.' He paused and she could hear the smile in his voice. 'I suppose you want to go there?'

'Of course. It sounds as though this is the end of the road, as far as the story of the filmmakers goes, so we'll need to film it.'

'When do you want to go out there? I'll have to let the locals know we want to cross the river into their land and film.'

'Thanks. Well, if I don't have any more leads, there's not a lot of point marking time here in Darwin – much as I'm enjoying it. Dougie is on standby, so I can go to Wild Man's Crossing as soon as you can get away.'

'Dougie? Not Eddie?'

'I'll explain later,' said Veronica. 'Say, I was wondering if you could help me buy a painting. I'd love to have something to remind me of the Territory. But I'm a bit confused. Every place I see has wonderful art, or so it seems to me. But so much of it is so different and I don't know what's good and what's tourist stuff.'

'Ah, you're right, some of the local art is wonderful and some is rubbish. The Western Desert art was the big breakthrough but not many artists work on bark anymore and now some of the contemporary art is very different from the old school. You need to talk to Mum, or better, Great Aunt Nellie in Katherine.'

'Your mother's aunt? Her mother's sister?'

'Yes. Funnily enough, when Nellie went into a nursing home in Katherine she was taken to the recreation centre. Having never been to school she didn't want to know about knitting and playing cards but she took to drawing and colouring in. Then she wanted her own paper and crayons and she started doing some amazing stuff. Mum has since set her up with proper canvases and acrylic paints.'

'And she'd never painted before? What does she paint?' asked Veronica.

'Her country and the old stories she was told, before people lived on the station or the mission came. She enjoys painting and it keeps her happy.'

'What happens to her artworks? Are they any good?'

'They're different. She doesn't have anyone to influence her. Mum gave her books on Aboriginal art and showed her around a gallery. But Auntie just does her own thing. Mum wants to take her back to Brolga Springs so that she can paint her country the proper way.'

'Gosh, Jamie, that'd be really moving.'

'You talk to Mum about her,' said Jamie.

Veronica smiled. 'Okay, I will. I'm doing the interview with Doris tomorrow morning.'

'I'll be in touch about the trip to Wild Man's Crossing. Hopefully we can get away Thursday morning.'

'Thanks, Jamie. I'll alert Dougie.'

The following day she and Dougie went to film the interview with Doris at her home. Dougie was quite spellbound by Doris's stories and the allotted two hours sped by. Veronica already had more footage than she needed, but Dougie was finding lots of good cutaways and Doris was in the mood to talk so Veronica wanted to hear more about her childhood at Brolga Springs and how her life changed after she went to Melbourne.

Finally Doris rose and apologised, saying that she had to go to a meeting. She hugged Veronica and added, 'Jamie mentioned you're interested in the local art. Would you like to see a couple of Auntie's paintings?'

Doris led them to her study and pointed to a wall hung with bold and dramatic canvases. Some were sweeping landscapes seen from an old woman's perspective. Other paintings were crammed with animals and plants, another was a frieze of figures depicting mundane tasks. Her choice of bright, strong primary colours amazed Veronica.

'They're unique. A genre or category of their own. Folk art, naïve art, tribal things, just wonderful,' said Veronica. 'I love them. But you need hours to absorb them.'

'Then you'll have to come back. I like to sit with a cup of tea and lose myself in them. They take you away to another place,' said Doris.

'I'd love to come back, if I may.'

Doris hugged her. 'Any time. Consider yourself part of the family.'

Andy listened as Veronica told him what she'd unearthed in the archives about Topov's death.

'Poor old bugger. No-one deserves to be eaten by a bloody great lizard.'

'I've got a pretty good idea of where it happened so I figure we should go and film the location.'

'Be careful. There are probably even more crocs around now.'

'So I hear. There wasn't much in the police report. Everyone in the group was interviewed and corroborated the story, but now that I think about it, there's wasn't an interview with Colin. I wonder why that was. I'll double-check. And it seems all Topov's personal effects were handed over to Olga.'

'And we don't know what became of Madame Olga?' said Andy thoughtfully.

'No. That's another angle we could chase. So, I'm heading out to Wild Man's Crossing.'

'How do you like the outback?' asked Andy.

'It's amazing. Beautiful. Intriguing. I must say it's quite swept me up.'

'Hmm,' said Andy. 'Now, do you want to hear my news?'

'Oh, sorry. I've been caught up in my stuff. Marta? Did you have any luck?'

'Sort of. We've found her listed with the Screen Actors' Guild of America in 1959. Of course that address is out of date . . .'

'That's exciting. It would be great if we can find her. There are so many questions to ask!' exclaimed Veronica.

Veronica felt better equipped than for her first outing with Jamie as she packed her backpack for the trip to Wild Man's Crossing. This time she and Dougie travelled with Jamie in his National Parks four-wheel drive.

For Veronica the journey was enjoyable and companionable as she and Jamie talked while Dougie sat in the back, staring out the window, his iPod in his ear. They turned off the main highway and were soon in the dramatic landscape of rocky red escarpments broken by splashes of vivid green palms, cycads and tawny spinifex. Veronica fell silent, trying to imagine how the vehicles in Topov's expedition picked their way through this same country with barely a road to follow.

Jamie had warned her there'd be no hospitality like Rick and Vicki had offered at Brolga Springs this time. 'There's a basic roadhouse and store with a few motel rooms, unless you want to camp. But for the short time we'll be here, camping doesn't seem worth the trouble,' he said. 'Sure to meet some colourful characters, though.'

'I'm a bit over colourful characters,' confessed Dougie. 'Seems I'm always filming them for one reason or another. I was told they were people who had opted out of the mainstream, who like to keep to themselves, be known by one name and yet they're happy to be on camera and talk for an hour.'

Veronica laughed. 'I know what you mean. The really interesting people don't want to be filmed at all.'

Dougie wanted to stop along the way to film the landscape. He was so enthused that Veronica agreed to the breaks. Once, while Dougie set up the camera and filmed scenic shots as well as close-ups of plants and tiny marsupial footprints in the soil, Jamie led her a short distance into the scrub, away from the road.

'Turn your back to the track. Take a deep breath, close your eyes,' he said.

Veronica did so and then he asked. 'What do you feel, hear?'

After a few minutes she said, 'I hear silence. But now I can hear all kinds of things – buzzing of insects, birds a long way away, the scrunch of an animal scratching under a bush or something, wind sort of whispering.' She stood a moment longer, then opened her eyes. 'Amazing how alert your senses get out here. There isn't the bombardment of city sounds, yet it's a busy world when initially it looks . . . empty and silent.'

Jamie smiled. 'Yes. You're starting to attune to the landscape.'

'Is this how it's done? Is this how you teach people about the country and what it means?' she asked.

Jamie nodded. 'It's a starting point. I used to walk with Billy blindfolded, holding his hand, to give him a sense of what was around him. Then you have to learn to use your eyes properly, because you'll start to see small things, details that surprise and enchant.' He stopped and spread his arms. 'I walk along a city street and things just pass me by. Here I walk through what looks like empty scrubby rubbish country to some, but I see beauty and layers of life that have continued for hundreds and hundreds of years.' He looked at her. 'It's a learning process. Especially for those of us who grew up some place else.'

'Yes, I can understand that. But then it begins to make sense?'

'Yes, it's as though somewhere there's a switch that connects us to where we come from and belong, no matter where we've been. It turns on and you just know. This is the right place. I find the land seems to speak to me.'

As they drove, Veronica thought about the dichotomy of Jamie's double inheritance. His life in Melbourne and his life out here were poles apart and yet he apparently fitted in so easily to both. She stole a look at his profile, his fine features, slim brown hands on the steering wheel, the slope of his shoulders and she tried to imagine him naked save for a loincloth and white clay paint, dancing by firelight. He caught her studying him and she looked the other way, hoping her face wasn't flushed.

Dougie was worried. Scattered clouds had drifted

in, shading the sun, fading the brilliant colours of the landscape.

'Will this cloud last long?' he asked.

Jamie glanced at the sky. 'No. It's between seasons, so you get the odd cloudy day, but it's not going to set in. Not like the build-up of the wet.'

A high wind was blowing as they rolled into the roadhouse at Wild Man's Crossing. Several battered and muddy vehicles laden with swags, tents and fishing gear were parked out the front. As she got out and stretched, Veronica was dismayed to hear a jukebox playing and raucous laughter coming from the bar. Jamie turned to her and said:

'Wait here, I'll go get the keys. Our rooms are at the back.'

'Jeez, this looks a bit rough,' said Dougie.

'We're only here a night.'

'Might've been better to pitch a tent or thrown down a swag away from here,' said Dougie.

'I agree. Except that Jamie says that the river and billabongs around here are infested with crocs. I don't know about you, but I wouldn't sleep much,' said Veronica.

'This camping area and roadhouse wouldn't have been here, back then when the group came through,' said Dougie, looking around.

'No, there would have been nothing but bush. Do you want to do a bit of a recce before dark?'

'Yes, and hope that it's fine in the morning. Do we know exactly the spot where the man was taken?'

'Not really. Jamie is taking us to the Crossing in the morning.'

They drove round the back past a generator, some forty-four gallon drums overflowing with rubbish, a work shed where two blue heeler dogs were chained and a toilet block. Next to a tall eucalypt tree was a low building – four basic bedrooms. Jamie handed them each a key.

'Keep your rooms locked. Pilfering, drunks and wild-life are rampant.'

'We were thinking we'd like to drive around a bit, just have a look-see about the area, is that possible?' asked Veronica.

Jamie handed her the car keys. 'Go for your life. I've got to find one of the land owners from the other side of the river and do a bit of paperwork. Just don't get out of the car anywhere dicey and don't get off the tracks.'

'We'll be an hour or so. If we're not back in two, come and find us,' laughed Veronica.

'Okay. I'll eat your share of dinner! But seriously that's how it works out here. Always let people know where you're going, what your plans are. There's a log book in the shop which they get visitors to fill in.'

Veronica felt comfortable driving Jamie's heavy-duty vehicle. She and Dougie headed along the dirt road and then took a turn off along a smaller track.

'Bit different from city driving,' commented Dougie as they bumped across deep dried mud ruts from the last wet season.

'I feel like I'm on safari,' said Veronica. 'I love it out here.'

They drove through the scrubby bush stopping once as a large goanna crossed in front of them.

'He's beautiful! Look at those markings,' exclaimed Veronica.

'He must be a metre and a half long! I bet the minute I get out with the camera he'll take off.'

'Of course he will, Dougie. And probably run straight up you. Isn't that what they do when they're frightened, run up the nearest upright object thinking it's a tree?'

'Hey, look. There's the river. And there's the track in. Let's take a look,' said Dougie.

Veronica drove slowly towards the river, following the tyre marks made by other vehicles. They reached a rough clearing that held an improvised barbecue plate on a stone base and at the water's edge they saw a cement landing, sloping into the water.

'Boat launching spot,' said Dougie. 'Must be good fishing.'

'I wouldn't be out on the river in this weather,' said Veronica looking at the trees whipped up by the wind and the turbulent muddy grey stretch of the river.

'Looks like a washing machine. It's rough for sure,' said Dougie. He opened the car door and they realised how strong the wind was as the door was almost wrenched from his hand. 'This must be beautiful on a calm sunny day. I might just take a shot of this.'

Veronica sat behind the wheel looking at the river and had to agree, this must look idyllic when the water was glassy smooth and the day was sunny.

Dougie tried to hold his camera steady against his shoulder as he started filming. 'Wind's too strong, I need the tripod. I'll just grab a few hand-held shots from the landing.'

Veronica got out of the car and pressed the central locking button, put the keys in her pocket and followed Dougie as he headed to the landing. But as she looked at the murky churning river and heard the howling wind in the trees, she was gripped by a sudden fear. The place was deserted and looked and felt utterly sinister.

'Dougie, no! Come back,' she shouted. 'Don't go there.'

'Just be a tick. One shot.'

'No! Please, Dougie.' She started to hurry after him and stopped. She simply couldn't bring herself to take one more step closer to the river. She glanced around quickly. 'Dougie! Come back. There's a crocodile here!'

'What! Where?' He stopped, looking around.

'I know it's here, quick. Come back to the car!' Veronica turned back and started running.

Dougie laughed. 'Come on, how do you know? I can't see anything.'

'Dougie, I'm ordering you,' shouted Veronica. She'd seen pictures of crocodiles and how amazingly fast the reptiles could move on their short legs. Visions of snapping jaws, the horror of being caught in such a mouth, made her start to shake.

Dougie hesitated as Veronica dashed to the car, fumbling with the keys. 'It won't open!' She kept pressing the electronic car key button. 'Oh, God, we're locked out!' She glanced around. With the wind they couldn't hear any sounds but she was sure that she could feel the presence of the crocodile.

Dougie caught up with her. 'Why'd you lock it?'

'I didn't think, but now it's jammed or the key has a flat battery.' She kept clicking the key with no success. 'Should we climb up on the roof?'

'What and spend the next two hours sitting there like a pair of dummies? Here let me try.'

He fiddled with the key as Veronica kept telling him to hurry up. Finally there was a click as Dougie manually turned the key and unlocked the doors. Veronica scrambled inside slamming her door shut. 'Get in Dougie, just hold the camera tightly, I want to get out of here.' She started reversing quickly.

'Why're you so spooked? I'm sure that the river's too rough for anything to be out there.'

Veronica didn't answer, relieved to be heading back to the road. Within a few hundred metres they came to a narrow bridge and stopped. 'You can take your shot from here, looking back at that landing spot on the bank,' she said.

Dougie shook his head still feeling bemused and leaned against the railing and lifted the camera to focus. But then he suddenly lowered the camera and pointed at the river. 'Oh, God, look!'

Veronica peered at the river. In the water was a massive crocodile, its mottled hide the colour of the choppy river. It lifted its large head out of the water and with it's tail flashing, it swam only a few metres from the landing where Dougie had been standing just minutes before. She caught her breath. The croc looked so evil, so cruel.

'Man, that must be three and a half metres long!' breathed Dougie, looking pale. 'Glad I didn't hang about. How did you know it was there?'

Veronica was too shaken to answer as they turned back towards the roadhouse.

It was a very different scene the following morning when they headed out after breakfast. The previous night had been noisy with music, laughter, shouting and a fight erupting in the bar. The ruckus continued till the small hours. Now the day was still, clear and sunny and Veronica was looking forward to visiting the notorious Wild Man's Crossing.

'Was there a wild man?' asked Dougie as they drove through the bright warm morning, already promising a hot day.

'Wild Man Johnson was a buffalo hunter, I've been told,' said Veronica, remembering Collette's comment.

'Yes, he was another one of those characters from the old days. He ran some cattle but mixed more with the local tribes people than he did with white people,' said Jamie. 'I'm sure he was a visitor to Brolga Springs in the early days. Apparently he'd periodically get on the grog and run amok, hence the nickname.'

'I wonder what happened to him,' said Veronica.

'Hard to say, don't think he had an official family,' said Jamie.

'You mean he had a black wife?' said Veronica.

'Probably. It was quite common and another reason he didn't mix in white society. Anyway his legacy is his name attached to a very notorious spot.'

The road they were now on was graded and seemed well used. As they turned past a ranger station they came to a bitumen parking lot where a tourist bus was parked. Beside it were public facilities, toilets, a picnic shelter and a barbecue. A bus driver in shorts, long white socks and a shirt with a company logo on it was setting out plastic glasses on a picnic table, an Esky of cold drinks beside him for a group of foreign tourists. A pathway wound a short distance to the broad river that glinted benignly in the sun. Even from where they'd stopped Veronica could see the now familiar large yellow 'Achtung' beware notice above the zigzag jaws of a croc's head. These signs seemed to be everywhere in the Top End, even beside the smallest pool of water.

Jamie came over with one of the local tour guides. The girl was dressed in a bright yellow T-shirt with an NT logo.

'This is Justine, she's going to take you down the river, give you a bit of a talk about her country on the other side.'

'You comin', Jamie?' asked Justine.

'Oh, I guess so. See if your spiel is up to scratch.' He smiled.

'Spiel? I'm talking true story here, fella,' she kidded him back.

'Right. This is Veronica and this is Dougie, they're making a bit of a documentary for TV.'

'Yeah, is that so? All right, let's go.'

'What about the tourists over there, are they coming with us?' asked Veronica.

'Yeah, once I get them rounded up. Backpackers can be a bit hard to organise, sometimes.' She pointed out her shallow, blunt-nosed aluminium boat with a canopy to shade passengers. There was a narrow portable aluminium walkway from the boat to the small wooden landing on the bank.

'Walk smartly, don't linger by the water,' advised Justine as she ushered them onto the vessel.

Veronica gave Jamie a questioning look and he nodded.

'Yes, there are a lot of crocs in here.' He pointed at the opposite bank. 'Keep your eyes peeled. Several of them will drift to the middle of the river. Justine knows where they are, most of the time.'

Dougie settled himself in the bow with the camera and Jamie sat beside Veronica, waiting for Justine to organise the tourists.

'This is a great initiative, these indigenous tours,' said Jamie. 'You can't beat the local people talking about their own country. They've all come back here from various places and work with the tourists.'

'There wasn't work here for them before this?' asked Veronica.

'No. Tourism is the way of the future, that's for sure,' said Jamie. 'What the hell?' He stood up as he heard raised voices.

Veronica swung around. Some of the tourists were at the landing and Veronica watched in horror as they peeled off tops to reveal swimsuits. Two or three had snorkels and one was putting on flippers. Justine was remonstrating with a large red-faced man who was gesticulating and shaking his head.

'We pay. We come to see everything. We good swimming people.'

'Swim! Are you nuts!' snapped Justine with a raised voice. 'See that sign? No swimming! Danger. Crocodiles. Yum yum. Eat people.' She made wild gestures but the visitors continued to prepare themselves for a swim.

Veronica looked at the river framed by cabbage tree palms, pandanus and reeds while its crystal clear water flowed gently past. The air was balmy, the water bathtub warm. It all looked very inviting. Jamie scrambled to the stern of the boat where Justine was standing, holding the rope and arguing with the apparent leader of the group.

Jamie stepped ashore and went up to the man, speaking calmly to him. But the man remained adamant and shook his head.

Jamie turned back to Justine. 'Bring the bus driver down here, please.'

The driver hurried to Jamie, relieved to see someone with some authority dealing with the situation. 'They won't listen, I've told them . . .'

'Why do they think they can do this?' asked Jamie. 'Surely you've explained the danger.'

The driver wrung his hands. 'Mate, they have all the info. But they've had a few let downs, these things happen, so now they don't believe a thing anyone tells 'em. I've tried to tell them they could get killed, but they've laughed it off. They tell me that I don't want them to enjoy themselves. I think they've mixed up their crocs, you know, freshies with salties. I'm not responsible for any of this. I've told them. They understand enough English.'

'Okay, calm down. Go back to the ranger station and make a report, tell them these people are ignoring your warnings.' Jamie turned back to the tourists and spoke in a soothing voice. 'Sir, there seems to be some misunderstanding. I'd like to ask you and your friends to join the rest of us on the boat. Come for a short trip down the river. Let us show you what it's like before you go for a swim.'

'We swim later?' asked the man.

'If you still want to. I'd like you to learn a little about this area first. Justine, our tour guide, knows this river very well. Just a short trip downstream. I think you might find it instructive,' he added.

The man turned to the rest of his group and as one woman began to head to the water Jamie spoke firmly, 'Everyone must come or no-one comes.'

After more discussion the group agreed to board the boat. Jamie smiled and helped them all to settle into the rows of seats.

It was not just Dougie filming the scenery. All the tourists had cameras and they took photographs as the boat nosed into the river and chugged slowly along. Jamie glanced at Justine and she slowed the engine when a break in the vegetation along the bank revealed a small sandy patch of red soil while at the water's edge it was grey-brown mud. The bank was marked by two smooth slides and at the bottom, with the tip of its snout in the water, basked a very large crocodile. Jamie tapped one of the women on the shoulder and pointed to it with a smile.

The woman turned and looked, then screamed. Suddenly everyone was shouting, looking shocked and dazed as the reality of the maneater's presence finally dawned on them. They rushed to one side of the boat to photograph the huge reptile.

'Hey, steady on, stay on both sides of the boat, please,' called Justine. 'There's another one up ahead on the other side. See, in the shallow water.'

She nosed the boat a shade closer to the floating croc than she normally would, so that the foreigners could take in its long snout, protruding teeth and mean-looking eyes that watched this boat cruise past twice a day. Further along there were two smaller crocs on the bank and the tourists began chattering amongst themselves.

'These ones, they attack men?' asked the group's leader.

'And women,' said Jamie affably. 'And children and cattle and dogs and fish.'

'That's why there are signs saying "No Swimming",' added Justine, just in case they'd missed the point.

'Can we shoot them?' asked the man.

Jamie shook his head. 'Sorry, mate, these animals are protected. Endangered species, so you can only shoot them with a camera.'

'But so many are here! Why are there no safaris to shoot these ones?'

Veronica imagined they were now reassessing this place no longer as a recreational spot but more as a big game experience.

Jamie was polite and patient and carefully explained how the crocodiles had almost been hunted to extinction, but since they had been protected their numbers had increased. Now there were special farms that bred them for their skins and meat.

Justine turned the boat around and returned the foreigners to the landing where they shook Jamie's hand and made a hasty return to the picnic area.

Justine set out again in the boat, with just Jamie, Veronica and Dougie and they motored back down the river.

'Justine has a lot of stories about this country,' said Jamie. 'The tourists love her.'

She took them further down river to a strip of white sandy beach, which she assured them, was safe as there were no resident crocs in the immediate vicinity. A few metres up on the bank the land was cleared and a bough roof suspended on slim tree trunks shaded some woven mats on the ground below. They went ashore and sat down and Justine handed around examples of weaving, carvings, utensils and digging sticks made by the local women.

'We bring people here for a bit of a talk about this country and my people, then we take the women out to look for bush tucker and medicine plants and the men go for a sort of hunting walk. They can learn to throw a boomerang or a spear and learn how to catch goanna and snake and that sort of thing. Then we make a campfire and have a bush tucker lunch. Just gives tourists an idea of how we live,' said Justine with some pride.

Dougie, who had been filming her, asked if she'd show him some bush plants which were important to the Aboriginal way of life. 'Where's the white sand from?' he asked. 'Not from the river. It's too muddy.'

Justine pointed to the distant range of jagged hills. 'It blew down from up there quite recently. It got dumped in the river and blocked up one of the entrances. I used to take the boat much further along, closer to the gorge so people could see the rock art and carvings up on the cliffs. It's harder now.'

'Have you always lived here?' asked Veronica.

Justine shook her head. 'Nah, I worked for a mining company to make money, but after a year I had to leave. I couldn't stand what they were doing to my country, digging it up like that. The old men cried when they saw all the sacred places getting dug up, buried or carted away. So now we want people to know the real story 'bout this land.' She got up. 'C'mon Doug, I show you plenty good things for your camera.'

Jamie smiled at Veronica. 'Shall we sit in the shade? Or do you want to go with Dougie?'

'He'll be right. I'll look at the footage when we edit it. He can get Justine to explain what things are.'

'She will, she's a good talker and knowledgeable.'

'That was funny with those tourists wanting to swim. You handled them very well, Jamie.'

'Yeah. Could've been interesting. Dealing with the

public can be a challenge. I try to leave that to the other people.'

'But you're very good at it.'

'It wears me out, I can be impatient.' He smiled. 'You don't know my bad traits.'

'There's a lot I don't know about you,' said Veronica, then felt embarrassed.

'And I about you,' he said.

'I'm not very interesting. You have two cultures, a huge, wonderful family, a fascinating job and lifestyle,' began Veronica, but he held up his hand.

'And a lot of baggage comes with that, Veronica,' he said seriously. 'And I have a son and a commitment to him.'

'Surely that's a good thing,' said Veronica.

'Sometimes. But it means I'm not a free man,' he added awkwardly and stood up, gazing at the river with his back to her.

Veronica looked at his lean, straight back and saw the tension in his shoulders, the taut muscles in his neck. 'What would you be doing if you didn't have such a sense of duty and responsibility?' she asked gently.

He shrugged, turned and ran his fingers through his hair, his gold and hazel eyes soft. It was a gesture that tugged at her. Then he smiled. 'Ah, I'd probably take off to Sydney, ask you out to dinner. Take you somewhere silly.'

'That sounds nice.' She smiled back at him and saw the intensity in his eyes belying his easy smile.

He looked away and his smile faded. 'It's not going to happen, Veronica. I really like you. But Sydney is a long way away.'

She didn't know what to say. She had felt drawn to him since they'd first met and while irrationally she longed to leap up and put her arms around him and kiss his perfect mouth, she understood what he was saying.

'That's okay. We all have commitments. I have my

job . . .' Her voice trailed off as she realised what she'd said. She'd put her job first. 'What I mean is, my family are all good, comfortable and can look after themselves. I'm a free agent, I suppose. I've never considered these things,' she finished lamely. Then seeing Dougie and Justine returning she asked, 'Where to next?'

'The Crossing. Are you ready?'

'Yes. I just wish Topov's ghost could appear and tell us what happened.'

'I don't think there's much chance of that,' said Jamie with a laugh.

'Okay, let's go. This might be the final curtain call,' she said. 'Unless we find Marta to tell us more.'

The country changed yet again. From the vast red spaces stretching to a distant horizon it plunged into lush emerald jewels of palm-fringed pools, paperbark swamps and rich grass marshes.

'Buffalo country,' said Jamie. 'Buffaloes make a dreadful mess environmentally and since being introduced they've became a feral pest.'

'Weren't they culled from Kakadu?' asked Veronica.

'Yes. There was an eradication program for ten years up to the mid-nineties, but they're still out of control in parts of the Top End.'

'Good for big game hunting,' said Dougie.

'Some buffaloes are shot for pet food and there's some live export trade. I have a friend who has a herd and he makes cheese from the milk,' said Jamie.

'I filmed a big mob from a chopper, once,' said Dougie. 'It looked beautiful, a stampede of huge beasts through the floodplains in the wet, but apparently they gouge tracks that become swim channels in the floods and this has caused a lot of problems.'

'This a field you're interested in then, Jamie?' said Veronica.

'Can't you tell?' he said with a smile. 'There are so many environmental problems here in the Territory.'

'Have you thought about entering politics?' asked Veronica. 'You and your mother have so much to offer.'

'I've thought about it. I'm in no position to do that just yet.'

'Billy?'

'And I need to learn more.' He changed the subject. 'There's the South Alligator River again. We turn off the track here, Wild Man is further downstream.'

'It's very pretty,' said Veronica. 'I can see why you'd want to camp here,' she said thinking of Topov and his party.

'Up here you're pretty safe. But I wouldn't be washing dishes in the river,' said Jamie.

They arrived at the Crossing ten minutes later. Jamie parked on the rise and Dougie leapt out to get the camera.

'I'll shoot you both going down to the Crossing,' said Dougie, then paused. 'There's water going over it. Can we get through that?'

Veronica looked at the smooth river meandering to the stone wall that made a causeway between the two banks. The green water slipped across it and cascaded a short distance into the deeper part of the river on the other side. 'I have no sense of danger here,' she said. 'It's deceptive. Can we drive through that water?'

'In this vehicle, no problem. But the water's actually deeper than it looks, probably a foot or so, and the current can be quite strong.'

'There's no-one here,' said Dougie. 'That's good.'

'Let's explore. Veronica, do you want to take photos as well as film?' asked Jamie.

'Absolutely. Jamie, could you tell me on camera about Wild Man Johnson?'

Jamie took her arm as they made their way down the steep track towards the river as Dougie filmed. At the bottom, Jamie talked easily and entertainingly about the Crossing and how it got its name. Then he added, 'There are negotiations underway to lay hundreds of kilometres of fibre optic cable through Arnhem Land, including under this river bed, to connect communities to broadband.'

'That must be a challenge, given the terrain and the wildlife,' said Veronica.

'Yes, indeed. So shall we cross and explore the Arnhem Land side?'

It was the perfect cue to get back into the car. Jamie drove Dougie to the other side as Veronica waited, taking photographs of the bow wave swirling around the vehicle. Then Dougie filmed Jamie driving her across.

'It feels different, knowing that I'm in traditional country,' said Veronica as she stepped from the car.

'It's the biggest Aboriginal freehold area in Australia and its culture is still very much alive here,' said Jamie, aware Dougie had his camera trained on him. 'This is where the yidaki, or didgeridoo originated.'

'Can you play one?' asked Veronica.

He shook his head. 'Not very well. Let's go a little further on foot, see what wildlife we might find.'

Veronica nodded to Dougie but he'd already turned his camera on the bird life swarming around them. Graceful white egrets, dainty jabiru, flocks of magpie geese and the flash of a sacred kingfisher diving into the river, all ignoring their presence.

'Look at those colours,' said Veronica, pointing to a spectacular plant beside the track. 'Pink flowers and red seeds.'

'It's a turkey bush. The branches are nice and straight, good for spears and the seeds are poisonous but the women make necklaces from them.' As Dougie filmed a close-up of the bunches of red seeds, Jamie continued, 'Aboriginal people look at flora and fauna differently from white people. For example, there aren't just the wet and the dry seasons. They have five seasons and the weather dictates what food to find and when and what to hunt.'

Veronica looked around her. 'There's a whole language and history here isn't there that we can't see?'

'It's why white engineers, mining people, government officials, developers, can't understand why they shouldn't dig the ground, or move rocks and fell trees. They see physical structures like buildings or bridges or roads or stockyards as evidence of civilisation that should be preserved, but Aborigines have a different concept of what heritage means.'

Veronica nodded. 'I see. Those hills over there, that ridge line, it's very distinctive. It looks like a huge mushroom.'

Jamie smiled. 'Yes it does. There are so many other interesting things in this region. Plants and minerals just waiting to be discovered.'

They walked a little further until they came to a waterhole below a small flat-topped jump-up.

'I guess these formations are called jump-ups because they just jump out of the ground, like a little plateau,' said Veronica as she took a photo.

'This is Palm Tree waterhole. There's been one palm tree growing here for years. I heard some old fellas tried to plant other palms but they won't grow. Just this one old one survives,' said Jamie. 'Let's stop a minute.'

They sat on a flat rock by the pool of water ringed with small waterlilies. Dougie wandered around looking for things to point his camera at and Veronica took off her shoes and splashed her feet in the cool water.

'Thanks for bringing me out here, Jamie. I'm trying to imagine whether Topov came here, sat here.'

'He would've been in this area if he walked over the Crossing, but he might not have come this way.' He lifted his arms in a vague gesture. 'Who knows?'

They returned over the Crossing and Veronica glanced back at the benign scene. 'Poor old Topov.'

On the way back to Darwin the next day Jamie announced, 'I have to make a small detour and call in at the Jabiru Land Council office. Would you like to stop and have a coffee at the Croc Resort?'

'That hotel shaped like a crocodile? I'd like to see it,' said Dougie.

'You can always get something to eat, to go with your coffee,' suggested Jamie.

'Sounds like a plan to me,' said Veronica.

Back in Darwin Jamie dropped Dougie and his gear at the TV station and Veronica at her hotel.

'When can I see you?' he asked. 'Billy wants to cook for you again.'

'That's lovely, but I feel it's my turn. How about I take you and Billy down to the wharf for dinner? Or is there somewhere else you can suggest?' asked Veronica.

'He'd love the wharf. And if he gets bored he can wander around while we share a bottle of wine.'

'Done. What time would suit you guys?'

Jamie glanced at his watch. 'Is an hour enough for you? We could catch the sunset and it won't be a late night for Billy.'

The lights and neon signs from the various restaurants reflected on the dark water. Fishing boats and pleasure cruisers glided past the long crowded wharf. Music from a party boat outlined in lights could be heard above the din. But Jamie had asked for a table tucked in a corner out of the evening breeze. They were screened from the rest of the diners by potted palms and Veronica thought it one of the most romantic places she'd eaten in a long time.

They'd all chosen the mud crab, which was a messy but hilarious meal. After dinner Billy was allowed to leave the table and go and buy an ice-cream.

Jamie topped up Veronica's glass of wine and touched his glass against hers.

'I've enjoyed your company, Veronica. I hope you come again.'

'Of course I will,' she said. Then she thought, what if I have no reason to return? The thought bothered her. She was very attracted to Jamie. Not just for his looks and charm; she found him interesting, they'd talked about so many different things and she was discovering that beneath his rather shy reserve he could be quite beguiling. 'I love your company. And Billy's. And you've been so helpful. You know what Dougie asked me?'

Jamie shook his head, a smile lurking at the corners of his mouth, warmth shining in his eyes.

'He wanted to know how long I'd known you as we seemed such good friends. He figured we'd known each other down south or somewhere.'

'There you go, then. But I feel like that too.'

'So we have to keep in touch,' said Veronica firmly. 'If you come to Sydney, I'll show you some of my favourite spots.'

'I don't know when that might be, but I'll take you up on it.'

Billy was dozing in the back seat of the four-wheel drive as Jamie pulled up at the Mantra.

'Say goodnight to Billy for me,' she said softly. Jamie got out of the car, opened the back and returned with a parcel.

'I will. This is by way of a souvenir of your time in Darwin. I hope you like it, it's one of Auntie Nellie's paintings. Let me know your plans.' He leaned over and kissed her cheek. She didn't move but her eyes closed in pleasure and he brushed her lips with his. 'Thank you, Jamie. Thank you for everything.'

In the morning she called Andy. 'Well, the Crossing was a bit of a dud. Beautiful, serene, empty. The Crossing's a sort of weir, a wall with no sides. Tricky with water running over it. But who knows what went on. Maybe Topov fell off it, maybe he walked too near the bank.'

'And on the other side of the Crossing?'

'Interesting country but who's to say what Topov did or even if he was there. I took a heap of photos. It has a kind of distinctive landscape. Perhaps I'm getting my eye in. It all looks so different from when I first arrived. Jamie has really opened my eyes.'

'Is that so?'

She could hear the amused tone in Andy's voice. 'So is he planning a trip to Sydney anytime soon?'

'I don't know, Andy! I hope so but it's unlikely. He's such a dish. But more, a lovely man with integrity and intelligence and he's so interesting to talk to. I mean, not just about Aboriginal culture, but everything. And most importantly, he makes me laugh. Not belly laughs, but he has a gentle humour.'

'And a son and a family.'

'Yes,' sighed Veronica. 'No wife though, she died. So, I think he's lonely even though he has hundreds of relatives. But Andy, it makes me seriously wonder what I ever saw in Eddie. He is such a selfish egotist. What was I thinking when I hooked up with him? I don't think that I ever had an intelligent conversation with him and now we can't even work together.'

'Well, unless you're planning to move to Darwin, that's unlikely to happen.'

'Hey, enough of me,' said Veronica. 'Tell me, what news on Marta?'

'Ah, yes. I almost forgot in the machinations of your love life . . .'

'I wish. Go on.'

'We have her current address and phone number.'

'Yay! Where is she? Is she still in LA? Should we go and knock on her door?'

'We've tried ringing, but all we get is a woman saying she doesn't know Marta Johanssen. But I'll keep trying. I'd hate to send you all the way to Lake Como for nothing.'

'Lake Como! Italy?'

Andy chuckled. 'How about that? She must have retired there.'

'That's a pretty upmarket place to live, isn't it? She must have done very well in the film industry to afford a place like that, although I've never heard of her. Well, it's all very confusing.'

'I've couriered her a package, tapes of our show and a long letter detailing what we know and why we want to pursue this story and assuring her that you are a person of the highest integrity.'

'Are you serious? About me going over there, I mean?'

'We have the budget now, if you recall.'

Veronica was stunned. 'I won't say no. Gosh, Darwin to Lake Como. Bit of a jump. Now we just need to find Madame Olga.'

'She'll be long gone, I imagine. She must have been pushing fifty when the expedition set out,' said Andy.

'Yes, you're right. Still, it'd be interesting to find out how she ended her days,' said Veronica. 'Colin said that she had a couple of daughters. Perhaps you could find them.'

'I think it's going to be hard to find out about anyone unless they kept in touch with Marta.'

'Or John Cardwell.'

'Somehow I don't think that would've happened,'

mused Andy. 'As you say, the whole project came to an ugly and tragic end so I suppose they all went their own ways after that.'

'So the final scenes of the story rest with Marta. I hope we can get her to talk to us,' said Veronica. 'I wonder what she remembers of the last night at Wild Man Crossing.'

11

Cloud obscured Veronica's view as the plane began to descend. When it broke through the cloud cover, mist swirled through soft rain and mauve haze above the grey industrial city beneath. The scene looked utterly bleak and she realised that her eyes were still used to the bold, bright, strong colours of the Northern Territory. What a change this was from the warmth and openness of the outback.

She'd barely had time to adjust to being back in Sydney after her trip to the Top End when Andy had called her into his office.

'Glad you're back. I'm looking forward to seeing your footage.'

'It looks good. Hard not to get great shots as everything is so scenic. I just wish I had more specific stuff that related directly to Topov's expedition, but at least now I have a sense of how it must have been. I'd love to go back and see more of that part of the country.'

'And more of Jamie McIntosh?'

She sighed. 'He's lovely. But I'm here, he's there. Now, what news do you have? Any luck with talking to Marta?'

'No. We still haven't spoken to her.'

'I've left that to you.' He slipped a piece of paper across his desk. 'We found her because she did some small roles in Hollywood so she still gets residual payments from SAG. Here's her current address and phone number.'

Veronica glanced at the paper. 'Lovely Lake Como. Do you think she'd know George Clooney?'

'I'll ignore that comment. She also has an address in Los Angeles and one in London. Let me know what she has to say. That will determine our next move. If she agrees to talk to you I've got an ace cameraman in the London office on standby. Give Geoff the word and he'll zip over to the Continent.'

'I'll call her after I've checked the time difference.' Veronica's mind was spinning as she tried to plot what to say to Marta. Three residential addresses. That was interesting. She hoped that Marta would be willing to hear her out and not dismiss her because the Topov expedition was a distant, brief episode in her life.

When she rang the phone number, a woman's voice, very clipped and curt, finally answered it.

'Pronto.'

'May I speak to Marta Johanssen, please?'

'Scusi?' There was a pause. 'There is no Marta Johanssen here.'

'Oh, I'm sorry. I don't know her married name. She was Marta Johanssen when she was an actress. Is she available, please?'

'Who is speaking?'

'I am Veronica Anderson. I work for Network Eleven television in Australia.'

There was a brief pause. 'Momento,' and the phone was put down with a clatter.

Veronica heard voices speaking in rapid Italian and at last there was a response.

'Hello? This is Marta Luccosa.' The accent was difficult to pin down, European but musical. It was the voice of a mature woman but it was light and curious and sounded as though laughter came easily to it.

Veronica introduced herself and briefly explained what she was doing. 'I know this must be a bit of a bolt out of the blue after all these years. I've just come back from the Northern Territory and I've been to Brolga Springs. It's a stunning place,' finished Veronica.

'Yes. I have special memories of the scenery,' answered Marta. 'Tell me again, why are you interested in our little excursion all those years ago? I received a package but I haven't looked at it thoroughly.'

Andy's parcel probably hadn't even been opened, thought Veronica. 'It's to do with the history of the Australian film and television industry. I know how little the outback featured in documentaries and films in the fifties and, when I heard the story of Topov and his brave idea, I thought it would be an interesting part of the whole story. Especially the films that didn't get made because the landscape defeated the filmmakers. It would be wonderful if we could see some of the film Mr Topov did shoot.'

'There wasn't so much. But I doubt any film exists anywhere. It was a wild idea and we were all crazy to go. Though it had its moments.' She hesitated. 'How did you hear about this?'

Veronica chose her words carefully. 'Some of my professional colleagues are film and TV veterans who met

Colin Peterson at a dinner and he mentioned the trip in passing. That sparked my interest.'

'Oh, I see. Have you, yourself met Colin? How is he? We haven't been in touch for several years.'

'He seems well. I met him briefly but his reminiscences are sketchy. I was hoping you could perhaps tell me what you recall of the trip.'

'Right now? I'm sorry I have no time, my dear. I am leaving for a luncheon party in my honour tomorrow. Besides, it would take days to drag through all that scenario.'

If Marta thought she'd put Veronica off, she was caught by surprise with Veronica's response. 'Of course. I can imagine you'll need time to think about things. I was planning to be in Italy next week. Is it possible we could meet?'

There was a short hesitation. 'I couldn't say . . .'

'I'll call you again and give you my details. Or would you like me to email you my background, the company I work for . . .?'

'Oh, I don't deal with such things. Dominico handles that sort of thing.'

'Great. I'll call back and talk to Dominico and then send him my details. I'd love to meet you Mrs Luccosa. I feel I know you.'

'And why might that be?' She sounded bemused rather than put out.

'I read a reference to your visit to Brolga Springs homestead in Mrs Johns's diary in the archives in Darwin. And do you recall the little Aboriginal girl, Doris, whom you met there? You gave her a silver bracelet.'

Marta was silent for a moment. 'Yes. I remember her,' she said softly.

'She's never forgotten you. And she still has the bracelet. It's one of her greatest treasures,' said Veronica.

'That's incredible. Is she still at that station? It was quite primitive.'

'You couldn't imagine – in your wildest dreams – what has become of Doris,' said Veronica. 'It's good, all good. I have some photos I can show you of Doris, if you'd like. Will you be staying there at Lake Como much longer?'

'Till the season is over and then I go to London. And I will be in California for Christmas.'

'I was hoping to talk to you soon. And as I'll be in Italy . . .' Veronica tried to sound as though she was a frequent visitor, even though she hadn't booked a ticket and was vague about its geography.

'As you say. Please, call again. In a day or so. I must think about all this.'

The arrangements had fallen into place easily and here she was flying to Milan where she was staying overnight before taking the train to Varenna on Lake Como. Before leaving Australia, Veronica had emailed Jamie to ask him to tell Doris that she was going to see Marta. He rang her to say that his mother was thrilled with the news and passed on Billy's 'hello hug'.

'It would be great if you can keep us all updated,' he said. 'Besides we all miss you, especially me.'

In Milan Veronica told the taxi driver, 'Hotel Straf, Via San Raffaele, please.'

He nodded. 'I know. Very trendy, nice hotel. Around the corner from the Galleria. You go take espresso there in the morning.'

'I'll do that,' said Veronica.

Her hotel was charming and she quickly gathered it was the haunt of artistic, bohemian-looking guests. She decided to telephone Marta to set up a meeting as soon as possible. The brusque-sounding lady who answered the phone, seemed surprised when Veronica asked to speak to Mrs Luccosa in order to find out a time that was convenient for her to visit.

Marta came on the line, sounding slightly vague. 'Oh, you're here.'

Veronica could hear the pages of a diary being turned. 'Tomorrow. Is it convenient?'

'Ah, yes. Of course.'

'Please come around before lunch. I will tell my staff to expect you.'

Veronica caught the train to the romantic village of Varenna on the lake, with its promenade, tiny harbour, narrow lanes and cafés beside the lakeside walk. The Hotel Olivedo conveniently faced the ferry dock and her room, with its tiny balcony, had a view of the lake and the distant snow-capped Alps. The following morning the businesslike hotel manager explained that Bellagio, where Marta lived, was just a ferry stop away.

From the water the full impact of the luxurious old mansions, now turned into exclusive hotels, the grand villas and busy villages with their squares, piazzas, fountains and boutiques confirmed that this was a place for the mega wealthy, a playground for the rich and famous.

When she arrived at Marta's summer home, Veronica was awestruck. The house was an imposing old pink stucco villa of three storeys with high windows framed with deep aubergine shutters. It had small turrets and a balustrade with stone eagles. There were gargoyles on each end on the roof and a circular wall on one corner gave the villa the look of a magical castle. Chimney pots dotted the gabled tiled roof. Shrubs and trees scattered flowers onto an emerald lawn. There were Juliet balconies on the windows facing the lake and striped awnings shaded the side windows from the full sun. The lawns swept down to a stone wall at the water's edge where an ivy-covered stone cottage sat beside the boat landing. Tall dark pine trees behind the villa screened it from the bald, grey rockfaces of the cliff and protected the grand old building from winter weather.

Veronica walked from the boat landing up a flight of lichen-covered stone steps guarded by stone gargoyles and across a flagstone path that wound past brilliant shrubbery to another flight of stone steps leading to a carved wooden door flanked by matching topiary orange trees in ornate pots. As she walked up the steps, the massive door swung open and a severely dressed woman with a matching expression waited for her with her hands folded.

'Good morning. I'm Veronica Anderson.'

The woman nodded and turned inside. 'Please follow me. Signora Luccosa is waiting for you.'

Veronica followed the taut-shouldered woman who gave the impression that Veronica was tardy when in fact she was early. Veronica wished the woman would walk more slowly as she wanted to absorb the beautiful interior of the house. The pale terracotta stone floor of the ground-floor entrance hall was covered in antique rugs. Tapestries hung along the walls. She followed the woman through the main foyer and up a curved staircase to the first floor. The thick, deeply burnished wooden floorboards were scattered with Persian rugs and portraits of dour-looking relatives in dark oils hung in ornate gold frames along the walls.

The woman opened a tall white door and gestured to Veronica to go in, announcing, 'Signorina Anderson.'

'Grazie, Allegra. Café e torta, per favore.'

Veronica stepped into the room and blinked at the burst of sunlight after the dim hallways. Floor to ceiling windows looked towards the lake. The room was pale lemon and white, feminine and elegant and this seemed to reflect its occupant.

Marta rose from a gold brocade wing-back chair and came towards Veronica. She was petite and dainty. Her curvy figure was neatly outlined by a fitted cashmere top. Her hair was bright auburn, curling fashionably round a face that belied her years although Veronica noticed that her jaw line was a little too sharp and her face a little too smooth. But for a woman eighty years of age, she looked twenty, even thirty, years younger and she radiated wealth and good taste.

Veronica shook her soft white hand and wished she knew the name of the alluring perfume that drifted around Marta.

Marta gave her a dazzling smile. 'How charming, such a pretty woman you are. And to come all this way. Surely not just to see me? Take a seat. Allegra will bring coffee and a sweet cake.' Marta sat and crossed her ankles, her feet shod in soft grey leather ballet flats with the Chanel double C silver buckle on top. Her heavily made-up blue eyes studied Veronica.

'This is a stunning home and you don't live here all the time?' asked Veronica.

'No, only in the season. Our other home is in Brentwood in Los Angeles. We have a townhouse in London as my husband goes there on business but I tend to go there less these days. I like the sun and warmth.'

'You had a lot of sun in Australia,' said Veronica.

Marta gave a small musical laugh. 'We did. I thought I would shrivel like an old prune. I hope you look after your skin, it's a cruel climate. Do you live in the north of Australia?'

'No. In Sydney. But I fell in love with the outback. The Territory is so special. Kakadu National Park is magic and I was lucky enough to go into Arnhem Land. And to Brolga Springs.'

'Some of those places I remember but I haven't

thought about them for a very long time,' she said softly. 'You mentioned the little Aboriginal girl, Doris?'

'She is an impressive woman now. She has a wonderful family.'

'Of course, she would be all grown up now. It was a long time ago, but I remember her beautiful eyes, that wild curly hair and a smile to break your heart. She was shy but wild like a horse. What do you call the wild horses . . .?'

'Brumbies.'

'Yes. That time in Australia was really very short, yet I have some very vivid memories.' Marta looked out the window and was saved from further comment by Allegra entering with a silver tray that held two glasses of steaming coffee in silver holders and a plate of sweet pastries.

'Grazie, Allegra.' Marta gestured to Veronica. 'Please help yourself.'

Allegra gave Marta a questioning glance and when Marta shook her head, the woman quietly left the room. Veronica glanced at the angular woman as she closed the door behind her.

'Allegra has been with this villa since she was a child. Her mother worked here also.'

'How interesting. Is your husband Italian?' asked Veronica.

'Paolo is from an old Milanese family. We met in Hollywood. But he has nothing to do with the film business.' She gave Veronica a smile. 'I had just done a small role in a film and was being promised big things. But I fell in love.'

'Did you work again?' asked Veronica.

'I chose not to. We have such a full life. Paolo is an industrialist. His family own factories and with three homes and a very busy social life, my little acting career seemed rather self-indulgent and unimportant.'

'I heard you were a very good actress,' said Veronica.

'I saw the write-up of the one-woman show you put on in Darwin.'

'You did! Yes, Colin helped me so much with that. It was the only way I could think of to make some money, as we were stranded there.' She lifted the tiny glass of espresso. 'That man Topov caused a lot of problems and angst,' she said mildly. 'On reflection I wonder about him. I wish we'd known more. He was a secretive fellow, loose with the real facts, but he lived life to the full. I also have been privileged to live a full life.'

Veronica could see Marta must have lived a life of great wealth. She reached into her handbag and took out several photographs. 'Please, let me show you the photos I have of Doris and her family.' She handed them to Marta, explaining, 'This is Doris, her son, two daughters and their husbands and her grandchildren. This is Doris and her husband Alistair, he's a Scottish academic. Well, he was. He's retired now. And this is Jamie, her son, with Billy, her grandson.'

Marta lifted the photos and studied them closely. Veronica suspected she might need glasses but was too proud to put them on. 'Oh, my. This lady, this is little Doris. And what handsome children!' She glanced at Veronica. 'Where is the wife of this beautiful young man?'

'Jamie's wife was killed when Billy was a baby. Very sad. Doris and her husband help to look after the little boy.' Veronica quickly sketched a potted history of Doris's life.

Marta shook her head. 'How different our lives have been. But Doris, she has done well for herself, especially when one considers where she started.' She glanced again at the photos. 'May I keep one of these?'

'They're for you. Doris has very fond memories of you because of the silver bracelet you gave her. She always felt a lucky star was watching over her.'

'I remember that. It was a spontaneous gesture. I thought she would have lost it or given it away within a day. She was such a tomboy. That's very touching.' She straightened up in her chair, coming to a decision. 'So, Miss Anderson, what exactly do you want to know?'

Veronica felt a surge of relief. Marta would talk.

'I want to ask you some questions so you can tell me the sequence of events after you left Brolga Springs. But I'd like you to tell me on camera. That way it's spontaneous.'

Marta gave a half smile. 'You forget I was an actress. I can reproduce spontaneity. But I understand the line of questioning. So we do not need to rehearse. Now, have you a cameraman who knows what he's doing, who can light me properly? I don't want to sound vain at my age, but there's no point in looking worse and older than I need to,' she said firmly. 'And I'll need my hairdresser to come over. Where would you suggest filming this? There's a sheltered corner of the terrace with the garden and lake behind it which might look pretty. It's quiet so there won't be any sound problems.'

The way she took control made Veronica smile to herself.

'Perhaps early tomorrow morning, when the light is soft. Say nine?'

'That would be wonderful. And I can assure you Geoff is a terrific cameraman. He's out of London and has shot a lot of celebrity interviews and is very particular about keeping women subjects happy.'

'I appreciate that.' Marta glanced at the small diamond watch on her wrist. 'Miss Anderson . . .'

'Please, Veronica.'

'Then you may call me Marta. I have a table waiting at Villa d'Este. I was going to take a light lunch there. I go there several days a week. Would you care to join me? Perhaps we can talk about Australia.'

Veronica was so relieved that Marta had agreed to do the interview that she didn't want anything to go wrong and the lure of dining at the fabulous hotel was too good an opportunity to pass up. 'I'd adore that. But please, you must let me treat you, as a guest of our show.'

Marta airily waved a hand. 'Nonsense, your employer will not be happy with such an extravagance. I have an account, it is my pleasure.' She lifted the small bell next to the coffee tray and within moments of its tinkle, Allegra appeared and Marta asked her to call the boatman.

Veronica followed Allegra who pointed to the guest bathroom and added, 'Augustus will meet you at the front steps.'

Veronica was expecting Augustus to be an aged retainer, but the man who waited for her was in his late thirties and handsome in a boyish Dustin Hoffman kind of way. He was dressed in crisp linen slacks and a white golfing T-shirt.

'Buongiorno.' His accent was soft, sounding more French than Italian. Augustus sprinted up the steps as Marta appeared at the front door wearing dark glasses and a silk scarf tied over her hair. Taking her arm he escorted her to the dock, settling her in the small, sleek motor launch.

As they travelled across the lake, Marta pointed out some of the more spectacular villas and mentioned the names of the people who owned them. The list included European royals, American movie stars and world-famous businessmen.

Augustus guided the launch into the steps of a grand hotel where a huge floating swimming pool bobbed on the unswimmable water of the lake. He escorted Marta through the marble foyer of the hotel and out onto the terrace, where he left her in the company of the maître d', who greeted her warmly and led her to her regular table overlooking the lake. Within minutes sparkling mineral water and two crystal glasses of pink chilled wine were set before them.

'At lunch we only drink rosé. This is Provençal, quite good,' said Marta lifting her glass. 'Here's to you, Veronica.'

She rolled the 'r' and Veronica touched her glass to Marta's. 'Thank you for bringing me here. I can now say I've seen the best of Lake Como.' Veronica tried not to stare at the intriguing guests around them, but Marta ignored them and gave Veronica her undivided attention.

'So now it is my turn. Before you interrogate me, I want to know about you.' Subtly and sometimes quite forthrightly, Marta probed Veronica about her family, her life, her job and her love life. She was chatty, amusing and paid great attention to everything that the Australian girl said, so Veronica found herself confiding in the beautiful older woman.

The lunch was delicious and after two glasses of wine they finished with a small coffee and Marta's favourite biscotti.

'You should be an interviewer, Marta, I've told you more than I've told anyone about myself,' laughed Veronica.

'Surely you and this Jamie have talked about yourselves when you were at Brolga Springs,' said Marta. 'I remember the confidences shared under those stars in the outback of Australia.'

'Colin?' asked Veronica. 'Do you ever wonder about him? Would you ever try to see him again?'

'Do not pre-empt the story,' teased Marta. Then she added, 'No, a card occasionally is enough. I haven't the patience for doddering old fools. I prefer to be the pampered one. And I'm very fortunate, Paolo has always spoiled me.'

She signed the bill and Augustus hovered discreetly near the table. As the waiter pulled her chair away, Marta reached for Augustus's arm without looking, knowing he would be there. Veronica followed them as they weaved between the tables and she realised that Marta was indeed a very pampered woman who could demand and receive the very best of everything.

With Allegra hovering behind her, Marta watched from the front door as Veronica waved goodbye and followed Augustus back to the boat. Her hostess had insisted her boatman take Veronica back to her hotel in Varenna.

'To your hotel?' asked Augustus. 'Or would you like a short scenic trip around the lake?'

'Yes, please.'

When Augustus didn't volunteer any chitchat, Veronica asked him, 'Have you worked for Signora Luccosa a long time?'

'A few years. I work mainly for Signor Paolo and his assistant, Dominico. I haven't been with the family as long as Signora Allegra.'

'That's such a pretty name,' said Veronica, wondering how to find out more about the stern housekeeper without broaching good manners and professional etiquette.

'It means cheerful and happy,' said Augustus. As he glanced at her they both burst out laughing.

With the ice now broken, Augustus pointed out the sights and told her about some of the characters, famous and infamous, who came to the lake each summer.

'I shall collect you tomorrow morning with your cameraman at eight-thirty,' said Augustus as he helped her off at the wharf at Varenna.

'Thank you,' said Veronica. 'I'm very excited the Signora has agreed to be interviewed.'

'I'm sure she will have an interesting story to tell,' said Augustus politely.

But Veronica was sure that Augustus had no idea that his wealthy and cultured employer was once the glamorous young Marta who, with lots of ambition but little money, had followed the dreams of a crazy Russian filmmaker into a country of danger and wild beauty where secrets remained silent.

The following morning Augustus collected Veronica and Geoff the cameraman, who was an Australian working for Network Eleven in London. Although he'd been sent a brief by Andy, Veronica filled him in, aware Augustus could hear their conversation.

'She's a very beautiful woman who has looked after herself and having been an actress, she's very aware of how she'll look on camera . . .'

'No probs, been there, done that. Even the young stars are fussy. Any particular angles we're after? When to zoom in or hang back?'

'Just run with it. It's a long story and I'm not sure how open she might be or if she's going to censor anything, or how clear she will be about details, though she seems as sharp as a tack. She's very charming,' added Veronica.

Geoff was taken aback at the sight of Marta, carefully made-up, hair softly but immaculately in place, dressed in elegant pale aqua pants and jacket, a soft cream silk blouse and a few heart stoppingly beautiful pieces of jewellery. She shook Geoff's hand, thanked him in advance for his consideration and patience and had him eating out of her hand in a flash.

'I have some lovely soft blondies and redheads – lights that is,' he smiled. 'Very flattering. Could you show me where you think it is best to film our conversation?'

'Ah, nice lighting, not just a video camera pushed in my face. I like this.' Marta led him through the French doors to the terrace.

Indoors, Allegra placed a large silver tray set with coffee on the desk in the library where Veronica sat checking her notes.

'Buongiorno, I am Marta's husband,' said a quiet, warm voice.

Veronica turned and pushed her notes aside. 'Buongiorno, I am Veronica Anderson.'

'Please, call me Paolo. I hope you have everything you need?' He waved an arm. 'Allegra will bring you anything you wish, iced water, something to eat?'

'Thank you, but no. The coffee will be lovely. This is very kind of you, I trust we're not interrupting you,' said Veronica, rising to shake his hand. She hoped that she wasn't obviously staring. Marta's husband was tall, straight, tanned, with a head of silver hair and perfect teeth. Even Veronica could tell his clothes were especially tailored for him: a pale-blue, fine, light cotton shirt, white linen trousers, soft leather shoes and a watch with an understated leather band that she imagined probably cost more than she made in a year. While his skin and face carried signs of his age, his bearing and movie-star looks put him in another league. He was a rich and handsome man, but there was a softness about him and the way his exquisite manners focused on her, made Veronica realise what a knockout couple he and Marta were.

'You are most welcome. I'm sorry I wasn't here to greet you yesterday. I have just returned from London.' He waited till she sat back down before lowering himself into a deep armchair and crossing his ankles, revealing smooth, tanned skin. 'Your visit has brought some excitement into Marta's life. I think she is rather elated to be in front of a camera again.' He paused. 'Though this time there is no script. While I do not understand your fascination with this moment in my wife's life, she seems very occupied with the black child she met.'

'Yes, Doris McIntosh. From the wild bush girl with no prospects she's become a very distinguished woman, looked up to as a leader and an educator,' said Veronica.

'Interesting. Australia prides itself on being egalitarian, isn't that so?'

'That's the theory. In practice, sadly, there are too few women like Doris. Despite our image we are probably like most other places,' said Veronica.

Paolo gave her an amused look. 'And are all Australians as frank, clear eyed and honest as yourself?'

'Possibly not. Though as a nation we don't take ourselves too seriously. Being able to laugh at ourselves is a national saving grace.'

Paolo chuckled. 'I like that. European arrogance and English pomposity are tiring. So, would it be fruitful for my wife to visit Australia again? Meet this Doris and her family?'

Veronica's eyes widened as she saw the potential for her story. 'I don't know about fruitful, but I had the impression Marta has a very busy life. I'm sure Doris and her family would welcome her. In fact, I believe it would mean a lot to Doris. She has always kept a memento that Marta gave her.'

Paolo shrugged. 'Australia is far away. It was an idle thought. Perhaps I might mention it to her.'

'It might not be my place, but I would be interested in her reaction,' said Veronica.

Paolo stood up. 'I have board reports to write. I hope your discussion with Marta is what you wish. It has been charming to meet you.'

'Thank you,' said Veronica holding out her hand, which he took and then gently kissed her fingertips.

Marta was sitting in the shade beside a small stone table, a potted clipped orange tree behind her and a vista of the lake in the distance. Geoff had bounced soft light from a reflector onto her skin and the camera was mounted some distance from her using a long lens for a soft effect. It also intruded less on the two chairs at the table.

Veronica sat opposite Marta, put her notes in front of her and smiled. 'Your husband is lovely. I see why you fell in love with him.'

'At first I was attracted to his good looks and the way he courted me so lavishly,' said Marta candidly. 'But then I discovered he had a very caring heart. My life with him has been a very happy one.'

Veronica was tempted to ask if she had ever wondered how far her own acting career might have gone if she had not become an elegant wife and superb hostess managing a complicated life. Veronica still found it hard to believe the transformation of this exquisitely groomed and gracious woman from the feisty and fun-loving Marta she'd come to know through Colin's recounting of their trip with Topov. She pushed the thought away and nodded at Geoff.

'Rolling,' he said quietly.

Marta straightened her shoulders, tilted her head, gazed at Veronica and waited.

Veronica briefly filled her in on the story that Colin had already told her. Then she took a deep breath and said, 'Marta, could we go back to the night before you arrived in Darwin. You'd just left Brolga Springs, said goodbye to Len Buchanan and camped for the night. The following day you headed for Darwin. Could we pick up the story there . . .'

The morning was clear and fresh, the sun beginning to tinge the horizon red and gold. Peter was stirring the hot ashes of the campfire, waiting for the twigs and dried grass to catch. Slowly a thin curl of blue smoke wound skywards and the fire burst to life. Colin poured water from the jerry can into the billy and set it to boil for tea as Marta sleepily emerged from her tent.

'I love the smell of the fire first thing in the morning,' she said, rubbing her hands above the flames to warm them.

'It's the leaves that make it smell so good.'

'What's in the camp oven?'

'Johnny's damper. Warm bread and cocky's joy for breakfast.'

Marta smiled. 'I love that golden syrup.' She sighed. 'I'm going to miss these breakfasts at the campfire.' She perched on a log that they'd dragged beside the fire the night before.

'We'll be camping in Arnhem Land,' said Colin.

'If we get there. We have to get things sorted in Darwin,' said Marta.

'We need to be paid and Drago says he's almost out of film,' said Peter.

'I'm sure Topov has made arrangements with Madame Olga to fix things up,' said Colin optimistically.

By the time everyone was assembled for breakfast, having first packed their gear, the mood around the campfire was friendly, almost jovial. Topov was last to appear. He ate his breakfast and when everyone had finished and started clearing up the campsite he disappeared into his caravan and emerged with the map.

'Johnny, Drago, who driving cars? Come, I show you way on map.'

'Don't worry, Darwin's straight out thataway,' said Johnny.

'We take detour,' announced Topov.

'What?' exclaimed Marta and even Helen looked surprised.

Muttering under his breath, Peter stomped over to Topov who was waving the map.

'Bloody hell, Topov. What sort of a detour? We want to get to Darwin,' said Johnny.

'Ah, this very exciting. Topov make survey, enquiry. We go to Rum Jungle, very close. Secret place, maybe make fortune,' beamed Topov.

The group simply stared at him with varying expressions of anger and annoyance.

'What the hell is Rum Jungle?' demanded Drago. 'What's there? Why do you want to go there?'

'Ah, I hear all about this place when we are in Birdsville. It's place where they find uranium,' said Topov triumphantly.

The group exchanged looks.

'What's uranium for again?' Marta asked Colin.

'What's that got to do with us?' demanded Peter.

Topov lifted his arms in mock surprise. 'This very valuable . . . for making atomic bomb. All world wants uranium.'

'We're not out here to find uranium, we're making a film, aren't we?' said Drago and there was a murmur of agreement.

The mood had now shifted and the brief feeling of camaraderie at breakfast had dissolved. Tensions began to mount but Topov was unswayable.

'We go. Topov hear many things about this place. Big boom in jungle.'

'Boom? You mean like a bomb?' asked Marta fearfully.

Topov clucked at her with a smile, rubbing his fingers together. 'No, boom time. Is big business. Maybe there is much money.'

Peter shook his head and turned away. 'He's a crazy man.'

'We go see. We leave now.' Topov walked to the Land Rover, got in on the passenger's side, opened his map and waited.

With a resigned air the rest of the group finished packing up.

'It's not much of a detour,' said Helen. 'Who knows? Something might come of it.'

'Don't make excuses for him,' said Drago.

'How does Topov know these things?' muttered Johnny.

Johnny took the lead in the Land Rover with Topov beside him. The landscape was not the jungle they'd imagined but once they'd turned off the highway onto a dirt road marked with a hand-painted sign 'Batchelor', they began to notice where heavy machinery had torn through bushland and that a river they crossed was lined with dead paperbark and pandanus trees. Bulldozers and trucks had gouged huge bites from the earth and then seemed to have abandoned the spot in distaste. The open wounds of large ditches scarred the scrub.

'This is all abandoned,' said Drago. 'Not being worked.'

'Just testing I suppose,' said Colin.

'Why such big holes, can't they make a small hole and see what's there?' asked Marta.

The sudden sight of the small township of Batchelor surprised them with its power station, blocks of prefabricated houses, gardens and amenities such as a small school, hotel, shop and community centre. As soon as they drove up to the centre two men came out to meet them.

'You looking for work?' they asked Johnny.

'We were wondering if we could have a look around,' he said with a smile. 'We're just passing through.'

One of the men scowled. 'Nothing to see here.'

Topov leaned across Johnny to speak to them. 'I wish to see mine.'

The men shook their heads. 'Sorry, mate, no sightseers.'

Drago got out of the Jeep and walked over to the men. 'Can we get a cold drink at the store here? We have women with us, they'd like to use the amenities, is that possible?'

The two men looked at each other and shrugged. 'S'pose so. Toilets at the centre, drinks at the shop. Then be on your way.'

The group stood outside the shop as Johnny and Helen passed around bottles of cold drinks.

'Nothing to see here,' said Peter.

'The man in the store said the mine is six miles away anyway,' said Drago. 'And you need a security pass to get in there.'

'What for? What's going on?' asked Marta.

'Who knows?'

Topov came out of the shop looking pleased. 'We go back way. Man in shop Bulgaria man, he tells me way.'

There was a round of groans.

'Forget it, we'll get lost or chased away,' said Peter.

'Shop man say mine very big. Australia has plenty uranium. Everybody look,' said Topov. 'I wish to see mine. Important for film.'

Drago shrugged. 'Six miles isn't too far.'

'I don't know what it has to do with the film,' said Peter.

'I don't like the idea of sneaking in the back way,' said Marta. 'Is that what we're doing?'

'It sounds dangerous to me,' said Colin. 'They're being so security minded and secretive.'

Topov ignored their comments and got back in the vehicle, explaining directions to Johnny. The others followed and it didn't take long before they found themselves in a landscape of levelled trees, the ground scraped clear and a network of bulldozed roads weaving between dumps of ore, pits and an open-cut mine. There were shafts disappearing into the ground that were big enough to drive through. They could also see a complex of sheds, workshops and machinery behind barbed-wire fences.

They drove unimpeded past the mine site and realised that they were at the rear of the township. Then they saw that between the mine site and the neat, if temporary-looking town, was a city made up of scores of tents and small, rough-looking huts. Two men in shorts and boots were sitting on an upturned box. Topov jumped out and went and spoke to them, then waved at Drago to come over.

Drago understood the signal and took the small camera with him. By now the men were on their feet, pointing at the tents and gesticulating. The others got out and went to see what it was all about. Drago was speaking Yugoslav to one of the men who seemed quite agitated.

'What are they saying?' Colin asked Johnny.

'I think they're complaining about the work conditions. Topov wants them to show him round.'

Drago turned to Colin. 'We're going to look at their camp and take some footage. We said we'd show it to their big bosses back in Sydney. In return they're taking us around the mine. Sorry, ladies, no women allowed underground.'

Helen shrugged. 'We'll wait with the vehicles.'

'I'll stay with you,' Colin offered. 'I'm not so interested in all this mining.'

When the men came back an hour later, it was clear that Topov had been in his element. He was enthusiastic and his pockets were bulging with rock samples. 'One man picked up a rock and poof! He finds uranium.'

'They said they didn't know the importance of the rock for years, though,' interjected Peter.

'We hear many good stories.' Topov grinned.

'So why is it called Rum Jungle? Is that what they all do? Drink rum?' asked Marta.

'They told us that about seventy years ago a bullock

team carrying rum got bogged in the jungle near the river so the drivers let the bullocks go and drank the rum and passed out until they were rescued,' said Drago. 'It is known as a very famous piss-up.'

'What is piss-up?' asked Topov.

'Over drinking,' said Colin.

'How Australian to commemorate such an event, especially with such a vulgar term,' said Helen tartly.

'So what is it like over there where the men are living?' asked Marta. 'Did you film anything?'

'We met some new Australians like us,' said Peter. 'Bulgaria, Romania, Hungary. They live worse than the Aborigines. Old tents, huts with holes for two men. Mud, cold at night, flies and they have to walk a long way to share a toilet with a hundred men. Very bad.'

'Why complain? They make good money, no communists here,' said Topov.

Peter glared at Topov. 'They should get the union people, go on strike. Drago has it on film.'

'Look, it's not our business,' began Colin.

'Plenty of commo bastards in unions,' said Johnny.

Topov cut the discussion off with a wave of his hand. 'We go little drive then Darwin.'

'What do you mean, a little drive?' asked Drago suspiciously.

Topov ignored him. 'I get map. Johnny, come.'

Johnny shrugged. 'Let's get out of here. It's like a concentration camp.'

'This is a holiday camp compared to a concentration camp,' said Peter darkly as he headed for the Jeep.

For the next two hours they bumped and careened through the scrub leaving the devastation of the mine site at Rum Jungle behind. Periodically Topov called a halt and he scrambled out using his director's lens as a telescope to peer at the rock formations, picking up a small rock or two and examining it before discarding it or adding it to his collection.

It was almost dark when they arrived at the Darwin Hotel and while everyone was furious with Topov the overwhelming feeling was relief to finally be in a large town. The luxury of clean rooms and a proper bathroom down the shiny wooden hall that smelled of cedar floor polish put them in good spirits. Topov was especially expansive and was already entertaining a group he'd met in the bar. He was perched on a high cane stool, his foot on a brass foot rail. Further along a group of cattlemen had hooked their Akubra hats to a pole at the end of the bar.

Marta, Helen and Colin sat at a table in the Green Room, a lounge next to the bar. The concrete floor was painted green and the cane furniture had green-leaf fabric cushions. It looked out onto a garden, a square of green lawn and tropical plants, open to the sea breeze blowing across the Esplanade. Helen had booked a large table for dinner and they were looking forward to receiving the payment due to them and the chance to shop for necessities as well as do a little sightseeing.

Topov sauntered to their table. 'Now, we eat.' Then he went through the swinging doors into the dining room.

Everyone found it pleasant to dine amongst other people and they made up for their last spartan meals by ordering three courses. Helen had a few words to Topov but he waved her comments aside and ordered more wine. After the meal they returned to the Green Room. There was an excellent pianist and, in a jovial mood, they all settled around two tables as Topov called for drinks.

Marta wanted Colin to dance but he shook his head. 'I'm not much of a dancer.'

She pouted and jumped up and went and spoke to

the pianist who was partly screened by a large vase of ginger plants and palm leaves. After a few moments he swung into 'I Can't Give You Anything But Love, Baby' and Marta stood by the piano and sang the lyrics in a strong throaty voice. In a few moments the chatter in the room diminished and when she finished all applauded and called for more.

'She's very talented. You haven't used her enough,' Drago said to Topov.

'Plenty time. We film more adventure after Darwin in Arnhem Land,' he said.

'I don't think such a place exists,' said Helen. 'Well, I'm going to bed. Goodnight, everyone.'

'When do we get our money?' Johnny asked.

'After the banks open tomorrow. Goodnight.' Helen glared at Topov but he ignored her.

When Marta returned to the table, Colin took her hand, his eyes shining. 'That was wonderful.'

Gradually the group broke up, Topov and Johnny heading for the bar.

'Feel like a moonlight walk?' Colin whispered to Marta.

'Just a little one. It's been a long day. Mad Topov and his mining,' sighed Marta.

They left the hotel and walked a short distance along the Esplanade, their arms around each other. Then they turned back to the hotel and went upstairs.

'My room is eleven. I have a nice big bed. Come and stay with me,' whispered Marta as Colin kissed her.

'I'm sharing with Drago. I don't s'pose it matters that everyone will know,' said Colin.

Marta gave a low laugh. 'You are so proper. Drago doesn't care.'

Colin had planned to return to his room at daylight. But he couldn't bear to leave Marta's warm and soft embrace. When he finally made his way down the hallway to his room, the housemaid mopping the polished floor gave him a big smile. There were also smiles and knowing glances at breakfast. Marta was unperturbed but Colin kept his head down and busied himself buttering his toast. Topov didn't appear, but Helen, who'd been collared by almost everyone asking about their money, announced she'd meet them all at morning tea time.

But when the time came Helen looked at the expectant group apologetically and said, 'I'm sorry. I have to say there's been a bit of a delay . . .'

There was an explosion around her.

'Delay?'

'Where's our money?'

'Where's Topov? What's happening?'

'This is impossible! It can't happen,' shouted Marta.

Helen made placating gestures. 'Please, listen to me. Madame Olga is flying into Darwin this afternoon with the money and more film.'

'We don't want film stock, we want to be paid,' said Drago firmly.

'And you will. In cash. The flight gets in at three pm,' said Helen.

'Did you know about this?' asked Johnny.

'No, I did not. I thought the money was coming through the bank,' said Helen.

'So why's she coming up here?' asked Peter.

Helen shrugged. 'She wishes to discuss matters with Mr Topov and hand over the film and take back what we've shot.'

'Well, I for one will be at the plane to meet her,' said Drago.

'Good idea. We'll all be there,' said Johnny. 'With bells on.'

*

Madame Olga inched her way down the steps from the aircraft, dressed in a bright red silk dress with an orange scarf wound about her head. The reception party all noted that she carried a large black leather handbag looped over her arm.

'How lovely of you all to meet me!' She beamed as everyone gathered around as she waited for her suitcase. 'But where is Maxim?'

'We're not sure,' said Marta. 'Helen will know. Where is Mr Topov?' Marta asked Helen.

'He said he is meeting with some people who can help us. And he is making arrangements for your accommodation, Madame Olga,' said Helen quickly.

'What sort of help is he arranging for us?' said Johnny. 'All we want is our money.' He looked expectantly at Madame Olga.

She fanned herself. 'This heat, it is excruciating. Yes, all in good time. Please, I must get into the cool air. Ah, there is my bag.'

Drago and Peter leapt to retrieve her expensive leather suitcase and then led her to the Land Rover. But Olga balked at the dusty vehicle with its high wheel base.

'I cannot travel in that. Get me a taxi,' she demanded.

'It's too high off the ground,' Colin whispered to Drago.

Marta stepped forward and smoothly said, 'Madame Olga, allow me to accompany you and help with your luggage.'

Helen seemed relieved. 'Madame Olga is in the Squatter's Suite at our hotel. Once she is settled we can all meet on the terrace outside the Green Room.'

'We want our money now, before the shops close,' said Johnny.

Madame Olga frowned. 'I wish to take a rest.'

'I could come back to the hotel with you to make sure

that you're comfortable and that the money's safe,' said Marta.

'I think that someone else should go, too,' said Johnny. 'Not that we don't trust you, Marta, but I think I'll come with you anyway.'

Madame Olga shrugged, happy to see the taxi pull up. 'As you wish.'

Johnny got into the front seat of the taxi as Madame Olga and Marta settled themselves in the back. 'Darwin Hotel,' said Johnny.

On arriving at the hotel, they escorted Madame Olga to her large, airy room with its own bathroom on the specially sectioned-off end of the verandah. They passed a tall man in an immaculate white suit who gave them a brief nod.

'A pearling master,' said Johnny.

'You should buy a pearl while you're here, Marta,' said Madame Olga.

'I have better things to spend my money on – like food and personal necessities,' said Marta, but the comment passed Madame Olga by.

'Open the louvres, please. The heat,' sighed Madame Olga.

Johnny pulled on a pole attached by a metal ring to the louvered windows, allowing the sea breeze to rush in. 'At least it's nice to sleep in a comfortable bed for a change,' said Johnny. 'This room is very nice,' he added, placing her suitcase on the small wooden stand.

'I'm sure you're comfortable. Your trip has been eventful,' said Madame Olga sitting on the bed and pulling the scarf from her head.

'Eventful! Yes, it certainly has. Sleeping on the ground, running out of food, going to crazy places. But comfortable, no. Helen at least had a bed in the caravan. I never want to see a sleeping bag again. I want to buy a collapsible camp stretcher for the rest of the trip,' said Marta.

'Add it to your shopping list,' said Johnny, then paused as he saw the expression on Madame Olga's face.

'Helen is sleeping in the caravan? Alongside Mr Topov? Why is this?'

'Oh, it's all above board, she was suffering with her back,' said Johnny hastily.

Marta stared at Madame Olga's furious face. Suddenly she wondered if Helen had been sleeping with Topov, literally. There'd been initial speculation but it seemed so unlikely and typical of Helen to look after her own comfort that the group hadn't considered the two might be lovers. But Marta quickly realised that Madame Olga was a woman consumed by jealousy.

Madame Olga snatched up her handbag. 'Send Topov to see me.'

'As soon as we find him. Ah, what about the money, Madame Olga? We're all a bit desperate,' said Johnny.

'Why you do not have money?' She pursed her lips as if she knew the answer, then opened her handbag and drew out an envelope. 'Divide this as a downpayment.'

'Downpayment? Where's the full amount?' asked Marta crossly.

'I will have to discuss the money with the financial lady,' she answered.

Johnny looked at Marta and shrugged, glad he wasn't in Helen's shoes right now. 'How long do we have to wait for the rest of what we're owed?' he asked.

'But you do have it with you?' persisted Marta.

'I need to speak to Topov. Oh, and you can take the heavy cans of film from my suitcase,' she said to Johnny.

'Will you take the exposed film back then?' Johnny asked.

'Yes. That is the plan.'

Marta had glanced at the money in the envelope. 'Madame Olga, we are owed much more than this. We have all paid upfront to make this film, but we can't be expected to pay for incidentals when that was part of the budget.'

'The film is not yet finished. The returns will come when it is sold. The expenses have to be justified. I wish to speak to the business manager, Helen,' insisted Madame Olga.

'Very well. But the whole film will be threatened if we are not paid what is owed to us,' snapped Marta, surprising Johnny with her vehemence.

'And you do not threaten me,' responded Madame Olga with equal strength.

Johnny started to back out of the room. 'We'll leave you to rest and see you at dinner. Come on, Marta.'

'Bring me that film,' called Madame Olga as they shut the door to her suite.

Marta strode down the hallway, ignoring the maid now wielding a polishing machine over the waxed wooden floor. 'This is the limit, Johnny. I will not go any further without being paid. Topov has wasted money or hidden it and she knows it. And now she is going to eat him – and Helen – alive because she thinks they are lovers.'

'Are they, do you think?' asked Johnny.

'I don't care. Topov might be sleeping with the fat old hag because she's rich. But I don't know about Helen. They think I am a stupid actress. Well, they will know that I am strong,' she declared.

'Let's wait and see, after she has consulted with Topov,' said Johnny. 'Perhaps that's why Topov isn't around.'

Nevertheless, as the sullen group gathered for dinner, Topov sailed in with Madame Olga at his side. She was dressed to the hilt, a fresh display of jewels on her bosom and seemed to have not a care in the world.

'Where've you been today?' asked Johnny.

'Topov is making plans. Big plans,' he said mysteriously. 'Appointment with important people.'

Madame Olga settled herself at the table. 'Yes, it all sounds quite interesting. However, like many things, it requires some organisation.'

'Is this to do with our film?' asked Peter.

'There won't be any film if we don't get our money,' said Johnny.

'It is coming. Money coming. Plenty of money,' said Topov, waving to the waiter.

Marta glanced at Helen who was sitting quietly at the far end of the table. 'Helen, do we go shopping tomorrow?' called Marta gaily.

Helen shrugged. 'I wouldn't rush, we'll have time before we move on.'

'And when might we move on?' Colin asked.

'Not until we're paid,' said Peter.

Topov told the waiter to bring wine and beers to the table. 'Madame Olga is taking film to Sydney, then we get more money. So we stay little while in Darwin.'

'And who's paying for this pub?' demanded Johnny. 'It's not coming out of my pay.'

'Just little misunderstanding. Helen explain to Madame Olga but she not understand well. So Madame Olga send money when she go back to Sydney.'

'I'll be returning there tomorrow,' added Madame Olga. 'It's far too hot here.'

'Yeah, I bet it is,' muttered Johnny.

'So when do we get the rest of our money? What we got today is barely a third of what we're owed,' said Marta.

'I will send it by telegraphic transfer to the bank. Colin, you are in banking, you know how these things work,' said Madame Olga. Then she turned her attention to the menu.

Everyone looked at Colin.

'Can you get things speeded up?' asked Drago.

Colin looked at Madame Olga who looked unconcerned, her biggest problem seemed to be what to select for dinner. Whatever had passed between Helen, Topov and Madame Olga would not be discussed, but Helen didn't look happy.

Dinner plates were cleared from the table. Marta gave Colin a secret smile that seemed to say, Let's make the most of tonight while we're here with a big comfortable bed. Johnny decided to drink and headed to the bar. Peter and Drago were discussing the camp at Rum Jungle over a bottle of red wine knowing that some of their compatriots were sleeping rough. Helen excused herself and disappeared to her room.

Topov escorted Madame Olga into the Green Room, where he walked up to a table of well-dressed cattlemen and the pearling master and introduced himself.

'I am Maxim Topov, this Madame Olga Konstantinova. We making amazing film in outback Australia. So, where we go for exciting pictures?' The well-to-do group invited this odd couple to join them and soon it was the locals who sat spellbound, listening to Topov talk while Madame Olga sat by, smiling and nodding.

But amongst the other filmmakers there was festering resentment. The following morning Helen made the point of talking to each of them.

'Look, the problem with the money is that it's just a misunderstanding on Madame Olga's part and she's overreacted. She's rather an emotional lady and she has it in her head that I am having an affair with Topov!' She gave a laugh. 'I hope you don't think the same. I have been quite particular about my male friends. Frankly, I wouldn't have cared if an orangutan was in the other bed as long as I had a mattress and a pillow off the ground.'

For the first time they saw Helen as a genuine person

without airs and graces and they believed what she told them.

Then she went on. 'Madame Olga is flying back to Sydney this morning. She's taken the film we've shot and left us fresh film. The hotel bill is paid up until breakfast this morning. After that, we're on our own until she releases the rest of the money.'

This was not well received. But as they discussed their predicament, there was general acknowledgment that they were stuck.

'I'm not leaving till I get what I'm owed,' said Johnny.

'We can't leave anyway, we have no money,' said Peter.

'We can't give up now, we have to finish the film,' said Colin.

'I think Topov is up to something,' said Drago.

'Helen you have twenty-four hours to pay me the money I'm owed or I'm going to go to a solicitor and sue,' said Marta.

The others stared at her.

'That will cost money. How can you afford it?' said Colin calmly. 'Let's just wait it out.'

'For how long? And where are we going to stay? How can we pay for a pub without any money?' said Johnny.

Marta shrugged. 'Then there's only one thing for it. We camp again, but this time at the beach, where we can have some fun!'

There was an immediate outbreak of chatter and some enthusiasm and they began planning how they would organise the sleeping arrangements. No-one knew where Topov was but later, when they told Helen their plan she turned up with her belongings looking tired and harassed.

'You can have the tent we used. Colin and I will share,' said Marta.

'Thanks, Marta. I won't be moving back into that smelly caravan,' she sighed. 'He's moved into it. I guess now we wait for Madame to calm down, send the money, and then we can go and finish what we started.'

'Do you really believe Topov wants to make this film?' asked Marta. 'I just feel we're all part of some play he's devised but we don't know the plot.'

'He does want to make it, but he gets sidetracked so easily. He's got this bee in his bonnet about finding minerals, gold, gemstones, uranium,' said Helen. 'He sits up at night reading geology books.'

'Might make us more money than this film. I don't care, really. I'm not expecting this to make me a star. But we all invested in good faith to get the equipment and vehicles and be paid expenses,' said Marta. 'I'm not a charity, I'm not funding some Topov fantasy,' she continued. 'So I'm not going anywhere till we get what's owed to us.'

Helen nodded. 'I understand. I feel badly that this is partly my fault. I really don't understand the relationship between Maxim and Olga.'

Marta's eyes widened. 'Do you mean financially and business, or personally?'

Helen shrugged. 'It is a mystery and I don't probe into other people's business.'

'Well, I'd like to know,' said Marta bluntly. 'Because it affects all of us. Never mind, let's see what happens in the next few days.'

That night when the campfire on the beach had dimmed and everyone had rolled into their swags and tents, Marta snuggled into Colin's arms.

'This is cosy,' he murmured. 'Are we sharing this when we set out next?'

'Of course. I just hope there aren't these little biting mosquito things sharing it, too. But you know, Colin, I won't go if we don't get our money. It's not right.'

'I agree. And we can't afford to buy food or petrol if

we haven't the cash.' He kissed the top of her head. 'Are you disappointed at how things have turned out? Because I have to admit, I'm not.' He didn't want to think about what might happen when this strange journey was over.

Marta gave a low laugh. 'I try not to make plans. I've been disappointed before today so now I've learned I have to stand up for myself.'

'Marta, you're so beautiful. You should be spoiled and looked after and have the world at your feet,' whispered Colin. 'I wish I could give you that.'

'Colin, let's live for now, where we are and with what we have. That's something else I've learned.' And Marta pulled his face to hers and kissed him with an urgency that obviously surprised Colin.

'I'll remember this for the rest of my life,' he murmured.

12

It was a short tropical shower that swept from the sea onto the beach, warm and humid and it would soon pass. But Marta was fed up.

'I am sick of this place. I want to move on. This is crazy,' she fumed. 'It's so hot and the ants and mosquitos are driving me crazy. I'm going to see a solicitor about getting the money from Topov, or Olga. They just keep stalling.'

'How are you going to pay a solicitor?' asked Colin. 'That'll cost you a bit. Anyway, Topov says Madame Olga is sending the money.'

'Topov says! Pissh,' scoffed Marta. 'Helen and Topov upset her and Johnny says Olga is holding back the money to teach Topov a lesson, so we all have to suffer.'

'We're caught in the middle,' agreed Colin. 'We're stuck

here. Some of the others are talking about getting work to get some money to get out of Darwin. It would be a shame about the film, when we've come so far. Maybe Arnhem Land will be where we finally get all the action and adventure.'

Marta studied Colin. 'You're so nice, Colin. So trusting. You always want to believe the best of people, but soon it's going to be everyone for themselves.' She chewed her lip, hugging her knees, feeling claustrophobic in the tiny tent. Colin sat beside her, staring at her adoringly thinking he couldn't believe the overwhelming joy of his proximity to her, day and night.

Suddenly Marta reached out and grabbed his arm. 'I know! I know how I can get the money.'

'You do? How?'

'A play! I'll put on a show. Sell tickets. People will come and then I'll have enough money to pay the solicitor, get the money from Topov and we can do what we want.'

Colin shook his head in admiration. 'Marta, you're amazing. But how? I mean, that's a big undertaking. How can we do it? Won't it take money to put on a show?'

'Not so much if we are clever.' She jumped up. 'Let's go and check out a few things.'

They took the Jeep and went into town and Colin trailed after Marta as she charged from the city council to a small theatre restaurant in a pub, to the local cinema, asking their managers if she could stage a one-woman show. Colin stood quietly by, awestruck by her bubbling enthusiasm, her charm and the persuasive description of the show she planned.

'It sounds fabulous. I'd buy a ticket straight away,' said Colin as he followed her backstage at the cinema.

'The stage is quite small, but they've done a couple of eisteddfods here, a prize giving, a Christmas recital. We held the world premiere of the new Australian film *Jedda* here earlier this year,' said the cinema manager proudly.

'What about the lighting?' asked Marta peering up into the dusty roof above the stage.

'Wouldn't know. You'd have to look after that, miss. We don't provide anything but the space. And a girl to run the ticket office if you want her.'

'How much does she want?' asked Marta in a business-like tone. 'Why don't we get a girl from the high school who's interested in drama? And she could help with props as well.'

The man shrugged. 'I could ask my daughter, she'd probably want to do it.'

Marta was excited but practical. 'Drago can help with lights. Create the mood. I will ask the pianist from the hotel to record some background music on Topov's machine, to play during the blackout moments while I change my costume and rearrange props. You and I can make up posters and stick them up all around town. We'll go to the local radio station and newspaper for some publicity. Next stop is the library to find some plays.' She smiled at him. 'I'll have to brush up on some speeches and scenes.'

'What sort of plays will they be?' asked Colin, bowled over at the speed of Marta's thinking and planning.

'I shall act scenes from some of the classics. It will be a smorgasbord! Some comedy, some drama, some mystery. But I'll keep it simple, just a few props, a hat, a cloak, a veil. Maybe I can find those at a church charity shop.' Marta was now enthusiastic. Colin was happy to see that her mood had changed but had serious doubts about her pulling off this public performance.

'How long is this going to take to get ready?' asked Colin.

'A few days, maybe a week. We want to get the word out so people know about it. The first thing is to find the venue.'

After leaving the library with a pile of plays and having discussed with Colin possible places to mount a show, Marta's mood became churlish.

'The town hall isn't finished, the cinema is too big, the Catholic palais isn't suitable and I don't like the recreation hut at the army camp. It has no windows and a leaky roof and is too big. I need something intimate.'

'What about the hotel?' suggested Colin.

'Noisy. Not the right atmosphere.' She stood for a moment in the street, then thrust the library books at Colin. 'Please put these in the car. I'm just going to ask that taxi driver.'

She walked with determination to the taxi driver who was leaning against his car, idly smoking a cigarette. There was a brief exchange between them and Marta returned triumphantly to Colin, while the driver appreciatively watched the sway of Marta's hips.

'It sounds perfect. A little outdoor cinema down at the harbour, people sit in deckchairs. Let's go.'

'What if it rains?'

'Colin!' she pointed to the sky which was clear blue. 'I won't let it,' she added confidently.

The others in the group seemed to have found diversions around Darwin. Topov was nowhere to be seen and Helen said he was busy dealing with some sort of bureaucratic government department, about what she wasn't sure except it had to do with permits and paperwork connected to Arnhem Land.

When Marta asked Drago to help with the lighting for her play, he agreed, but added, 'Just as well it's in the evening. Peter and I got a job today.'

'A job? Doing what?' asked Colin.

'Signwriting. Peter has some experience. We're making some advertisement signs.'

'Maybe I should look for work,' said Colin. 'Though

I'm not sure what sort of work. I've only ever worked in a bank.'

'You're too busy helping me,' said Marta quickly. 'You are my producer.'

'What about you, Johnny?' said Marta.

'I have a few ideas I'm working on,' he said.

'At the races?' said Helen.

'Mind your own business. I reckon that we should give Topov a week to raise the money or we all find our own way out of this mess,' he said.

'If we all get some sort of work and pool our money we could bail ourselves out and finish the film,' suggested Helen.

There was an instant outcry of derision.

'What for? Why should we help Topov?' said Peter. 'Besides, we have paid already.'

Drago shrugged. 'I'm not siding with Topov, he's behaved badly, but we do have half a film and Colin is right, maybe it can be salvaged in Arnhem Land.'

'I'll keep working on him. I wish I knew what Topov was up to,' said Helen. 'He has a knack of pulling irons out of the fire and coming up with the goods at the last moment,' she added.

'His silver tongue won't get him far up here,' said Johnny. 'These bush people know bulldust when they hear it.' He eyed Helen. 'What about you, Helen? Are you getting a job?'

'What sort of work have you done, Helen?' asked Peter.

Helen lifted her chin. 'I have been fortunate in my personal life, but I am not lazy. I drove an ambulance during the war and made myself available for volunteer work.'

'Why don't you get money from your toffee-nosed family then?' asked Johnny. 'Sell some of your thoroughbreds.'

'That's none of your business,' said Helen. 'My being here has nothing to do with my family. Besides, people's circumstances change. I prefer to lead my own life. But I am willing to look for a job to get money to help us continue.'

'Thank you, Helen,' said Marta. 'Don't let him bait you.'

Johnny shrugged and grinned at Helen. 'Well, I bet I can earn more than you can.'

Helen stood up. 'Very well. I shall look for work, although the only jobs for women in this place seem to be as a barmaid or a waitress.'

Johnny burst out laughing and the other men couldn't help smiling at the idea of the cool, aristocratic Helen pulling beers in a pub. But Helen surprised them all by landing a job with a Stock and Station agent as a bookkeeper.

Marta ploughed on with plans for her show. Colin need not have worried about publicity. One small write-up in the newspaper, which he had organised, brought a flurry of requests for tickets.

'There is no culture here,' said Marta. 'They are starved for it.'

In their little tent at night she ran through her lines as Colin followed along by torchlight, gently correcting a word or two where she faltered.

'First my fear; then my courtesy; last my speech. My fear is, your displeasure; my courtesy, my duty; and my speech, to beg your pardons.'

'What's that from?' asked Colin.

'Henry IV. Next, let's do Shaw's St Joan speech. Find the page.'

'I don't know how you remember all this,' said Colin in admiration.

Marta was a whirlwind. Peter helped them by designing a flyer which they had duplicated at the high school and Marta and Colin stuck them up all over town. She hired a young girl who was working at the Darwin Hotel to handle the box office and sell tickets. The outdoor cinema manager showed Drago the lighting system and Bobby, the pianist from the Green Room, agreed to record some music to entertain between scenes.

Marta sent Colin from the front of house to backstage to check on every detail, while she sat in the tiny dressing room preparing to go on stage. She wore elaborate, heavy make-up and a black dress which she would accessorise with the costume props. She maintained an air of distraction, at once removed from the normal, while remaining razor sharp about every small detail of the production.

'When it goes black at the end of the first scene, wait and count to ten before cueing the lights and the music. Don't forget to change the props and don't lose the order of my wardrobe. They are laid out as I need them. And did you get flowers for me? They must be presented at my curtain bows,' she told Colin.

Colin nodded. Marta was rather imperious and although she said she was nervous, she looked self-possessed and confident. 'You really love doing this, don't you?' he smiled.

'Don't you love doing something that you know you're good at, that sweeps you away, that fulfils you?' she asked, her eyes shining. 'Now go. Sit in the front row and clap very loudly!'

There was an almost full house. Some people had made an effort to dress up and there was an air of anticipation. The lights dimmed, the stage was in darkness. Suddenly, the spotlight blazed onto the stage showing Marta standing, hands folded, head bowed. There were a few half hearted claps. By the end of the first scene, however, the audience were mesmerised and the loud applause was enthusiastic. Her clear voice reached to the back row and the audience stared, transfixed by her accomplished performance. The time seemed to speed past and at the interval Colin raced backstage to double-check on the props, but before he could say a word, Marta held up her hand.

'Do not say anything. Not until the show is finished. Now, make sure everything is in place. Don't forget the music.'

After Marta, who'd been word perfect all evening, had finished her final speech and taken three deep bows, Colin presented her with the bouquet of flowers. The thunderous applause continued until Marta blew a series of kisses and gave a small signal to Drago who darkened the set, allowing her to make her way off the stage.

'You were wonderful, fantastic!' Colin hugged her.

'It went well. But there were small problems. Ask Drago to come and see me.'

The Wednesday opening night was a great success. Marta was interviewed on the radio and the show was given a rave notice in the paper and so it was booked out for the next few nights. Yet no-one seemed aware that this famous European actress was camped at the beach. Colin kept telling Marta how proud he was of her and how stunned their little group was by her remarkable performance and Topov announced that he would grace the show with his presence on Saturday night.

After that show Topov came backstage to Marta's crowded little dressing room. He grandly embraced her and announced, 'Now, we make big film role. You be famous star.'

'Not unless I'm paid a lot of money,' retorted Marta.

Topov threw up his hands, waved to everybody and sailed from the room. 'I go. Topov has very important business. You wait. Soon we have big success.' But no-one took much notice.

After the visitors left, there was another tap at the door and Colin went to open it.

'More fans, I suppose,' he said.

However, standing in the doorway, almost unrecognisable in his town clothes, was Len Buchanan from Brolga Springs.

'G'day, mate. What a show! Had to come and congratulate the star.'

'Len! This is a surprise. What are you doing in Darwin?' asked Marta.

'I'm living here for a bit. Saw a piece in the newspaper about your show, thought I'd come along, see how things're going.'

Helen came forward and shook his hand. 'Wouldn't have recognised you. Good to see you again.'

'You mean you don't know me without me horse?' he grinned.

'Well, you look a lot more spruced up than when we saw you last,' said Helen.

'So do you lot,' said Len. 'Tell me, what's happening?' He accepted a glass of beer from Colin and looked around the group.

'We've come to a temporary standstill,' said Drago. 'The budget is bust.'

'No money?' said Len. 'That's a bit steep. What are you doing about it?'

'We've got jobs to tide us over. Doesn't pay much,' said Peter.

'Anytime you want to come out with me to make a few quid, let me know. I'm shooting crocs. Skins fetch a good whack.' He glanced at Helen. 'If you want to come for a ride, I've got me horses here in Darwin.'

'That would be nice. How do I find you?' she asked.

'I'm staying at a mate's property while he's away. I'll write his number down, if I can remember it. Not used to having a phone.'

*

Marta did not sit back and bask in her sudden fame and money. She paid the box office girl and Bobby the pianist and, with Colin, marched into a solicitor's office where she explained her situation. Colin watched quietly as Marta put on another performance about being stranded in Darwin. The solicitor agreed to represent her and said he'd send a letter to Topov demanding that he pay Marta what she was owed.

Topov ignored it.

Marta told Colin not to mention the solicitor to the others until the case was resolved. Several days later she stood before the local magistrate in the Court of Petty Sessions.

Topov, now unable to avoid the issue, made a dramatic entrance into the hearing room at the last moment and when asked if anyone was representing him, Topov announced with a flourish, 'Topov speak for Topov.'

He studiously ignored Marta and when directed to a chair before the magistrate's bench, he flicked imaginary dust from the seat with his large handkerchief, sat, crossed his legs and smiled at the magistrate. But every time Marta's solicitor began to outline the facts of the case, Topov leapt to his feet, protesting.

'This is rubbish talk. Not so, this crazy story.'

The magistrate's patience soon began to wear thin and he admonished Topov, threatening to fine him if he kept interrupting. 'Wait until it is your turn to speak, Mr Topov.'

Marta's solicitor reiterated the facts of her investment in the film project and her being hired to appear in the film as an actress for which she would receive an extra payment over and above the expenses due to all the investors on the trip. When, at last, Madame Konstantinova's name was mentioned, Topov seized the moment.

'Is true, true. Madame Olga holds all money. I, too,

am employee of this lady. She very strict money lady. She keep money. She mad because Helen sleep in my caravan. I do not invite this woman to my caravan. She cold English fish. She is . . .'

'That is enough, thank you, Mr Topov. The fact remains, it was you who auditioned and hired Miss Johanssen. Made promises to her.' The magistrate peered over his glasses at the angry, red-faced Topov. 'You are in charge of this filming expedition. Did it not occur to you that you were ill-equipped, that your plans were hazy to say the least? Under these conditions, a lady requires some comforts and certainly some security.'

'I make promise, yes. Topov make successful film. Everyone come with Topov because they know Topov brilliant director. We make film to amaze world, make plenty money.' For the first time he spun around and directed his gaze at Marta. 'Everyone share Topov dream. We know it is not easy, not piece of cake. Marta, you are spoiled girl. Selfish girl.'

'That will do, thank you, Mr Topov.' The magistrate banged his gavel on the desk.

Marta shifted uncomfortably and refused to look at Topov, but she too was angry.

Her solicitor put a restraining hand on her arm. 'Say nothing.'

'Mr Topov, I must find against you. You must pay Miss Johanssen the money owed to her.'

Topov exploded from his seat, gesticulating wildly. 'Impossible. Topov cannot. Olga has money. Why Marta not sue Olga? Topov innocent man. Topov making brilliant film, make everybody rich. Now this silly little girl stop great film.' He reefed out his large handkerchief again, this time to dab his eyes, saying in an emotional voice, 'Topov has no money, how he pay this girl? What about all other people? They stay with Topov, but now . . .'

Marta looked down at her clasped hands as Topov, now on his feet, paced in front of the magistrate.

The magistrate was unmoved. He gave Marta, looking pale and upset and dressed in a clinging blouse, short skirt and high heels, a swift and appreciative glance, then looked at his notes. 'I direct you, Maxim Topov, to pay this young lady the two hundred pounds that is currently owed to her . . .'

Topov's pathos turned to red-hot fury. 'I cannot pay. Topov has no money. Olga has money. Topov sacrifice everything to make great film.'

'Then you'll have to sell whatever you can,' said the magistrate firmly. 'Your vehicles, your camera, to raise the money that you owe Miss Johanssen.'

Topov froze, his power and energy suddenly drained from him. 'Sell? You make Topov sell camera? Sell my soul, sell my passion, sell my life?' he demanded incredulously. 'I do not make this film for Topov. I make this film for Australia, for world.' He began shaking his head as he paced like a caged lion. 'No, no, is impossible.'

'I'm sorry Mr Topov, that's the law. You owe Miss Johanssen two hundred pounds. You have broken an agreement and she is entitled to restitution. That is all. This case is concluded.'

Topov suddenly dissolved like a snowman in the sun. He walked in front of Marta, opened his arms and fell to his knees, his voice trembling.

'Marta. Why you do this? You are beautiful actress. I make you star. We all work hard, we all one family. Why, why you do this?' His voice broke.

The solicitor grabbed Marta's arm and bundled her out of the room. 'The man is mad.'

Marta wiped her eyes as Colin hurried after her, watching her distressed face.

'What will happen?'

'He has to pay her,' said the solicitor. 'Will you take her home?' He turned to Marta and handed her an envelope. 'My account. I do hope you can settle it quickly.' He gave a weak smile. 'Don't want any more money troubles, do we?'

Seeing Marta's expression change from distress to haughty disdain, Colin stepped forward and took the envelope. 'Your bill will be paid. Thank you.' He took Marta's arm and they walked away from the court.

'I didn't want him to have to sell everything. I didn't think this through,' she said. 'It's Madame Olga who should be paying. Topov's right. Anyway, Colin, I have enough from the show to pay the solicitor.'

'Fine then. Maybe this has taught Topov a lesson. Why don't you let me or Drago or Helen talk to him when he's calmed down? We'll tell him to talk to Madame Olga and get some money up here straight away.'

'Perhaps I have been selfish. I was so angry. I was promised extra money for appearing in the film,' said Marta. 'I am a professional actress. I am not some cheese-cake model . . .'

'I know you aren't,' broke in Colin hastily. 'Everyone knows now. You were brilliant in your stage show.'

'I just don't want to be a woman that men tramp all over,' said Marta vehemently.

'I respect you, Marta, for standing up for yourself. No-one else thought of confronting Topov,' said Colin.

'I bet that he won't sell anything. He'll weasel his way out of this, like he always does,' said Marta. 'At least I have a moral victory. And it might get him to spur Madame Olga into action.'

'So then everyone won't be too angry,' said Colin comfortingly.

*

But when Marta told the others what had transpired, they stared at her, quite shocked. Then they became annoyed and agitated.

'Why didn't you tell us what you were doing? We could have all applied to the court,' said Drago.

'You knew I was doing my show for money,' said Marta defensively.

'We didn't know you were just looking after yourself!' said Johnny.

'If he sells the gear we can't go on,' said Drago.

'We're all stranded,' said Peter.

They all glared at Marta and Colin looked down at his feet not knowing what to say.

'I'm not sorry for suing Topov,' said Marta heatedly, 'but I am sorry that I have put you all in this spot. Perhaps we can find the money another way, without having to sell everything.'

It was Helen who spoke up, 'We all need money. Why don't we do what Len suggested?'

'Hunt crocodiles? I'm not very happy about that,' said Peter.

'Well, according to Len, it's good money. Very good money,' said Johnny and everyone looked at him, thinking the same thing.

'You wouldn't tackle a croc, would you?' asked Drago.

'I'll do anything for money,' said Johnny cheerfully.

'It wouldn't do any harm to talk to Len. Find out what's involved,' said Helen.

'It'd be good if we could film some of it,' said Drago. 'Now that'd be real action.'

Marta had kept quiet but now offered to help. 'If you all want to risk your lives to go on with this craziness . . . I will contribute any money that I have left over after I've paid my solicitor's bill.'

A huge smile broke out on Colin's face and he grabbed her hand and squeezed it. 'I'll go along too.'

'We'd better see if Len is keen on a bunch of amateurs tagging along,' said Helen. 'I'll talk to him.'

That night everyone, including Topov, who didn't want to be left out, met Len in the bar of a pub he frequented down near the harbour. Helen quickly took control, calling the meeting to order. 'Len and I have already been talking and he'd be happy to have us join him in a business arrangement.'

'We make film business,' said Topov.

'We need to buy petrol, supplies,' said Helen patiently. 'So we need money.'

'Who can handle a gun?' asked Len.

'I can. I have in the war. But I'm not much of a shot,' said Peter.

'I can, too,' said Helen.

'Gee, that's great,' replied Len.

'So how dangerous is this business?' asked Johnny.

'You just have to be careful, have your wits about you and listen to me,' said Len. 'We're trapping the crocs as well as hunting them in the boat. And there's more work after they're caught. It's not pleasant dealing with the skins, skinning, salting, packing them, but they fetch bloody good money.'

'How you catch these monsters?' asked Topov. 'We want to see plenty action. Drama. Excitement.'

Len tried not to smile. 'Reckon you'll see a bit of action, Mr Topov.'

'So how would it work, with all of us?' asked Helen.

'In small groups, you'd each have a different job, provided you're physically up for it,' said Len.

'I don't have to go if there are too many of us,' offered Marta.

'No, we need you to be on camera,' said Drago.

Topov quickly added, 'Marta be damsel in distress.'

'I'm not going anywhere near a crocodile,' said Marta quickly.

'Once they're tied up, they're pretty harmless, you can jump on them and wrestle them a bit,' said Len nonchalantly.

Marta turned up her nose.

'Where do we get money for the skins?' asked Johnny.

'I sell 'em in Darwin. And a couple of blokes buy 'em and take 'em to Broome, too. Flog them in Asia.'

'Can we catch crocs in daylight?' asked Drago. 'I'm thinking it'll be hard to shoot them in the dark.'

'Nah, night is best, spot their eyes, they glow red in the dark,' said Len.

'We'll need spotlights in the dark.'

'Once we've found the croc,' said Len.

'So where do we go?' asked Helen. 'Is it public land or someone's property?'

'I have a few Abo mates I go out with. It's their territory so they know where the crocs hang around. Couple of spots are quiet backwaters, never been fished much either. You can't believe the size of the fish in there.'

'Well, we won't starve,' said Johnny. 'You catch 'em, I'll cook 'em.'

'Croc is beautiful meat to eat,' said Len. 'How soon do you want to set off?'

'As soon as possible, I guess,' said Helen looking around the group.

'Marta need costume for part. Safari clothes,' said Topov. He turned to Marta. 'You have money, you buy hunting clothes.'

'I've got enough suitable clothes already,' said Marta. 'And why am I the one in the front line here? Shouldn't we film Len and the others in action, too?'

'Let's just shoot it as it happens,' said Drago quietly.

'Topov make big story,' began Topov but they ignored him.

Helen broached the subject that was on their minds. 'How do we share the profits?'

'That depends how many skins we get, how big they are, the demand and the going price for them. But look, I'll do the right thing by you blokes. I don't mind helping you out a bit,' said Len, smiling at Helen.

'So, our convoy hits the road again,' laughed Marta. She was surprised how happy she felt to be travelling out into the bush again.

'Where are we headed?' asked Helen who was sitting in Len's vehicle with Marta also squashed into the front seat.

'Round the South Alligator River region. Might cross into West Arnhem Land where there're some special spots. It's wild blackfella country out there and I have a couple of them lined up to help us.'

'Are we allowed to hunt on Aboriginal land?' asked Helen.

Len shrugged. 'Depends who catches us, eh? The black-fellas don't care, it's open slather as far as they're concerned.'

They'd left the organisation of the supplies to Len, the cost of which would come out of their share of the profits. They set off, travelling east in a small convoy consisting of Len's truck carrying a runabout, a wooden dinghy tied on top, the Land Rover, the Jeep and, bringing up the rear, the old Dodge towing the very battered yellow caravan. They left the main road and followed smaller ones until they petered out. Then they trailed behind Len as the bull-bar of his truck tore through the scrub, snapping saplings, exploding termite mounds in a shower of red dirt while eucalyptus trees and cycads flailed at them as they passed.

They drove beside a magnificent billabong seething with honking ducks and geese and squawking, flapping ibis amongst the giant pink waterlilies.

Len turned towards a nearby low escarpment that had a deep overhang as though a bite had been taken from the solid orange rockface. As the rest of the party followed him through the crushed grass, they could see a thin plume of blue smoke rising from a rough camp where a group of Aborigines and several skinny dogs waited.

There were two women, one of whom had straggly white hair, a teenage boy and an older man whose bare chest showed deep initiation scars as if witchetty grubs had burrowed beneath his skin. Both men wore loincloths, the older woman wore the remains of a faded cotton dress, while the younger woman had a small woven apron strung from her hips as she sat cross-legged, cradling a baby at a drained and sagging breast.

'Who these people?' said Topov as they stopped and watched Len greet them. 'We make film with them. Where big hunter warrior men?'

'Come 'n meet the mob,' said Len. 'These're my mates. They're hunting with us.'

'Do we share the profits with them too?' asked Johnny.

'Ah, bit of tucker and tobacco is all,' said Len as he shook the hand of the broadly smiling older man. 'This is Clive, his son George. And that's Mary and Violet, his wives and little baby. What piccaninny name?' Len asked Mary, the older woman.

'Lisabet. Like queen lady.' And she burst into giggles.

Marta and Helen laughed too, peering closely at the chubby, long-lashed infant.

'You hunt old man croc?' asked Clive.

'Yep. We want special big fella for these people. Seen any?'

'Plenny big one. Some little fella,' said Clive.

'Do they attack humans?' asked Helen.

Len began to pull some of the gear off his truck. 'The crocs are well fed round these parts, no humans to bother them. They've been living off the land here for millions of years, mate, but it don't mean that they wouldn't try.'

Clive signalled to George to help Len take down the camping equipment and the boats. 'We bin walkin' down river, long way. Big croc took one dog. We get 'im, eh?' said Clive.

'You bet. My friends want to see plenty catch 'em big croc for pictures. Click, click.' Len mimed holding a camera. 'Don't think they know about moving pictures out here.' He turned to Topov. 'These Aborigines very good actors. You tell 'em what you want them to do. And you should see 'em dance!'

'I take scene of family walking along river,' said Topov. 'Maybe they do something? Get food, make something?'

'Let's get our camp set up first, eh? By the way there's some fantastic old cave paintings up there in the shelters if you want to take a look.'

'I'll help you set up,' said Johnny. 'I'm not into art.'

The others pulled out their tents, sleeping bags and personal bags and left them in a pile as Len, helped by Clive and Johnny, directed where to set things up.

'You blokes go up the hill, there. Take Clive and young George with you, he'll show you where the cave paintings are. They're real old, special creation ones apparently,' said Len.

'What about the ladies?' asked Peter, looking at Violet and Mary. 'Do they want to come?'

'Some of them pictures can't be looked at by their women. If you climb up the side of that escarpment and to the top, it's pretty precarious, but amazing paintings. Clive has to come and touch 'em up every so often. Traditional business.'

'What do you mean, touch them up?' Helen turned to Clive. 'These paintings, are they old ones? Have they been there for, say, many generations?'

Clive nodded emphatically. 'Them old, for sure.' He made a curling movement with his hand as if waving across hundreds of generations. 'We keep painting 'live one. Keep 'im story going.'

Helen turned to Len. 'But surely they are not *defacing* ancient rock art?'

Len glanced at Clive who was smiling proudly. 'Look, Helen, they have their ways. I don't pretend to understand what it's all about but these people have kept a culture alive for centuries. It's not our place to tell them that what they're doing ain't right. As a matter of fact, they did a lot better before the white man came along, if you ask me.'

Johnny smirked. 'It's a Pommy thing, init? Gotta be in control, tell the natives that what they're doing isn't how it should be.'

Helen bristled. 'Think what you like. I am trying to learn and understand these people. I do believe they have a far more sophisticated culture than we give them credit for.'

Surprisingly, Topov came to her defence. 'Helen is right. Native people wild, dirty, no clothes, but up here, big brains.' He tapped the side of his head. 'Smart people. And here, also very big.' Topov touched his heart. 'They live wild life, free life. Good life.'

'I just want to know more about this rock art,' said Helen.

'Let's go see it then,' said Marta.

'We saw paintings at Katherine Gorge,' said Peter.

Len shook his head. 'Not like this. This is magic stuff. And I mean magic. Some of the caves are burial sites. The Abos bring the bones back there after they've been picked clean by birds.'

'Ouch, that's awful. Birds eating your flesh,' said Marta.

'No worse than being cremated,' said Len. 'It's all a ritual. The body is taken to their home country and hidden in a tree tied to a bark frame. Then a year or so later they go back and get the bones, wrap 'em in paperbark and sometimes they're painted and then there's a big ceremony when they get put in their secret burial place.'

'Can we film this?' asked Drago.

'Who's to know, mate?' Len shrugged. 'You should get Clive to take you up when he does his touch-up painting. That's one of the reasons they're camped here, as well as helping me. Then they're going walkabout. They can take some croc meat with them.'

Topov listened to all this, nodding his head. 'This good. Topov take Bolex and make pictures in cave. Topov go hunting too, sometime.'

'Yeah? For buffalo? Crocodiles? Emu?' said Johnny disparagingly.

Topov stomped away to the battered yellow caravan and rummaged for a while before emerging with a large canvas-wrapped parcel. Throwing off the canvas, he revealed a machine.

'This Geiger counter. I find uranium,' he said triumphantly to the startled group.

Johnny was the first one to react. 'You're crazy! Uranium! What for? Damned needle in a haystack, mate.'

'Where did you get it?' asked Peter.

'I buy in Darwin.'

'We're making a film and trying to make money, aren't we?' said Drago with some heat.

'Who says there's uranium out here?' asked Len.

'Topov great geologist. I find uranium here. This is good place for uranium.'

'What would you do if you found it?' asked Helen.

Peter just rolled his eyes then muttered to Drago,

'Keep him away from the filming. He's not going near crocodiles.'

'So you go hunting minerals while we hunt crocodiles?'

Len saw the same opportunity. He'd been concerned about having the large and erratic Russian in a tiny boat at night with a big dangerous croc close to them. 'Plenty of work for everyone. We don't all have to be in the boat and hanging about. Crocs can take off and cause problems. Might be best if the ladies hung around the camp at night.'

'No, Marta is star, she must be in boat with hunter,' insisted Topov.

Drago stepped in. 'I understand what our director wants. I'll follow the action in the second boat, Peter can hold the spotlight, Johnny can steer,' said Drago soothingly.

'Colin and Marta can come with Clive and me,' said Len.

Marta hissed to Colin, 'Unbelievable how Topov gets out of the work.'

'Sounds like keeping Topov out of the way suits Len,' answered Colin.

'Y'know, Topov, you can't just peg a claim anywhere,' said Len. 'You gotta have a licence and register it.'

Topov dismissed their talk. 'I make find, we film it and government know I discover uranium.'

'Steady on, mate. Do we want another Rum Jungle out here?' said Len in alarm. 'Leave it there.'

'He's not going to find any minerals,' said Helen. 'Let him go and play.'

Topov dug into the pocket of his baggy pants and pulled out a folded paper, smoothed it out and waved it at them. 'Topov have licence. We find money in this ground. Lots of money.'

Helen snatched the piece of paper. 'What's this?' she glanced at it and looked at Len. 'It's a fossicker's licence.'

'So let him fossick. Come on, let's get this camp sorted out and you do a bit of rock climbing while I get the gear ready for tonight,' said Len.

The group ignored Topov as he fiddled with his Geiger counter.

'These dogs are pathetic,' said Marta as the skinny dogs hung around them.

'They look like dingoes, don't they?' said Colin.

'They'll keep you warm at night,' Len explained. 'That's why this mob keep 'em around. You've heard the expression, it's a two- or maybe a four-dog night?'

Marta burst out laughing. 'Really! I'd rather have something else keep me warm.' And grabbing Colin's hand she picked up her small bag and headed for their tent.

Eventually the group, without Len and Johnny, set off, wading through waist-high, brittle, sun-faded grass towards the small escarpment, led by Clive and his son George. Topov came with them carrying his Geiger counter, a stills camera and a notebook. As they neared the rocky outcrop Clive lit a small fire then smothered it with green branches and, as the smoke rose, he called out, chanting to his ancestors.

'Maybe he's telling them we're here and asking permission so we can go to the caves, that sort of thing,' suggested Colin.

The group stood quietly, while Topov signalled to Drago to use the Bolex to film the ceremony. Clive then set off again but, at the base of the rise, everyone looked up wondering how they were going to reach the craggy overhangs. Topov paused to wave the tube of the Geiger counter over a pile of rocks.

It was a tricky climb, very steep, but there were obvious footholds that helped them reach the first level. They crouched in the first overhang where smoke from centuries of fires stained the shelter. There were paintings of animals, large kangaroos, emus, birds and lizards as well as hunting implements which retold the tale of successful hunts. Several white handprints walked over the roof. But the main painting, winding across the shelter, was of a massive crocodile.

Drago was glad the shelter was so open as it allowed in plenty of light and, with Clive's nod of agreement, he filmed the paintings and the view from the shelter across the landscape to the river in the distance. Down below, Len and Johnny were just specks in their little campsite.

But when Clive indicated that they had to squeeze through a crevice and climb further up, it became more difficult. Clive led the way, his semi-naked body scrambling with sure-footed ease, while George helped the rest of them by placing their feet onto tiny footholds that they couldn't see in the dark. When they reached a slightly more level, if narrow, ledge they edged along it following Clive until he ducked under a low overhang and wiggled out of sight.

'Where's he gone? This is scary,' said Marta, holding onto Colin.

Colin went through first and soon there was a muffled call. 'It's not too bad, you can stand up.'

One by one they inched through the narrow labyrinth of passageways until they found themselves standing in an extraordinary domed gallery lit by a narrow funnel that let in light from the sky above. It acted as a foyer to a series of cleft shelters going back into the rockface. On one side was an opening that had a view of the landscape, unseen by those below.

Once they'd all squeezed through, even a surprisingly agile Topov, they stood in silence and looked in awe about them. High above, narrow slits were decorated with stylised symbols and strange stick-like figures. They were so high that it was hard to imagine how the artists had reached up to paint them. The impact on the party of the hidden gallery was as powerful as though they had entered a temple or a cathedral. Each one felt that they were in a sacred space, with a feeling of aloneness, of privilege, with the innate knowledge that they were seeing something unique that was the embodiment of a spiritual and living culture. It was not a museum, this was a space that had been lived in, with discarded shells, bones and blackened fire rings showing that here was a seasonal place for feasting, celebration, mourning and artistic endeavour to ensure future good seasons.

Clive, familiar with possibly every inch of this internal landscape, was nonchalant. 'Up there, that old one paintings. See old boat, come here, 'fore whitefellas.'

'It looks like a canoe with a sail, or a kind of raft,' said Peter. 'They must have come from Asia. I know my Dutch people explored this part of the world. Arnhem Land is named after a part of the Netherlands,' he added.

'I'm going to sit near the opening,' said Helen. 'I feel I'm being smothered in here.'

'Drago, take shots of Marta and Clive with paintings,' ordered Topov. 'I look outside, at view. Maybe I see good place to find minerals.'

They spread out through the monastery-like complex while Drago had Marta and Clive stand in the best available light. Marta gazed up at the dramatic figures etched in white ochre.

'They're strangely flat. And these look like they're fresh, newer,' she said to Clive.

'We touch 'im up. Paint over for ceremony.'

'So you said,' exclaimed Marta. 'But some of them look very, very old.'

Clive nodded in agreement. 'White school fella say mebbe forty thousand.'

'Years?' Peter looked amazed as he wandered over.

'Look at the ones back here, they're a deep colour, like old wax,' said Colin, joining them. 'The patina has almost become like the rock surface.'

'It's incredible,' agreed Drago. 'I hope Topov appreciates this footage.'

'He's so preoccupied with the minerals and that infernal machine,' said Helen, reappearing.

'If I'd known about Topov's obsession with geology I might have thought twice about this trip,' said Peter.

'We'll talk about that later. Let's look around a bit more,' said Marta. 'There's so much here.' She glanced at George, who must have been eighteen years old. 'You come here very often with your father?'

He shook his head. 'Not much.'

'So this is a secret place?' Colin asked Clive.

Clive nodded. 'Some of our people forget 'bout here. They forget ceremony, painting up, look after old people. They no hunt, they want whiteman tucker. You take good picture dis place. So we can keep 'im, eh?'

'This be big scene in movie,' agreed Topov enthusiastically.

Drago checked the film in the Bolex. 'Yes, we'll take good pictures. Then when you're an old man and can't climb up here, you can look at them,' he smiled.

Clive gave a huge smile. 'Ah, my bones come back here. Sleep long time. George den do painting, eh.'

George nodded, looking down at his feet, but somehow the group of visitors were not convinced. They saw a future in which young people would not be carrying on the traditions in the same way.

The climb down didn't seem as precarious as they chattered about the amazing art gallery in the escarpment. They walked back through the long grass to the camp and Clive took them on a detour past a crystal, glittering lagoon where Mary and Violet, with the baby in a sling on Violet's back, were wading amongst the waterlilies pulling up tubers and putting them in pretty woven dilly bags.

After dark they all crammed into the Land Rover and Len's truck and drove down to the river where Len had set up the boats. Topov, who'd spent the rest of the afternoon fossicking, nervously accompanied them although he complained his eyesight at night wasn't very good.

'I be director on the shore,' he decided.

'It's too dark and we're going down river,' said Drago.

'I wouldn't be standing on any river bank in the dark with crocs around, mate,' said Len.

'You can watch from the back of the truck with me,' said Helen. 'I know I can help out in some way, but there's not much room in the boats.'

'Don't worry, I'll put you to work one way or another when we have to skin 'em,' said Len cheerfully.

'You can have my place in the boat. I'll join Helen,' joked Johnny to Topov.

Topov squared his shoulders. 'Topov go in boat.'

'Fine by me. I'll call the fire brigade if something goes wrong,' said Johnny.

Len wasn't happy with Topov's decision but he settled the director next to him in the stern while he held the tiller of the small wooden dinghy. Clive, holding a roughly made metal harpoon on a rope, squatted in the bow. Marta, pale and quiet, sat in the middle.

'We'll motor quietly up to where I'm pretty sure the old bloke hangs out. We might row a bit too, so as not to disturb him. If there's an unusual noise like the motor or if the spotlight upsets him he can sink and keep out of sight. They're cunning buggers.'

Drago, Colin and Peter were in the slightly bigger runabout. Drago sat in the bow with the camera, Peter steered the boat, which also had an outboard motor and he handed Colin the spotlight as he sat in the middle.

Len gave them all a quick briefing on running the boats and suggested the best angle for filming. 'Wait till I give the signal before turning the light on,' he said to Colin.

'You show us big crocodile, for Drago,' said Topov. 'Drago, get close-up pictures.'

Drago didn't answer.

'Have you ever hunted in the daytime?' Marta asked Len, thinking that it would all feel less threatening if the sun were shining.

'Yeah. Some nights if I haven't been able to get a croc, I put out a marker buoy and come back in daylight and have another go. Crocs tend to sit on the bottom. If it's clear water I might dive down and take a gander to see what he's doing.'

The two boats set off, close together, the engines so quiet that they could still carry on a conversation.

'You ever had a croc attack you?' asked Peter.

'If I had I wouldn't be here to tell the tale,' said Len.

Marta shuddered. 'Imagine those jaws eating you up.'

'Crocs don't eat you right away,' said Len in a chatty tone. 'They grab whatever takes their fancy then roll and roll, the death roll it's called, and drown their prey. Then if it's something big like a dog, a 'roo, a big lizard, they shove it somewhere, under mangrove roots, under a submerged log, to let it rot a bit. Then they come back and eat.'

'Ugh. That's horrible,' said Marta.

Clive, squatting quietly in the bow, scanned the dark water. He lifted his arm and Len cut the engine. Clive pointed up ahead, held up a light and swung it across the surface of the water.

'Do you see anything?' Marta whispered across to Colin.

'No. Do they make any noise?' Colin asked Len in a low voice.

'They have a bark-like call I've heard on occasion. There, look up on the right. See the two red dots, that's his eyes. They're on top of his head which is why they can lie there submerged and still hunt.'

Len signalled Drago who called softly. 'Yes, I see. Too far away to film. Clive, can you stand up?'

Topov took the light from Clive. 'Good picture, take him,' he told Drago who had already been filming Clive's loose-limbed body balancing easily as he held the heavy, sharpened harpoon head while Len took an oar and paddled the boat towards the red eyes.

'Where is monster?' asked Topov in a loud voice, swinging the light across the water.

'Quiet, Topov, don't alert him,' hissed Peter who'd seen the red glow of the crocodile's eyes.

Len chuckled. 'He's right. This is a monster . . . You can tell by how far apart his eyes are.'

The dark surface of the water was crumpled over the spiny back of the floating crocodile. Len rowed slowly forward. Clive lifted his arm and hurled the harpoon. Drago swung the camera onto the thrashing croc, which disappeared from sight as the rope spun out of the boat. Suddenly the rope went taut and the dinghy was towed roughly through the water by the fast-swimming crocodile. Marta screamed and clutched one side of the boat.

Topov leapt to his feet shouting.

'Sit down, Topov,' shouted Drago. 'I can't see what's happening.'

'Keep up,' called Peter.

Clive began hauling the rope, inching hand over hand, his face creased with effort.

'It's too bloody big, mate,' cried Len.

'Be careful,' screamed Marta. 'It'll pull you in!'

There was a moment of tension when everything seemed to stop. Clive stood motionless, not relaxing his hold on the rope. The crocodile had stopped swimming. A second or two later and seemingly out of nowhere, the croc spun forward, charging the boat and leaping out of the water in front of Clive.

Marta screamed. Clive fell backward into the boat as Len scrambled between Marta and Topov with his rifle. Topov grabbed the oar that Len had dropped and stood up, poking at the thrashing crocodile as it twisted, rocking the boat alarmingly and preventing him from taking aim. There was a crunching sound and the croc dropped back into the water.

'You all right, mate?' Len asked Clive as he got back to his feet. 'Bring the light here.'

He grabbed the light and they saw that the wood had splintered and that part of the bow was now crushed. Len checked the damage and turned around and gave Marta a tooth. 'He left some teeth behind. Have to dig the rest of them out with a knife.'

'Where is it? Will it come back?' asked Marta fearfully.

'He got 'em harpoon, boss,' said Clive ruefully.

'That's going to slow him down a bit,' said Len. 'Where do you reckon he is?'

Clive inclined his head and Len shone the light across the water.

'Where is monster? Bring him back for pictures,' shouted Topov.

Len glanced back at Marta. 'Struth, the man is crazy.' He waved at Topov. 'Why don't you just jump in and haul him up? He's down there, under the boat.'

Len cut the motor and they drifted quietly for a few more minutes, slowly waving the light across the river. Then Clive pointed and as Len steadied the spotlight they saw the frayed end of the thick rope on the surface of the water.

'I'll paddle us over there,' Len said quietly. Dipping the oar in from side to side, he inched the boat towards the rope. In a swift move Clive leaned down and grabbed it as Peter brought the runabout closer. Topov began issuing instructions loudly to Drago.

'Cripes, hit Topov over the head will you,' said Len.

They were in shallower water now, but as Clive anchored the ropes around the small front seat, the croc suddenly resurfaced, making another lunge at the middle of the boat where Marta sat. It flung itself upright on its tail, flashing the pale yellow skin of its underbelly. Marta shrank back and the boat rocked dangerously. Amidst the cries, shouts and shrieks there was an explosion as Len fired his .303 rifle into the head of the crocodile, which went limp, almost instantly.

'Stand up, Marta,' shouted Topov. 'Shoot with rifle!' cried Topov as Peter brought their boat close to the action for Drago to film.

'Got 'im 'tween the eyes, boss. Good shot, eh.' Clive, who'd grabbed the croc started lashing it to the side of the boat as Len ripped the motor to life.

The weight of the croc slowed the boat, but as soon as they were back at the clearing where they'd left the vehicles, the men all helped drag the croc onto the bank. Helen and Johnny hurried down to see what was happening. Johnny let out a low whistle, for once at a loss for words.

'My God! It's enormous,' said Helen.

'It's so much longer than the boat,' said Marta who had started to shake.

'Get lights on him! Marta, you get close,' called Topov, dancing around the scene, waving his arms.

'Bloody oath. Come on, get down close to him, here's a rifle,' said Len, helping Marta into position as the spotlights splayed over the muddy scene. Drago moved in for close-ups. Clive returned from the truck with a huge hook on a length of wire and a chunk of putrid meat.

'What's that for?' asked Peter.

'Goin' fishin',' grinned Clive.

'How many more are out there?' asked Helen.

'They're pretty territorial. But Clive knows where another old female hangs out. We'll set this bait.'

'Did you get some good shots?' Colin asked Drago.

'I hope so. It wasn't easy.'

'Let's get this fella into the back of the truck,' said Len. 'You can take some more pictures of it in daylight. Then we'll skin him.'

Helen stood by the truck, holding one of Len's rifles, as Johnny held up a spotlight. Marta and Topov headed for the vehicle and, further along the river bank, Peter and Drago pulled the runabout ashore. Len and Clive untied the crocodile lashed to the side of the dinghy, Len standing knee deep in the water as they pulled the heavy animal out of the river. It was chaotic and everyone was excited at capturing the large croc.

Helen suddenly snapped at Johnny, 'Lift the light, lift the light. There, to the left.'

Johnny swung the light to the side. 'What? Oh Jesus! Is that another one? Len, look out!'

Before Len and Clive could move, there was a rush of water as another crocodile lunged from the river, jaws snapping. As it leapt forward, Helen raised the rifle she'd been holding and fired without hesitation. The water churned and bubbled, then the croc sank from sight. Clive and Len rushed out of the river.

'Did you get it?' asked Len. 'Careful, Clive, it might make another dive at us,' said Len breathlessly.

Johnny held the spotlight aloft as they waited, staring at the dark water.

The others came racing to the truck.

'What was that?'

'Another one! Stand back.'

Len looked at Helen holding the rifle. 'You might have got it. Quick reactions, mate. Thanks.'

Marta looked at Helen. 'You shot a crocodile?'

'I believe so.'

Clive headed to the water's edge. 'Yep. Dis fella gone, boss. Gone dead.' The Aborigine turned and looked at Helen with a big grin. 'You good shot, missus. Quick one.'

It was late by the time they got back to the camp. The Aboriginal women were curled up with their dogs by the smouldering campfire. By now everyone was on a high, especially Topov. He produced a bottle of rum from the caravan and passed it around.

'Topov say we go north and get action! Man-eating monster! Good, very good, eh?'

'Yeah, thanks for lining up the croc attack,' said Johnny dryly. 'What's next?'

'Tomorrow you can help Clive with the skinning,' said Len. 'Then we'll head out and see what else we can find. We need a few more skins than this to make a quid or two.'

'What about buffalo? We hunt buffalo, plenty action,' exclaimed Topov.

Len finished rolling his cigarette and licked the paper. 'Yeah. We could do that. Not much money in it, but.'

'Topov, we're here to make money, remember,' said Helen.

'We make film and Topov find mineral. We be rich!' he exclaimed.

'I'm going to bed,' said Johnny.

'In daylight we'll check the hook,' said Len. 'Bring your camera.'

'Yes. We'll be there,' said Drago.

Topov tossed back another mouthful of rum, screwed

the cap on and said to Len, 'You keep teeth of monster for Topov,' before marching to his caravan.

Len rolled out his swag. 'Don't know how you blokes put up with him.'

In their tent, Marta snuggled into Colin's arms. 'Ooh, I was so afraid. I kept imagining that the crocodile was grabbing me, or that one of us was falling into the water.' She shuddered.

'You probably won't be involved anymore in croc hunting. Drago got some good shots, he thinks. But we need a few more skins to sell, that's for sure,' said Colin.

'Topov is dangerous. He could cause an accident. He's crazy, I think,' said Marta. 'It's all his fault we're out here.'

'He does seem a bit mad at times,' said Colin. 'All this mineral and uranium stuff. And why'd he get a fossicker's licence?'

'I wish he would go away. Fall down a hole, disappear,' said Marta sleepily. 'Then Drago could finish the film.'

Colin kissed her ear. 'I think everyone is running out of patience with Topov. Come on, let's not think about him. He just makes me cross.'

For the next few days Drago, Peter and Johnny worked with Clive, George and Len, capturing five more crocodiles, although none were as big as the first ones. Topov lost interest in croc hunting and began roaming further afield in his hunt for minerals but he refused to talk to the others about where he went and whether he'd had any luck.

Helen helped Len roll up the skins and carefully store them under a tree in the shade.

'I reckon that you'd make a great croc hunter,' said Len shyly. 'Maybe when we get back to Darwin I could take you out on my horses. We haven't had a chance to yet, have we?'

Helen smiled. 'That'd be nice. What will you do with the crocodile skins?'

'Ah,' said Len, 'It depends. The best quality belly section is cut out and sold for a good price, while the rest of the croc skin will have to be sold for less. I know this bloke in Darwin, he'll give us good prices.'

Remembering the time she had spent at Brolga Springs, Marta enjoyed the company of Mary and Violet. They went out food gathering and she spent hours sitting with them as they showed her how they soaked thin strips of pandanus leaves in a dye solution made from sandstone ochres and tied several of the strips together in a coil which they bound around each other to make mats, baskets and a lid for the cooking pot. Marta especially loved their long dilly bags decorated with feathers, bits of bark and twisted twine and leaves. She tried her hand at weaving but was not dexterous enough and the women giggled as they expertly showed her again what to do. In the end they gave her a bag in return for one of her shirts. Marta was amused to see the women taking turns in wearing it.

While their life was basic, they enjoyed their meals of crocodile meat and wonderful fish. Most of them fished in their spare time, though it was scarcely a sport. The area was so unspoiled that the fish almost leapt into the boat or onto their hooks. Queen fish, barramundi and giant mud crabs became staples in their diet. It was a wonderful existence.

Only Colin was out of sorts and he finally confessed to Marta that he was suffering from a toothache that was getting worse by the day. By the middle of the next morning Marta could see how swollen his jaw had become.

'Colin, you have to go back to Darwin and see a dentist. Len, he has to go to Darwin.'

'Topov does not go Darwin,' said Topov. 'You go, we stay.'

'I don't want to interrupt things here,' said Colin miserably, knowing Len had plans to try and snare another big croc.

'Clive can yank out your tooth,' said Len. Then seeing the expression on Colin's face, he grinned, 'No worries, sport. Take one of the vehicles, George will go with you and see you onto the road to Darwin.'

'Good. I'm happy to drive but I need some guidance to get back out of here onto the main road.'

Discussion flew around the camp. Clive, George and the women spoke together. Clive then spoke to Len.

'We all move camp. Go to other place. Make business, ceremony.' He looked questioningly at Colin. 'Okay. You take us to camp, you and George go to start of Darwin road.'

Colin looked at Len, who shrugged. 'If you need to see a dentist then drop the mob off and you go to the big smoke. You might as well stay there, won't take us long to finish up here, just a couple of days or so.'

The knowledge that his dreadful pain might soon be eased came as a huge relief to Colin. 'If that's okay with everyone, I suppose I can stay in Darwin.'

'See how you go, mate. We'll see you there in a couple of days, if all goes well,' said Len.

So it was agreed that Colin would take the Jeep and drop off Clive and his family at a point where they'd meet up with ''nother mob from over west'. George and he would then head west and onto the road to Darwin. Colin packed quickly and hugged Marta.

'No, Marta, don't think of coming. I'll be all right. I don't want you to miss anything exciting,' said Colin, kissing her. 'I'll find somewhere to camp on the beach again. I just want this tooth fixed.'

'I think I've had enough excitement,' said Marta. 'We'll celebrate when we're all back in Darwin. And hopefully Len will get a good price for the skins.'

Marta waved Colin off with young George confidently driving the Jeep with Clive, Mary, Violet and the baby in the back.

Marta felt lonely without Colin, Violet and Mary. Suddenly everyone was busy with their own tasks. She was so bored that she even asked Topov is she could go and watch him fossicking.

At first he was surly and negative, which didn't upset her as Topov was always grouchy first thing in the morning. So she shrugged and decided to tidy the tent and pack and wash some clothes in the tin of water set by the fire. But later Topov came to her carrying his Geiger counter and a bag with water, his notebook and some food. A hat was crushed on his head, his director's viewfinder, as usual, was around his neck and his long socks were rolled over his boots and his fancy belt holding up his baggy shorts. His sunglasses were in his top pocket and the remains of his toast were sprinkled on his beard.

'You come if you want. Just short way, first stop near crossing. Later Topov go hunting for more minerals, you come back here.'

'Okay. Sounds like a nice walk,' said Marta agreeably.

Topov and Marta walked along the flattened grass tracks to the river downstream. There was a shallow crossing of boulders with ankle-deep water splashing across it. Marta was very hesitant to cross.

'Isn't this dangerous? Aren't there crocs around?'

Topov gave a dismissive wave. 'No-one eat Topov. Too tough,' he shouted.

Marta smiled to herself. Topov was a tough old nut, prickly and hard to crack. She wondered if under the rough shell there was soft heart. If there was, she'd never glimpsed it.

They splashed over the crossing and into the bush on the other side. Topov soon became engrossed with his Geiger counter and Marta quickly became hot and bored.

'Where are you going?' she asked.

He waved vaguely towards some rock in the distance. 'Where rocks are. Very interesting.'

'How much longer will you be? I'm just so hot here and looking for rocks and minerals is boring.'

'I look until it start to get dark. Then I come back.'

'Well, I'm going back now. You be careful of crocs.' With that she turned and made her way back towards the camp.

Marta walked back the way they'd come. She stopped under a eucalyptus tree and saw a line of red hills and a strange mushroom-like rock. The landscape before her was coloured in unbelievable hues of reds, blues and greens, spread before her like a brilliant painting.

No-one would believe that these colours are real, she thought. She stood there as the silence enveloped her. She closed her eyes, straining to pick up even a minute sound, a rustle of the yellow grass, a swish of wind, a creaking branch, the cry of a bird. But all was silent. She opened her eyes and looked around, absorbing the images she'd keep with her for a lifetime.

'I know there are stories, secrets, out there,' she said aloud. 'This land is too old and has seen so much. But it's a silent country that will never speak to me. Only to its own people.'

She turned and made her way back to the camp.

13

THE WARM AND FLATTERING TV lights around Marta hissed and died as the plug was pulled, leaving her features still beautiful in cold daylight, the spell broken. Geoff readjusted the reflectors, the gauze and gels as both Veronica and Marta caught their breath. Then Marta undid the microphone on her lapel and Veronica glanced at her notes. She hadn't really looked at them after Marta had started talking, for Marta's memories had flowed fluently with no pauses or struggles to recall a particular moment.

'Marta, you were wonderful,' said Veronica. 'I feel I was there with you. Crocs and all.'

'My husband couldn't believe I did all that,' she smiled. 'It really was a lifetime and a planet away from where I am now.'

'Your life worked out very . . . comfortably, for you,' said Veronica, searching for the right word.

'Eventually,' Marta sighed. 'I know Colin loved me. But,' she shrugged. 'He was naïve, unsophisticated and meek. I knew that he could never make me happy.' She gave Veronica a steady look. 'You have to face these decisions in your life. And take control. I was never one for laissez faire. I was not going to wait and see what came along. I went after what I wanted. And Paolo has been a magnificent husband. He is kind, courteous, generous, smart, amusing, sophisticated. Everything I ever wanted.'

'It does seem almost too good to be true,' said Veronica. 'But I doubt it works out that way for everybody.'

'Maybe not. But for some of us, who are strong, determined and go for it, you'd be surprised. Don't be passive in life, Veronica.'

Marta stood up and Geoff rushed to assist her. 'Is that the end of the interview? I was just getting into your story. What happened next?' he asked as he rolled up the cable of her microphone.

'A lot,' she said giving him a flirtatious smile. 'This is the intermission.' She glanced at Veronica. 'How much more do you want to know for your program?'

'Well, my biggest question is, what happened to Topov? He was taken by a crocodile, wasn't he?'

'Ah, yes.' Marta glanced at Geoff. 'Perhaps it's best we discuss this first. Then you can decide how much you want to tell in your show.' She glanced at Veronica. 'You can keep your tape recorder running, if you like. I'll ask Allegra to bring us coffee.' Marta pushed a button on the phone. 'Then I will tell you the truth.' She looked at the shimmering lake and the steep dark hills. 'It all seems so long ago, so far away. I never thought I'd revisit those days,' she said softly.

'I'm sorry if this is difficult for you,' said Veronica. 'I didn't think . . .'

Marta lifted a hand, her diamond ring catching a shaft of sunlight. 'I have nothing to hide. I know Colin and I are innocent.'

'Innocent?' asked Veronica. 'I thought that Topov was taken by a crocodile.'

Was it a smile, a sigh, a shadow, that touched Marta's face? Veronica waited.

'It's getting late. I don't understand why Topov hasn't come back,' said Marta. 'Maybe I should go and look for him.'

'I'll drive you. Can't have you driving round the scrub by yourself this time of day when 'roos are about,' said Len. 'Anyone else want to come?'

Everyone was occupied, they had been all day. Johnny had been fishing, Drago had gone out looking for suitable filming locations and Peter, as usual, had kept to himself. Helen and Len had packed up most of the croc skins, ready to take back to Darwin. Now, as daylight began to fade, they all sought the comfort of the blazing campfire. Without the Aborigines and their dogs the camp seemed unsettled, unsafe almost. Drago and Peter had dragged extra wood onto the fire and Johnny was busy preparing the fish he'd caught.

Then it was Helen who spoke up. 'I'll come with you.'

'Bring the gun, might try and get a 'roo to cook for tomorrow,' said Len.

They set off, Marta squeezed between Len and Helen. They reached the river crossing and waited. Marta got out and looked around. There was no sign of Topov.

'Where was he going?' asked Len gazing at the small jump-ups nearby.

'In that direction, I think,' said Marta, pointing into the gathering gloom. 'We walked across the river and then I wanted to come back and he said he'd return to the camp later.'

Len rolled a cigarette and smoked in silence, waiting for Topov to show up. But by the time Len had pinched the end off his cigarette and ground it under his heel, Helen had become impatient.

'Why don't we drive over there and find him? The silly fool could be lost.'

'Righto.' Len got back behind the wheel. 'Let's go. It's easy to lose your way out here. Especially once you get among those rocky outcrops.'

'Do you think he'd discover anything out here worth mining?' asked Marta as they drove over the Crossing.

'Finding anything is probably like finding a needle in a haystack,' scoffed Helen.

'Dunno, he could be lucky. They say the Rum Jungle is making a decent quid for the blokes that found it,' said Len. 'And the same might happen in Queensland for the prospector who pegged that Mary Kathleen uranium mine he found last year.'

They drove a bit further before Len stopped. 'Don't want to go too far in the wrong direction.'

'Blow the damned horn,' said Helen.

Len gave three long blasts on the horn, then turned off the motor and waited.

Forty-five minutes later it was almost dark so Len decided to drive around and look a bit further afield.

'Helen and I will stay here. Just in case he turns up,' said Marta.

Len drove off, his headlights brightening the rocky terrain.

'Do you suppose anything has happened to Topov?' asked Helen.

'He's probably just lost,' sighed Marta. 'Really, we should leave him out here for the night and teach him a lesson.'

'He is a headache,' said Helen forcefully.

They sat in silence a few moments. 'Look how quickly night comes,' said Marta. 'One minute it's light, then the next it's dark.'

'No lingering twilight in the northern Australian bush,' agreed Helen.

'Do you like it here?' asked Marta suddenly.

'Australia? Or this outback?'

'Both, I suppose,' said Marta.

'I didn't at first. I hated the loneliness and the vast spaces, but I like it more now.'

They heard Len's truck returning.

'About time, now we can get back for dinner,' said Helen.

'He's driving very fast. Len must be hungry too,' said Marta as Len's vehicle careened towards them, the headlights bouncing up and down.

He pulled up, flung open a door and kept the motor running. 'Get in. Quick.'

'What's up? What's happened?'

'Where's Topov?'

The door had barely slammed before Len took off again, crashing the gears.

'He's out there.'

'Is he hurt?'

Len concentrated on the terrain, turning the wheel to avoid a boulder. 'Yeah, he's hurt all right. He's dead.'

'What?'

'My God! How? '

Len didn't answer but braked to a stop. In the glare of the lights they saw Topov, slumped against a rock, his head at an unnatural angle.

Helen was first out of the truck. She raced over to him, feeling for a pulse.

Marta was horrified. She stood shaking. 'What happened? A heart attack?'

Helen straightened up. 'There's blood on him.' Gingerly she tried to move him.

'Do you think he fell?' asked Marta.

'From where?' said Len. 'Anyway, look at his face.'

'Bruises. Bad cut on his nose.' Helen looked at Len. 'How could this happen?'

'I've seen enough fights in my time to recognise one. He's definitely been on the wrong end of a blue.'

'Well, we can't leave him here,' said Helen briskly.

Marta watched, hand over her mouth, as Len and Helen struggled to lift Topov.

'Come and help, for goodness sake,' said Helen.

It took the three of them to lift Topov's bulk into the back of the truck.

Drago and Peter stood up as the truck sped towards them. Johnny remained in his fold-up chair nursing a mug of black tea. When the three got out without Topov, Drago and Peter went over.

'Don't tell me the silly bastard is lost.'

'Not exactly,' said Len. 'There's a problem.'

'He's dead!' exclaimed Marta, her voice rising.

'What?'

'Christ! What happened?'

Johnny hurried over. 'What the hell happened to him?'

'Where is he?' asked Peter.

Len nodded at his truck. 'Help me get him out.'

'What're we going to do with him?' demanded Johnny.

Len didn't answer as they lifted Topov off the back of the truck and laid him gently on the ground. 'You don't have to treat him with kid gloves, he isn't going to feel a thing,' said Len. 'Get a light.'

'Look at the blood,' said Drago.

In the light from a torch, they could see a nasty head wound as well as the bruises on his face and his bloody nose.

'He's been in a brawl by the look of him,' said Johnny. Everyone began talking at once.

'What went on, for God's sake?' muttered Drago.

'He wasn't the most popular man in town, was he?' commented Len.

'Who would do this to him?' asked Helen.

'So what do we do now? Get the police?' asked Marta.

'Out here? And what for? He's dead. Nothing is going to change that. He's done nothing but cause problems for us from the start. Now here's another one,' said Johnny.

'It must have been an accident, surely,' said Marta. 'Because there's no-one else out here but us.'

There was a sudden tension in the air as everyone looked at each other, the same question in their minds.

Johnny was first to react. 'Hey, hey, don't look in my direction. I didn't beat him up. I was fishing.'

Len held up his hand. 'No-one's accusing you of anything, but then, no-one liked Topov. He was a con man, he took your dough, he was a bastard.'

'That's for sure,' muttered Peter.

'But we have to let the police know,' said Marta.

'I don't think that's a smart idea,' said Johnny. 'Questions and more questions. Alibis, explanations, checking into our backgrounds.' He shook his head. 'For what?'

'So is this a murder?' asked Peter. 'Or a terrible accident?'

At the mention of murder, everyone looked horrified. It looked as though someone had either deliberately killed Topov, or, at the least, left him to die and it had to be one of their party because there was no-one else out there. But no-one raised an accusatory voice. It was incomprehensible to any of them that there was a killer in their midst. Then Len spoke up.

'Look, the man is dead. It might've been an accident, tempers can get out of hand, but it might not have been, so the cops are going to ask a lot of questions. We could be hanging around for a long time. Inquest, coroner's report, God knows what else. Frankly, I'd find that a pain in the bum. Red bloody tape.'

'Oh no, we could be stuck in Darwin for weeks and weeks,' cried Marta.

'And who's going to pay for that?' asked Johnny.

'It's all very inconvenient,' said Helen.

'We'll have to notify Madame Olga,' said Drago.

'Maybe somebody did everyone a favour,' said Len quietly.

All of them avoided eye contact, but no-one disagreed with Len's comment. They turned and stared accusingly at Topov lying on the ground near the truck.

'Should we cover him up?' asked Marta. She was trying to raise some sympathy for the old director, but she, too, was secretly relieved. She was sick of Topov's film, it was not just stupid, it was dangerous and she'd had enough of it all.

Helen must have had similar thoughts because she looked at Drago and said, 'And what's going to happen about the film? Can you finish it? It seems a shame to have come this far, done so much, for nothing.'

'There are some good scenes, but I can't see how it was ever going to cut together,' Drago replied. 'I could finish shooting, but I don't know what Topov had in mind, it's all been a bit . . . disjointed.'

'I'm not hanging around to finish this project. We don't owe the old bastard anything,' said Johnny.

'Let's at least look in his caravan and see if he left any

notes about the film. Get something to put over him,' said Helen.

'I'll go and look in the caravan,' said Johnny, 'And I can raid his rum, too. He won't be needing it.'

'I'll see if he has any personal documents. It's such a pigsty in there,' said Helen. Helen and Johnny took the torch and headed to the now pathetic-looking, battered little caravan that Topov had so loved.

Marta pulled a canvas chair closer to the fire, her back to the lump on the ground which Len had covered with an old oilskin. 'This is like a horrible dream. A nightmare,' she said. 'So why do I feel so relieved?'

Drago and Peter also pulled their chairs closer to the fire as Len stood, his back to the flames and rolled a cigarette.

'Nasty business. Wonder who he upset,' mused Len.

'Everyone,' said Drago and Peter almost in unison.

'Might be worth going back to the scene in daylight, see if we can pick up a few clues,' said Len. 'Too bad Clive's gone. He's a good tracker, that one.' He glanced at them. 'What's done is done. Whoever did it will have to live with it for the rest of their life.'

They were wrapped in their own thoughts as the torchlight in the caravan flickered at the window.

Then Johnny came out, closely followed by Helen. 'Bloody hell, you're not going to believe what the bastard's done,' he called.

'Or didn't do,' said Helen. 'It's outrageous.' She was shaking her fist, waving something in it.

'What did you find?' asked Marta.

'Look at this. Our money. He had it all the time!'

Marta jumped to her feet. 'I don't believe it! Where did he get it? How come he didn't pay me! How long has he had it? We're out here in the wild, risking our lives and he's sitting on *our* money!'

'It must have come from Madame Olga. She must have sent it to him in Darwin and he hid it from us. That's outrageous.' Helen shook her head.

'Why didn't he pay me the two hundred pounds he owed me?' asked Marta.

'He really must have wanted to come out here to Arnhem Land,' said Drago thoughtfully. 'I suppose he knew that we were getting annoyed and figured we would only stay because of the money he owed us.'

'Yeah, if I'd known he had the cash, I would've taken what he owed me and pissed off,' said Johnny.

'Well, that's what we can do now,' said Marta. 'We can go back to Darwin and buy plane tickets out.'

'But what abut the film?' asked Drago.

'It's not our film,' said Peter. 'I agree with Marta. We go.'

'But we can't leave Len stuck out here, we agreed to help him. He agreed to help us, actually,' said Helen.

Everyone looked at Len.

Len dragged on his cigarette. 'We probably have enough skins to make a few bob. But no-one's flying off anywhere while there's the problem of Topov's body. Are we going to tell the cops?' he said matter of factly.

They were all silent.

Then Johnny spoke up. 'What if there wasn't a body? If Topov had just . . . disappeared.'

Len sucked the last drag from his cigarette and tossed the soggy end into the fire. 'Was a bit of luck finding him, actually.'

'And if we hadn't found him? We would be on our way to Darwin,' said Marta.

'And how would you explain his disappearance?' continued Helen. 'Wouldn't the police have to come and look around?'

'Possibly. They need to know how he died,' said Len.

'We could just bury him,' said Marta.

'We can't just go back without him and not say anything,' said Peter.

'We could do that,' agreed Len. 'But it doesn't stop the police looking for answers. But I think there is another way . . .'

They all looked at Len as a bit of a smile lurked at his mouth.

'What if poor old Topov was taken by a croc?' There was an intake of breath as Len continued. 'Mind you, we didn't actually *see* the tragic event, but I'm a professional and despite our warnings he wandered down to the river, which I know is a big croc's territory. And the signs of what happened were obvious.' He sighed. 'Sadly, no remains were found.'

Johnny picked up the story. 'We shot a number of crocs and opened them up, looking. But no luck. Terrible thing. Scared us all. So we packed up and left straight away.'

They all looked at each other, the mood shifting.

'Sounds good to me,' said Peter.

'There's one thing, though,' said Len, gazing at each of them in turn. 'This is not to go past this group here tonight.'

'Obviously,' said Helen.

'Of course,' agreed Marta.

'That includes your friend Colin,' said Len.

'Why? He's trustworthy,' said Marta.

'Because Colin is dead honest and bloody naive. He'd think it was his duty to tell the police what really happened,' answered Johnny.

'Yeah, he wasn't part of this, so why tell him,' said Len practically.

'Are you sure such a story is believable?' said Helen, looking at Len.

'Easier than the truth,' said Len. 'How do we explain that?' he pointed towards Topov's body, 'Without implicating one of us?'

'So we're all agreed,' said Marta, wanting to resolve things.

'Do we need to make a pact, like blood brothers or something?' said Johnny.

'Pass the cup of rum and we'll toast Topov and that'll be the end of it,' said Peter.

There was a sense of a blood pact, a secret shared, as the enamel mug with the rum went from one to the other, each shaking the hand that gave it to them.

A hasty meal of damper, fish and a leafy green which Mary had showed them how to pick and cook was soon dispatched. The last of the rum was passed around the circle. The moon rose above the distant ridge that Topov had been so sure held riches deep in its heart. The air was clear and cool. The fire burned brightly, a beacon in the darkened landscape around them.

It was Marta who rose shakily to her feet. 'I want to propose a toast to Maxim Topov. Director, cinematographer, entrepreneur, irritating rascal, a mad, wild ira . . . iras . . .'

'Irascible,' supplied Helen.

'. . . Irascible man who drove us crazy. But also made us laugh and who believed in himself and his dreams, although no-one else did.' She lifted her mug. 'Dream on, Topov.'

'To Topov. Who brought us here,' said Helen. 'Which we will never forget.'

'That's for sure,' said Johnny.

'To Topov's dream and film,' said Drago quietly.

Everyone drank and there was a short silence. No-one was going to raise the issue of how Topov died.

Johnny broke the spell. 'So, what're we doing with him?'

'Bury him,' said Helen.

'We can't just leave him out here. He deserves a bit of a service,' said Drago.

'Oh, Topov wasn't religious,' said Marta.

Len stood up. 'We'll bury him in the morning and we'll mark the place with our own cave painting, eh?'

This broke the solemn spell as everyone discussed the sort of picture that would sum up Topov without identifying him. There were ribald and ridiculous suggestions until finally they settled on Drago's idea of a stylised interpretation of his director's viewfinder.

'That'll give the Aborigines something to ponder,' grinned Len. 'There's a lot of white and red ochre around here. We'll do it properly.'

It was after midday before their convoy drove away, heading back to Darwin. Marta looked back at the mushroom-shaped outcrop below which they had buried Topov, the spot marked by a symbol painted on the rockface above the grave.

Len had made sure they dug very deep, to stop the dingos from retrieving the body and he was meticulous in brushing away signs of digging and footprints from around the site. Then they had gone to the river and Len pointed to the spot where Topov could have been taken by a croc, describing its mudslide, the location of its nest and what might have happened to Topov's body. After the excruciating detail, Marta thought it better that Topov had died the way he did and had not been taken by a giant reptile.

Marta turned her back to the lake and smiled at Veronica. 'The police accepted every word we said. Len convinced them that Topov had been taken by a crocodile. We handed all Topov's personal things to the police and told them to forward them on to Madame Olga.'

'So, the story I read in the paper was not true,' said Veronica.

'No. That story was made up by Len. Anyway, it was the beginning of the end for us, too. Colin and I went back to Sydney, but without the film we had nothing in common. He went back to the bank, I looked for work as an actress. Television started and I made some TV commercials. To me that wasn't acting but it paid better than the theatre. When I had an offer to go to Hollywood it seemed like a lifeline out of Sydney and I was pleased to go.'

'The adventure was over,' prompted Veronica.

'Yes. The outback, that wild, wonderful, beautiful, dramatic country swept us along. I imagine everyone went back to mundane lives, but none of us could forget that country and lifetime we travelled through.'

'Did you ever see the others again? Do you know what happened to them?'

'I exchanged cards with Colin over the years. I believe Drago went back to Europe and became a very respected cinematographer in feature films. Peter went to Western Australia looking for work. Johnny stayed in Sydney but I don't know what he did. The most surprising thing was that Helen stayed up north with Len. They got married and Helen bought a property and they bred horses or some such thing. One never knows how life will turn out.'

'You might be surprised to know that Johnny became very rich, though his business interests have come under some suspicion . . . gambling, casinos, nightclubs, entertainment connections and so on,' said Veronica.

Marta gave a small laugh. 'That sounds correct.'

'He's still alive. In fact, he was not at all happy that I started investigating this story.'

Marta raised an eyebrow. 'Really? We might not have done the right thing. But we just wanted to get away from there. And frankly, most of us despised Topov. He did the wrong thing by us all. I don't think that anyone wanted justice for him. Besides, none of us wanted to believe that one of us had caused his death and, frankly, no-one was brave enough to make an accusation.'

Veronica looked at her notes, trying to phrase her next remark. 'Marta, later on, did you ever discuss it with Colin and tell him what happened?'

She shook her head. 'No. We agreed on that. It was better he believed that Topov was taken by a crocodile.'

'So you never found out what really happened to him?'

'You mean, who in our group was responsible for Topov's death?' Marta shrugged. 'I have thought of scenarios but I know that I did not do it. Nor did Helen . . . The bruises on his face. That was ugly, I'll never forget that. Only a man could do that.' There was an interruption as Allegra appeared with the silver coffee service on a trolley.

'Thank you for being so open with me,' said Veronica. 'I still have unanswered questions of course. But there are some happy endings – you, Doris, Helen, Drago.'

Marta nodded. 'Poor Colin. He married but I suspect he wonders what his life might have been like if the film had eventuated. Johnny sounds like he achieved what he wanted, to be rich. But he is a man always looking over his shoulder, I imagine, even now in his old age.'

'Marta, would it be possible for me to find where Topov was buried?' asked Veronica suddenly.

Marta lifted the ornate silver coffee pot. 'Yes, perhaps, but what would it achieve if you found him?'

'I don't know,' said Veronica. 'Closure, perhaps. The film, I know nothing came of it, but what happened to the film that was shot?'

'The cameras, Topov's notes, his personal things,

403

everything, were all given to Madame Olga. I have no idea what happened after that.' She poured the coffee and handed a cup to Geoff with a brilliant smile. 'Sugar?'

As Veronica waited in the departure lounge before boarding her flight home, she felt a tap on her shoulder and saw her old friend Gordon smiling at her, dressed in his immaculate flight attendant's uniform.

'Where've you been?' he asked. 'A holiday?'

'I wish. No, an interview in Italy. Can we chat later, when everyone is asleep?' asked Veronica. She couldn't think of a better person with whom to share her story about Marta and her experiences with Jamie.

'I'll find you when I have a break.' He waved and went on board.

The movie was halfway through and most of the passengers seemed to have dozed off when Gordon tapped her on the shoulder again and motioned her to the galley at the rear of the plane.

He handed her a glass of wine. 'From First Class, it's a good drop. Now, tell me what's been happening. I heard that you'd gone bush somewhere.'

'I did. I've been in the Territory. I loved it, especially Kakadu. I've been chasing a story about a film expedition that happened more than fifty years ago. Then Andy dug up a woman who was on the original expedition and now lives in Italy. She did well for herself. Married a billionaire and has houses around the world. I went to interview her at her summer house on Lake Como.'

'Woohoo! So tell me more. Have you met anyone else interesting in your travels?'

Veronica sipped her wine. They were speaking quietly as Gordon tucked into his dinner tray. 'Actually, I have, in Darwin. His name's Jamie McIntosh and he's an environmentalist. He's been very helpful.' Seeing Gordon's raised eyebrow, she smiled. 'Yes, he is dishy. Very special.'

'Too bad he's in Darwin.'

'I'm going back up there. Marta, my contact in Italy, gave me some interesting information.'

'What a glam job you have. Like me.' He rolled his eyes.

Veronica smiled. 'People do think our jobs are fabulous but they don't understand the gruelling side of it. And I'm not happy about the great new idea of shoving me in front of the camera all the time. I've had the cameraman shooting me doing the most mundane things . . .'

'I hope you did your hair and make-up!'

'That was the last thing on my mind. See, I'm not cut out to be a front of camera person. I hate the idea of losing my privacy. I wish Andy would come up with something different and not make me the focal point of the show,' Veronica said.

'I can see the thinking. It's a good idea because you'll look great and the show will get good ratings and you'll get a bigger budget and everyone will say it's all because of you. By the way, did you hear the news about your boss, William Rowe? He owns your network, doesn't he? He's been nominated for Australian of the Year,' said Gordon, pleased to impart news she didn't know.

'Is that so? He seems a decent sort of man. Even cynical Andy likes him and says that he has business integrity. He's given a lot of money to various charities, too,' said Veronica. She took another sip of her wine. 'Oh, and you'll never guess who I worked with up north,' she continued. 'Eddie. That's where he went.'

'No way!' Gordon loved this piece of gossip. 'How was it? How did you feel? Did the ol' heart go pitter patter?'

'Absolutely not. It was fine for a while, very professional. He is a terrific cameraman. But I'm glad we broke up. The man is a serious male chauvinist pig. He certainly objected to taking instructions from me.'

'I'd been telling you that for ages, darling heart.'

'Y'know, Gordy, since I've been up in the Top End I've realised how debilitating city life can be. Rush, rush, rush, all the time. I never thought I'd question my career, but I'm starting to feel like I'm treading water.'

'Been there, done that? Maybe being in front of camera will give you a bit of a boost once you get used to it,' said Gordon.

'I love working, but this whole story of the original expedition and the people back then and those people I've met in Darwin have opened my eyes to a lot of things.'

'Hmm. Like?' Gordon gave her a shrewd glance.

'How life can work out so differently from the way one imagines or expects it's going to.'

'Would this have anything to do with this Jamie guy?' He hastily swallowed the last mouthful of his dinner as a passenger's bell rang. 'Blue light calling. Better see what 32A wants. Here, have the rest of the wine. Let's catch up soon.' He kissed her quickly and disappeared behind a curtain.

Veronica thought about her chat with Gordon as she headed into the office to see Andy. Why had this particular story, these people, these places and events, affected her more deeply than any other story she'd done?

Andy gave her a hug. 'Good to have your cheerful presence back in the joint.'

'It's good to see you,' said Veronica. 'We have a lot to catch up on. How are the other stories working?'

'Pretty well. Of course, they aren't monsters like this one, but then we are still doing them in the old format. This one is really going to break new ground for us.'

'Pleased to hear it,' Veronica said, smiling at her boss.

'Did you get my emails? Where have you got to in your investigations?'

'I've got a few leads. But first, tell me what you made of Marta. Is she telling you the truth about Topov?'

'I don't doubt her for a moment. She's very beautiful, self-centred as mega-rich people can be, but her story was really compelling. It turns out that they all lied to Colin and the police about Topov's death. Colin still believes that Topov was taken by a croc.' Veronica filled Andy in on all Marta had told her.

'Well, that does half answer why John Cardwell doesn't want the story to come out,' said Andy.

'Half answer?'

'It seems from what Marta says that any one of them could have been responsible for Topov's death,' said Andy slowly. 'Apparently they all disliked the man and on the day he died, everyone had an opportunity to confront him.'

'Are you thinking Johnny – John Cardwell – might have been the one that did?' asked Veronica.

'Why else would he put the heavy hand on Colin and us?'

'But Colin didn't know anything.'

'Well, maybe Cardwell just didn't want any of the events brought up again because he doesn't want to be implicated in Topov's death, even after fifty years,' mused Andy.

'But that's not going to stop us, is it?' said Veronica.

'Not until we've found out as much as we can,' said Andy. 'But we still need more facts.'

'Like?'

'Like finding Topov's grave. It might still be there, untouched. Finding his remains would make the program even more interesting and verify Marta's story. The icing on the cake, as it were.' Andy gave her a swift look. 'I don't suppose you'll have any objection to going north again?'

'To find Topov? That could be a long shot.' She tried to remain professional but she could feel a huge smile breaking out on her face at the thought of seeing Jamie again. 'Marta gave a fairly detailed description of the place where they buried him, I'm sure Jamie could help us find it. It's worth a shot.'

'I think so. Use Dougie again, his stuff was good.'

'Well, we'll go out and see what we can find.' But Veronica had difficulty reminding herself Topov's body, if it was there, would be mere bones by now. To her he seemed still very much alive, a much larger than life character.

'I know that you believe Marta, but it still sounds pretty wild. I think we'd look a pair of jackasses if we dragged the police into this now on a rather flimsy premise. But if we do find a body, it will change things and it won't just be a vague story of a forgotten journey,' said Andy.

'Do you want to see some of the interview with Marta?'

'I certainly do. Especially the bit where she talks about burying Topov,' said Andy.

'She wouldn't say that on camera,' said Veronica. When Andy's face fell, she added, 'I did, nevertheless, get it all on my personal tape recorder.'

'We can't use it without her permission.'

'She agreed I could use the tape and it does give the details of where they buried him.'

Andy slapped her on the shoulder. 'Excellent. We could use her voice over the scenes of your finding the remains, if and when you do.'

'Maybe. Now, what leads do you have?'

'While you were slumming it at Lake Como, I haven't been idle. I've been on the trail of Madame Olga Konstantinova.'

'Really! Did she stay in Sydney?'

'On and off it appears. I haven't been able to ascertain

much about her relationship with Maxim Topov. But she was quite the social doyenne in her time. There're lots of reports of social functions at her Darling Point home and references to the Count, presumably her husband, who was always abroad it seems.' He paused. 'And she had two daughters who were at school in France, improving their accents.'

'So did she stay in Australia or go back to Europe?'

'She went back and forth to visit her daughters. Her husband's career seems a little shadowy and vague. The daughters eventually came back to Australia . . . and stayed here.' He paused for effect and then continued, 'One of them, Valma, still lives in Olga's house.'

'Really! We can film the place where it all began!' exclaimed Veronica. 'I wonder what ghosts might lurk. Have you talked to her about this?'

'Indeed I have. She has heard of Topov, but never met him and never took much interest, though she recalls her mother mentioning him. She's rather ambivalent about the whole thing, so I thought I'd leave it to you to meet her and whip up some enthusiasm and get permission to film there. The other sister is younger and doesn't recall much either. She lives in Paddington but is overseas at present.'

'What's the older sister like?'

'She's never married and I got the impression she's not fond of men. So I told her you'd be in touch. Use your charm.'

'So she's in her late sixties at least . . . How do I handle this? Maybe I have to explain what a wonderful entrepreneur her mother was and how she supported this film project . . . Do you think that's the way to go, Andy?'

'You understand women better than me, Veronica. Whatever works. My antennae say Valma holds a key.'

*

409

That evening, after unpacking and heating up a frozen meal, Veronica curled up in her bed. She was glad to be back in her own surroundings and she decided to ring Jamie.

'Hi. What are you up to?'

'Watching some rubbish on telly while I put off making a lot of notes for a talk I have to give. Have you recovered from Italy?'

'I'm a bit jetlagged, but I can't relax, I have so much spinning around in my head.'

'About?'

'The story, of course. I found out a lot in Italy and Andy's come up with some new info.'

'Ah, of course. So the story's going well?'

'It's certainly proving to be interesting. Actually, I'm planning to come back up to the Territory. I need to get out to Arnhem Land again.'

'You do? Happy to help.' The warmth in Jamie's voice flowed down the phone line.

Veronica found herself curling into the bed, cradling the phone. 'I haven't had a chance to tell you all that Marta told me.'

'No, I got your text messages about the scenery, the food, some amazing house. What's the good news that's going to bring you north again?' asked Jamie. 'Work or not, Billy – and I – will be happy to see you.'

Veronica told him at length what Marta had related about the fate of Topov. It felt good to share it with someone who was really interested, other than Andy. And it helped her to go through the details once more.

At the end of the story, Jamie seemed quite amazed. 'That's a heck of a story. Do you have any theories about who might have thumped him? And why?'

'Everyone had a motive, I guess. But now Andy wants me to come up there and try to find the place Marta described, where they buried Topov and see if we can find his remains.'

'If you do find it, are you going to show it on TV? If you are, you'll have to follow correct procedures. That means police, forensic people, coroner, too.'

'I know, but it means some sort of closure to the story.'

'True, but it will still leave a lot of unanswered questions, won't it? What kind of info have you got to help find the place where they buried him?'

'Quite a good description. I'd like to talk to John Cardwell to see what he remembers, but he's very media shy,' said Veronica, yawning. 'I'm sure that he doesn't want this to come out.'

'That sounds a bit suspicious. Maybe he's the one who had the fist fight with Topov. You sound tired, shall we talk more tomorrow?' said Jamie gently.

'Yes, I'd love to, after I've had a good night's sleep. I'll let you know when I'm arriving up there. I'll have to alert Dougie, too.'

'I'll meet you. I'll tell Mum and Dad, they'll be happy to see you again. In fact, would you like to stay with them? Mum loves visitors.'

Normally Veronica would have refused such an offer because she liked her peace and privacy when she was working and she'd liked the place she'd stayed before. But Doris and Alistair were another matter. 'I don't want to put them out . . .' she began.

'I'll get Mum to ring you. If it's not convenient, she'll say so. Go to sleep. We'll talk tomorrow.'

'G'night, Jamie. Thanks.'

Andy handed Veronica a piece of paper. 'Valma Konstantinova. Olga's daughter. Phone number and address. You'll see her before heading north?'

'Thanks, I'll check her out. Tom is free, so I can line him up to film an interview if she agrees to one. I told Jamie everything Marta described about where they buried Topov and he thinks he knows the spot. There's a mushroom-shaped rock formation over the river crossing and that seemed to pinpoint it for him.'

'Excellent. You said you plan to stay with Jamie McIntosh's family?' He raised an eyebrow.

'Saving the company money,' said Veronica shortly. 'Besides, Doris is part of the story.'

The house at Darling Point was as Colin had described it, grandly brooding, the sandstone walls smothered in dark ivy and, Veronica thought, probably looked little changed since Olga and Topov gathered together the hopeful investors in their plan to film the Australian outback. The house seemed locked and the shutters were closed, the French glass doors were sealed and the blinds drawn. She went up the flight of stone steps to the heavy front door and rang the bell.

Eventually, as she was about to turn away, Veronica heard the doorknob rattle and the door swung open. A tall, plump woman with braided graying hair wound around her head, porcelain skin with red cheeks and pale eyes stared at her.

'Miss Konstantinova? I'm Veronica Anderson. From Network Eleven. This is Tom, my cameraman.'

'Yes. We spoke on the phone yesterday. Please come in.' She stepped to one side. Veronica followed her inside and was immediately hit by a slightly musty and dusty smell of age, a faint trail of faded flowers.

Valma Konstantinova was heavyset but carried herself well, her shoulders back, and had an air of superiority about her. She had clearly been an attractive woman.

'I'm afraid I've just arrived home, so I haven't had time to prepare any biscuits or cake.'

'Please, nothing for me, I'm fine. We'll try not to take up much time.'

'We can sit in here. I'm not sure I'm going to be very helpful, I really know very little.' She led them into a glassed-in conservatory that looked out onto the rear garden.

'This is a magnificent garden,' said Tom. 'A lot to look after.' His unasked question about the house hung in the air.

'I do what I can. I have some help,' said Valma. 'Now, make yourselves comfortable.' She sat in one of the old armchairs and folded her hands in her lap.

Veronica took her notebook and small tape recorder from her handbag. Tom unhooked his digital video camera from his shoulder and gave Veronica a questioning look.

'Miss Konstantinova, may we film our little chat? I think I explained what we're doing on the phone . . .'

'As you wish. I'm sorry I can't tell you very much. My sister and I were away at school in France at that time. We didn't come back here very often, we had only the occasional holiday in Sydney.'

'So when did you come back here to live?'

'After my mother died. My sister, Sacha, married an Australian, so I decided to join her here and I took over this house.' Valma had a faint accent, almost American.

'Your parents were Russians who escaped the Revolution?'

'Yes. They lived in China for many years and my father made a lot of money there. My mother was very outgoing and rather flamboyant.' Valma gave a small smile. 'My father was rather taciturn. From what I understand Mr Topov was also . . . colourful.'

'Do you know anything about Maxim Topov even though you never met him?' Veronica glanced at Tom and saw him zoom in on Valma's face.

'No. I have seen photos of him. I believe that my mother was helpful to him because he was Russian, too.'

'Was it a relationship based on a special friendship or was it just a business arrangement?' asked Veronica tactfully.

Valma shrugged and smiled. 'Who is to say? Maybe both of those things. While I don't wish to paint my mother in an unfavourable light, I believe she was fond of Maxim. She could be quite volatile but I believe that she was very distressed when he died. She said that she thought he was a great filmmaker. I suppose that's why she funded him.'

'Do you think he might have been?'

'I don't know. Mama seemed to have faith in him. I suppose that's why she kept his personal things, which the police sent to her after he died.'

'Where are Topov's belongings now?' asked Veronica, barely drawing breath.

'Still in the attic where my mother put them. But I don't think there's anything of any value,' said Valma.

'Could we see them?' asked Veronica.

'I suppose so. But I will have to ask my sister first. It may take some time to unearth them. My mother had a lot of things up there. She never threw anything away.'

'That would be very, very helpful,' said Veronica.

'It might take a few days, but I'll see what I can find,' said Valma.

'Thank you so much. You also mentioned photographs of Topov. Where are they?'

'Oh, they're around. Have you seen pictures of him?' asked Valma.

'Only one, which I got from the internet.'

Valma continued. 'I think there are a few around the place, I'd be happy to show you. He does look quite a character. I can see why he might have appealed to my mother. You know, beret, beard, long scarves, a polka dot silk cravat. He was theatrical looking. Like Mama. My father was more the business type.'

'Miss Konstantinova, I can't thank you enough,' said Veronica trying not to appear as excited as she felt. 'You've brought a shadowy person to life for us.'

'I doubt Maxim was ever called shadowy.' She smiled. 'And please, call me Valma. I think, however, that it was a terrible thing that he was eaten by some awful creature.'

Veronica paused. 'There may be some doubt about that now. We believe that the circumstances of his death were not quite what your mother was led to believe. It appears that it was easier at the time to bury him and to say that he was killed by a crocodile than to face a police inquiry.'

Valma stared at her. 'Why would anyone do that? I'm so glad my mother isn't alive to hear this. It was bad enough his dying . . . Who were the people that lied?'

'Some of them are still alive. I'm trying to piece the story together, which is why I'm anxious to see if there is anything in Topov's possessions that could give us a clue.'

Valma shook her head. 'I wouldn't imagine so. But then neither my sister nor I have gone through them.'

'I'm going back to the Northern Territory to try and find out more. Perhaps when I come back you might have had a chance to find Topov's things?' said Veronica. 'And I can fill you in, hopefully, on anything I learn.'

'That's kind of you. I'll talk to my sister and I'll make a foray to the attic. It's a job that has been in the back of my mind. We are not getting any younger and all this is quite a . . . museum.' She waved her arm around the living room which Veronica assumed hadn't altered since

Olga lived there. The faded brocade curtains looked very dusty and old and the furniture was already unfashionable fifty years ago.

Veronica stood up and Tom turned off the camera and took off his earphones. 'Could we take some shots of the garden? It's quite magnificent. As is the view.'

'You used to be able to see much more of the water,' said Valma. 'But the trees are taller and there are more new homes. Sydney is very crowded now. Please walk around the garden. I'm afraid it's not as immaculate as when my mother kept it. Gardeners are expensive these days.'

While Tom got the exterior shots of the house, Veronica sat in the car excitedly relaying the news of Topov's belongings to Andy.

'Did she say what sort of possessions? We don't want old boots and a Russian hat,' he said. 'The photos would be good, though.'

'Yes. It could be interesting,' said Veronica. 'I really don't know what there is. We'll just have to wait and see.'

The heat and brightness hit Veronica the minute she stepped from the plane. Sydney had been dull and cool when she left and now she felt her spirits lifting. But she was unprepared for how excited and moved she was at the sight of Jamie and Billy waiting for her.

'This is so good of you!' exclaimed Veronica as Jamie kissed her cheek and Billy jumped up and down.

'We're going on a picnic and lots of things! Are you staying a long time, Veronica?'

'She's here to work, Billy. Now come on, let's get going. Is this all you've got? The one small bag?'

Veronica nodded. 'I want to go back to that nice shop with the camping gear. I love their clothes for this climate. So, Billy, tell me what you've been up to.' She took his hand as he hopped beside her as they headed to Jamie's car.

With Billy chattering excitedly about school, his art project and his soccer team, Jamie and Veronica barely had a chance to exchange a word before they arrived at Doris and Alistair's home.

Jamie took her bag from the car and Billy raced inside to find his grandmother while Alistair greeted her warmly. 'Welcome back, dear girl. Doris is so looking forward to having you stay. She'll chew your ear off, so remind her that you have to work or just go to your room and close the door.'

'I'm looking forward to chatting with her,' laughed Veronica.

Doris embraced her warmly. 'Cup of tea and a biscuit? Or do you have something to do right away?'

'Cup of tea would be wonderful. I have to touch base with the station and my cameraman to make plans but I'll need to talk to Jamie first.'

'I thought we might talk over dinner tonight, if you'd like,' said Jamie. 'Billy has a sleepover at a mate's place down the road.'

After their cup of tea, Jamie and Billy left and Alistair retreated to his study, so Veronica filled Doris in on what had happened to Topov.

'It is quite a remarkable story. Odd, though. The personal dynamics are most interesting,' said Doris.

'There must have been a lot of suspicion among the group over which of them had punched Topov and been responsible for his death. But they made a pact about a fictitious crocodile attack and stuck to it.'

'You must remember the times too, Veronica. They were in a remote area and communication and travel in that country in 1955 were difficult. And I can believe that they didn't want to get held up with a lot of red tape. I'm not condoning what they did, but I'm putting myself in their position,' said Doris. 'Now, tell me about Marta. What's she like?'

'She's beautiful, looks younger than she is and seems to have had a life of luxury once she married Paolo, who is charming in that Italian aristocratic kind of way . . .'

'I don't know many Italian aristocrats,' said Doris and Veronica smiled.

'As a young woman she was so independent and such a talented actress but once she had security and a life of glamour and indulgence, it seems to me her ambition evaporated. I don't know what she's done with her life, but she obviously enjoys it.'

'Did she remember me?' asked Doris.

'Of course she did! She asked me to send you her warmest wishes. She was very touched when I told her you'd kept her bracelet.'

'So she told you about what really happened to Topov. I suppose she had no reason not to tell you,' mused Doris.

'She was a bit surprised when I told her I was going to try and find his remains,' said Veronica. 'At first she said we should leave the past alone, but then she agreed that since I'd gone this far with the story I should try to resolve it. She gave me as many details as she could about where they'd buried Topov and Jamie seems to think he can find the spot.'

'He's very happy to see you back here again. And not just for professional reasons. He's rather fond of you, I think.' Doris gave her a penetrating look.

'As I am of him,' admitted Veronica.

'I saw that possibility,' said Doris gently. 'Naturally I want my son to be happy, he's had a lot of heartbreak and he's retreated inside himself, emotionally.'

'You're saying you don't want to see him hurt again,' said Veronica.

'I'm talking to you, woman to woman. I want you to

be aware of the fact that Jamie is committed to living up here. Not just because of his job, but because of his obligations to his family and ties to his country here.'

'And a city girl like me doesn't fit?' asked Veronica, the full implication of Doris's words sinking in.

'I'm not saying that at all. I'm asking you to consider that, should you fall in love with my son, perhaps your life with him could be very different from your current life.'

'I understand, Doris. And thank you.'

Veronica thought about what Doris had said. She did not take it as a mother protecting her son but saw Doris as an older, wiser woman alerting a younger woman to the pitfalls of a complicated relationship. And she had done it in such a way as to make Veronica feel that she cared about her as much as she did her son. She was even-handed and not judgmental.

It was Saturday afternoon and only a skeleton staff was at the TV station when Veronica arrived, but Dougie was working and greeted her cheerfully. 'Hey Veronica! Good to see you. So we're going bush again?'

'Yep. You up for that?' She hadn't told Dougie or Murphy, the chief of staff, exactly what she hoped to find.

'Yes, trouble is I'm in the middle of a shoot, so it might be a couple of days before I can get away. I s'pose you could talk to Murphy about getting one of the other guys . . .' He looked crestfallen.

'No way, Dougie. I want the continuity of the same cameraman. Your stuff looks great.' He was also good at thinking on his feet and was beginning to read her mind.

He beamed at her. 'Thanks, Veronica. It's been really interesting and I liked getting out there, especially with Jamie. I learned a heap.'

'Me too. As I said, I was wondering if I could look at the footage we shot when we went out to Arnhem Land, especially at Wild Man's Crossing.'

'No prob. And thanks, Veronica. This trip'll be very cool. Wish you worked up here all the time.'

The young cameraman's words struck her. Could she work in a small affiliate station in Darwin after the pressure and power of producing a top-rating Australian show, especially in the same television station as Eddie? Uh, uh, she answered herself. No way. What was she thinking? She thought Jamie was a lovely man, attractive, sexy and thoughtful, but after her talk with Doris, she could understand his reluctance to start a relationship. All very well for her to come in to town occasionally and have a fling, but past that? Forget it. She could see it was all too hard.

The video Dougie had shot, brought back strong memories as she watched it in the editing suite. The variation of landscape – from stone country and billabongs, paperbark swamps, towering escarpments, floodplains and mangrove forests – gave her again a sense of what a special place it was. No wonder Jamie enjoyed visiting it so much.

'Thanks Dougie, that's refreshed my mind, but I can't spot what I'm looking for. I'm trusting Jamie will find the particular place I'm after.'

'Righto. Talk to the boss. I should be free in a day or so. See ya then.'

'Good one. I'm off to see my mate at the paper.'

Jim Winchester was pouring over the racing form from the morning newspaper as she tapped at the door. 'G'day. You busy?'

'Hey there, Veronica. Got a pin? Might be just as good at picking a horse for me.'

'I thought you were working hard and giving up your Saturday afternoon. How's Mary?'

'Great. She has the gardening club at the house for a chitchat and cake and pruning tips. I thought I'd get in the way so that's why I suggested we meet here.' He folded the paper. 'Good to see you back.'

'I'm really glad to be back. I love this climate. And the people, of course.'

'That's a truism. Bloody wonderful people up here, even with the industry expansion and population explosion. Great comradeship once you're out of the city shallowness. Want to go to the pub for a beer?'

'Sure. I need to give you the full run down on what I'm doing.'

'Yeah, Andy mentioned there was something afoot. Remember, you've promised us the exclusive.'

'Only after it goes to air, though a teaser to promote it would be good.'

'So what's the story?' asked Jim, ordering drinks after their short walk to the pub and carrying the frothy cold beers to a corner table.

He listened, sipping his beer, as she told all she knew.

'Strewth. Are you insinuating there was foul play? Be careful of legal action. I wouldn't go near that one with John Cardwell involved. Is this why he warned you off?'

'Perhaps. I just don't think he likes any unwanted attention. I also get the sense that there was a strong pact between them all to let sleeping Topovs lie,' said Veronica.

'I take your point about saying nothing till you know if the body is out there. It's a good story. A death-by-default solved fifty years on. But you know, there's any number of unknown deaths, bodies languishing in never-never land. It's harsh and lonely country and people disappear.'

'A land that doesn't give up its secrets easily,' said Veronica.

'Nope. It's a silent country all right. Back in the fifties there was no Aboriginal voice or presence, or acknowledgment of their culture until the famous anthropologist W.E.H Stanner talked about the "Great Australian

Silence". Some things are simply never spoken about. I think your filmmakers must've embraced the silence theory and you must ask yourself, what will it achieve to crack that agreement made by them all those years ago?'

Veronica was thoughtful. 'I hadn't thought of it like that. But even with an argument like that, I can't walk away from this story now. I'd fail as a journalist and as a curious woman.'

'So, you're going to do this?

'Come on, would you leave the story this far in? You wouldn't,' said Veronica firmly.

'Okay, you're right, I wouldn't. But I like to play devil's advocate. Final piece of advice: as well as having Jamie, I'd take Reg Sculthorpe along, the Aboriginal guide you met at my place with Bonza. He will balance the story. While it's true that Jamie is an intelligent and educated part Aborigine, who knows a lot about his culture, Reg talks as a blackfella.'

Back at Jamie's parents' house, Veronica joined Alistair and Doris for a drink before dinner. She told them she planned to take Reg Sculthorpe with them and Doris agreed it would be a smart move.

'I was talking to Jim at the *Darwin Daily* and he mentioned something called the "Great Australian Silence",' said Veronica and Alistair nodded.

'Ah, yes, Stanner. He was a very fine anthropologist in the fifties and sixties who challenged the way Australians thought about themselves and this country. According to him, Europeans practised what he called "the cult of forgetfulness", which relegated Aborigines to the past, but not to history.'

'It seems that Topov, in his crazy way, was trying to break that silence,' said Doris. 'He simply wanted to show people what there was beyond the cities and the suburbs.'

'Perhaps without knowing it, everyone was drawn to

go on that expedition to find out more, not only about this country and landscape and people, but about themselves,' said Veronica slowly, trying to clarify the thought.

'And perhaps what they found was not always to their liking,' said Doris. 'Australia can be confronting, for some, but for others it can be comforting when you find you belong.'

Veronica looked at Alistair relaxing in the deep armchair, nursing his scotch and smiling at them. 'What about you, Alistair? Your homeland is very different, very far away. You have a wife with extremely strong ties to her Aboriginal heritage. Where do you feel you belong?'

Alistair looked fondly at his wife. 'I found I belong wherever she is. My life would be very colourless without her.'

They heard Jamie calling down the hallway.

Veronica stood up. 'You are very special people. I'm very glad I've met you both.'

'Enjoy your evening, Veronica,' said Alistair.

'Have fun,' said Doris, smiling broadly.

'I thought we'd go out to Cullen Bay. We've missed the sunset, but it's still pretty by the water and there's a very good fish restaurant,' said Jamie.

'Seafood sounds good.'

Jamie made her laugh with funny anecdotes and stories of local characters and events. He was so easy to be with, to talk to and share confidences. Maybe it was the wine, but Veronica found herself occasionally not paying attention to what he was saying and instead studying the way his eyelashes curled and the shape of his lips over his even, white teeth. He really was too beautiful to be true, she thought.

As they left the restaurant, hand in hand, Jamie asked, 'Want a nightcap at my place? I just need to nip down the road and check everything is okay at the sleepover,' he said.

'Love to,' she said.

He parked in his driveway and handed her the key. 'There's a bottle of white wine in the fridge, I'll just see how our friends have survived the onslaught of five small boys.'

Veronica opened the wine, found glasses and took them onto the back patio, settling herself into the big cane lounge.

'Glad you've made yourself at home.' He dropped a kiss on top of her head, reached for a glass of wine and sat beside her, stretching his long legs.

'Billy okay?'

'Was a bit of a struggle getting the boys to settle down, but they're all out cold. They're having a big barbecue breakfast so I can sleep in.' He glanced at her. 'Seeing you have a couple of days before we can leave for the bush, would you like to go somewhere? See anything special? I'm all yours.'

She closed her eyes thinking, I wish. 'Um, I'm open to suggestions. It's your country.'

'Okay, I'll take you to places other people don't know about. It'll just be us.'

'I like the sound of that.'

He leaned forward to top up her wine, but instead put his glass down and took Veronica in his arms. In minutes their kisses unleashed the feelings that had been simmering beneath the surface for a long time. Their bodies were entwined, damp with the heat of the tropical night and the surrendered passion they both felt.

'Come inside. It's cooler,' murmured Jamie, picking her up and carrying her into his bedroom where the overhead fan turned softly.

Veronica awoke as daylight sliced through the wooden slats of the window shutters. She looked at Jamie's lean brown body against the tangle of white sheets thinking how wonderful their lovemaking had been and how hard it would be to leave this bed.

He opened an eye and gave her a quizzical look. 'What are you thinking?'

'What will your mother say? I hope she's not worried.'

'She won't be surprised. I sent her a text last night anyway.'

'Saying what?'

'That I was hoping you'd stay the night.' He reached for her as he whispered in her ear. 'It's been so long, so long. And now to find you . . .'

She kissed him, stemming his words. Veronica didn't want to think past this moment. All she wanted was to lose herself in the joy of Jamie's arms.

14

FOR THE NEXT TWO days Jamie, with Billy, Doris and Alistair, showed Veronica around Darwin. She saw many delightful facets of the city she might never have discovered as a tourist. One of Jamie's school friends was up from Melbourne with his family and they all went fishing. Veronica couldn't help comparing Jamie's family with her own and wished that she could share the laughter, discussions, friendly debates and closeness with her own parents as Jamie did with his.

She had visited her parents on her return from Italy and while they'd been interested in hearing about Lake Como and Marta's house, the story she was pursuing, its ins and outs, held little interest for them. When she told them she was off to Darwin again, they merely nodded, recognising that this was what she did as part of her job.

Veronica had told them that she thought the outback was wonderful and had explained how Jamie McIntosh was helping her with the story. But even when she said how much she liked him they'd asked few questions, so she dropped the subject. When she'd rung her sister, Sue had been full of her own news but sighed at the mention of Italy.

'We so want to go to Florence and Venice, but the trouble is finding the time and the money. Do we take the girls? Let us know any time you can come and take charge. Oh, Vee, I wish Mum and Dad would act more like grandparents.'

'They do, Sue! But they're both working and have busy lives. Taking care of two youngsters is a full-on job. I can't see when I'd be free to do it, either.' It seemed to Veronica that they had this conversation regularly.

Veronica had rung Andy and explained that she would be delayed a few days as she'd prefer to wait till Dougie was free and then she'd set off for Arnhem Land with Jamie and Reg.

'I'll take a couple of days leave, Andy. I'm just playing around, having fun,' she explained.

'Is Jamie looking after you? Relax, have a bit of a break, you must have accrued a ton of overtime. Don't worry about it,' he said.

'I'm having a great time,' said Veronica. 'I can't tell you how marvellous this is. Any other news?'

'No. I've looked at your footage of Marta. Lake Como is quite a contrast to what you've shot in the Territory. She's very glamorous. Be good for publicity when we get this whole thing together.'

'I just hope it does come together,' sighed Veronica. 'I don't know what we're going to find.'

'Do what you can. I'm sure you don't mind getting back out in the long grass with that handsome Jamie bloke.'

'Andy, that's not an appropriate thing for a boss to say! Though I have to admit it's been one of the best jobs I've ever had to do. Apart from sticking my face in front of the camera all the time.'

Andy chuckled. 'The big boss cruised through the other morning. Asked how our new star is doing.'

'Oh, God, no. Why is he asking about me and not the story? I just hope he doesn't cut our budget – before we tie this one up.'

'Seems okay so far. He's looking forward to the story, even though he doesn't know much about it, as we'll be breaking new ground with this program. I have to say that Rowe grows on me. I think he's a great nominee for Australian of the Year. He certainly seems to be more hands on since being nominated,' said Andy.

'Well, I'll know more in a few days, I guess. Jamie is taking me to one of his favourite spots today. I'm really loving it up here.'

'Don't get too attached, Veronica,' said Andy. 'I'd hate to lose you to the wilds of the north. Keep in touch.'

'Will do, though I don't know what the mobile reception's like once we get out of Darwin.'

She dressed carefully even though she was only wearing shorts, shirt and sandals and a floppy straw hat. While Jamie said he'd bring their picnic, Doris suggested that Veronica could pick some bananas from a bunch hanging in the back garden.

'Enjoy Howard Springs, it's lovely. Nice swimming hole, big barra in there, too. Some good walking trails and there's a lovely orchid farm,' she said as she kissed Veronica goodbye. 'Sorry I can't chat, but I have to dash off to work.'

Alistair had gone into town to do some work and have lunch with a friend from the university so Veronica sat on a cane chair in the front garden waiting for Jamie. These last few days had been different from anything she'd experienced before. Doris and Alistair had ignored her comings and goings between Jamie's house and theirs. Because she and Jamie had agreed that it was better if she was not at Jamie's place when Billy got up at breakfast time, she was madly looking forward to being with Jamie all night out in the bush at the Crossing.

She was still in wonder at the feelings Jamie's love-making had aroused in her. His ardent and passionate nature emerged without overwhelming her, and his sweetness and gentleness made her ache with longing. She couldn't wait to be with him.

Veronica glanced at her watch. In her romantic musings she hadn't noticed the time pass. Jamie was running late. She checked her phone but there were no messages. She hoped everything was all right. Then her phone rang and she started to smile as she saw it was Jamie. 'Hi. I'm all ready . . .'

'I know you've been waiting. I have a bit of a drama. An emergency has come up. Sorry, Veronica, I can't go today. I'm really sorry, but this is a family thing . . .'

'Billy? Is he all right?' she asked anxiously.

'Fine. It's my cousin, Travis. You met him, remember, at Mum and Dad's anniversary party? I have to sort things out for him. Look, I'll get back to you as soon as I can. Sorry, but this is how it is.'

'What's happened?'

'He's been arrested. Again. We've helped him before. It's been such a long haul and I guess there's still a long way to go. Will you be okay?'

'Sure, no problem. I'll fill in the day. When will I see you?'

'No idea, but I'll be thinking about you. Thanks, Veronica. Sorry.'

'Okay. Take care.' He hung up and Veronica was surprised at how disappointed she was. She'd so been looking forward to having this day alone with him. Between Billy, his parents, his friends from Melbourne and his work, Jamie always seemed to have someone making demands on his time. And this trouble with Travis sounded very stressful. She was tempted to rent a car and drive to Howard Springs herself but decided against it and went inside to make herself a cup of coffee when Doris rang.

'I just heard. Sorry, Veronica. Travis has been arrested over a punch-up in a bar last night. Jamie will have to step up and try and sort it out and spend some time with him. Travis has a chip on his shoulder and drinks too much. A bad combination.'

'A lot of young men fall off the rails for a bit,' said Veronica, feeling inadequate, wishing she had something constructive to say.

'I wish it were just that,' sighed Doris. 'I'm afraid Travis is like many of our young people. His parents were both institutionalised and didn't really have much idea about raising children. Actually, his father died a few years ago. He was quite young, too. Anyway, Travis has had very little formal education. Neither he, nor his parents cared about school. As much as we try to help him, he remains adrift.'

'And Travis won't listen to Jamie? Or you?'

'Oh, he'll listen. Be contrite, plead and promise – all to avoid going up before the court or the police. But it's likely that he'll slip back.'

'Travis seemed a lovely guy. Good fun, charming, good looking,' said Veronica.

'Often the way. Travis hides under a gregarious exterior but he has very low self-esteem. But we are very fond of him and of course he's family so we try to give him hope. Anyway, I've finished my meeting and I thought you might like to come out with me for a while.'

'Oh, Doris, you don't have to entertain me. I'm fine. I'll do some work.'

'But I'd like to take you somewhere. And perhaps you'd like to talk about your story, sometimes that helps clarify things.'

'I just hope we can fit the last pieces of the jigsaw together,' said Veronica. 'But I have to wait and see what we find out past the Crossing.'

'Veronica, would you like to come with me to a community school? It's the initiative of a government agency and the local indigenous TV station. One of the things I'm supposed to be is their media communication advisor, though my job is more to do with fundraising. But you know far more about this area than I do, perhaps we could pick your brains a bit?'

Veronica was intrigued with the Indigitel Media School and its students who ranged in age from their late teens to their mid-thirties. Glen Weyburn, the head of the school, an Irishman with a faint brogue, had worked as a teacher and an actor. He seemed cheerful and very amusing. But he was quick to admit that he had limited television experience.

'Stage is my forte. And I've had small roles in a couple of films. But I taught drama in media courses and now here I am trying to educate, inspire and train these students for a career in the media.'

'And doing a remarkable job,' said Doris. 'We have a couple of people who are knowledgeable in technology, computers, radio gear, cameras, that sort of thing, who are training the students, but I'm sure they'd love to hear from a professional like you who works on a national TV show. Give the students a few tips. Would that be all right?'

'I've never done anything like this before, but sure, I'm happy to chat to them,' said Veronica.

'I'll go and rustle them up after the break. There's a tea room, if you want to help yourself,' said Glen.

'Where are the students from? What's their background?' asked Veronica.

'Quite varied. All are indigenous, some come from outstations, some from remote communities, some from the islands and some are from Darwin. Some come from troubled homes, others from very stable homes,' answered Doris.

'Anyway, all our students take a keen interest in media and most of them hope to work in the field,' said Glen. 'I think this is a terrific initiative. It's based on a similar school in the Alice which has been very successful.'

'I think it's a great project, too, and I love being involved,' said Doris.

'What sort of opportunities are there for the students?' asked Veronica.

'We're working on that,' said Doris. 'There are plans for more local stations and community networks, that sort of thing. But Glen's dream is for his students to be good enough to get work at any media outlet anywhere in the country.'

What started as a half-hour chat to the forty students became more than an hour as the students continued to ask questions. Veronica found them all highly motivated and she enjoyed the discussion.

Over a late lunch with Doris, she began to outline suggestions and ideas for the school.

'You should be telling Glen all this,' said Doris. 'We should make you a consultant.'

'I enjoy their enthusiasm and their fresh approach and their ways of looking at things so differently from many of the people I know down south,' said Veronica. She told Doris about how she entered television and how important mentoring and guidance had been to her career. 'And still is. My boss Andy is such an old hand. Technology might have changed but certain things never do. Sensing and shaping a story, for example.'

Doris glanced at her watch. 'I'm going home to change and head out to the farm. Why don't you come and see my horses. Do you like riding?'

'Oh, I'd love to see the farm, but I'm not sure about riding.'

'Do it another day with Jamie. I have a foal and a few other things to check on. It's only forty minutes out of town.'

It amused Veronica to see Doris change from her businesswoman's attire of tailored skirt and blouse into old jeans, boots and a sleeveless shirt. Her hair was curly and tinged with grey but her brown arms were muscled and strong and her figure youthful.

Veronica had assumed that what Doris called 'the farm' would be a couple of paddocks and stables where she kept her horses. So she was surprised to see a neatly graded road, good fences and a small ranch-style bungalow. The stables were well kept. There was a small training ring and several fit horses were standing in the shade of trees by a dam.

'This is amazing! I thought you just had horses in a couple of paddocks.'

Doris smiled as she got out of the car. 'It's my little retreat. Well, it's for all of us, but I seem to be the one who uses it most. When I have a lot of thinking or reading to do I come and stay overnight. I have a friend who comes by most days to feed, water and check the horses as I don't get out here every day. I bring Billy out here too. He's developing into quite a good little rider.'

'Have you always had horses? After you left Brolga Springs and went to Melbourne, how long before you started riding again?' asked Veronica as she followed Doris to where a mare and foal were standing in the corral waiting for them.

'Not till I was a young teenager.' She clicked her tongue and the mare trotted towards her. 'But I've always wanted my own horses to breed and train and when Alistair and

I moved to the Territory, I got my chance. I believe that Lord Vesty and some others let a few English thorough-bred stallions loose in the north and that accounts for the good brumby stock we have now. It would be great to develop some really excellent breeding lines. I'd like to get into it more seriously when I stop work.'

'And when might that be? You don't seem the type to retire, Doris.'

Doris leaned on the railing, one hand caressing the mare, then looked at Veronica. 'No. I feel I owe it to my people to keep fighting for better circumstances for us all. I was lucky in many ways. I lost my mother and nothing can change that, but I also got an education and a won-derful husband and Jamie has had advantages too. So that makes us feel obligated to help our people.'

'Do you ever think back to your childhood, to Brolga Springs?' asked Veronica.

'Occasionally. Even now those early memories can be very sad because while I had lots of the opportunities the white world offers, I've lost most of my own family. I sometimes wish I'd made the move back up here ear-lier and become involved with my own people sooner.' Doris drew a long breath. 'Because there is still shameful inequality in this country, you know. Half the people in gaols across the country are Aboriginal and yet they make up only two per cent of the population. Our people have shorter life spans and suffer dreadful health problems. Time isn't fixing it. We are losing the next generation, like Travis, to despair. Old people haven't been able to fit in and young people don't respect them. Traditional knowl-edge and lore is being lost.'

Veronica looked at Doris's earnest face and asked, 'But there must be something that can be done to improve this.'

'There are no easy answers. It is true that education,

better health and housing are part of the solution, but it's a very complex problem. I just want to be able to help constructively where I can and I know that Jamie feels the same way.'

'You've given me a lot to think about, Doris,' said Veronica quietly.

Doris relaxed. 'Let's go and see the other horses. I want to see how the foal responds to the touch of a human hand.'

Veronica was fascinated watching Doris work with the horses and it was almost dark when they drove back into Darwin.

'Will Jamie be back?' asked Veronica.

'Who knows. He'll call us.'

'Did he ask you to take care of me today?' asked Veronica suddenly.

'No. It was my idea. I liked spending the day with you.'

'Me too,' said Veronica warmly. 'It's been a wonderful day.' But she wished she could talk about it with Jamie.

Alistair and Billy had dinner prepared for them even though it was something pulled from the freezer. Alistair poured drinks and put out a plate of cheese and biscuits as Billy was dispatched to do his homework.

Veronica's mobile rang. 'It's Jamie.' She picked up her wine and moved outside.

'Hey. How's it going, things all right?'

'Forgive me, Veronica. It's been full on. I'm so sorry about today. I hope you found something to do.'

'I certainly did. I've had a fascinating day with your mum. Where are you? When are you coming back?'

'Hopefully tomorrow. I've organised a solicitor and Travis is out on bail. Some of the family want to take him bush and give him a good belting, teach him some respect but the old ways don't work. Mum and I will have to keep an even closer eye on him in the future, or he'll end up in gaol.'

'That sounds like a full-on job,' said Veronica.

'We'll share it. He knows he's let me down so he'll probably be fine for a while. I'm sorry about Howard Springs but we can leave the day after tomorrow for Arnhem Land if Dougie is all set.'

'We're ready.'

'What did you and Mum do today? I hope she hasn't roped you into anything.'

'She took me to Indigitel Media School, which I loved,' said Veronica.

Jamie laughed. 'So you gave a talk? I bet the students enjoyed that.'

'Well, I certainly answered a lot of questions. They were great. I got swept up in their enthusiasm.'

'Terrific. Listen, I have to go. Tell Mum all is in hand. I'll check in tomorrow. Give Billy a hug for me.'

When Jamie finally returned, there seemed to be endless family conversations. He was also busy getting their trip organised so Veronica saw little of him until the following morning when he turned up with his vehicle packed and looking very professional.

'Reg is collecting Dougie, we're meeting them on the highway. You got everything I told you to bring?'

Veronica hugged Doris and Alistair goodbye and they drove off in silence. Jamie finally lifted his shoulders and sighed.

'Man, am I glad to be getting out of town. Sorry if I've been a bit preoccupied.'

'That's okay,' said Veronica slowly. 'Does this sort of thing happen very often?'

'Travis? This is his second time, we don't want three strikes . . .'

'No. I meant the pressure on you to deal with family crises. I can see your role and the responsibilities. I was thinking how I would juggle those things. You do have a lot

436

on your plate. And I realised, here we are taking you away to the bush again on what might be a wild goose chase . . .'

He smiled and seemed to relax. 'I could say it's part of my job.' He reached over and touched her knee. 'But I wouldn't miss this for anything. A chance to get away to the old country, be under the stars around a campfire and share my tent with a gorgeous woman called Veronica Anderson. Nah, I wouldn't miss this.'

'You think we're going to find something, don't you?' she said suddenly. 'I hope you haven't done all the permits for this trip for nothing. I wish it was just the two of us,' she added wistfully.

'Another time. I promise you that.' They glanced at each other, both sensing that deep waters lay ahead.

At the roadhouse they met Reg and Dougie and ordered tea and hot meat pies. Reg was cheerful and practical and when Veronica asked if he thought they stood a chance of finding Topov's remains, he nodded.

'Dunno. You'll find something that's for sure. That area is a well-known burial area. Bones are always turning up. Animals tend to disturb them bodies, especially the ones left in caves. Every time we get a new young cop in the area he'll get all excited when bones turn up. I know of one old blackfella whose bones have been "found" two or three times.'

Veronica was amazed at how familiar some of the landscape looked. She loved the paperbark swamps, the pale trees of soft shredding bark standing guard over dark, still pools spotted with giant waterlilies.

When she saw the rugged sandstone ridges of the Arnhem Plateau in the distance, she asked, 'I don't suppose that anyone has ever explored every bit of that land? Looked in every crevice and cave?'

'No secrets in the stone country,' said Jamie. 'I doubt there's a spot that isn't known, or hasn't been touched, by the local people in the last forty thousand or so years. But the knowledge is dying out and not being passed on so a lot of special places have been forgotten. When ceremonies aren't performed and the custodial care is gone, the land is lost. But the old stories remain in the rocks and the rivers and the trees.'

'That's sad,' said Veronica.

'So part of my job is to try and find out from the old people some of their knowledge before it's gone.'

'What are you finding out?

'A lot about land management, for one thing. Aboriginal people had thousands of years to perfect the use of fire. Now we realise that people aren't burning off as much as they used to so while there aren't as many fires, when there are they're much hotter and cause more damage and changes to the vegetation. Working with the old people helps to put the pieces of the puzzle back together and maintain the country properly.'

As Veronica listened to Jamie talk she looked at the landscape and could hardly wait for the opportunity to walk slowly through it, observing its detail.

It was almost dark when Jamie pulled into a clearing near Wild Man's Crossing.

'We can pitch tents here for the night. Safer on this side of the river. There's a toilet in a shed over there with an outdoor shower. The water comes from the river so it might be a bit brackish.'

'A campfire with a hotplate, very useful,' commented Reg. 'Who's catching dinner?'

'I'm not going near that river,' said Dougie looking at the last of the light glinting steely silver on the water in the distance.

'Don't worry, Dougie, we have an Esky full of goodies,' said Veronica. 'Steaks, salad, bread rolls.'

'Then I'll help cook,' offered Dougie.

Reg unrolled his swag, Dougie put up his pup tent and Jamie pitched the small tent for Veronica and him. When he threw both of their sleeping bags into it neither Dougie nor Reg commented. Sitting round the blazing campfire, feeling the closeness of Jamie beside her and gazing up at a night sky so full of stars that you couldn't stick a pin between them, as Reg had said, Veronica was utterly content. Later in the tent she slept, rolled in Jamie's arms.

They had a hasty breakfast and talked excitedly about what they hoped to find that day. Then they piled into Jamie's vehicle, after checking that they had all of Dougie's camera gear along with everything else they needed for the day.

The water running over the Crossing was clear and calm. No-one was out on the river as Dougie grabbed a few shots of the peaceful morning.

Veronica had transcribed Marta's interview and she read aloud Marta's description of the area as she'd remembered it. It seemed as though little had changed. Jamie drove among the boulders and scrubby grasses, past a termite mound and slowed as they began to study the rock formations and jump-ups carefully. With the escarpment as a backdrop, they wound slowly among the outcrops. Veronica was trying to imagine Topov with his Geiger counter testing the different types of rocks and soil. And then rising before them so that they spotted it simultaneously was a large rock formation in the shape of a mushroom.

'Jamie, didn't you point this out to me last time we were out here?' asked Veronica.

Jamie stopped and they got out. Dougie filmed them as they picked their way towards it; Jamie in the lead, Veronica close behind and Reg with a spade over his shoulder. They walked slowly around the outcrop seeing nothing unusual, not sure what they were looking for. The ground was strewn with rocks and hard-packed earth, there was no overhang or obvious shelter. But directly behind was the lower end of a sandstone cliff. Small trees and saplings sprouted from its crevices. They came to it and began walking slowly in front of its face.

Veronica found she was studying the ground as if some marker to indicate Topov's grave would be obvious.

They circled the rock as Dougie followed with the camera.

'Here! Look,' shouted Reg.

'What is it?' Veronica stumbled in her hurry.

They all quickly moved to where Reg was pointing. 'There, see those scratchings. That's no blackfella picture. See, it's been done in ochre but not very well,' said Reg, peering at the little image. 'The ochre, not the picture.'

'What's it supposed to be?' asked Dougie, taking a close-up.

'I think it's supposed to be a director's viewfinder,' said Veronica.

'Oh, yeah. Thought it was some sort of telescope,' said Dougie.

'Quick, where do we start digging?' asked Veronica.

Jamie glanced at Reg who shrugged and put his foot on the top of the shovel, pushing it into the sandy soil.

'Here's as good a place as any,' said Reg.

Two hours passed and they had dug a trench on both sides of the little painting on the rock. The three men had taken it in turns and all were hot and dripping with sweat at the exertion.

'There doesn't seem to be a thing here,' said Dougie, his voice filled with disappointment.

'There has to be. Just has to be,' said Veronica in frustration. 'Let me have a turn.'

'No, no. Can you pass the water? We'll try a bit longer,' said Jamie, knowing how much it meant to Veronica.

Reg leaned on the shovel. 'I'm just wondering if we need to go deeper.'

'The hole's pretty damn deep already. If these people wanted to get away after he died, why would they go to the trouble to make such a deep hole?' asked Dougie.

'Animals, especially dingoes, would find a body pretty quickly if it was in a shallow grave,' said Reg.

'And scatter the remains about. That'd give the show away,' added Jamie.

'In that case, let's dig deeper right under the picture,' suggested Veronica.

They had dug down nearly another metre when there was a dull thud as the shovel hit something hard.

'Hello, what's that?' Jamie started to shovel the soil away more quickly.

'It's just stones,' said Veronica.

'A whole heap of 'em. But that's not a natural formation. Someone's put them there,' said Reg.

Dougie picked up his camera. Veronica leaned in closer as Jamie cleared more dirt away. He put the shovel to one side and Reg jumped in the hole beside him and together they began lifting the stones out.

'There's just dirt under them,' said Veronica as the last few stones were lifted out of the hole.

'Nah. There's something else under here.' Reg looked at Jamie.

'I'll give you a hand.'

'Hope it's the whitefella you're after, Veronica,' muttered Reg. 'Otherwise the spirits going to chase me for disturbing some brother's resting place.'

'There's something there?' Veronica knelt at the edge as Dougie stood on the opposite side filming Reg and Jamie as they held up a frayed old rope.

The two men gingerly lifted a sack of rotting oilskin out of the hole and laid it carefully onto the ground.

Veronica sat stunned. 'I can't open it. Jamie, you do it.'

Veronica couldn't help giving a small scream and clamping her hand over her mouth as the rope was removed and oilskin was opened to reveal the remains of what had obviously been a human being. Some shreds of material and leather remained on the bones and they stood there staring at Topov's skeleton in shocked fascination, while Dougie continued to film.

Jamie said quietly, 'I think you've found your man, Veronica.' He leaned down and pulled a leather strap that was around the neck of the body, lifting up a rusted metal object.

'The viewfinder,' said Veronica in a whisper.

'What's this?' Reg lifted a square of metal. He scratched at it and handed it to Veronica.

'It's a belt buckle,' she said. She rubbed the rusted artifact and saw an elaborate design. 'It's a two-headed eagle with a sceptre and a ball, no, an orb. It does look Russian.'

'This has to be Topov,' said Jamie.

Dougie took a lot more shots of the grave and the rock face as the others sat in the shade. No-one spoke for a while as they savoured the moment of their amazing discovery.

Finally Jamie said, 'Well, I think we should put him back where we found him. I wouldn't like the animals to get him after all this time. Reg, would you get a plastic tarpaulin out of the truck? Then we can head back. Mission accomplished.'

Dougie began packing up his camera and Veronica sat quietly with Jamie, gazing at the monsoon forests and the distant spine of the stone country.

'How do you feel?' Jamie took her hand.

'I'm not sure. Pleased the whole thing has been justified in the end, concerned and wondering what it all means – is this what John Cardwell didn't want us to find? And sad, for Topov.'

'I can understand that. Of course the authorities and the elders will have to be notified. Reg will be able to look after that.'

Dougie stared at Reg carefully returning the remains of Topov, now wrapped in plastic to the hole and filling it in. 'So it's really him?'

'Has to be. It's just as Marta described,' said Veronica.

Back at the campsite Reg announced that he was off to see the elders to tell them what they'd found.

'Why don't you lot boil a billy while you're waiting? I won't be long. The elders will probably want to let the police know. You'll have to make a statement.'

Jamie nodded. 'Yeah, we'll do that in Darwin.'

'You will keep this quiet won't you, Reg? No newspapers or anything. I don't want my story nicked,' said Veronica.

'Mum's the word,' said Reg cheerfully.

Reg wasn't gone long. When he returned he announced that the traditional owners had been notified and everything should be fine with the authorities. So they all packed up and headed back to Darwin.

'We could take a bit of a break after we've seen the police. Call over to Brolga Springs, if you'd like,' suggested Jamie.

'Thanks. Another time. I know you have a lot to do for Travis and you've been away from Billy for a bit. I need to get going on this story now.' But seeing the sudden set to his jaw as he nodded, she quickly added. 'But I really want to spend time with you, Jamie.'

They drove back over the rocky ground and the Crossing, the silhouettes of pandanus standing high on their roots like massed stilettos. A bird swooped low after a dragonfly and then headed towards the monsoon forest.

'This is so beautiful. It reaches out to you. It's hard to describe but it feels somehow . . . alive,' said Veronica.

'Yep. I can just feel it. Sense it. Sometimes when I touch a rock or a tree it's like there's a heartbeat there. Especially in my mother's country.'

'Yes. You get a sense of some connection. Even for me. I'd love to see this landscape in the wet season,' added Veronica.

'It's magnificent and I'd love to share it with you. But my heart belongs to my mother's country,' said Jamie.

'What about the farm where your mum has the horses?'

'It's handy but it's real estate. It has no meaning for me. Not like Brolga Springs where Mum was born.'

'And what about where your father was born? Have you no desire to go to Scotland?'

'I went for a brief trip to meet some relatives and it was lovely in the springtime. I'll go again but it's not as meaningful to me,' said Jamie. 'Dad understands that. What about you? Where do you feel your roots are?'

'I feel a bit embarrassed to say I don't have a deep feeling of connection to any place in particular, not like you do,' confessed Veronica. 'I like parts of Sydney, but I like a lot of places.'

'Lake Como?'

'Yes. For a holiday,' laughed Veronica. 'But the idea of having homes in different countries sounds exhausting.'

They were both silent a while, then Jamie said, 'Would you show me your favourite places in Sydney? I have to go down there soon for a conference.'

'Really? That's fantastic! When did you find this out?' exclaimed Veronica, her eyes shining.

'It's been on the agenda for a while and I've been trying to get out of going, but now I've changed my mind.' He gave her a sidelong glance. 'What do you think?'

'Jamie, I would really, really love that. Would you stay with me?' asked Veronica shyly. 'I mean, I can reciprocate Doris's hospitality in a small way.'

He reached out and rubbed the nape of her neck. 'I want to be with you,' he said simply. 'I just wish it could be more often.'

Veronica's mind was spinning. 'I'd love you to meet Andy and my parents. I mean, if that's okay with you?' She also wanted Jamie to meet her girlfriends but she didn't want to overdo things.

He smiled. 'Perhaps I could spin out the trip a bit longer if I'm not imposing?'

'No. This is good. Really good,' said Veronica, quite overwhelmed at how happy she felt. But as Jamie took her hand and squeezed it, another thought struck her. And after his visit, what then? Was this how it would be? Sporadic trips between the north and the south whenever their work permitted?

Veronica rang Andy. He was silent as he listened to her news about finding Topov.

'So? What do you think? I was right!' bubbled Veronica. 'And the best part, Jamie is coming down to Sydney. I can't wait for you to meet him. You there, Andy?'

'I am. I'm a bit stunned. I guess I wasn't really expecting things to follow Marta's script like this. Good on you. So we wait for the coroner's report?'

'I guess so. Reg has done everything correctly so we won't have any backlash anywhere. The police are going out to the site with him and one of the custodians of the land to be sure that the body isn't Aboriginal.'

'Not much chance of that with his buckle and view-finder carefully preserved with him,' said Andy. 'Where are they, by the way?'

'With the police. They'll be handed over to Olga's estate, I suppose. So Valma will get them. Any word from her?'

'Yes, she says you've started her on a mammoth clean-up. Says she's found a box and suitcase labelled "Maxim" and they're waiting for you. I figured it'd be a crucial scene in the show so you should be the one to open it.'

'Fantastic. Well, I'll be on the way back the day after tomorrow. Just going through the footage with Dougie to check we don't need any pick-up shots or anything. He modestly said it looks very good.'

'I looked at your NT footage here. That Jamie pal of yours is a talent. Good looking, nice, warm, calm personality. Knowledgeable. He could kick around a TV station if he wanted.'

'I know. But he doesn't want to be in Sydney. Or any southern city.' Veronica sighed.

'Hmm. Shame for you. You sound pretty keen,' said Andy. He'd never heard her this enthusiastic about a man before but it was early days. The distance would probably defeat the relationship. But it was nice to hear her so happy.

'So, how are you going to wrap this story up? Will you go back to Colin and Marta? What about Cardwell?' he asked.

'Poor Colin doesn't know anything of this. He'll be very surprised to find out what really happened to Topov. He still thinks he was taken by a croc. Marta will be amused, vaguely interested because of Doris and possibly pleased she led us to this. But Cardwell . . . Now there's another story. It's ironic when you think about it. If he hadn't scared Colin off, we might not have approached Marta and found out the truth about Topov's death and like Colin we'd believe the story about the croc, too. I suppose that's why he didn't want this to come out.'

'Yes, well the fight, the bruises on Topov. Someone had a fight with him and even if they didn't actually kill him, they left him to die,' said Andy. 'That night when they discovered the body – who do you think made the decision not to tell the police? Johnny? Or the others?'

'Actually, I think it was Len. He was the bushman, the most practical and he knew the tiresome consequences if they reported it,' said Veronica thoughtfully.

'Why would he want to involve himself in someone else's hassle? But I suppose he must have been in love with Helen as they stayed together,' said Andy.

'Do you think he was protecting Helen?' mused Veronica.

'Why? If there was a fight, the women would hardly have been involved, but the men . . . There was no-one else around, so it had to be one of them and my guess is that it was John Cardwell, ' said Andy.

Veronica glanced at her watch. 'I'm getting a head-ache trying to think this through. Anyway, we'll probably never know for sure.'

'Listen, enjoy your last day in Darwin. When we sit down and start editing, you'll be surprised how well this will hang together,' said Andy.

'Thanks, Andy. I don't know what Valma will have for me, I just hope that it's interesting. And yes, I plan to enjoy my last hours with Jamie. It won't be so bad leaving him knowing that he's coming down to Sydney soon.'

'I'll take you both to lunch as a way of thanking him.'

But saying goodbye to Jamie was harder than Veronica could have imagined. She clung to him at the airport, glad now that she'd farewelled Billy with Doris and Alistair at their house.

'It won't be too long before I lob into town,' whispered Jamie as he held her.

'Can we talk every night?' murmured Veronica into his shoulder.

'As often as you like.' He kissed her long and hard, drew back and stared into her eyes. 'I'll miss you. I'm just realising how much.'

Arriving in Sydney was jarring. The cold wind, the queue for a taxi, the honking car horns of impatient drivers. She went home, but her tiny place was lonely and felt too neat, too impersonal. She missed the warmth and clutter of Doris and Alistair's house, the calm feeling of being in an oasis at Jamie and Billy's home. She rang her mother.

'I'm back. Can I come over for dinner tonight? Tell you all about it?'

'It would be lovely to catch up, Vee. Seems you've been gone for ages. Your father and I were going to a movie, but we'll get take-away instead. Chinese? What have you missed?'

'Eating? Not much, there's fabulous food up there. I even ate kangaroo and buffalo and crocodile.'

'Yuk,' her mother shuddered.

'And fabulous fresh seafood of course.'

'Well, I'm sorry we can't match any of that. I haven't got time to cook anything,' said her mother.

'It's fine. How's Sue?'

'Oh, don't get me started,' began her mother.

'Tell me about it at dinner.'

Over dinner her mother, with interjections from her father, filled her in on events at work, her sister's latest drama, the machinations of the local council and the disaster of a tree branch falling onto the guttering.

It was her father who finally asked. 'So what have you been up to?

Veronica was pleased that at last she could introduce Jamie into the conversation. 'This story has really taken off, we have a stunning ending but I've been so lucky to get help from this great guy that I met last time, I think I've already mentioned him. Jamie has been wonderful.'

'Don't let anyone else take credit for what you do,' broke in her mother.

'It's not like that. He has great local knowledge. He's good on camera and I stayed at his parents' house. They're lovely. His father's a retired professor. Scottish with a delightful accent and his mother was a teacher but now works with government agencies. She's half Aboriginal and quite a political activist. She has a connection with the story. In a couple of ways . . .'

Before Veronica could elaborate further, the phone rang and Joan sighed. 'That'll be Sue or Philip, they're anxious to talk to you, dear. Roger, can you take it, please? Tell them Veronica will be there in a minute.'

'I'll call her back,' said Veronica.

'Oh, they'll be going out I'm sure. Just have a quick word, Veronica. So when does this fascinating story go to air?'

'Not sure. I haven't quite finished tying up what ends I can. Anyway, as I was saying, Jamie is coming to Sydney so I'd like you to meet him.'

'Of course, dear. Your friends are always welcome. Especially if his parents hosted you up there. Though really why your office couldn't pay for decent accommodation in Darwin is beyond me,' said Joan.

'Yes. Especially now you've got this mega-rich boss. Or is he saving his own money and cutting corners?' said Roger, returning to the table.

'Actually Big Bill has increased our budget. My show will launch the new season. And I'm it,' said Veronica.

'Speaking as a marketing man, they need a new launch pad, a bit of a change without tampering with the bits that were successful,' said her father.

'Roger, that's just moving the deckchairs around. Veronica told us she was going to be The Face of the show. I hope you know what you're doing, Vee,' added her mother.

'Yes, if it sinks, you go down with the ship,' said her father.

'Thanks for the vote of confidence,' said Veronica getting up to go to the phone. 'We've got quite a story.'

Her father made her pause as he called after her, 'And then what? What'll you do for an encore?'

Veronica's hand hesitated as she went to lift the phone in the quieter sunroom. That, she thought, was a very good question. If the story on Topov's expedition came together the way she hoped, it would be hard to top it. She suddenly longed to get home and phone Jamie, but instead rang her sister.

'Hi, Sue. How're the girls?'

'The usual, full of energy. When are you coming down? Did you bring them something from the wild north?'

'Miniature crocodile handbags,' said Veronica facetiously as she felt guilty she hadn't brought anything special this time.

'Oh, how divine! Do they make little girl croc shoes? Are the skins dyed? I saw some pink snakeskin shoes last week and I thought how cute small ones would be . . .'

'Sue, I was kidding. I have a lovely painting that was done by the aunt of a friend of mine and there's such a wonderful story to it . . .'

'Oh, that's all very well, but the girls wouldn't be interested in that. They're little girls, remember? You haven't been to see us in so long, you think they're teenagers,' said Sue.

'I'll come and see you as soon as I can, I promise. I might even bring a special friend to visit.'

'Really?' Sue was interested. 'How come you've had time to date when you've been away so much? You are the dark one.'

'Actually he's from up there. He's coming to Sydney for a conference and we might go down to Melbourne. He's originally from Melbourne.' Veronica had just decided that she wanted her sister's approval of and admiration for Jamie.

'A conference? So he's not moving down? You can't have a boyfriend in Darwin, for God's sake. We've met some lovely, lovely men here in Melbourne. So much easier to socialise and meet people here than in Sydney. We'll have them lined up. Better leave the Darwin man behind,' advised Sue.

Veronica just laughed. 'No chance. Wait till you meet him. Have you got your house organised?'

Sue launched into their latest plans and Veronica's news was pushed to one side.

In bed that night, when she phoned Jamie, she talked about the differences between her family and his.

'Veronica, you can't compare them,' he said calmly. 'Your family has different priorities, but it doesn't mean they love you any less.'

'It's hard to explain. I hate to say it but I feel I have more in common with your mother than my own. I really admire my mum, she's a hard worker, but I guess I'm more interested in what Doris is doing.'

'That's okay, Veronica. Like I said, it doesn't mean that you don't love them any less, do you?'

'No,' said Veronica slowly. But she was thinking of the warmth of the interaction between Jamie's family and the superficiality of her own.

'Anyway, I'm glad you like my mob. There are quite a

lot of us, when you take in my extended family and as you know that can mean a lot of obligation and responsibility.'

'I understand, Jamie.'

'How're things going?'

'I'm off to see Valma tomorrow. I'm hoping to wind this up fairly quickly. I want to have some free time when you're here.'

'I can't wait to see you, Veronica.'

'Me too.'

She hung up the phone, the thought of seeing Jamie uppermost in her mind. The strength of her feelings surprised her. Their lovemaking was passionate and tender. They enjoyed each other's company. They had common interests. Veronica knew that Jamie was very, very special.

The next day she went into work, fighting for a parking spot at the production office and found Andy.

'Hi. I've just seen the stuff you shot finding the body. Great pictures. Like a movie!'

'I hope viewers realise it is for real and not a set-up,' said Veronica, suddenly worried.

'We'll have to reiterate Marta's description of what happened so that this just confirms it. I'm keeping the footage under wraps, everyone working on it is keeping mum.'

'Yes, I told Dougie the same thing. His stuff is good, isn't it?' said Veronica. 'I've arranged for him to go over and chat to the students at the Indigitel School. He's young but very enthusiastic.'

'Oh, that's the indigenous media school you mentioned? Very good idea. Next time I go to Darwin, I'll offer my services. Do you think that they'd want to hear from an old bloke like me?'

'Andy, when were you last in Darwin?' Veronica laughed. 'But seriously, they're hanging out for contact with other professionals. I promised I'd do a workshop next time I'm up there.'

Andy raised an eyebrow. 'Next time? I thought this story was nearly finished.'

She looked embarrassed. 'You know, that just slipped out. I'm assuming I'll be going back up there. Gosh, Andy, the thought of not seeing Jamie, Billy, his family, I can't imagine it.' She looked stricken.

'Well, if this show is a success you can ask for a raise to pay for all the trips to Darwin,' said Andy shortly. 'Now, grab Tom and get over to Valma Konstantinova's.'

Veronica, Tom and a sound man were ushered into the house by Valma, who was still what Veronica's mother would call reserved. While not unfriendly, she was businesslike.

'You've started something. But not before time. I had no idea the rubbish my mother had stored upstairs in the attic.'

'I hope we haven't inconvenienced you,' said Veronica.

'Not really. Now, there's a suitcase and a carton marked "Maxim", so could your fellows bring them down?' said Valma.

'Certainly. But, er, would you mind if I took some shots of them in situ?' asked Tom.

'Valma, would you mind if we're all in it? You showing me the box and then perhaps me opening it?'

'Please yourself. Take anything you want. There's nothing I want to keep of his.'

'Too bad we know nothing about his family. If he had one,' said Veronica as she followed Valma upstairs, Tom trailing behind with the camera, two portable lights and the sound recordist.

Veronica and Tom exchanged glances as they saw the upper level of the house with its long dark panelled hallway and tantalising glimpses of crowded bedrooms behind ornate doors. Veronica did notice the contrast of a near-empty bathroom, cavernous and cold with an old-fashioned claw tub in the centre of a black and white tiled floor and large curtainless windows. Tom hoisted the camera and turned on the camera light to film Valma and Veronica as they headed up yet more stairs.

The narrow flight of stairs led to the smaller third floor, which was mostly a storage attic although there was also a maid's room and kitchenette in one corner. When she looked around, Veronica was reminded of old films with haunted attics. The casement windows, the sloping eaves, the trunks, a rocking horse, dark paintings, an overstuffed chair and piles of boxes couldn't have been arranged better if it had been part of a movie set.

'I see what you mean. This is quite a collection of memorabilia,' said Veronica.

'Most of it is junk. Mother bought us everything a little girl could ever want, but when my sister and I came back from France we were young ladies and had outgrown the toys.' Valma pointed to a large suitcase and a box. 'They are the things I found relating to Topov.'

Veronica knelt beside the dusty, battered suitcase running her hands over it. A tag was tied to it with 'Maxim' pencilled on it.

'I haven't opened it,' said Valma.

Veronica glanced at Tom to be sure he and the sound man were ready.

'Rolling,' said Tom quietly.

Veronica opened the suitcase as Valma watched.

There was a bulky jacket, some sweaters and trousers and a tailored jacket, which Veronica held up. 'There's a small gold pin in the lapel, don't know what that is. I hope it's not just old clothes.' Beneath the clothes layer were some old books, a pair of black shoes and then a series of notebooks filled with handwriting. 'These are notes. I think it's about the film, a sort of script. It's in terrible English. I'll go through them some other time.'

Reluctantly she put them to one side. 'Ah, photographs. This is good.'

'Do you know who they are?' Veronica asked Valma as she handed her several of the pictures.

'These look to be when he was young. And here's one with my mother. I wonder where it was taken?'

Other than a few more personal effects there was little else of interest in the suitcase. Veronica then pulled the cracked tape from the carton and opened the flaps.

'What's this? Oh, heavens, it's a camera! What a funny old thing.' She pulled it out and read, 'Bolex. Let's see what else is in here.' She delved some more and pulled out a larger, bulkier camera. 'This must be the professional camera. And another box. What's this thing?'

'Looks like one of those old geiger counters,' said Tom.

Excitedly Veronica felt to the bottom of the box and came up with an envelope. 'This was on the bottom.' She opened the envelope and pulled out a printed form.

'What's that?' asked Valma.

Veronica skimmed through the document. 'It's a fossicker's licence. A permit to stake a mining claim in the Northern Territory. So he really was serious about looking for minerals.'

Veronica put the licence to one side with the notebooks. 'Can I take these away to study, please, Valma?'

'Take them all. None of it is of any use or interest to me. I can't imagine why Mother kept them, especially after she knew he was dead and wouldn't be coming back to claim them.'

'Yes. Like everything to do with Topov, it's all a bit mysterious,' agreed Veronica. She signalled to Tom to stop filming and he quickly picked up the old cameras.

'Brilliant old machines. Probably still work after they've had a bit of a service. Not that anyone uses film anymore.'

'Is there any film still in there?' asked Veronica hopefully.

Tom opened a camera. 'Nope. Nothing. That's a pity.'

'Valma, thank you for this. I'm not sure what to do with these things either, but we'll take them back to the studio to get them out of your way.'

Andy was intrigued with the cameras and the notebooks and tried on the musty jacket.

'Gosh, three times too big for you,' said Veronica. 'Take it off, that's creepy.'

'The fossicking licence is interesting. But it doesn't shed much light on the story,' said Andy.

'Look at the date. It confirms Marta's story that it was issued just before they set off to Arnhem Land,' said Veronica.

'Well, off you go to the editing suite. Put all the pieces together,' said Andy cheerfully.

'Yeah, right. Easy peasy,' she said. But she was looking forward to the challenge.

'Hi. I've been calling you. What're you up to?' Jamie's warm voice woke Veronica who had gone to bed, not bothering to eat, exhausted from two days of being locked in a small cubicle going through hours of video tape.

'It's good to hear from you. Sorry, I've been locked in an editing suite going back to day one and viewing every shot, making notes and trying to figure out how to tell this whole story in under an hour when I must have five hundred hours of tape!'

'Sounds like a nightmare. How's it coming?'

'My head is spinning. I feel like I've done the entire trek over again. And then I get to scenes with you and I go over and over them, wishing I could make you materialise in the room.'

'I wish I was there, too. I miss you.'

'Me too.'

'Not long. Another week. And then I'll be there.'

'I'm trying to get this story in some sort of shape by then so I can hand it over to the editor. It'll be okay.'

'Just okay? Don't rush it.'

They talked about Billy, a project Doris was doing and Jamie's upcoming conference.

'Dad's writing a paper for some academic journal,' said Jamie. 'Mum's pleased. She didn't think he was keeping himself occupied enough. Now, he's buried in his study and we can hardly get him out.'

Veronica laughed. 'I'm anxious to hear more about it. Give them my love.'

'Go back to sleep. Sorry I woke you. Sweet dreams.'

She dreamed of a track through the landscape of Jamie's country, the smell of a campfire and the warmth of his body close to hers. The sounds of traffic, of a city day beginning, woke her and she put her pillow over her head trying to recapture the gentle sounds of the outback. But it was futile. She got up and went to work.

Andy came and found her in the editing room. 'I know you've got your head down, but Valma Konstantinova has called. Said she has found something else for you. Maybe call her back. She sounds a bit fed up. I think she's tossing everything she can into a rubbish skip.'

'I was ready for a coffee break.' Veronica stood up and stretched.

Valma sounded tired and frustrated. 'There are more of these Maxim things. Some huge tins in with some boxes and papers in the fridge in the maid's room.'

'Tins? Tins of what?' asked Veronica.

'They're round flat ones filled with film. Why they've been kept in the refrigerator I don't know,' she sighed. 'My mother must have run out of storage space. Do you want them?'

Veronica could scarcely speak. 'I certainly do!' Whether the film was unused or was exposed footage she had no idea. She could only hope.

Tom was about to go out, but when she told him they might have one more shot and that it could be the old film footage, he was as excited as she was and jumped in a taxi with her to go to the old Darling Point mansion.

Valma rolled her eyes at the sight of Tom and his camera and turned and took them back upstairs to the third floor. The maid's room was still cluttered with boxes and belongings and Valma flung open the door of the old Kelvinator in the corner. 'Can you believe I found these in here?'

The film cans were quite cool to touch and were two different sizes. Tom filmed Veronica taking them out of the fridge.

'Some of the film is sixteen millimetre, the others, thirty-five millimetre,' she read. 'Ektachrome. Supreme Sound Studios.' She held her breath as she managed to unscrew one of the cans and looked at the large roll of film. She saw written in black ink, 'Day 7. Fishing and bog'.

'Oh God. This must be Topov's unfinished masterpiece. And it looks as though it's been developed.'

Tom broke protocol and spoke from behind the camera. 'Don't expose it. It might be dry and crack. We'll open it up in a dark room.'

Veronica was silent in the taxi on the way back to Network Eleven. At her feet were two old-fashioned

458

maroon-coloured Qantas flight bags Valma had given her to hold the precious cans of film.

It was all that remained of Topov's dream. She just hoped the film had survived and would show them how it had really been.

15

Veronica spread her notes across the old pine table in what had been the lounge room of the cottage where the production offices of *Our Country* were now housed. She laid them out in sequences and scenes, shuffling and rearranging them, trying to construct a comprehensible and interesting structure for her story.

Stu stuck his head around the door. 'Hi Veronica. What's your favourite colour?'

She stared at the editor. 'Huh? Why?'

'The set. They're fluffing up a new set for the show for when you start fronting it.'

'Oh, no! I'd better talk to Andy.'

She hurried into Andy's office.

'What's this about a new set and me fronting the show in the studio? It's bad enough I'm on camera all through the story!'

'Don't be so modest! Actually, the directive came from above. Big Bill is taking quite an interest. They all seem to be locked into the idea of having a face up front. A presenter who's promotable, you know the kind of thing.'

'But that's what we agreed we wouldn't do!' exclaimed Veronica. 'We want to let the story speak for itself. If they do it this way, then the next thing we know, the stories will be told through my eyes, my point of view. It's overkill to have me front the show as well as relating the story.'

'No offence, but I agree,' said Andy. 'I think that you're right and it will change the focus of the program too much.'

'Can I speak to the boss?'

'Leave it for the moment. Let's put this first big launch story together for the new-look program and give him a sneak preview and tackle it then,' said Andy soothingly.

'It's almost together. I'm banking on that old footage being good enough to use. It'll fit in perfectly and illustrate Colin and Marta's stories as well as contrasting with the modern stuff we filmed in the Territory.'

'The old film's with the film lab, we won't have it back for a day.' Andy hesitated then asked, 'I realise this mightn't be the time to raise this, but have you thought about what you might like to do next?'

'Do?'

'Story-wise. Television is a voracious eater of time, talent and material, you may recall. We have to find next month's feature before this one goes to air. The team will have to start working on it. But the story has to be one that excites you.'

For the first time in a long time Veronica didn't feel enthusiastic about her job. Normally, once a story was in the editing stages she mentally put it to bed and then the search to find the next assignment consumed her. Why was she not feeling that same adrenaline surge now?

'I guess this story has taken so much out of me, I've got so involved with it, been such a part of it that I'm having trouble letting go, let alone thinking about what to do next,' she confessed to Andy.

He looked at Veronica and then down at the papers on his desk. 'Hmm. I thought this might happen.'

'What do you mean?'

He leaned back in his chair, folding his arms behind his head. 'You're better at your job than you know, Veronica, but perhaps you need some time off before tackling the next story.'

'I'm sorry, Andy.' Veronica didn't know what to think. 'I'm just tired. I'll be fine after I have a break when Jamie comes down.'

'Veronica, I will eventually retire and you could easily fill my shoes. I want you to think about that.'

'I understand, Andy.'

'Now, we have a job to finish.'

Later Tom appeared in Veronica's office.

'It's back already. The old film. Transferred to DVD. Andy thought we should look at it together. A sort of a screening with popcorn and coffee,' he said. 'After the production meeting, just you, Andy and me. I'm keen to see how it comes up. Lucky it was stored so well.'

'Did the lab say how much of it was useable?' asked Veronica, not daring to get too elated.

'Most of it, apparently. The tech guys were pretty intrigued with what they saw.'

'I can hardly wait to see it.'

Andy and Veronica settled themselves in a small editing suite and Tom cued up the computer.

'This DVD has all the stuff from the big camera, the

one you said Topov mainly used, the thirty-five mill,' said Tom. 'The sixteen-millimetre footage is separate.'

'That's the smaller camera that Drago used a lot, though Marta and Colin said Topov used it sometimes, too,' said Veronica. 'I'm keen to compare their footage with the stuff we shot.'

'It was a shoestring production, obviously,' said Andy. 'If Topov hadn't died and they'd finished the trip, I wonder what he'd have made of the film.'

'I guess we'll know when we see it,' said Tom.

'Let's all make notes for editing purposes. Just in case we have anything useable here,' said Andy.

'Gosh, I hope so,' muttered Veronica. She sat very still, her coffee untouched and watched the images unroll before her.

Immediately Veronica was swept away as everything came to life. Marta, curvy and sexy, looked wonderful. There were glimpses of the others, including a smiling Colin, who was pointed out by Veronica.

'Yes, I recognise him from the Pioneers' Reunion,' said Andy.

'I bet that's Drago, he looks Slavic,' said Tom. 'That handsome, wide face.'

'No mistaking Helen, she does look a bit proper. And sensible,' said Andy.

'Who's that with the car?' Veronica strained forward. The young man, who'd been tinkering with the engine, gave a salute with a spanner. 'Cocky. Could that be Johnny?'

'You said Peter the Dutchman knew more about cars,' said Tom.

'Pause it, please, Tom,' said Andy. 'Yep. That young cocky lad is our Mr J. Cardwell,' said Andy firmly.

'So the dour fellow over there must be Peter. But where's Topov?' said Veronica. 'Oh, of course, he's filming this.'

'There's a cut. Aha, here he is,' exclaimed Andy.

Topov stepped in front of the camera, lifting his view-finder to his eye and gesticulated as he posed, pretending to direct Marta. He wore a small hat, a scarf around his neck and occasionally stroked his beard earnestly. He dominated the screen, turning to the camera to direct Drago, who must have been filming this sequence. His flamboyant actions, cheeky lifting of an eyebrow, eye rolling and dramatic gestures caused the three watching to break into laughter.

'God, what a ham,' said Tom.

'He's magnificent!' said Andy.

'Even without sound,' agreed Veronica.

There was a lot of scenery and they were staggered by the road conditions as Topov filmed the group digging the cars out of deep sand.

'There's virtually no road at all, just space that might be a track between the dunes and grasses,' said Veronica. 'I'm amazed they got those vehicles through there. I thought it was tough going off-road in Jamie's big four-wheel drive.'

'Look, there's Peter letting the air out of the tyres. That helps driving in sand,' said Tom.

'It's a good bit of action that gives a sense of how desolate the country they travelled through was,' said Andy. 'Wouldn't have been too many travellers out there in those days.'

Veronica joined in the laughter at a scene of Marta staggering down a sandhill and 'dying' at the bottom.

'God, talk about melodrama. It's a wonder Topov didn't have his heroine tied across the railway tracks,' chuckled Andy.

'I thought she was supposed to be a serious actress,' said Tom.

'She's doing what the director says, obviously. You can see that she's sending herself up a bit,' said Veronica.

'Now where's this? Isn't this river pretty,' said Andy. 'What a lovely place to camp.'

Veronica looked at her notes from her interview with Colin. 'I'd say this could be Cooper Creek.'

'Ah, I wonder if they knew what an historic place Cooper's is,' said Andy. 'Bit of voice-over explanation needed there. Now here's a place coming up, not much to it by the look of it,' said Andy. 'Inland Mission Hospital. And a nice nurse out the front. Blimey, she's in the full uniform, starched veil and all! Way out there.'

Veronica flicked through her notes. 'Birdsville, I think.'

'Pretty isolated isn't it?'

'Hey, here's Topov again. Don't you love him?' laughed Veronica. 'What's he dragging? He looks very pleased with himself.'

'Some sort of bird,' said Tom.

'Oh, it's the bustard! The one the white drover and his Aboriginal mate caught,' said Veronica.

'And there's Johnny cooking it over the campfire. The rest of them don't look very impressed,' said Andy as the camera panned around the rather sullen group.

'That must be Topov filming. He looked so pleased with himself and with the bird and look at everyone else. They look really pissed off,' said Veronica.

'Now what's this, where are they here? The Devil's Marbles. Amazing, that's a good shot,' said Andy.

'They camped there, apparently Drago filmed a lot at this spot. Some must be on the other camera,' said Veronica consulting her notes from the interview with Colin.

'So here they are back on the road. People up ahead, walking,' said Andy. 'Oh, dear, what a sad looking bunch.'

'These could be the Aborigines from the awful camp,' said Veronica. 'Drago didn't want to film them, but Topov thought they should show the appalling conditions.'

'I expect that part will be on the other camera as well,' said Andy.

There was little talk as they watched the scenes of the changing landscape from the gibber plains to spinifex country, to raw-looking red dirt.

'Look, 'roos. I bet that caused a bit of excitement,' said Tom as they watched a large mob of big red kangaroos bound across the road, taking no notice of the little convoy.

'What's this coming down the track? A mini tornado?' asked Andy.

'A dust storm?'

'A couple of horses. Two drovers.'

'I'd like to have seen more of that,' said Tom. 'Have you noticed that when Topov is filming and something happens, he stops filming? Probably goes up to do all the talking.'

'Look at that drover. He's got a packhorse and a kid behind him,' said Tom. 'Oh, it's a little girl I think.'

'What a cutie,' said Andy.

'It's Doris!' shouted Veronica. 'So that must be Len. Oh, I wish there were more shots of her. Andy, that's Jamie's mother! I think Drago took a lot of film of her as well. I can't wait to see it. Isn't she adorable?' said Veronica excitedly.

'Cute eyes and hair, but she looks like a scruffy little boy,' said Andy.

'If you meet her one day, Andy, I'll tell her you said that,' said Veronica. She felt quite emotional and suddenly this was all very real to her.

'So where is Len taking them? Looks like they're off the track,' said Andy.

'It's Brolga Springs. It has to be,' said Veronica, studying the building, which she recognised as the original old homestead of Brolga Springs. 'And that woman, that must be Annabel Johns. Oh, I have to get a copy of all this for Doris and Jamie. This is their place. Doris was born there.'

Andy gave Veronica a slightly amused glance but he was touched when he saw the light in her eyes and her excited expression.

'Okay, what's next? Hey, look at this,' Tom leaned forward. 'Aborigines. They look in better shape than the ones they passed on the side of the road.'

'Wonderful-looking men. And painted up, too. It's a corroboree.' Andy folded his arms, watching shots of the group getting ready for their performance.

'Look, there's Drago with the little camera following the men and the boys,' said Veronica. 'He must have filmed their preparations.'

The scenes of the corroboree were not well composed and it was difficult to make out what was happening in the limited light.

'I hope Drago got better shots with the Bolex. This is magic stuff,' said Andy.

'This isn't a tourist show, that's for sure,' said Tom, quite fascinated.

Veronica was mesmerised. She wondered what Jamie would have to say about this unique material.

The next scenes were of quite a different terrain. 'These people saw this country in its natural state,' said Veronica as they looked at shots of termite mounds, lagoons, grasslands and several distant water buffalo.

Suddenly they were looking at an open-cut mine and all manner of mining operations beside a shanty town reminiscent of a third-world slum.

'Rum Jungle,' said Veronica. 'This is where Drago filmed some of the workers protesting.'

'He must be filming this too, because there's Topov, in a hard hat no less, talking with some miners,' said Andy.

'He's showing him some rocks. He really was interested in geology, wasn't he?'

'That's what Marta and Colin both said,' replied Veronica. 'It seemed that they made this detour after Topov heard stories in some of the pubs about uranium mining.'

'And here's civilisation. Darwin,' said Andy. 'The old pub, damn shame it was pulled down.'

'The Darwin Hotel, what a great building,' said Veronica looking at the old Queenslander with its tropical architecture of lattice and wooden decorative fretwork, and its deep upper verandah, glimpsed through waving palms. 'I love the old tropical buildings. There're a few new places built in that style which are lovely.'

There were several views taken from a verandah looking across the Esplanade to the sea but then the group were back on the road again. There was one shot of their convoy and this time Len appeared posing with Topov beside Len's vehicle, which had a small boat on top and one on the back.

'This must be when they set out to get the croc skins,' said Veronica.

'To make some dough, eh?' added Andy.

The next series of shots were taken by the river as the group divided themselves among two small boats.

'That must be Clive, the Aboriginal guide that worked with Len,' said Veronica.

'Look at the tiny little wooden boat,' said Tom. 'To go after crocs! Man, they'd want to know what they were doing.'

The next scene showed a monster crocodile laid out beside the boat, with everyone posing beside it.

'Okay. That's the end of the first disc. Here's the other one, the sixteen-mill film in the Bolex camera,' said Tom.

'So most of this next one was filmed by Drago, as

a kind of second-unit back-up,' said Veronica. 'Though Marta and Colin both said Topov grabbed the little Bolex and used it on occasion too. According to Colin, Topov was going to use this film to make a TV doco and sell it overseas.'

'I hope we can see more of that crocodile hunt, that croc was a bloody monster,' said Andy.

As they began to watch the footage transferred from the small camera, Andy said, 'You can see the difference. Drago was obviously the better cameraman.'

'That sunset over the river with those birds going home to roost is just beautiful,' said Tom.

It was fascinating for the trio to see the same journey and events filmed by Drago instead of Topov.

'Here's Marta lost in the desert again,' chortled Tom. 'Did they have a dolly? They're doing a tracking shot. It's so bumpy he must've taken it from a car. Strewth, that's pretty good.'

'Good grief, the car is tipping!' Veronica leaned forward as the Jeep fell onto its side. The camera stopped rolling.

'Bugger. I wanted to see how they got out of that mess.'

They were silent at the scenes of the Aboriginal camp outside Tennant Creek.

'These shots with the malnourished Aborigines are horrific,' said Tom.

'Ah, this is better. Very pretty,' said Andy.

'Katherine Gorge,' they all said together.

'I've never been there. I must go,' said Tom. 'Looks a bit rugged.'

'Jeez, look at the tourist facilities. Everyone crammed into one little boat. I'm sure that's changed since then,' said Veronica.

'Pretty stunning scenery. What's Topov waving at?' asked Tom.

'Rock art.'

There were a lot more scenes along the way and a few shots around campsites.

'Now look at the way Drago has filmed the mob of cattle, from amongst them and close on their heels. The shots of young Doris are heartbreakingly sweet, especially the interaction between Marta and Doris,' said Andy.

'And at the mining camp, shot on the other camera, he showed the miserable conditions the miners were living in. They were obviously asking for some kind of help,' said Veronica.

'He's good,' said Andy. 'Quick on his feet to spot things as well as take time to line up the arty shots.'

'Those Devil's Marbles shots were brilliant,' agreed Tom. 'He certainly captured the setting sun brilliantly. A real work of art.'

They all admired the wonderful and evocative shots Drago had taken of the old Dodge ploughing through clouds of dust and rough herbage where no road was visible.

'I like the camp shots. You get a better idea of how they lived and their different personalities,' said Veronica, thinking of Topov and his little caravan and Colin erecting a small tent as Marta watched. So much of it was exactly as Veronica had imagined that she felt that she had actually been there.

'Here, this must be the crocodile hunt. Look at that rope and the harpoon thing,' she said. 'There's Topov in the boat with Marta. What a shame that it's really too dark to see exactly what's going on, except that there seems to be a lot of thrashing about and waving the light around. Still he does manage to convey a sinister setting, doesn't he?'

'The vision is nearly at an end,' said Tom.

'Now where's that?' asked Andy. 'Camera shots are a bit erratic. All those bloody rock formations.'

'Topov must have filmed this. It's not very good, is it? Marta said that he went out by himself to look for minerals with his Geiger counter and sometimes took the Bolex,' said Veronica.

'He's filming everything around him, like he wants to remember exactly where he is,' said Andy thoughtfully.

'Hang on, who's that? There're two men,' said Tom.

'They're picking up rocks, or hammering something,' said Andy.

'So there were other people around,' said Veronica. 'This is very surprising.'

'Oh, they've spotted the camera. Topov must have called to them.' Andy craned forward as the two men walked towards the camera. 'God, I wonder . . . Surely not . . .'

'They seem to be arguing . . . Oops he's dropped the camera. He must have been waving his arms around,' said Tom.

'Wish I knew what they were saying, they don't seem happy,' said Veronica.

'Stop the DVD, Tom. Rewind it. I want to take another look,' said Andy quickly.

'Why?' Then seeing Andy's intent expression, Veronica asked, 'What's up?'

They all studied the screen.

'See that young bloke on the right. Know who that is?' said Andy.

'You know him?' exclaimed Tom, who stopped the DVD, freezing the image of the two men striding towards the camera.

'Pretty sure. That's a very young Big Bill. Our esteemed leader.'

'William Rowe! You're joking. How can you tell?' asked Veronica.

'I've been digging up old pictures of Rowe for a little

doco, just in case he's made Australian of the Year,' said Andy. 'I've seen pictures of him since he was born and every photo and bits of newsreel he's ever appeared in. That's him all right.'

'What was he doing out there?' asked Veronica.

'He made his millions in mining,' Tom reminded her.

'Well, we'll have to ask him! I wonder what he can tell us. It's incredible that he was there . . . Maybe he saw something that would give us a clue about how Topov died.'

'He's at a conference in Europe and won't be back for a week or so,' said Andy. 'But it certainly is worth asking if he remembers meeting Topov.'

'Topov doesn't seem to be a character you'd forget,' said Tom.

'That's true. So what else is on there?' asked Veronica, curious to see what other surprises the DVD might hold.

They forwarded through the rest but it was disappointing. There was one final shot of Rowe and his companion hammering or chipping at a rock and it had been taken from some distance away. Then there were more shots of rocks, a pan around the landscape and then a close up of a sheet of paper nailed to a wooden peg.

'What's that?' said Tom.

'It's Topov's claim!' exclaimed Veronica. 'He took out a fossicker's permit in Darwin. I think he's trying to show he had a mineral claim.'

'Well, he never got to work it,' said Tom.

'So what now?' Veronica leaned back in her seat.

'You start putting your story together. If Big Bill can shed anymore light on events, we'll certainly work it in with the rest,' said Andy.

'When did Topov die?' asked Tom.

'Some time after that, because Marta said on the day he died he went off with just his Geiger counter. No camera,' said Veronica.

Andy stood up. 'You've got a big job incorporating that old film into the modern story. But it's going to bring the whole thing to life. You've got a winner on your hands with this, Veronica.'

She worked hard to piece as much of the old and the new vision together so that the story was almost completed before Jamie arrived in Sydney. Veronica called Andy in to the editing suite to have a look at the rough-cut version.

'I've given it the working title of *The Expedition*, but I think it's hanging together quite well,' she said. 'We end the program with the excavation of his remains. I feel it needs something else to close with but I'm not sure what.'

'Could you get a reaction from Colin? He still thinks a croc took Topov,' suggested Andy. 'And you could start the story with him.'

'Unlikely after being scared off by Cardwell. And what about young Johnny? We've seen nothing in any of the footage that incriminates him specifically.'

'I wonder how he'll react when the publicity for the programme starts,' said Andy. 'Maybe when Big Bill comes back from Europe he might recall something that could give us another angle. So, let's roll it and see what you've done.'

Andy watched it through in silence. Even though he knew the content well and had seen the pictures before, Veronica had matched the best scenic shots from the old film with the footage she had taken in the Territory beautifully. And while it showed the majesty and magic of the outback landscape, it was the characters that captured his attention.

'It's wonderful, Veronica,' said Andy quietly. 'I feel I've been along with them through the whole thing. You have a great feel for the country. Topov, interestingly enough, seemed to appreciate the land and had a sensitivity to the

Aborigines. I love the contrasts too, especially between that shy little bush girl and then seeing articulate, strong Doris today.' He shook his head. 'It's a journey all right. You've done well. It's a bit of a magical mystery tour. People are going to be fascinated. And, Veronica, like it or not, you're brilliant on camera. I suggest we show this rough cut to publicity to get them excited and thinking about their PR and advertising campaign.'

'Okay, but I don't want to show them the final bit about finding Topov,' said Veronica. 'I don't want any leaks to give it away ahead of time.'

Andy nodded in agreement and, as he left, he dropped his hand onto Veronica's shoulder. 'You've done good, kiddo.'

She gave a slight nod, not trusting herself to speak.

Veronica couldn't believe how nervous and excited she felt as she paced around the airport waiting for Jamie's plane. She'd arrived ridiculously early, had twice checked how she looked and was trying to imagine the scenario of what they'd do and say to each other. Would they still feel the same? It had been so easy in Darwin when work had thrown them together. Now she was hesitant to tell him how she missed his company, how she missed their lovemaking, how she missed being around him and his family.

The plane had landed and Veronica stood watching the passengers, her heart fluttering, butterflies in her stomach. This is crazy, she thought.

And suddenly there he was, tall and handsome and coming towards her, a huge smile breaking out across his face. It felt like a slow-motion movie with everyone around them blurred and she wasn't conscious of any sounds other than the thump inside her chest. In two more strides he was before her, dropping his bag and enfolding her in his arms, pulling her tightly to him as if to imprint her onto his skin. Their lips locked and she didn't want this moment ever to end.

Finally they pulled apart. His iridescent hazel eyes were sparkling and neither of them could stop smiling.

'Wow, what a welcome,' he finally said, taking her hand and picking up his bag.

'I thought I knew how much I missed you but seeing you is . . . overwhelmingly great.'

As she drove out of the carpark, she caught up on news of Billy, Jamie's parents, his work and Travis's case. 'Everyone sends their love,' he said.

'That's nice, thanks. I've taken a break for a few days while the editor finishes putting the story together, so we can play in between your commitments,' she said.

'Sounds great. But listen, don't go to any trouble and feel that you have to entertain me. I just want to see you.'

'Me too. But there are some people I want you to meet, like my parents. Is that okay with you?' asked Veronica.

'You make it sound like a chore. I'm happy to do whatever you want. I just hope they like me,' he said.

'It's just that they're not like your parents. They're pretty easy going though and I know they'll like you. And how would you feel about going to Melbourne for a day or so? That's where my sister and her family live.'

'If there's time, sure, why not? And while I'm on show, do you want me to meet your boss?'

'Oh, dear. Do you feel like you're going to be on parade?' asked Veronica.

'Kind of. But that's all right. I'd like to know what your life down here is like and your family and friends, then I can visualise it all when I'm back in Darwin.'

'Let's not talk about that, you've just arrived,' said Veronica, suddenly feeling a sense of panic at the idea.

'I hope I survive,' said Jamie as Veronica changed lanes in the hectic Sydney traffic.

'You have crocodiles, we have crazy drivers,' said Veronica.

She carried drinks and a plate of cheese and olives into the small sitting room where Jamie was relaxing, his long legs stretched out, watching the early evening news.

'I don't expect you to wait on me,' he said, taking the tray from her.

'I've made a reservation for dinner at the local Italian,' said Veronica.

But they never made it to the trattoria. They made love, they took a bath, they lay on the bed and talked and then made scrambled eggs, which they ate by candlelight while they shared a bottle of wine before returning to the rumpled bed. They went out for breakfast and then Jamie set off for his conference. Veronica went to the local farmers' market to look for fresh ingredients to cook for dinner.

Veronica's parents had invited them over for Sunday brunch, as her father liked to grill bacon and sausages and fry the eggs on his barbecue. Her mother had bought croissants, strawberry jam and cream.

While Jamie and her father were at the barbecue, Veronica helped her mother.

'So what do you think of him?'

'He's certainly good looking, my goodness. And he seems very charming. Quiet, a gentle sort of person. Not your sort at all,' added her mother.

'What do you mean?' demanded Veronica.

'You've always been so competitive with your boyfriends. You can be quite bossy, Veronica,' said her mother affably. 'It's nice to see you actually listen to what Jamie has to say. And he is very intelligent.'

'So you like him?' asked Veronica.

Her mother smiled at her. 'What's there not to like? I just hope he can find a job down here. I can't see you hopping up to Darwin regularly.'

Lunch with Andy and a tour of the *Our Country* offices and Network Eleven was a success. Andy and Jamie hit it off, as Veronica knew they would.

'I've said this to Veronica, having seen the segments in which you appear, you could kick around a TV station on a regular basis, Jamie. Just a matter of finding the right show for you.'

'Thanks, Andy, but that's not my thing at all. Veronica brought out the best in me. She's easy to talk to and was genuinely interested in what I had to say,' said Jamie, giving Veronica a warm smile. 'I'll leave the showbiz scene to her.'

'I thought I'd show Jamie the rough cut of the show tonight,' said Veronica. 'I have it on DVD. See what he thinks. He's trustworthy,' she added.

'Yes, I'd be interested in your reaction and comments, Jamie,' said Andy. He stood up and shook Jamie's hand. 'I've very much enjoyed meeting you. Really, very much. I'd like to see you again.'

'Any time you're in Darwin, my turn to reciprocate,' said Jamie.

'Who knows? I might make a trip up that way. I've got a standing invitation with my friend, Jim Winchester,' said Andy, giving Veronica a smile.

After dinner that night, Veronica played the DVD of the show for Jamie, who watched it intently. Even though Veronica had seen the vision countless times, watching it with Jamie was special. The places they'd been together made them laugh and reach out to touch each other. Jamie was bemused at seeing himself on camera and interested to see the interviews with Marta and Valma and touched at the scenes with his mother.

'It's still only roughly put together as my editor is still working on it and it needs a better ending, but what do you think?' asked Veronica, realising how anxiously she wanted Jamie to approve.

'It's excellent. Intriguing, entertaining, but what I like most is the impact of the landscape. Maybe I'm biased as it's about country that I love, but I hope that the people watching it will be moved and inspired and understand what's important about keeping land, like Kakadu, in as natural a state as possible.'

'I thought you explained the indigenous connection to the land very well. It's a story on a lot of levels, isn't it?' she said.

He leaned over and kissed her lightly. 'It's a stunning opening show. You are sensational. I can hear the accolades . . . fresh, exciting. You'll be able to write your own ticket. If it's promoted properly, it will rate through the roof.' He raised an eyebrow. 'So what's next?'

'Oh, I can't bear to think of moving on from this. I can't let this story go,' she said slowly. 'And you know what? I miss the north. I miss the air, the sun, the big sky, the things we did, like fishing . . .'

'Oh, we haven't done anything yet! I still owe you a picnic at Howard Springs. But you know, if you had longer up there . . .' He paused. 'Well, we could have a great time. I'd love to show you so much more of the Territory.' He cleared his throat. 'Can you ask Andy for some leave? You said you had a lot of holiday time owing to you.'

The following morning as Veronica lay in Jamie's arms, she sighed. 'I'd like to start every day like this.'

'Me too.' Jamie was about to lean over and kiss her when the phone rang.

'Veronica, it's Amber Delaney here from publicity. Congratulations on your story, it's fascinating! So intriguing. A kind of detective story, too. We want to start promoting it, so I was wondering if you had any stills we could use of you and that gorgeous Jamie and any of the original group?'

'Yes, we can take some stills off the original film and I have some lovely shots of Doris as a grown woman.'

'Far out! That's great!'

'Jamie is here in town at the moment . . .'

'Fantastic! Would he do some press interviews with the papers ahead of time? What's his number?'

'Let me ask him first,' said Veronica, suddenly glancing at Jamie. 'I'll get him to call you.' She looked at Jamie as she hung up. 'Sorry, I got carried away. Is that okay? Would you mind doing an interview?'

'Sure. And what about Colin?' asked Jamie.

'I don't think that I'll contact Colin until after the program goes to air.'

'How do you think John Cardwell will be after he hears about it?' asked Jamie.

'I don't know, but once he sees the story he'll see that no-one is pointing a finger at him,' said Veronica. 'Cardwell knew that Topov wasn't taken by a croc but I think he thought that if Topov's body were found, he could be incriminated.'

'Hmm. It's still all a bit of mystery, isn't it?' said Jamie.

'Veronica, it's Amber here again.'

'Ah, yes. How did Jamie McIntosh go with the press?'

'Brill. Brilliant. What a talent. Boy, is he wasted up in the bush. But there's something that's just come up. Bit worrying.'

'What's that?' asked Veronica.

'Legal just rang. The first teaser went out yesterday and there's been some fall-out.'

'Lordy, what?' asked Veronica.

'An injunction's been taken out to stop the story from going to air.'

'Oh, no! Damn. Let me guess. John Cardwell, right?'

'Yes, how did you know? The man is a big mover and shaker and has legal heavyweights by the score. Our legal advisor wants to discuss it with you,' said Amber, glad to pass the buck.

'Don't worry about it, Amber,' said Veronica firmly. 'Cardwell is panicking for no reason. I'll get straight onto the legal department. We're running with the story.'

Andy thought Rowe looked exceedingly fit and relaxed despite having had a hectic schedule in Europe and the long flight back to Sydney.

'Sit down, Andy. I hear *Our Country* has a very exciting opening show. When do I get a preview?'

'I have it right here,' said Andy, holding up a DVD. 'It's a bit open ended though. Veronica Anderson was looking for a wrap-up to finish as there are still some unanswered questions. We're hoping you might be able to help, actually.'

'Me? How? I don't even know what the program's about. I gave you free rein,' said Rowe.

'The story revolves around an outback filming expedition which set out in '55 to make a documentary. There are three surviving members of the trip, two of whom we have used to piece the story together and fortuitously some of the old film footage turned up.'

'Terrific. Should be interesting,' said William Rowe. 'I'm keen to have a look.'

'There's a small scene we discovered on the old film,

480

one of the last things shot, that is a bit puzzling and we're hoping you might be able to throw a bit of light on it. You were up in the Top End in 1955?' said Andy.

'That year I was all over the place. Started in the Western Australian goldfields, went to the Alice and travelled through Queensland and the Cape with a geologist partner.'

Andy nodded. 'It looks like you fellows ran across one of the members of this expedition, a large, bearded Russian named Topov and we're wondering if you recall anything. The man died soon afterwards. I know that it was over fifty years ago but I expect that you would probably remember meeting Topov. I don't think that he was the sort of person you would forget easily.' Andy paused as Rowe took off his glasses and rubbed his eyes.

Rowe drew a long breath. 'Dear God, that Russian man. A movie director or something? Had a camera. I certainly remember him.'

'You do?' Andy said.

'Yeah. He was a bit pugnacious. A loud fellow. Got Norman, my partner, offside, big time.'

'What happened?' asked Andy.

Rowe leaned back in his chair. 'Andy, it was a helluva long time ago. But things like that happened out there in those days. The poor bloke was taken by a crocodile, you know. We read about it in the paper. Norman always thought it some sort of odd justice.'

'Why was that?' Andy leaned forward.

'Now we were pegging a claim. Uranium had been found in the Territory and we thought that there could be a whole lot more minerals out there. We had been prospecting in the area of what is now Kakadu and parts of Arnhem Land and had some promising finds when out of nowhere literally this wild, big, fat fellow with a beard, appeared and started abusing us. He was shouting that he had the rights to the area. Kept jumping up and down waving a bit of paper and telling us to bugger off. He and Norm had words.

'Anyway, I think it was the following day and Norman insisted that we go back to the claim that we had pegged out and, would you believe it, this Russian fellow was taking out our pegs and putting in his own. That sort of thing happened occasionally, but generally out in the backblocks there was a code of honour that you didn't jump another man's claim, but we caught this chap redhanded.

'Norman hated foreigners at the best of times so he went a bit crazy and before I knew it he flew at the Russian bloke. Got stuck into him and there was a fight. The Russian was big but not a fighter. Norm gave him a bit of a hiding before I could intervene.'

'What happened next?'

'The big fellow went down like a ton of bricks. Then Norman grabbed me and pushed me towards the car insisting that we head straight for Darwin to establish our claim. I was worried as the fellow's face was a bit smashed up and he'd fallen heavily but Norman kept insisting that he would be fine and if we didn't get to Darwin before he did, we could lose our claim. First person who registers it owns the rights, you know,' said William Rowe.

'So you left him?'

Rowe continued, 'Norman was so angry that I just wanted to get away. But I felt badly. The bloke, however, must have been all right, because a couple of days after we got to Darwin and registered the claim we read about a Russian bloke being taken by a croc around Wild Man's Crossing. So we knew it had to be him, couldn't be another Russian out there. Norman said that it served him right for trying to diddle us out of our claim. But no-one should end up like that, fodder for a croc,' said Rowe with a shudder.

'He didn't die from a croc attack,' said Andy. He paused then said, 'Veronica dug up the remains of his body where it had been buried more than fifty years ago.'

'What!' Rowe sat upright. 'How is that possible? Good lord, what happened?'

'I've brought you the DVD of the edited story that Veronica has put together. That will tell you what the film makers did with Topov's body. There's a character in it called Johnny, the cockney cook. Better known these days as John Cardwell.'

'The business operator? Casinos? You name it, unsavoury type?'

Andy nodded. 'When he heard we were doing this story he tried to stop us because the group thought there was no-one else around when Topov died and so suspicion for his death would fall on them. Obviously, under these circumstances, Cardwell doesn't want it to come out that Topov wasn't taken by a crocodile.'

'Christ!' Rowe stopped, then looked at Andy. 'This doesn't make me look too good, does it?'

'Is Norman still around?'

'No, I parted company with Norman not long after because I got tired of his temper and his unpredictability. He died quite a few years ago, long before I raised the capital to operate mines in the north. So it's just my word against a dead man's?'

'What are we going to do about this?' asked Andy slowly. 'Cardwell has taken out an injunction against us screening the show. He's always been a bit paranoid about media exposure but I guess he has some justification this time.'

'Telling what I know will clear all of them, won't it?' said William Rowe, staring at Andy. There was silence in the room. Finally Rowe said quietly, 'You're the Executive Producer. You're the only one who knows my story so it's your decision what to do with it.' Rowe didn't break his steady gaze and Andy looked away first.

'I'm thinking this story could be very damaging to your reputation,' he said.

'You have to tell your producer Veronica Anderson,' said Rowe.

'Yes. I should,' agreed Andy. 'But because you own the network, I feel it's your call.'

Rowe looked thoughtful. 'For a couple of days, until that newspaper report about the Russian being killed by a croc turned up, I lived with the thought that I had left an injured man in the bush. We left him pretty badly cut up. But then I was able to go on with my life thinking that he'd met a different fate and I was off the hook. And I went on to make a lot of money. Now I realise that my original guilty feelings were justified. '

'Did that make you become a philanthropist?' asked Andy suddenly. 'You've given money away, helped a lot of charities and set up a big foundation to help others in the community who aren't as fortunate as you've been.'

Rowe shrugged. 'It seemed the right thing to do. Maybe remnants of that guilt were still there.' Rowe stood up and shook Andy's hand. 'You'd better share this with your producer and let me know what you plan to do.'

'No instructions from you?' asked Andy, wishing Rowe would make the decision for him.

'I said the day I arrived I would not interfere in the production decisions of my staff or in the content of programs.'

'And you're a man of your word.' Andy turned to leave the office, his shoulders slumped.

'Andy.'

He turned to look at the man behind the desk.

'If it helps, you can tell your producer that I intend

484

to decline the nomination for Australian of the Year. It will help the judging panel if I withdraw and they don't have to make such a contentious decision.' William Rowe smiled.

'That's a damn shame,' said Andy.

Andy sat on the sofa in his office, his face in his hands.

'Hey, what's up?' Veronica sat down beside Andy.

'I saw Rowe.'

'And?' Veronica was trying to fathom Andy's expression. 'Did he see anything? Did he remember being out there?'

'Oh, yes.'

She stared at Andy. 'You don't look happy. What happened?'

'I'll tell you the story as he told it to me.'

Veronica sat still, trying to digest the details of the full story of Topov's death.

'Poor old Topov,' she managed. 'I suppose that there can't be any doubt, not when you put together Marta's story and see Topov's film footage. It all adds up.'

'Hopefully he didn't recover consciousness. Better than being eaten by a crocodile, you'd hope,' said Andy. 'But now we're left with a bit of a moral dilemma, aren't we?'

Veronica nodded. 'It's a shame that William Rowe is such a decent man. If I hadn't found Topov's body and confirmed Marta's story then no-one would have been any the wiser. Perhaps I should have taken Jim Winchester's suggestions and left things alone.'

'Even though Big Bill has said he'll decline his nomination for Australian of the Year, this story will be a big blot on his character,' said Andy.

'And he really didn't put any pressure on us?'

'No. You're the producer, what do you think we

should do? Should we ignore the truth about Topov's death to save the reputation of a good man?' asked Andy.

'Andy, you can coat the story in as many layers as you like to push extenuating circumstances and so on, but the fact remains, Rowe walked away leaving a man to die in the wilderness.'

'And at the end of an illustrious career, he's to be damned for an incident that happened fifty years ago?'

'I know all that. But the fact remains, we are journalists and we have to tell the truth, no matter how unpleasant. If Rowe wasn't our boss, would we think twice?' argued Veronica.

'Yes, the decision would have been easier if Cardwell had been responsible for Topov's death,' said Andy. 'You're right, of course. It's a heck of a surprise end to the whole episode.'

'Which is why we have to tell the truth,' said Veronica firmly. 'I hate my job sometimes.'

'Has he made it easier for us by declining the nomination?' asked Andy.

'I don't know. Putting the program to air will affect his standing around here as much as it will in the public domain. He might retire because of this. And just when we had someone running the place whom we all liked and respected and who seemed to have the right idea about television,' said Veronica.

'Which is why he expects us to do the right thing,' said Andy.

'Yes.' Veronica stood up. 'Is he prepared to tell his story on camera?'

'I assume so. Once he knows we're running with it.'

'So who's going to tell him? I think I should,' said Veronica, answering her own question.

*

Tom followed Veronica into the editing suite, closed the door and put down the camera. 'That's been the most painful interview that I've ever had to do. What a decent bloke, though. I think he comes across well, despite the terrible facts.'

'He was certainly honest. Didn't try to make excuses, fudge or hide anything. And because he was so straightforward, his integrity shines through and you can't help feeling sympathy for him,' said Veronica.

'It's going to shock people,' said Andy. 'Especially Cardwell. And poor old Colin. Are you going to tell them ahead of time?'

'No. But the legal people are sending the DVD of the show to Cardwell. That'll get him to remove the injunction,' said Veronica. 'I'll send a copy to Marta, too. Now all we have to do is to shoot my wrap-up of this final segment. I'll have to think about how to do it,' said Veronica. 'I'll get a coffee.'

In the end she decided to just tell it as it happened. She sat on a seat in the garden outside the Network Eleven studios and explained how once they'd identified the young William Rowe on the film that Topov had shot a day or so before he died, they'd asked Mr Rowe for an interview.

Veronica looked into the camera lens. 'Mr Rowe had no hesitation in explaining in full the details of what had happened fifty years ago – as you have seen. Even though he is the owner of this network, he asked for no favours, nor did he put *Our Country* under any kind of pressure. However, by revealing a young man's weakness and fallibility he has shown that even a kind man, a philanthropic icon, can be flawed, as good men often can be. Because he does not want to place the judges in a difficult position, Mr Rowe has declined his nomination for Australian of the Year. But I still believe him to be a decent and caring man who, while ignorant of the results of his actions so long ago, has dedicated his life to helping others.'

Tom turned off the camera. 'Nicely put.'

Veronica stood up and unclipped her microphone. 'Maybe, but the media will still have a field day with this, especially the opposition TV networks. I'm going home, Tom.'

'You've earned a stiff drink. Is Jamie still around?'

'Yes. Thank goodness. But he's going back to Darwin in a few days.'

'Bummer. He's a nice guy.'

Veronica nodded. Suddenly she felt tired, over-whelmed, depressed and sad. She needed Jamie.

Walking in the door she suddenly saw that her little place was now as she'd always wanted it to be – a home. Even though Jamie wasn't back yet, his boots were on the little patio, his bush hat was by the door, his notes and books on the coffee table and his clothes in her wardrobe.

'I was going to take you out to dinner,' said Jamie as he came in and found Veronica in casual clothes, her feet up, sitting in silence, sipping a glass of wine.

'I'm not up for going out. I feel terrible.'

'Are you feeling sick?' He was immediately concerned.

'In a way. Sick in my heart and sick to death of the media. Especially TV. It's shallow, sensational and voracious. It eats your time, talent and energy.'

'Okay. Let me get myself a beer and you can tell me what's happened.'

He got a glass, poured himself a drink and sat beside her. 'Go for it.'

She told him about William Rowe and he looked at her in astonishment.

'Well, you wanted a dramatic ending. You've got your final piece of the puzzle. But not how you wanted it, huh?'

'I feel bad about Rowe because I think this story is going to destroy a good man. Maybe some others couldn't or wouldn't have gone all the way with this. But the ethics of journalism are strong in me and I have to tell the truth and the whole story.'

'That's who you are, Veronica.'

'Yeah. A good journo, but at a cost. And suddenly I hate myself, hate my job. I don't want to have to make decisions like this. I'm tired of peeling away the layers of people, exposing people's motives, histories, souls.'

Jamie was a bit nonplussed. 'I thought you loved your job, you're making a big career move and you work with people you like and admire and they think the world of you. Promotion awaits. I wouldn't be throwing that away easily.'

'But it's all more of the same from here on in. I don't want to be the best known face in the country or whatever. And, yes, Andy will retire at some stage and I could be offered his job. But doing this program has made me look at things differently, rethink a few things.'

'You've become very involved emotionally in this story. You've sort of lived it,' he said quietly. 'My mother would probably tell you to go away, clear your head, get things into perspective. She does that when she goes to the farm and rides one of her horses for miles.'

Veronica was silent a moment. And then it was as if a light switch just flicked on. She turned to look at the man whom she now knew she loved more than she thought it possible to love anyone.

'Jamie, you know what? I have the rest of my life waiting for me,' she said. 'And I don't know why I'm hanging around Sydney working long hours, under pressure, being pushed into a work role I'm not happy about and having to make terrible decisions like I did today.'

'So what do you want? Really want?' asked Jamie softly.

Veronica answered slowly, thinking aloud and enunciating her wishes for the first time. 'I want to feel happy. And that means being loved and loving someone back. Waking up every morning and looking forward to sharing the day with that person. To feel I'm doing something that's worthwhile and be in a place that makes me feel good. Calm. Contented. You know, when I looked at the footage we shot at that fabulous home of Marta's at Lake Como and then I looked at Brolga Springs, riding, swimming at the waterfall or just being in that extraordinary landscape, I thought, nah, I don't want Marta's life.'

'Sounds like you want my life,' said Jamie casually. 'Maybe you'd better move to Darwin.'

They looked at each other, the enormity of his casual remark sinking in.

'And? Do what?' she asked.

'Be with me. And Billy. Give yourself some space for a while. Decide how permanent you want it to be.' He glanced away, his long lashes covering the deep longing she suddenly glimpsed in his eyes. 'You'd find work. If that's what you want. Maybe not as a big TV star . . .'

'Been there, done that,' she said softly as she leaned towards his outstretched arms.

He held her tightly, resting his chin on top of her head. 'I love you, Veronica. I don't know how things will work out for us, but I'd like to give it a try, if you want to.'

She lifted her face to kiss him. 'I certainly do. I love you too. Seems a good place to start.'

'Welcome back,' said Andy as Veronica drifted into the office after seeing Jamie off at the airport. 'You must be feeling sad, eh?'

'Not really. Taking two days off was great. We went to Melbourne. I finally got to see my sister and her family in their new house.'

'And they got to see Jamie,' said Andy.

'They did. It's been a while since I've seen Sue stuck for something to say,' smiled Veronica. 'Now I'm wondering if you'll be stuck for words. I have some news.'

'Why do I think that it's not good news for me? I think I know what's coming. Jamie? You and Jamie?' He gave her a quizzical look.

Veronica nodded. 'I love him, Andy. I'm going to Darwin and we'll see how it goes.'

'Hell's bells! Veronica, Jamie might be special, but Darwin! What'll you do with yourself? And what'll we do? Everyone who's seen the show says it's going to be huge and so are you. It's a big kick-off, not just because of the sensational story, but because of you. The whole country is going to love you, going to want to know what you'll do next. You've hit your straps, Veronica.'

'I feel awful about walking out on the show. But it's not what I want, Andy. And I'm not deluding myself that my job will be here waiting if I've made a mistake. I'm cutting the ties and making a new start. I also know the show will need a new front person and I've put you in a terrible position.'

'We'll have to stagger along without you. Reinvent the format, though I liked the idea of following one of the crew. You were perfect.' Andy tried to put a positive spin on things as he saw how wretched she was feeling. 'I hope this decision isn't based solely on a tough call and putting Rowe on camera.'

'That's only part of the reason. This has been building up. And I know that Jamie and I are inevitable.'

'I see. You'll be hard to replace. Publicity can run with the love-story angle to explain your disappearance,' said Andy.

'More promotion for the show, eh?' She laughed. 'Andy, there is someone else you could try,' she said. 'What about Tom? He's very personable and a good talker.'

'He's used to being behind the camera, not in front, just like you,' began Andy. 'Hmm. Maybe it could work. We'll try him out. But so long as you're sure about this move. It's a big step. What did your parents say?'

'They're disappointed I'll be so far away. But they like Jamie and I think they want to go up and check out his family. Mum doesn't think I'm very maternal, but Billy is such a great kid, I can't see a lot of problems in that department.'

'What about finances? Work?'

'I do need to get a job. To keep me interested and make me feel I'm contributing to the world. That's a McIntosh thing. Actually, I've been thinking about that indigenous media school that Doris is involved with. Thought I could do something there. And I'm sure Doris will have umpteen other ideas. She and Alistair are thrilled, but not surprised, by our decision,' added Veronica.

'Well, that all sounds pretty good. I hope you keep me in the loop. It's no idle threat that I could head up north next holidays.'

Veronica was shocked at how easy it all was. She stored her belongings, rented her place. She had a farewell lunch at the network, dinner with her parents and got on a plane to Darwin.

Jamie and Billy were waiting for her at the airport.

Veronica looked at the red film of dust over her shoes. Why had she bothered to wear good shoes?

She smiled at Jamie. 'First time I've seen you in a tie.'

He fiddled with his tie, slightly loosening the knot. 'Take a good look, it doesn't happen very often.' He looked around. 'But I must say everyone's made an effort. Nice.'

Veronica glanced at the small group. 'Where the heck are Dougie and Reg? They should have been here thirty minutes ago.'

'Yeah. Could be a problem. Maybe I should go back along the track. There's no mobile reception out here. I hope there wasn't a hold-up in Darwin. Maybe the plane was late.'

'Yes, go and look for them. You could take Billy with you, he's getting bored. I'm going to stand in the shade with Doris and Alistair,' said Veronica.

'Don't be impatient, darling,' said Jamie calmly.

'I know. But after a couple of months of waiting, I want to close this final chapter.'

Veronica leaned against the old wooden railing beside Doris in the sparse shade of a youthful eucalypt.

Alistair was slowly pacing, his hands clasped behind his back, a panama hat pulled low to shade his face.

'How are you feeling?' Doris asked Veronica.

'A bit impatient. I just want to get this over with and move on and see friends and catch up a bit,' said Veronica.

'No, I meant about the move up here. With Jamie.'

'Oh, Doris, I couldn't be happier,' said Veronica, her eyes alight. She glanced down at the small diamond ring on her finger.

Doris looked pleased. 'It's a joy to see you both together. You sure about taking on all us mob?'

Veronica nodded, knowing this was lightly asked, but a serious question. 'I am. I'm learning. I appreciate how it is with the whole big extended family and its obligations. It's quite a package. I'm okay about it. When we have kids they'll enjoy having a hundred relatives!'

'They'll all want to come to the wedding, so warn your parents,' laughed Doris. She fanned herself. 'It's getting hot. Maybe I'll join Alistair and take a twirl around the place. Pay my respects to the Johnses and other old friends.'

Veronica watched Doris link her arm through her husband's and walk slowly among the scattered gravestones. I couldn't have wished for a better mother-in-law to be, she thought. In the three months since she'd moved to Darwin, each day had brought her closer into the fold of Jamie's family. And when Jamie told Billy that Veronica was going to stay, the boy had held on and hugged her so tightly that Veronica had felt that her heart would burst.

Darwin was feeling more and more like home. She'd had her things sent up and most of them fitted easily into Jamie's house. She had done some volunteer work, enjoyed outings with Collette and made other new friends. Now that she had regular work at the Indigitel Media School, her days were busy. She'd recruited Dougie as a volunteer to help to train camera people and take students out on work experience. She was finding the stimulation of being with the students exhilarating and most of them had definite media talent and abilities.

The air around her was faintly scented with gum blossom. The stillness, Veronica had once thought was lonely, she now found peaceful. She closed her eyes, enjoying the heat. Then she heard Jamie's car returning, followed, she saw with relief, by Reg's car.

Veronica hurried to meet them all.

'Sorry, Veronica, had to change a tyre, but we're here at last,' called Reg.

'Well, where on earth have we landed?' Andy smiled at her, holding his coat by one finger over his shoulder, his tie loosened in the heat.

'Andy! I can't believe you're here!' She hugged him. 'And, oh my goodness, Jim you've made it! And Colin, how lovely to see you.'

Colin, dressed in a shirt with a silk tie, looked dapper if a little flushed. 'What a trip. This takes me back! Veronica, congratulations. Thank you so much for including me in this event.'

She gave him a hug. 'We're all pleased you're here.'

'The show, it was . . . Words fail me,' said Colin. 'I had no idea, none at all.' He shook his head.

'I think a couple of other people were surprised and relieved when they saw it, too, ' said Andy. 'You know Cardwell sent Veronica a nice note.'

'But he doesn't want to be part of any reunion,' said Veronica. 'He's still a very private person.'

'He certainly seemed to change over the years. I suppose money does that,' said Colin. 'I'm thrilled to be here. I never imagined I'd get to the outback again. I wish Marta had come.'

'She sent a note too. Thanked us for the DVD of the program, said it brought back special and happy memories. She offered to make a donation or something. I said I'd let her know. She also sent a note to Doris and invited her and Alistair to Lake Como. They're going to take her up on the offer. Should be a very interesting reunion.'

Colin inhaled deeply and gazed around. 'Well, at least some things don't change.'

'You'll find Brolga Springs quite different, in many ways, but the old homestead is still over there. Rick and Vicki are putting on lunch for us,' said Veronica.

'Andy, Colin, come and meet my parents,' said Jamie.

'Andy, Doris will be pleased that you've agreed to be guest lecturer at Indigitel,' said Veronica.

'Yes, I'm looking forward to it,' said Andy. 'By the way, I come bearing gifts.'

'You didn't have to do that,' said Veronica. 'You're our guest.'

'The gifts aren't from me exactly. Big Bill thought you might find a set of editing computers for the school useful.'

'You're joking! How fantastic. Why has he done that?'

'He's a nice man. It's a funny thing, but after he went to air about his involvement in Topov's death, the ratings for the station climbed. It seems that his simple honesty had a very positive affect. When I told him I was coming here and, well, you know him. It's a gracious gesture.'

'It is. Wow, wait till I tell the students. Andy, could you make the presentation?'

Veronica watched Jamie lead Andy and Colin towards Doris and Alistair as Billy skipped behind them. She turned to Reg. 'Where is he?'

'In the back. Get everyone sorted and we'll start.'

'Veronica, you sure you don't want to shoot any of this?' asked Dougie.

'No, thanks. This is personal. I think we all feel the need to do this. You and Reg do the honours. I'll join the others.'

Slowly Veronica crossed to the other side of the old Brolga Springs cemetery where the small group waited for her, chatting animatedly.

Jamie nudged Veronica. 'Here he comes.'

They turned and watched Reg and Dougie slowly come towards them. Reg had his didgeridoo under his arm while Dougie carried a small metal box. The group parted, forming a respectful semicircle around the small, freshly dug hole next to the simple headstone.

As the haunting notes of the didgeridoo rang out across the cemetery, Dougie, helped by Jamie, knelt down and placed the box in the hole. Veronica stepped forward and gently placed Topov's rusty old viewfinder and his belt buckle with the emblem, now polished, on top of it.

Jamie picked up a shovel and threw the first sod of soil into the hole then passed it to Veronica. One by one they each threw in a shovel full of the red soil until the hole was filled. Dougie smoothed the dirt into place. Then they all looked at Veronica.

She looked at the headstone, simply carved with the name *Maxim Topov. Traveller and filmmaker. Peace at last.*

She leaned down and said quietly, 'Well, Topov, I wish I'd met you properly. We don't know much about you, where you came from or where your family rests, but I hope you are pleased that we found you and that your film will live on. You were right, Australia is wild and beautiful and precious. I hope in this silent country you will hear the rustle of leaves, the sigh of the breeze, the companionship of creatures, the footsteps of visitors and know you are not alone and not forgotten.'

Veronica stepped back and Jamie squeezed her hand.

Colin dabbed at his eye and then mopped his face with his handkerchief. 'I think he would have liked that, Veronica. Thank you.'

'Maybe not as flamboyant a production as Topov might have wished but, under the circumstances, I think it serves the occasion,' said Veronica.

'Maybe he'd prefer we raise a glass to him,' said Andy.

'Follow me,' said Reg. 'There's a small feast waiting.'

As they headed to the vehicles, Colin asked Andy, 'So what did the coroner's report have to say?'

'Cause of death unknown. Could have been his heart. Who's to say?' said Andy.

'True. He ate too much, drank too much,' said Colin. 'But I think he lived life to the full.'

Jamie kissed Veronica. 'I'm sure Topov is happy now. You know why we were late?'

'Reg said he had to change a tyre?'

'Yes. Which meant taking out the casket to get to the jack. He fixed the tyre and drove off. And left Topov behind. Fortunately he realised when they were only a couple of clicks down the track!'

'Oh, no!' Veronica burst out laughing. 'What a typical Topov story! Jamie, I've just had a thought. You know Marta offered to make some sort of donation, so why don't we have a perpetual award set up at Indigitel – the Topov Trophy for best student film?'

Jamie hugged her. 'What a glorious idea.' He took her hand. 'It would be nice to be able to fulfill someone's dreams.'

'Now, that is what Topov would call a good ending,' said Veronica.

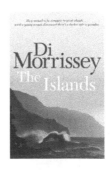

CPSIA information can be obtained
at www.ICGtesting.com
Printed in the USA
LVHW02s0019100818
586508LV00002B/258/P